Still Life and Death

and Death

A Shepherd Sisters Mystery

TRACY GARDNER

For David and Joni

Chapter One

WHEN SAVANNA SHEPHERD CAME THROUGH the door after work, she was nearly knocked off her feet. Fonzie, her wiggling, yipping Boston Terrier, greeted her like he hadn't seen her in days.

He was ready for his walk on the beach, but it would have to wait. They were headed to the roof of Libby's Blooms. After a day of teaching art lessons at Carson Elementary, Savanna was going to lead her still life painting class for adults.

She grabbed her well-worn smock from the hook in the hallway and maneuvered through the unpacked moving boxes in the front room. She'd seen her set of acrylic paints somewhere in here, but where? She shuffled through boxes until she finally found them.

To keep her long, auburn-brown waves out of her face, she pulled them back and fastened them with a barrette. With Fonzie at her heels, she went out the door again, locked it behind her... and paused.

Her wide front deck, complete with seating around a fire pit in the center, faced west over the dunes of Lake Michigan. It was her favorite part of the house. When she'd spotted this place last summer while walking the beach with Aidan, she'd known it'd be a fixer-upper;

she didn't mind. Two years ago when she'd returned to her hometown, she'd moved in with her sister Sydney, but she loved finally having her own place.

Her dog took off, kicking up sand behind him as he sprinted toward the lake. Though it was only early May, the deep blue waves were dotted with boats.

"Fonzie!" She whistled sharply, and he ran back to her. She ushered him into the back seat of her car, and in two minutes, she was on Carson's quaint, inviting Main Street.

The bell jingled over the door to as she entered her younger sister's dog grooming salon. The only pet-centric establishment in Carson, Fancy Tails & Treats was wildly successful. Overstuffed aqua seating and a vintage red-and-chrome café table sat in front of the large window overlooking Main Street. Savanna and her two sisters met here for lunch at least weekly, taking turns at bringing carryout. Sydney lived right behind the shop, and it was centered between Skylar's law office and Savanna's school, making it the perfect place for a quick catch-up.

Sydney smiled at her from the gourmet treat display case. "You brought my buddy back!" She bent down to scratch Fonzie's ears and slipped the dog one of her signature Chicken Churros.

"Do you mind if I leave him here during class?"

"Of course not—he loves it here. He'll get to see his friends. Willow has Caroline Carson's poodles in the bath right now. Jack is picking them up later."

"Nice!" Savanna had become friends with Jack, the librarian at Carson Elementary, when she'd painted a mural in his grandmother Caroline's mansion. "He's in my class tonight. I bugged him until he signed up. You should have Willow close up and come join us."

Syd laughed. "No, thanks. You're the artist in the family. I'd just embarrass you."

"Whatever. You're very artsy—these are gorgeous!" Savanna pointed at the variety of elaborately decorated goodies in the display case, all of which looked good enough to eat…if you were a dog.

"That's different than painting a picture," Sydney replied. "Maybe I'll try a class next week, just for fun."

"You should. Libby would love seeing you in the class. Maybe it'd get her to try it too."

"She's even more paintbrush-shy than I am," Sydney said. "But I don't buy it. Anyone gifted enough to create her flower arrangements would probably be great with a canvas. I'll work on convincing her next time we have our rooftop tea. If she does it, I will too."

Savanna loved that her sister had made such close friends with some of Carson's small business owners. Sydney and Libby met in Libby's greenhouse once or twice a week before their shops opened. She imagined early mornings must be peaceful and pretty up there, looking out over Main Street and the lake beyond.

She left Fonzie with Syd and crossed the street to Carson's flower shop, Libby's Blooms. Uncle Max circled the reception desk inside the store, coming around to hand her the colorful bouquet he'd preserved from Tuesday's class to continue work on today's canvases. He held the door open to the staircase, which provided access to second-floor storage for all of the building's business owners, and also to Libby's rooftop greenhouse.

She kissed him on his slightly scruffy cheek as she passed. "Thanks! Will you be here when I'm done, or are you heading out?"

"I'm closing tonight—I'll be here. Libby's been up there all afternoon working on a super-secret project. Go make artists of those students, love. Have fun!"

Savanna could listen to him speak all day. Uncle Max had left London years ago but hadn't lost his British accent. Today, repotting plants and working with the soil, Max was nevertheless dapper and put-together, his slim frame dressed in a double-breasted plaid vest and rolled-up shirt sleeves under his florist's apron. His short, dark hair was streaked with silver, though not much for his sixty years. Libby Kent had hired Max on the spot last fall after learning he was a botanist. Uncle Max hadn't even begun looking for a job yet after his move to Carson, but he'd immediately fit right in at Libby's Blooms, and he clearly enjoyed it.

Savanna wondered what kind of super-secret project a florist might be working on. She climbed the two flights to the rooftop greenhouse. Libby had pitched the still life class idea to her as a way for the flower shop to gain new customers, and for Savanna to make a little money exercising her creative muscles. The course ran Tuesday and Friday evenings over four weeks. Today was just the second class, but she was pleased to see all eleven of her students present. They were an eclectic group—more women than men, with a wide age range. She'd had them all introduce themselves at the last class, though she knew a few of them. Jack was seated in the front and was already working on his canvas. One woman, Jodie, had the same last name as fourth grade teacher Missy Vonkowski at Carson Elementary. Savanna would have to ask how they were related when she got the chance.

Counting herself, twelve people and their easels

filled the space Libby had cleared. The florist was busy working at the far end of the greenhouse, nearly obscured by an abundance of flowering plants. Savanna greeted the group and set up the flower arrangement. Once she'd provided some instruction, she circulated with the new paints and admired the renderings in various stages.

Libby stopped to chat before heading toward the exit. "These are all so lovely!" She beamed at the small group and then at Savanna, her eyes crinkling at the corners above plump rosy cheeks. "This turned out to be a great idea. It goes until six-thirty, right? Do you need anything before I head down to the shop? These stairs kill me, but I'll send Max up with more supplies if you're missing something."

"No, we should be all set, but thank you. And yes, six-thirty. I'm so glad you had the idea, Libby." Savanna smiled warmly at the older woman. "You know, in case I haven't said it, I'm also happy you hired my uncle. He really seems to love it here."

Libby carefully took off her florist's gloves. "Don't thank me for that. He's fabulous. He's got the eye, the customers love his arrangements, and look. All of my plants are thriving under his care." She made a sweeping motion with one hand across the greenhouse. "I've got to run. I'm so happy my Rachel's coming home for dinner tonight! Anthony's making my favorite—lasagna." Then she shook her head. "I should get home before he ruins it. The poor man thinks he can cook." She removed her apron and fluffed her short, curly blond hair.

Libby's husband Anthony handled the books for Libby's shop. Savanna had only met him once, last year, when Libby had been gone visiting her mother and he'd had to run the shop with help from their daughter Rachel. They'd made a good team, Rachel handling the flower orders and Anthony running the register.

"I hope you have a nice evening," Savanna said. "I'll stop by before work Monday morning to pick up those flowers for the kids' still life paintings."

"I'll be here," the florist promised. "Oh, if you see Sydney, tell her I'll call her. I can't wait to hear all about tonight's date. That beau of hers won't even give her a clue about where he's taking her!"

Savanna chuckled. "Sounds about right. I think he does it just to drive her crazy. Have a nice dinner!"

The rest of the class time flew by. Savanna gave a few demonstrations of shading and adding depth. By six-thirty, the still life paintings were vibrant and colorful, some quite realistic-looking. The easels remained in the greenhouse at the end of each session. She followed her class down the two flights of stairs and into the flower shop again, saying goodbye to them as they exited through the back to the parking lot.

Uncle Max reached past her to turn the key in the stairway access door. He moved through the shop, straightening displays and locking the front door as well, before turning out the lights at the rear entrance. "Ready? The blooms are all tucked in for the night."

Savanna walked with him out into the parking lot behind the shops. Libby's Blooms shared a brick building with Kate's Yoga on the westernmost side and was flanked on the other side by Priscilla's Dance Academy, where Savanna and her sisters had taken ballet and other dance classes in their youth. Savanna's older sister Skylar's law office was in the next building over, just before the Carson Village Offices, which housed law enforcement and township offices. Fancy Tails & Treats was kitty-corner across the street from Libby's. Savanna had often thought there must be a path worn by now between Fancy Tails and the coffee house in the next block, she and Sydney were there so often.

Beyond the picturesque downtown was Carson Park, at the end of the road before the walkways to the beaches of Lake Michigan. If you see Sydney, would you let her know I'm coming 'round tomorrow to replenish Lady Bella's biscuits?"

"I'll tell her. Have a good night!" She waved as he pulled away. Lady Bella fit her name. She was the most adorable, regal Corgi Savanna had ever met. To say she was spoiled was an understatement.

Savanna walked across the parking lot to head around the block and pick up Fonzie. There were still several cars in the dance school's designated parking area, and she caught the faint sound of classical music as she turned the corner onto Main Street.

Jack Carson was on his way out of Fancy Tails, both poodles leading the way and tangling their leashes together. He held the door open for Savanna. "I'm loving the class. I can't wait to show Grandmother my painting," he said, smiling. "You know her—she'll tell me it's beautiful even if she thinks it looks like Princess and Duke painted it."

She crouched down to pet both the poodles. "Give Caroline a hug from me. I owe her a visit."

"I promise I will." His trademark khakis and button-down oxford bore no trace of paint, which didn't surprise Savanna at all.

Her sister Sydney had a visitor, even though Fancy

Tails was now closed. Finn Gallager stood in the doorway to the grooming area, one hand resting on a broom.

"Hey there, stranger," he said, grinning. She still found it startling how much Finn looked like his older brother Aidan, though Finn was a bit slighter. Both brothers had thick black hair, Finn's stick-straight while Aidan's was wavy, and Finn's eyes as bright green as Aidan's were sky blue.

"Finn! How are you? How was Phoenix?"

"Hot and dry. How're things here? Other than furry." He cocked an eyebrow and said it over his shoulder to Sydney. His usual navy-blue Air Med Lifeteam jacket and aviators had been replaced tonight with an all-black ensemble. He was dressed up, right down to his shirt and tie and black high-sheen oxfords.

"It doesn't look like you're sweeping. I might have to fire you," Sydney said, moving past him to her desk.

"All done, darlin'. And you can't fire me. I'm free labor. Are we ready?"

"Almost." Sydney swapped out the ankle boots she'd worn to work for strappy heels that complemented her boho-chic dress. Her trademark collection of bracelets jangled on her wrists as she pulled the pin that held up her hair, and loose red curls cascaded down her back. "Ready." She added to Savanna, "We're going to dinner."

"Ooh, where?"

Syd looked up at Finn. "She wants to know where. See?" She tilted her head, straightening his collar. "People like to know where they're going for dinner."

He shrugged. "Too bad."

"Do you even have a plan? You don't know the area. You've spent a total of, like, five weeks here since last summer."

"More than that," he argued. "Trust me. I know things."

Finn had come to Carson last year to visit Aidan, and had ended up delaying leaving on his next Med Flight job after he'd connected with Sydney. It was also a win for Aidan's daughter, who seemed to believe the sun rose and set on Uncle Finn. Savanna had glimpsed the two of them watching *The Princess Bride* together last summer, sharing popcorn with the dog and poking fun at Wesley's "As you wish." Aidan had cautioned Sydney that his brother never stayed anywhere long, making a career of lucrative short-term paramedic assignments all over the country. So far, though, Finn and Sydney seemed to be making it work. Finn had been taking shorter travel contracts, though he was still gone a month or two at a time, and he worked for the ambulance service affiliated with the local hospital as a temp in between assignments.

"Have fun," Savanna said, patting her thigh for Fonzie to come with her.

"I'll lock up after you—we're going out the back," Sydney said, following her to the front door. "Wait, are we having coffee tomorrow morning? Have you heard from Skylar?"

"I'll call her again. I'll be here with coffee at eight-thirty, with or without our sister." She frowned. Skylar was stretched thin these days. Having a four-year-old and a newborn must be exhausting.

Savanna stood on the sidewalk and watched her sister dance through the shop toward Finn. He stopped her with one hand at her waist, pulling her to him. Sydney melted into his embrace, tipping her face upward. Savanna looked away before Finn kissed her. She didn't want to spy. But she'd never seen her sister smitten with anyone before.

Across the street, small clusters of people exited the Miss Priscilla's dance studio, mostly in twos. A pang hit Savanna. She missed Aidan. They had planned to catch a movie, but he'd been called into surgery. Dating a top cardiothoracic surgeon definitely had its downside.

Years ago, Aidan Gallager had moved to Carson from New York with his new wife, but tragically, she'd passed away. He'd stayed in town so their daughter Mollie would be close to her grandparents. He and a business partner ran Carson's family practice clinic, which never really cut into his off time, but the hospital was another story. Savanna saw him often during the week, at drop-offs and pick-ups in front of the school, but that didn't count. She was always professional, careful to portray a normal parent-teacher relationship.

Well. Tomorrow couldn't come soon enough.

She crossed the street, Fonzie by her side, and went around the corner to the parking lot behind the shops. Miss Priscilla was making her way to her car, her arms full with two large, stacked bins. A few pieces of sparkling material hung out one side—she must've been taking home costumes to alter. The tall, thin woman moved quickly, her posture erect despite all she was carrying. Even from several yards away, Savanna could see the scowl on her face, which instantly took her back to her childhood ballet classes and the admonishments for poor posture and lazy pliés. Miss Priscilla's intimidating presence hadn't diminished at all over the years. Savanna firmly quashed her childhood fear, knowing she should offer assistance.

"Um…Miss Priscilla?" Savanna cleared her throat,

hurrying in her direction. "May I help you with that?"

The older woman halted and turned. Dark hair pulled tightly back into her usual bun and severe, angled eyebrows only added to her unapproachable air. "No, thank you. I've *got* help." She spat the words, throwing a glance back toward the rear exit of the dance studio. "Such as it is." She resumed her pace.

A door banged open against the brick of the building and two men came out with more costumes, the older gentleman pushing a garment rack. Savanna recognized Priscilla Blake's husband, Dylan, and the younger man with him was the new tap instructor—she'd seen him when she'd taken Mollie to dance class after school. Miss Priscilla seemed to have plenty of help. Savanna reversed direction and went to her car.

As she was backing out of the parking space, Libby's daughter Rachel pulled in next to her. Savanna rolled her window down, waiting until she got out. Wasn't she supposed to be having lasagna right now with her parents?

"Hi, Ms. Shepherd!" Rachel bent down, peering into Savanna's window. "How are you?"

"I'm great! Everything all right?"

"Sure. Oh—Mom forgot something. I'm just grabbing it for her."

Savanna nodded. "Have a good night!"

Skylar was waiting outside the front door to Fancy Tails Saturday morning, baby stroller with her, when Sydney unlocked the shop. Savanna carried three coffees and a large white box to the table at the window, then rushed over to the stroller, peeking under the visor. "She's awake! May I?" she asked Skylar.

"Sure! Here." Skylar spritzed Savanna's hands with sanitizer.

Baby Hannah was five months old, with a shock of fuzzy hair a little lighter than Skylar's sleek blond bob. Savanna carefully lifted her from the stroller, saying, "Oh, look at you." Hannah pedaled her tiny feet in her Winnie the Pooh sleeper, then settled against her aunt. Savanna bent her head and closed her eyes, breathing in Hannah's scrumptious baby scent. "Ugh." She met Skylar's gaze. "How do you not just hug her constantly?"

"I do! Hug her quick—I stole her from Travis, but I'm going into the office to catch up on some things. He'll be here soon to get her." At thirty-three, Skylar was the oldest of the three sisters. A mom of two, with four-year-old Nolan and now baby Hannah, plus her career as attorney in one of Michigan's largest law firms, she somehow was still presentable at eight-thirty in the morning. Silver ballet flats and dark denim jeans were topped with a crisp pink blouse. Skylar reminded Savanna of one of her childhood business-themed Barbies, an organized, put-together, highly driven go-getter who looked equally comfortable in a courtroom or behind a stroller.

"You have to let us babysit eventually, you know," Sydney said. "Don't you and Travis need a date night?"

"We'll work as a team," Savanna added. "They'll be in good hands, I promise." She let Sydney take Hannah from her and distributed the coffees: black for Skylar, and caramel with whipped cream for herself and Sydney.

"Okay," Skylar said, sitting back in her chair.

"Yay!" Sydney squealed. "When?"

"Anytime. Really. I'm so tired. Hannah's not even much work at this point, but Nolan is sure giving us a run for our money. We enrolled him in the pre-K theater class at Miss Priscilla's, hoping to redirect some of his energy, but every time I turn around, he's up to no good!"

"Aw. Well, that makes sense," Savanna said. "He's competing for your attention."

Skylar nodded. "I know. Believe me. We make sure he gets lots of one-on-one time. I think it's a tough adjustment for him."

Sydney gasped. "Oh my God."

"What? The pediatrician says it's normal—" Skylar stopped midsentence at the sound of sirens.

Sydney stood, cradling Hannah, and stared out the front window. A police car pulled up across the street, siren screaming. An ambulance was close behind.

"What in the world?" They went out front, watching the action from the sidewalk in front of Fancy Tails. A uniformed officer entered the building across the street, weapon drawn, followed by Savanna's friend, Detective Nick Jordan, and his partner. Finn Gallager and a fellow paramedic waited just outside the door, their large red Med-Kit bag at the ready. Shop owners up and down Main Street emerged to see what was happening.

"They're going into Libby's," Savanna said.

Sydney frowned. "Is Uncle Max working this morning?"

"Is Libby?" Skylar asked.

"Oh, no. I think Uncle Max might be," Savanna said. "What if—what if something happened? What if he or Libby are hurt?" She'd never seen anything like this. It was broad daylight on quaint, idyllic Main Street, and an officer had just stormed into the flower shop with his gun drawn. Her stomach lurched. She didn't know what she'd do if something awful had happened to Uncle Max. Or Libby. She glanced at Sydney.

Her younger sister's face was drawn in fear as she stared at the scene across the street. "She wanted to have tea today," Sydney whispered.

"What?"

Sydney met Savanna's gaze. Her mouth was drawn down, and she looked agonized. "She asked me last night if we could have rooftop tea this morning. She wanted to hear about my date. And I told her no! I could've changed our plans—you two wouldn't have cared. I should've been there."

Skylar's husband Travis pulled up to the curb amid the chaos. He came around to the passenger side and asked, "What happened?"

Skylar shook her head. "We don't know. Everything was quiet until two minutes ago."

Travis turned and took in the scene across the street. His chiseled profile could've been cut from a *GQ* ad. He and Skylar made a striking couple. "I'll get her out of here. Are you coming? All of you? It might not be safe."

"No. Uncle Max or Libby might be in there. I'll call you, okay?" Skylar put a hand on his forearm and leaned up to kiss him. "Don't worry."

He frowned at her as he took the baby. "Call me. Soon."

She nodded. The sisters were across the street in seconds, stopped at the entrance to Libby's Blooms by a Carson police officer.

"What's going on?" Skylar demanded. "Our uncle

works here with Libby. We need to know if they're inside." Sydney was talking with Finn, still on standby outside the building.

"I can't say," the officer replied. "You'll have to wait out here. They're sweeping the place now."

"Is he hurt? Is Libby? What happened?" Savanna chimed in.

"I can't release any details. What's your uncle's name?"

"Max Watson." Her mind was racing. "What brought you all here? Was the alarm tripped or something?"

The officer met Savanna's gaze. She didn't recognize him, but it wasn't like she knew all the cops on Carson's police force. "We responded to a 911 call." His badge bore the name of Whitney. He turned his head quickly as the radio on his shoulder crackled.

Detective Nick Jordan's voice came through the static and made Savanna's heart drop into her stomach. "Whitney. Premises are clear. Send in the paramedics. We need them on the roof. Now."

Chapter Two

S AVANNA WAS ABRUPTLY JOSTLED TO one side by Anthony Kent, Libby's husband. Skylar caught and steadied her, hands on her shoulders.

"Sorry," Anthony murmured, already past her. "I just got here—this is my shop. I've got to get in there. What's happened?"

Officer Whitney stepped in front of him. "Mr. Kent?"

"Yes, yes. We aren't even open yet. Is my wife all right? I've got to—" He attempted to push his way past Officer Whitney and the other officer who'd just joined the group clustered around the front door.

Whitney put one hand on Anthony Kent's chest, stopping him. He unclipped his radio and spoke into it. "Jordan. We have Libby Kent's husband out here." Finn and the other paramedic entered the building.

"Copy. Keep him there. I'm coming down." Detective Jordan's command was loud and clear.

Two more people from the sheriff's department appeared: a young man carrying a large case, and an older woman with a camera. The word *Evidence* was emblazoned on their shirts and caps.

Whitney opened the door for them. "To the left and

up two flights to the roof."

Hot tears stung Savanna's eyes, threatening to over-flow. She stepped back, pulling Skylar and Sydney with her. "We have to call someone."

Sydney's brow furrowed. "Uncle Max isn't answering his phone. He always answers. Should I text Finn?"

"No, don't do that," Savanna said. "He probably can't tell you anything, anyway. What about—"

"No," Skylar said. "Don't call yet. We don't want to cause unnecessary worry. Wait until we know what's going on." Her tone left no room for argument.

"Folks." Officer Whitney moved away from the en-trance to the flower shop, leaving his partner there to guard the door. He spoke to the gathering crowd spill-ing out into Main Street, primarily made up of busi-ness owners and employees, though curious patrons were now emerging from the coffeehouse as well. Shops would all be opening soon for Saturday morning cus-tomers. "Everything's under control—you all need to head back inside."

"What's going on in there?" Miss Priscilla spoke up. She and her husband stood near the front door of the dance school.

"We've got students coming in," her husband added. "What happened?"

"We have a right to know!" another voice chimed in from the crowd.

Sydney's friend Kate from the yoga studio came over to the trio of sisters. "Do you know anything? My first class starts at nine. I'm thinking I should cancel it."

"No idea what all this is about. We think our uncle was inside opening the shop," Savanna said. "You didn't happen to see him this morning, did you?"

As Kate opened her mouth to speak, Uncle Max emerged from Libby's Blooms, followed closely by Detective Jordan.

"Oh!" Savanna was flooded with relief. Uncle Max seemed to be okay. He was talking with Nick Jordan. She pushed her way through the crowd, Skylar and Sydney behind her, and threw her arms around her uncle.

He patted her back gently, then embraced his other two nieces as they joined in. "Oh, my. I'm quite all right."

Savanna let go, now noticing how pale his face was. He looked shaken. Then she saw his hands, stained red. The white cuffs of his shirt sleeves were covered with blood. There were flecks of blood on his lavender waistcoat and his shoes, and she spied the faintest smear at his left temple. She gripped her uncle's arms. "My God. Are you—" She couldn't finish the sentence; she was too busy assessing him. There was no injury that she could find.

Detective Jordan stepped closer to their little cluster. "He's fine," he said firmly, addressing the three of them. "It's not his blood."

Sydney gasped. "Libby," she whispered, her eyes wide and fearful.

"What happened? Is she…" Savanna couldn't finish the question. Their poor uncle! What on earth had happened?

"Give me a minute," the detective said. He met her gaze, and for a split second she saw that he was rattled. The man normally had the world's most impenetrable poker face. Seeing him rattled sent a chill up her spine and filled her with dread.

Savanna considered Nick Jordan a friend after all

they'd been through since she'd come home to Carson. He'd expressed his gratitude to her last year for her major role in solving the murder of a Carson government official. And before that, she'd assisted with handling dangerous incidents going on at Caroline Carson's mansion. Savanna's knack for seeing hidden details, sometimes without even trying, was a skill she owed to her years in Chicago working as an art authenticator. Details like that scant trace of blood on Uncle Max's temple, which worried her more than his bloody sleeves. What had gone on inside the flower shop that he'd come out unharmed, but bloodstained from head to toe?

Detective Jordan was taking in the growing crowd. She was close enough to hear him as he leaned toward Officer Whitney and spoke quietly. "Run up and tell Taylor they've got to bring her out the back. I'm not putting that out on the radio."

Whitney nodded and darted through the entry door.

Savanna's breath caught in her throat. She turned to ask Uncle Max, but thought better of it. The man looked like he was still on his feet through nothing but sheer will.

Detective Jordan's face was stony. He raised one hand in the air, addressing the crowd in a deep, authoritative voice. "People. The show's over. No details will be released until we complete our investigation. There is no imminent danger. I need the sidewalk cleared now."

Little movement ensued, the onlookers obviously still curious.

Jordan exchanged glances with the other officer still stationed at the door, then continued, his tone calm, though Savanna heard the undercurrent of irritation. "Let us do our job. My officers will be happy to issue tickets for loitering if needed."

The crowd began to disperse.

Sydney asked, "Uncle Max, what happened?" She had an arm linked through Max's, and Skylar took his other arm. He seemed not to hear her.

Savanna followed his gaze to Libby's husband. Detective Jordan was speaking with him, and he put a hand on the older man's arm. Nick Jordan was a big believer in personal space. Savanna didn't think she'd ever seen him stand that close to anyone besides his wife. If Libby was only hurt, paramedics would've already brought her out and rushed away with her. Savannah's chest was pinched with anxiety over what Jordan must be telling Libby's husband. Libby was not okay. Not even close. She drifted closer, but their words were too quiet for her to catch.

Anthony Kent nodded, his eyes wide now. The officer at the door escorted him into her police cruiser, and they sped away, causing the few stragglers left on the sidewalk to stop and gawk.

Detective Jordan approached Savanna's little group. "Mr. Watson, do you mind if we finish with your statement now? We can use the office inside."

"That's fine," Uncle Max agreed.

Skylar took charge. "We're coming with him." Savanna could've kissed her.

Jordan didn't argue. He held the door open and ushered the four of them into the building, turning the manual lock on the inside of the door and pulling the shade down against the remaining onlookers.

Once in the office, Detective Jordan motioned to the chair behind Libby's desk. Uncle Max sank limply into it. Savanna pulled a chair over beside him for Sydney, who looked almost as pale as their uncle. Savanna had a terrible feeling about all of this. Where had they taken Anthony Kent? To the hospital, to be with Libby? Why hadn't they let him go in the ambulance with her?

"Walk me through your morning, from your arrival here until you discovered Libby," Detective Jordan said to Max.

"Weekends are the busiest," Uncle Max said. "So I try to do as much as possible ahead of time before we open."

Savanna shook her head to clear it, focusing on what her uncle was saying.

"I'd typically get everything running, set up the cash register, water the plants, that kind of thing. Libby never enjoyed opening."

"But she was here this morning," Detective Jordan stated. "Why?"

"I believe it was due to the upcoming Flower and Garden Show, Detective. The last several days, Libby was keeping early hours. She was often already in the greenhouse when I'd arrive. She was cultivating a plant for the show; she'd been going on about it, hoping it might win."

"Was the shop unlocked when you arrived?"

"No. It was locked—I had to let myself in."

"And you entered through the front or the back?"

"Oh, the back. We always do; best to leave the street parking for customers. Libby made a point of that. She liked us to park at the far end of the parking lot." Uncle Max raised a hand as if to run it across the top of his head. He froze, eyeing his blood-stained hand midair in front of his face. He dropped it back into his lap.

Jordan jotted something in his notepad. "Did anything seem out of place when you arrived?"

"No. Nothing that I noticed."

"Was it usual to lock yourself in when you opened the shop in the mornings?"

Max inclined his head, looking curious. "No, why? I didn't. I believe I left the back door unlocked after I arrived."

"Yes," Jordan said. "But it was locked when you arrived, yes? So Libby must've locked it this morning when she got here before you. You did say you found it locked?"

"Yes," Max agreed, frowning. "That's odd, but I suppose she was being cautious? As she was here early, on her own?"

The detective didn't answer. Savanna was glad for the small break in the questions he was peppering her uncle with. Nick Jordan was intense when he was digging for information.

"I know the front of the shop was also locked," Max said. "I had to let you in after I called 911."

"What about the door to the stairwell? Did you have to unlock it when you went up, or was it open?"

"It was locked; it's a key deadbolt. Libby and I always lock it behind ourselves, since it's a common-use stairwell for the building."

"Who has a key to that deadbolt and to the shop? Besides you and Libby?"

"Her husband Anthony, for when he does the books. And Rachel. I think that's it."

Skylar interrupted. "Nick, what are you getting at? What happened? Did someone attack Libby?"

Detective Jordan pressed a thumb and forefinger

against his eyelids for a moment. He sighed and looked at each of them as he spoke. "Someone shot Libby, likely with a silencer. Your uncle discovered the body—sorry, he discovered Libby—when he went upstairs to water the greenhouse plants. He called 911."

Sydney gasped. "She's *dead*? She's just…gone?" Her hand flew to cover her mouth.

Savanna squeezed Sydney's shoulder. "Oh my God."

"I tried," Uncle Max began, his voice shaking now as he glanced at Sydney and then back at Jordan. "I tried to help her. The operator told me how to do CPR, and I recalled a bit from our classes when Ellie was a child. But it didn't help. There was so much blood. Libby was… I don't know how long she'd been lying there," he finished softly, looking down.

Savanna kneeled beside his chair and hugged him. Her heart ached for him. She hated that he'd had to go through this. Uncle Max had never struck her as frail, but he seemed very small and unnerved right now. "I'm so sorry you were the one to find her. It sounds awful."

"There was nothing you could've done," Detective Jordan said, his voice kind. "My evidence tech estimates her time of death was at least a full hour before you discovered her."

The small florist office was quiet.

Sydney broke the silence. "Her poor husband and daughter. Oh, my goodness—Rachel. Oh, this is so awful. Someone's got to tell Rachel."

"I can't believe this," Savanna said. "I just talked with her." She didn't want to imagine what Rachel and Anthony must be feeling.

"You just talked to who, Savanna?"

She looked up at Detective Jordan. "Well, both of

them. Libby last night, during my still life class, and Rachel as I was heading home."

"They were both here? Did anything seem off to you?" Jordan asked.

"No, not really. Libby said Anthony was making lasagna, her favorite, and she was excited that Rachel was coming for dinner. Then Rachel stopped by to get something Libby forgot here." She shrugged. "Who would do something like this?"

"The daughter didn't say what it was?"

"What?"

"What did Libby forget?"

"Oh. I have no idea. Rachel must've been on her way to her parents' house. She probably just came from work or school—she was in scrubs."

"She's in nursing school," Sydney offered. "Does she know? I can't even imagine."

"Detective," Savanna said. "Libby's husband…your officer took him to the hospital, then? Does he know yet?"

Nick Jordan nodded. "He knows. He'll have a chance to see her, if he wants to. She had to be taken in; the county forensic pathologist will do an autopsy. Anderson Memorial will have a doctor and social worker ready to talk to Anthony Kent and his daughter, who we've also got coming in."

Skylar spoke, a hand on each of her distraught family members' shoulders. "Are we all set? I think Max should get home and rest."

Uncle Max didn't argue. Savanna glanced up at him from her kneeling position on the floor. His color hadn't returned, and his eyes were wide. The jovial, lighthearted demeanor her uncle always exuded was absent, and no wonder. He'd arrived at work thinking he'd be tending flowers, and instead had been a firsthand witness to the aftermath of Libby Kent's murder.

Detective Jordan opened the office door. "Of course. It might be wise if someone stayed with Mr. Watson for a while, make sure he's okay."

"Absolutely," Savanna said as she passed the detective.

"Thank you for your help, sir," Jordan said to Max.

Skylar was the last to file out. The detective stopped her briefly. "Listen. Your uncle isn't going anywhere, is he?"

Savanna and Sydney looked back, watching the interaction.

"He lives in Carson. He's not leaving town, if that's what you're asking." Skylar's voice was cutting, making it clear to everyone there that she knew exactly what the detective was really saying.

He said it anyway. "Good. He shouldn't. Not until we officially eliminate him as a suspect."

"Are you serious right now?" Sydney came back over and glared at him. "He finds Libby dead, calls 911, tries to save her, and you think he's the murderer?"

Jordan kept his cool. "I didn't say that. He was first on the scene. It's just how we have to work this. Shouldn't take more than a few days to rule you out, sir," he said, addressing Max.

"Completely reasonable," Uncle Max replied. "Girls. Please... I'd like to go home."

Outside, Sydney put a hand on Max's arm. "Really, I don't know what he's thinking, saying he has to rule you out. Nick tends to come off as a little cold, but I know he isn't. I'm sure he knows you had nothing to do with Libby's death."

"I always forget you two dated," Savanna said. "He can be tough to read, that's for sure."

"It was forever ago. He's a good guy. Don't worry," she said to Max.

"Of course. Don't give it a second thought." Max looked around. "My car is out back—"

"Nope," Skylar said. "I'm driving you. Savanna will bring your car. I already checked in with Mom, and I'm going to stay for the afternoon until Freddie gets home."

Max looked from Skylar to the other two sisters, starting to protest and then closing his mouth. "Thank you, love."

Chapter Three

O N Saturday evening, Savanna looked out over the sand dunes from her porch. She'd poured herself a glass of wine and had come out here to call Sydney. She'd left a message on her voicemail, saying, *I hope you're doing all right.*

Aidan would be here soon to pick her up for their date. She wasn't in a date kind of mood, but he was exactly who she needed after a day like today.

She'd gone through the motions of getting ready for their evening while her thoughts continued to spin, trying to make sense of what had happened this morning. It wasn't like violence never happened in Carson. It hadn't even been a full year yet since the councilman had been murdered. This was equally heinous. And Libby Kent was one of the nicest people she'd known. How could someone have shot and killed her? Why? If they'd wanted money from the cash register, she'd have given it to them. She couldn't imagine Carson without Libby. She hated thinking of what the woman's husband and daughter must be feeling right now.

A few hundred yards away, Fonzie bounded up and

down the deserted beach, pouncing at the waves rolling in. Lake Michigan was choppy tonight, scattered white-caps decorating the blue water with the wind picking up. Her vast lake was an ocean without the salt.

Dr. Aidan Gallager appeared at the railing on her deck, looking like something she'd conjured from a fairytale—bouquet of flowers in hand, he was strikingly handsome in a slim-fit navy blue button-down and dark straight-legged denim. His jawline was clean-shaven, and his close-cropped black hair was just unruly enough to make her want to reach out and touch it. She rose, and he met her halfway, handing her the beautiful pale pink peony bouquet.

Savanna closed her eyes and breathed in the sweet fragrance of the flowers. "Aidan, thank you. These are so lovely."

"So are you." His deep voice, his clean, spicy scent, his close proximity made her heart thump in her throat. He slid one hand along her forearm, and she stepped in, wrapping her arms around him.

"I've missed you," she murmured, her lips against his neck.

"We need to do something about that."

She looked up at him. "We really do. More hours in the day, maybe? More days in the week? Can you make that happen?"

He gazed up. "Hmm. I'll work on it. What are you doing Wednesday?"

"Um…probably nothing. Why?" She raised her eyebrows. "What about Mollie?"

Aidan's daughter was eight. When he wasn't at the clinic or hospital, he was with Mollie. His commitment to being a good father made him that much more attractive to Savanna. She viewed Aidan's family time as his own, though she loved it when he planned things for the three of them. Maybe he was inviting her on some fun outing Wednesday night?

"Mollie's social calendar is filling up. She and Grandma Jean now have a standing date every Wednesday volunteering at the nature center."

"Ah. So, what you're really saying is, you need a little something to occupy your time each week?"

The right corner of his mouth went up into a smile that began as devilish and finished with the corners of his eyes crinkling. "Hmm. You sound like you might have some ideas."

Savanna flushed. "I might."

Fonzie joined them suddenly, as if he'd just realized a guest had arrived. The little dog ran in circles around them while Aidan reached down, trying to pat his wiggly, squirmy black-and-white body. Tied around Aidan's wrist in front of his watch was a thin black-and-yellow braided string bracelet.

Savanna touched his wrist, turning the bracelet to reveal a tiny bumblebee charm braided into the threads. She looked up at him. "Mollie." She was growing to love that little girl. After Aidan's wife died, then-four-year-old Mollie had begun the tradition of choosing a childlike accessory or two for him to wear each day. She'd told her dad, when he'd asked back then, that it was so he wouldn't forget her when they were apart. Savanna had felt her heart swell when he'd finally explained his quirky rainbow-striped socks and turtle cufflinks to her.

He nodded. "To match her hair ties today."

Savanna opened the front door and ushered her

wild dog in, scratching his chin and promising she'd
see him soon. "Be good, Fonzie!"

Over a cozy, candlelit dinner that should've been perfect at the new small-plates place in town, Savanna's
thoughts kept returning to the traumatic events this
morning. "Aidan, I can't stop thinking about Libby."

He nodded. "I know. It's awful."

"It's completely crazy. She was fine twelve hours
earlier, upbeat and friendly and heading home for dinner with her family." She paused. "Finn was one of the
first responders. Is he doing okay? I know my uncle was
really shaken up. So was Sydney—she and Libby were
close."

"I saw my brother for a few minutes after work.
He seemed all right. He's unfortunately probably seen
worse. I'm sure your uncle is upset, stumbling onto that
scene. How are you handling it?" His brow wrinkled in
concern.

"I'm fine. I'm worried about Libby's family. I think
her husband and daughter were all she had, at least in
the area."

"It's going to be hard for them," he agreed. "Nothing I
said really helped calm her daughter down."

"You saw them?" She recalled Nick Jordan's words.
"Oh, Aidan. Were you the one who had to tell Rachel?"

He nodded. "It was me. I was working the ER when
Finn brought Libby in. The social worker and I had to
sit down with them."

"That must've been so hard." She squeezed his hand.

"Yeah. You never get used to those conversations.

Libby's husband held it together until their daughter got there. I hope they've got family somewhere, someone to lean on."

"Did you..." She couldn't think of a nice way to phrase what she wanted to ask.

He frowned at her, looking curious.

"Did you have to...see Libby?"

"No. She was pronounced dead at the scene. I heard it was a gunshot wound."

"Yes, Detective Jordan said she was probably shot using a silencer, which must be why no one heard anything."

"Do you or your uncle have any idea who'd want to do something like this? Maybe Sydney has some thoughts?"

Savanna shook her head. "No. Not at all. Libby was kind to everyone. She's had that florist shop ever since I was a kid, or maybe longer. I remember Miss Priscilla always had Libby supply their recital flowers every spring." She shook her head. "We used her last June for the art festival. She was so great; she'd never take any money for the flowers I use in my classroom when we work on still life paintings. I don't understand how this could've happened. Nothing about it makes sense."

"Well, I'm sure the police will get to the bottom of it. It's a small town. Someone has to have seen or heard something."

After dinner, they strolled over to the Carson Theatre. Main Street was lined with overflowing spring flower boxes in front of the shops, and the trees were adorned with tiny, warm white fairy lights. Soft music drifted through the air from the weekly acoustic concerts on the lawn of Carson Park. Savanna genuinely loved this town. But she couldn't keep a chill from crawling up her spine as she thought of Libby lying dead in her beloved greenhouse this morning. She hoped Aidan was right and Detective Jordan was able to catch the killer quickly.

They got in line at the Carson Theatre's outdoor box office window under the lighted red-and-white marquee. Savanna always looked forward to an evening here. She'd attended almost weekly since the grand opening last winter, sometimes seeing the same movie twice. Carson hadn't had its own theater in decades, until Jack Carson's pet project had finally become a reality. He'd created an inviting venue with two large screens; heated, reclining seats; and bottomless popcorn. The interior of the space was lush and beautiful, with deep-red carpeting, elegant chandeliers, and the Century of Cinema mural Jack had commissioned Savanna to paint, a tribute to film through the decades that took up an entire wall, with references from Hitchcock to Harry Potter to Captain Marvel.

"Wait," Savanna said as they turned to walk into the theater. Something had caught her eye. "Isn't that Anthony Kent's car?" She pointed to the baby-blue Ford Flex parked in front of Skylar's law office, next to the building that held Libby's Blooms. All the businesses at that end of Main Street were closed at this time of night, nearly nine-thirty.

Aidan shrugged. "Is it?"

"I'm sure it is. Nobody has that color Flex around here but him. I wonder if it's still there from this morning."

"Today was probably the worst day of his life. I doubt he'd make coming back to get his car a priority, right?"

Something nagged at her, though she couldn't put her finger on it. "Right, of course."

They were seated in the middle of the last row in the theater to watch the new summer superhero film, hands linked on the armrest between the seats, when Savanna heard a familiar voice.

"Oh my goodness! Well, how are you, Ms. Shepherd? And Dr. Gallager! I thought that was you." Tricia Williams, one of the teachers Savanna worked with, hurried down their row, pulling her daughter along behind her. Tricia's trademark blond pixie-shag had been teased higher for her night out, and her burgundy lipstick was perfect, as always. Her daughter kept her head tilted downward, brown hair falling forward like a curtain.

Aidan greeted them, and Savanna instinctively unlinked her fingers from his.

"Hello! Hi, Cassandra." She smiled widely up at Tricia and then at her daughter. Cassandra was in her fourth grade class. "We're so excited for the movie. Aren't you?"

Tricia replied for her daughter. "We are too! I almost didn't see you—it's so dark in here. But I thought, could that be our sweet Ms. Shepherd and Dr. Gallager? We just had to run up here to see two of our favorite people. Right, Cassandra?"

The girl nodded. Like a lot of children running into a teacher away from school, she seemed suddenly shy. Teachers were out of context out in the community; Savanna remembered the feeling. It could be a little disconcerting. Cassandra stuck a handful of popcorn in her mouth.

The lights went down even lower as the previews began. Tricia's phone buzzed in her hand, and she glanced down at it.

"Mom, it's starting." Cassandra's voice was an urgent whisper in the now-quiet theater.

"It's only the previews." Tricia flapped one hand toward her daughter before turning back to face Savanna and Aidan. "So, you two—"

A man in the next row cleared his throat, making a point of turning around in his seat to stare back at them.

"Mom!" The girl pulled at Tricia's sleeve.

Savanna took a deep breath, trying to quell her rising stress level. The last thing she wanted was to be the focus of Tricia Williams' scrutiny. And she certainly didn't need other theatergoers angry over the disruption. Plus, she always looked forward to the previews.

"All right, all right. We'd better get back to our seats. We'll chat on Monday!" Tricia followed Cassandra down toward the front. "I'm going now, Randall," she said to the man in the next row as she passed him.

Savanna stared wide-eyed at Aidan. *Oh my God,* she mouthed silently.

He smiled at her and shrugged, then took her hand again and put his lips close to her ear. "Don't worry about it."

Six rows in front of them, Tricia Williams was encased in a bubble of dim light as she furiously typed something into her phone. Cassandra leaned over to her, obviously saying something, and the light went out. *Good.*

Even so, tension snaked across Savanna's shoulders and the back of her neck. She did not want to "chat" on Monday with Tricia about her movie date with Aidan.

Maybe the woman would forget about it by then. Savanna resolved to steer clear of the teachers' lounge for a few days.

When Savanna arrived at her childhood home on Sunday evening, Skylar's husband Travis was at the grill. Sunday dinners were a longstanding tradition in the Shepherd family, with everyone taking turns at preparing the meal. Today was Skylar's turn, which meant Travis did the heavy lifting. Savanna stopped to pet the big orange tabby, Pumpkin, who was soaking up the sun in his usual chair outside the kitchen door.

"Something smells delicious." She peered over the top of the grill.

"Skylar's been wanting kabobs. It's finally nice out— perfect grilling weather."

"They look great!" Assorted chicken-and-steak skewers were loaded with green, red, and orange peppers and red onions. Travis brushed barbecue sauce over them one by one before he turned them over.

Nolan shot through the kitchen door, holding a frisbee as high as he could over his head. "Grandpa says Fonzie's here!"

Savanna's dog was immediately at attention, bounding around the giggling four-year-old.

"Hi, Nolan!" Savanna tousled his hair.

"Hi, Auntie Vanna," he said over his shoulder. He tossed the frisbee in a wild throw and took off across the green back yard after Fonzie.

Harlan joined them on the patio. Savanna's construction contractor dad was in his late fifties, his brown hair graying at the temples, though he still had the height and build of a linebacker. His tanned skin was the mark of time spent in the sun and wind, either working, fishing, or out riding his motorcycle. Underneath his sometimes intimidating exterior, he was a huge softie. His wife, Charlotte Shepherd, was the ruling force in their family, and Harlan was the sturdy foundation.

He handed a beer to Travis. A giggling Nolan sprinted by them, shooting a look over his shoulder to make sure Fonzie was still following him. "That boy sure loves your dog," Harlan said to Savanna. "I'll get you something to drink. What do you feel like?"

"That's okay," she said. "I'm going in. Are Uncle Freddie and Max here yet?"

Her dad nodded. "They're inside, passing Hannah around."

"Oh, I want a turn."

Around the large kitchen island, she found her mother Charlotte, Skylar, and her uncles. Uncle Max was cradling the baby. Savanna gave him a little hug around his shoulders, careful not to jostle him. "Are you doing okay?"

"We're brilliant," he said, looking down at Hannah. She wrapped one tiny hand around his pinkie finger. Her toothless smile tugged at Savanna's heart, and Uncle Max's too, judging by his expression. "Aren't we now? We certainly are."

"Hi there, kid," Uncle Freddie said to Savanna, coming around the island and planting a light kiss on the top of her head. A renowned architect for a Fortune 500 firm, Charlotte's brother Freddie had thick silver hair, perpetually tanned-from-the-golf-course skin, and the kind of square-jawed, confident smile that won over colleagues and clients alike. At fifty-two, he was a few years younger than Charlotte and Harlan. He ushered Savanna away from the cluster of people around the kitchen island. "What about you? It sounded like yesterday was quite the traumatic event. Were you close with the florist?"

"Sydney was closer with her, but we were friends. I can't believe it. I've tried to imagine who on earth would ever have wanted Libby dead, and I just can't."

"I'm sorry you girls have lost a friend."

"I'm sorry Uncle Max had to find her that way," Savanna said quietly.

Uncle Freddie nodded. "I am too. And I'm not happy with your sheriff's department. They could've ruled out Max as a suspect on the spot. He told them he was at the café with your mother before coming into the shop yesterday morning. Max and I talked about it, and I put a call in to that detective."

Uncle Freddie was probably right. Savanna hated the impression her uncles were probably forming of Nick Jordan, who was only following procedure. But they didn't know the detective; they'd only been in Carson since last November.

Freddie Quinn and his husband Max had visited Carson last summer when they'd moved their daughter Ellie into her dorm at the nearby university. When Freddie had called a month later to announce they'd put an offer on a house in Carson, he'd claimed it was so they could be on the water, and closer to family. Savanna knew it was so they could be near Ellie. Freddie and Max had been at every single one of their daughter's soccer games, parent nights, doctor visits, school plays, and a thousand other little things through the years.

Max had adopted Ellie a couple of years before he'd met Freddie. Ellie's biological parents had appointed Max as their daughter's godfather when she was born. He must've been shocked when he'd abruptly found himself a parent after the couple had perished in a tragic house fire. Two-year-old Ellie had somehow miraculously survived.

Savanna loved that her cousin was nearby now. And it was obvious from the way Ellie had gone from anxious and homesick back to her sweet, joyful self that she was much more at ease now that her dads were nearby. She'd often been part of their growing group around the Sunday dinner table.

Savanna fished around for something reassuring to say to Uncle Freddie. "I'm sure Detective Jordan will call you back. He's good at what he does. He'll get Uncle Max cleared quickly, I'm positive."

Uncle Freddie nodded. "He'd better." He must've caught Savanna's worried expression, because he went on. "Now listen, you know me. I was nothing but polite when I called. I'm getting the feeling the detective is also a friend?"

She tipped her head to one side. "He is. But I'm just as upset about this thing as you are."

"You know who isn't?" Uncle Max had moved closer to their private little chat. "Me. It'll all get sorted, and from what Savanna says about this detective, Libby's killer will be brought to justice."

Savanna turned toward him, seeing he'd passed Hannah on to Charlotte. "That's right," she agreed. "Mom, it was my turn. Don't monopolize the baby!"

Charlotte was making silly faces and cooing noises at her granddaughter. Savanna's mother was fine-boned and the shortest of the Shepherd women. Her auburn hair fell just past her shoulders; the glint of small gold earrings peeked through her waves. She carried Hannah over to Savanna, carefully transferring her. "Only because I have to go change. I've got a flight out right after dinner." Charlotte Shepherd worked as a management consultant and often traveled for business.

Hannah began to fuss the moment Savanna touched her. "Oh no, little one," she said, immediately launching into the gentle swaying, bouncing dance that settled most babies right down. "Let's go see what your big brother's doing, shall we?"

Sydney came through the kitchen door as Savanna carried Hannah out onto the patio. "The highlight of your evening has arrived, ladies and gents," Sydney announced, an oversized foil-covered pan in her arms. "I give you my own personal creation—banana split cake!"

"Ooh, really?" Savanna turned and followed her back into the kitchen. "Let me see!"

Sydney set the dessert on the counter and uncovered it, revealing a wide layer of yellow vanilla pudding across the pan.

"Oh," Savanna said. She'd expected to be wowed.

"Just wait. There are seven delicious layers to this masterpiece. But," Sydney added as Nolan sidled into the kitchen, "only people who eat their dinner can have banana split cake."

The little boy sighed loudly. "I know the rules, okay?"

Sydney scooped him up, whispering something in his ear.

Nolan shrieked and put a small hand on either side of Syd's face. "Are you for real?"

She laughed and set him on a stool at the counter. "One bite. A preview. And only because I'm your favorite red-headed aunt and I said so."

Skylar threw her hands up in the air, laughing. "Pure anarchy, I swear. You're lucky I love you," she said, making a kissy face at Sydney before exiting to check on Travis and the kabobs.

Savanna set a plate in front of Nolan, and Sydney cut the tiniest square possible from the corner of the pan. The concoction she served to their nephew was a mess of pretty: layer after layer of graham cracker, bananas, chocolate pudding, strawberries, cream cheese, more graham cracker, and vanilla pudding. Sydney added a dollop of whipped cream on top.

"Here you go, young sir." Uncle Max handed Nolan a spoon. "You're the official taste-tester."

"Thank you, old sir!" Nolan bowed his head deeply toward Uncle Max. Savanna clapped a hand over her mouth, and Sydney burst out laughing. Four-year-old Nolan had meant nothing but respect, despite how it had sounded.

Max grinned. "He's got my number."

Over dinner, with Hannah happily pushing baby crackers around her highchair tray, Savanna leaned over to Sydney. "I thought you said you were inviting Finn tonight." She kept her voice quiet; they'd discussed when might be the right time to invite Finn and Aidan to Sunday dinner, but hadn't reached a real decision.

"He has this thing about parents," Syd whispered. "They don't usually like him."

"What? That's ridiculous," Savanna whispered back.

"Where's Aidan?"

"I...um...forgot to invite him." Savanna couldn't quite imagine throwing Aidan into her large, loud family dinner, as much as a big part of her yearned to have him here.

Sydney scowled at her. "You did not forget."

"I wasn't ready! And it's a good thing, since you flaked on bringing Finn," Savanna whispered.

"Okay, do-over next weekend. For your birthday dinner."

Savanna's eyes widened. Nothing like upping the stakes. "I don't—"

Harlan cleared his throat at the head of the table. The family had gone quiet, all eyes on Sydney and Savanna.

"Care to share?" Charlotte asked sweetly.

"No, thank you," Sydney said.

"Mm-hmm." Charlotte speared a bite of chicken, her gaze moving to Harlan.

He sat back in his chair. "Girls. We hope you know friends are always welcome at our table."

"Yes," Charlotte agreed. "Anytime either of you wishes to invite a guest, perhaps a significant other, we want you to feel comfortable."

"Significant other." Sydney let the words roll slowly off her tongue. "That's some serious stuff."

"All right. I think they get our point," their mother said, chuckling as she looked at Harlan.

"Significant other." Savanna said the words to Sydney, enunciating each syllable.

"Boyfriend," Sydney said firmly.

Savanna laughed. "Okay then."

The evening wound down when Charlotte left to catch her flight to Denver. Skylar and Travis headed home to put the kids to bed, and Sydney covered the dessert she was leaving for her dad.

"I'll walk you out," Uncle Max offered when Savanna gathered her light sweater and purse to go.

"It's dark out. Use the front door," Harlan advised. "The bulb just went out on the patio."

Savanna hugged her father goodbye and walked through the living room with Max. She gasped. "The front door." She suddenly realized what had left her unsettled last night.

Max turned, looking at her curiously.

"The front door, Uncle Max. You said Libby always liked you to park in the back of the flower shop, to leave the street parking for patrons."

"That's right," he agreed.

"Did that include Anthony Kent? When he came in to do the books? Was it Libby's rule for all of you, Anthony and Rachel included?"

"Yes. Why?"

"Why did he come in through the front yesterday?"

"Well...he probably saw the hubbub outside the shop and just pulled up to go in," Uncle Max offered.

"But the Kents live in the neighborhood behind the shops. I've arrived at the same time she has before when I'm picking up flowers—she comes in the back way to the parking lot."

Max was frowning. "You're right. I pulled in to open the shop last Thursday just as Anthony did. We parked at the back of the lot, next to each other. He doesn't take Main Street."

"So why did he use the front entrance Saturday? Why did he park on the street? Unless he wanted the folks out front to see him arrive. After Libby was already found dead."

Chapter Four

S AVANNA SUCCESSFULLY DODGED TRICIA WILLIAMS all
day Monday. She'd brought her own coffee this
morning, and then joined Jack Carson in his
library for lunch. Jack was the kind of friend who'd
brave the teachers' lounge for her much-needed coffee
refill, and he did—twice. He'd reported back both times
that Tricia wondered why she hadn't seen Savanna at
all today.

"I kind of thought she'd just forget about it," Savanna said. "I don't get what the big deal is."

Jack was the first person at school to make her feel
welcome a year and a half ago when she'd come home
to Carson. Being a librarian meant he was the black
sheep in the Carson family, who all worked within the
family's commercial real estate corporation. Savanna
had thought him a little awkward at first, but she'd
quickly revised her opinion. He wasn't awkward anymore with her. He'd become a kind and loyal best friend.

He stood in her classroom doorway after the last
bell. "You don't know Tricia." He glanced over his shoulder into the long hallway before continuing. "She has
this burning desire to be the source—the person with
all the goods. It'd kill her if she thought you gave some-

one else the hot scoop about you and Dr. Gallager out alone together in the back of the movie theater."

Savanna laughed. "You make it sound so illicit! We were there because we both love superhero movies."

"Yeah, that's working against you too."

"What?" She frowned, curious. "How do you mean?"

"I think her exact words were *'Why wasn't Mollie with them? I know it was a date.'* Tricia figured if you and Aidan were out platonically, you'd have brought his daughter. She and Rosa Taylor had a whole conversation about it while I was getting your third cup of coffee."

"Hey, don't judge. You drink your share too. And in what world would it be appropriate for us to bring an eight-year-old to a PG-13 movie with violence and kissing?"

Jack shrugged. "Don't blame me. I don't write the news—I only report it."

She sighed. "Great. So, she just wants to be in the know, is that it? Maybe I'll be an adult tomorrow and inform her I'm dating Aidan. Not that it's any of her business."

"I wouldn't do that. The last thing you need is to have your relationship with one of the parents put under a microscope by the school district. Be vague. Or better yet, keep avoiding her."

"Hold on. Is it really a big thing? I mean... I'm Mollie's art teacher. I only have her in class two hours a week. And we've been so careful to never have any hint of impropriety whenever Aidan has to be at the school for something."

"I know. I've seen that firsthand. But I'd avoid starting that conversation. Keep flying under the radar as long as you can."

Savanna stood, gathering her purse and sweater. "I don't like this." She felt very uncomfortable, little fingers of worry tapping the back of her neck. "I'm not going to knowingly break the rules. Should I talk to Mr. Clay?" The idea intensified her discomfort. She loved the principal, who had complimented her again last week on how happy the children and parents were with her classes. Mr. Clay had hired Savanna after she'd left her art authentication career at Chicago's famed Kenilworth Historical Museum; she knew he'd rolled the dice by giving her the art teacher position, but she'd fallen in love with her job, and Mr. Clay seemed pleased with her work.

"I think that's a bad idea," Jack said. "I'm not even certain there is an actual rule, but Elaina and I try to keep things on the down-low too. Her son Carter's in my computer class once a week." Elaina Jenson taught at Carson Elementary as well. Now that Savanna thought about it, Jack and Elaina definitely kept their interactions platonic around school. "You're always respectful, and your…friendship…with Dr. Gallager hasn't impacted your teaching or treatment of Mollie. Leave it at that. Tricia will settle down at some point."

Maybe he was right. After all, he'd been at the school eight or nine years and knew all the teachers fairly well.

"Ms. Shepherd?" The small voice came from behind Jack. He stepped to the side, and Mollie entered the classroom, backpack on and sparkly pink tote bag in hand.

"Hi, Mollie." Savanna smiled at her. How long had she been standing there? Savanna tried to replay Jack's words in her head. She didn't think Mollie had heard anything she could decipher or worry about. "Ready for dance?"

"Yes. We get our costumes today!" The little girl clasped her hands, clearly excited, and then looked up at Jack. "For m-my recital. I have t-two costumes, Mr. Carson."

Savanna only ever heard the stutter at school. When Mollie was with Aidan, or in almost any other setting, it disappeared. She was making nice progress with the school speech therapist, who'd told Aidan the stutter would likely disappear as Mollie got older.

"How exciting," Jack replied. "What classes are you in?"

"B-ballet and tap."

"Really? I love tap! Did you know I used to take dance at Miss Priscilla's too?"

Mollie giggled, looking at Savanna and then back at Jack. "You did?"

He nodded. "I think I was around your age. Oh my gosh, it was so much fun."

"Mr. Marcus is s-s-silly," Mollie said, beaming up at Jack. "Did you like him too?"

Jack chuckled. "Oh, well, Miss Priscilla was my tap instructor way back then. She was not even a little bit silly." He glanced at Savanna.

She smiled. Mollie came right out of her shell around certain people, and Jack was obviously one of them. "Miss Priscilla was never silly," she agreed with Jack. "She was my ballet teacher, but I never took tap. Which is your favorite?"

Mollie turned both hands palm up toward the ceiling, shrugging. "I like my p-pink ballet tutu better than the l-leggings we wear for tap. But my tap shoes are m-m-my favorite," she said, her expression serious.

Jack checked the analog wall clock behind Savanna's desk. "You are so right," he told Mollie. "Tap shoes are the most fun. I've got to run. Enjoy!"

Mollie drank her juice box and munched on a cheese stick in the car during the short drive to Miss Priscilla's. Savanna had volunteered to bring Mollie to dance two days per week, since the girl's class time was right after school. She'd noticed Aidan taking turns with Finn, Mollie's grandpa, and even the neighbor who occasionally babysat, and figured it only made sense. The two dance classes were back-to-back on Mondays and Thursdays. Savanna was even starting to enjoy her time in the lobby where parents gathered. She'd made a few friends, and it was nice seeing Mollie so happy. The girl loved her classes, even with stern Miss Priscilla. It was a shame Nolan's theater class fell on alternate days with Mollie's classes. She could've helped get him there or back too.

She drove down Main Street, wanting to get a look at Libby's shop before she turned the corner to park behind the building. Wide yellow police tape crisscrossed over the front door of Libby's Blooms. A large black-and-red sign declared *No Admittance*.

Poor Anthony and Rachel Kent. And who was taking care of all the plants? The store's entire inventory would be useless without watering and care. Detective Jordan must be letting the two of them in for maintenance. Uncle Max was off work until further notice. Libby's husband had told Max he'd be in touch if and when the shop reopened. The idea of Libby's closing permanently hadn't occurred to Savanna until she'd heard that. But everything being up in the air made sense. She didn't think Anthony had any florist's training, and Rachel was in nursing school.

The door to the Studio A classroom in Priscilla's Dance Academy was still closed when they arrived. The three studios in the dance school each had a gleaming, professional dance floor, an independent sound system, and a barre along a wall of mirrors. Mollie went into a changing room to put on her leotard and leggings, and Savanna chose a chair in the corner of the lobby near a table. She had the baby blanket she was knitting for Hannah in her lap by the time Mollie returned to her side. The lobby was filled with young children in tap shoes. Class should've started a minute or two ago.

The rear entrance door swished open, and Mollie's tap instructor, Marcus Valentine, entered, wearing dark sunglasses. "So sorry I'm late," he addressed the group. "Are we ready? You know what today is, don't you?"

"Costume day!" A girl in short pigtails jumped up from the chair beside her dad.

"Costume day," Marcus confirmed, smiling at his students. "You'll try them on right over your leotards, and you can wear them during class if you'd like, *just* for today. After that, they'll stay safely in your closet until dress rehearsal. Moms and dads, I'll be sending an email on how to assemble the headpiece. Follow me, tappers!"

Over a dozen seven- to ten-year-olds clustered around Mr. Marcus. He was new to Miss Priscilla's, having replaced the former tap instructor three months ago. Savanna had thought the former teacher would be a hard act to follow, but Marcus Valentine had filled her shoes seamlessly. The kids loved him. Mollie said he was *"jokey, like Uncle Finn."* Marcus looked to be in his early twenties, and he carried himself like a dancer, spine perfectly straight, movements fluid. Tall and lithe, he dressed simply in black dance pants and tucked-in white T-shirt. His mass of dark hair was sometimes left loose, though today he wore a headband that kept it off his forehead.

Miss Priscilla spoke loudly from the doorway of Studio C. "Mr. Marcus." The words were sharp and clipped.

"Good afternoon!" He turned toward her as he opened the classroom door, allowing the students in. "You're looking exceptionally lovely today, Miss Priscilla."

"Your costume rack is in your studio, organized alphabetically. Each parent must sign that they've received the full ensemble. And take off those ridiculous sunglasses."

"Yes, ma'am." He removed the shades to reveal a large, vivid purple shiner around his left eye.

The lobby fell suddenly quiet.

"Put them back on." Miss Priscilla's voice dripped with irritation. "See me before you leave tonight." She turned back to the rack of costumes she was sorting.

Mr. Marcus stepped into Studio A, tossing a quick glance around the lobby full of parents. He donned the sunglasses, brought his shoulders up in a shrug, and shut the door.

"Did you see that?" A hissed whisper from one mom to another filled the silence.

"His eye looked awful!"

"He must've been in a fight."

The small room buzzed with speculation.

"With whom? Where? I didn't hear about anything happening."

"I can't believe he showed up like that! What will our kids think?"

"He tried to be discreet, until—"

"Shhh!"

Many of these parents had taken dance with Miss Priscilla as children themselves. Most of them were intimidated by her. Savanna was frankly glad the woman across from her had been shushed. She really didn't want Miss Priscilla to overhear, or think they were all talking about her, though they sort of were.

The older woman next to Savanna—Callie's grandmother, Savanna recalled—leaned over to her and spoke quietly. "Do you know anything about Mr. Marcus?"

She shook her head. "Only that Mollie loves his class. He seems like a nice guy."

"Someone didn't think so," the grandmother said. "He ought to be more careful, having to work around kids. That sets a bad example."

Savanna looked at her. She wasn't exactly wrong, but... "Well, we don't know what happened. For all we know, he might've taken a nasty fall in the tub or something. And he did try to keep it covered. It looked a day or two old; there was some yellow around the purple. Maybe he hoped it'd be mostly gone by the time he got to work today?"

The older woman nodded. "Yes, you're probably right." She frowned, her gaze moving to a dad in a yellow polo shirt a few seats down. "Tim, your little guy takes the optional Saturday classes sometimes, doesn't he?"

The man looked up from his newspaper. "What's that, Mrs. Holloway?"

"Your Zachary, he takes the Saturday classes sometimes, right? Was he in class this weekend?"

Tim nodded. "Sure. He hopes to get into the competition troupe, so he's been putting in extra time. But he only did jazz this past weekend. Tap was cancelled. Not sure why. Maybe Mr. Marcus was recovering from whatever happened to his eye."

"I'm surprised they didn't cancel all the classes, with the awful incident next door," Mrs. Holloway mused. "The police were just leaving Libby's when I came for my noon yoga class."

That began a brand-new round of speculation in the lobby about who had murdered Libby Kent. All the theories were outlandish. Savanna couldn't think of any reason someone would kill Libby. The shooting had to have been personal for the culprit to have gone all the way up to the rooftop greenhouse to find her. Savanna made a mental note to stop by and ask Detective Jordan if he'd officially cleared Uncle Max yet; maybe she could glean a little info about the case while she was there.

The door to Studio A opened. The dancers who had ballet next stayed, filing into Studio B after changing their shoes. Miss Priscilla's husband, Dylan Blake, came through the lobby, carrying two large boxes stacked on one another. In his late forties, and of medium height, he was younger than Miss Priscilla by a handful of years, and an inch or so shorter. Sandy-blond hair, dimples, and a mustache that somehow managed to look debonair rather than dated complemented his outgoing demeanor, a pleasant contrast to Miss Priscilla's more reserved attitude. He often partnered with her in her ballroom dance and swing classes in addition to directing some of the theater numbers the school performed at the annual spring recital.

Dylan greeted the parents and caregivers, glancing down and taking care not to trip over anyone's feet in the small space. A cloud of cologne followed him, assaulting Savanna's nostrils with a powerful evergreen-and-musk combination; she unconsciously turned and looked away, brushing the backs of her fingers momentarily against her nose. Wow. She'd noticed that about him before, but had forgotten how strong the scent was.

"I know," Mrs. Holloway whispered. "Miss Priscilla needs to take away his cologne bottle."

Savanna stifled a laugh. "Shh," she said, staring after him. He didn't seem to have heard. The poor man probably had no idea how he smelled.

"The rest of the recital props came. Where should I put them?" He set the boxes down on the semi-circular reception desk. The sleeves of Dylan's work shirt were rolled up to his elbows, revealing muscled forearms.

The receptionist looked up at him, then turned on her swivel chair to defer to Miss Priscilla, who was sorting the ballet costumes for her Studio B class.

"Put them in the office for now. We'll have to make room upstairs." Miss Priscilla crossed to the front door between two of the studios and poked her head out. "What in the—" She marched back over to the reception desk. "Why is the police tape still up?"

Dylan came out of Miss Priscilla's office. "Well, I'd say because they're still investigating over there." "I've got to start my class. I thought you were going over to the station to make them get rid of that mess. It's an eyesore for our school!" Her voice grew louder and higher toward the end. She stared at her husband, eyes wide and hands now on her narrow hips.

The man turned and took in the group of parents in the lobby, most of them watching the exchange, before focusing on his wife. He stormed past her out the front door. "Fine!"

Miss Priscilla slammed Studio C's door behind her, leaving silence in her wake. The receptionist at the desk ducked her head and scooted her chair closer to her computer screen, obviously avoiding acknowledging the argument or the parents watching.

Savanna looked down at her knitting needles, not wanting to be part of the low rumblings moving through the lobby now. Usually, when Miss Priscilla's husband came through the studio while Savanna was waiting for Mollie, he didn't converse much at all with his wife. Miss Priscilla was always all business, and Blake was more likely to stop and exchange pleasantries with parents or staff. Savanna was sure he was upset he'd been yelled at in front of customers. The police tape looked like just what it was: a device warning people away from the flower shop during the investigation. Savanna doubted it was hurting the dance school's business.

Sheesh. She hoped Miss Priscilla had calmed down enough to deal with her ten and under ballet class. The thought made her so uncomfortable that she set her knitting down. "Going to ask Kate about a class," she told Mrs. Holloway. "Will you mind my things, please?"

"Of course. I'll be here." Callie's grandmother was working on a sudoku puzzle.

Savanna casually strolled down Main Street from the dance school toward Kate's Yoga, stopping to peek through the window into Studio B. The curtains were closed, as Miss Priscilla maintained privacy for the children's classes, only opening them for the adult sessions. But when Savanna stooped low and caught a glimpse between the curtains, she saw Priscilla walking down the line of dancers at the barre, smiling and nodding as she appraised their form. All right, so at least she'd been able to turn off her anger at her husband and be calm for her class.

Savanna reached Kate's and read the store hours on the door for good measure, then walked back toward the dance school. Passing Libby's and the crime scene tape, she shivered briefly. It was hard to believe Libby was gone, hard to believe the way it had happened, and that poor Uncle Max had had the misfortune to encounter that scene. She hated that her sister had the constant view of her late friend's closed-down shop through the front window of Fancy Tails. She paused at the building access door. The plain door in the red brick storefront sat between Libby's Blooms' Main Street entrance and Priscilla's Dance Academy's front entrance. She'd seen it and walked by it so many times, she'd never given a thought to its existence. Just through the beveled glass window above the doorknob, she could see the stairway that went from Libby's shop up to the second-floor storage space and then to the roof. Small, simple black lettering on the glass bore the words *Owners / Occupants Only*. Without thinking, Savanna tried the handle. It was locked. Well, of course it was.

After handing off Mollie to her grandma Jean at Priscilla's, Savanna crossed to Fancy Tails. The little bell over the door jingled as she entered. Sydney was at the appointment desk on the computer, and her assistant, Willow, stood behind the treat counter on the other side of the shop.

"Hey, Willow! Syd. Got a minute?"

"Sure. What's up?"

"I'm going to stop by and talk to Detective Jordan and wondered if you want to come."

Sydney dropped the pen she was holding and grabbed her purse. "You just saved me from having to fabricate an excuse to see him. This is perfect timing; we have a little lull. Next grooming appointment isn't until..." She leaned over and checked the schedule. "Oh good, not for another half hour."

Sydney left Willow in charge and walked with Savanna over to the Carson Village complex just beyond Skylar's law office. They passed Dylan Blake as he was leaving the police station.

He looked exasperated. "I tried telling her the crime scene tape stays up until they're finished with whatever they need to do there. They must think I'm an idiot for asking."

"I don't think it's an issue," Savanna reassured him. "People love your dance school."

"Thank you." He turned his attention to his phone, probably texting Miss Priscilla what he'd been told. Savanna didn't really see what the woman was upset about. With or without the visual reminder, all of Carson was aware Libby Kent had been murdered this weekend.

Detective Jordan came down the hallway of the Carson Village Police Station. "Sydney, Savanna. What can I do for you?"

Svanna said, "I was just thinking—"

He put a hand up. "On second thought, let's talk in my office." He smiled, a rare enough sight that it still surprised her. Nick Jordan was a serious person, especially on the job. Before she'd gotten to know him, Savanna had assumed he was always cranky. She'd finally said something about it to him in a moment of frustration last year. She had to give him credit; since then he'd seemed to be making a conscious effort to come off a little less gruff. Sometimes. He held the door open for them. "Have a seat. You were thinking?"

She debated whether she should mention noticing Anthony Kent's car parked on Main Street Saturday, and the oddity of him coming in the front entrance at Libby's. Even in her head, it sounded ridiculous. The man could park his car anywhere he pleased. She pushed it to the back of her mind. "We wondered if anyone's been in to take care of the plants."

"Oh. That's it?" The detective rested his elbows on the desk. "You mean you don't have Libby's murder solved already?"

Savanna smiled. "Funny." He knew her well; probably why he'd ushered her into his office rather than chatting in the vestibule. "I don't. I really did want to make sure someone's been able to take care of the plants. My uncle said Libby was working on something important in the greenhouse. And aside from that, I think a lot of the shop's inventory is live plants that need care."

"You're right. We've had an officer accompany the daughter in twice a day—not sure why watering plants is a twice-a-day job, but I suppose I don't know much about plants."

"I think Rachel must know at least a little," Sydney said. "She fills in for Libby now and then when she's sick. Or when she used to—I mean—" Sydney's voice cracked. She frowned, unable to finish the thought.

Savanna spoke. "Detective, Libby was a good friend,

especially to Sydney. This has been hard on everyone. Including our uncle. Have you cleared him yet?"

"Working on it. We have to verify his alibi. That should happen tomorrow, but I can't make any promises."

"I don't understand. He and our mom had an early breakfast together Saturday at the diner. That should be easy to verify."

He nodded, noncommittal and poker-faced.

"You can't tell us what the holdup is," Sydney said, frustration in her tone. "We get it. But Nick. You know he didn't do it, right? It's ridiculous that you even have to rule him out."

Detective Jordan's expression changed nearly imperceptibly. The corner of his mouth twitched, and he raised his eyebrows but said nothing.

"He can't say he knows Max is innocent," Savanna said, glancing at Sydney. "I get that too. Procedure and all that." She placed her hands on the armrests of her chair to stand. "But so you know, Detective, Max Watson isn't capable of hurting a fly. I mean, maybe a fly. If it was on one of his plants. He was just the unlucky person who found Libby. He was pretty shaken up. My family would like him eliminated as a suspect as soon as possible."

"I understand," he said. "I'm sorry I can't be more helpful at this time. And believe me, I'm aware your family is upset. Max's husband was here first thing this morning to talk to me."

"Oh," Sydney said, exchanging glances with Savanna. "Did that, uh, go all right?"

"I assured him I hope to have it resolved by Tuesday."

Savanna suspected Nick Jordan could handle Uncle

Freddie, and vice versa. Both men presented an air of calm authority.

"So what are you doing to catch Libby's killer?" Sydney leaned earnestly forward in her chair. "Can you tell us that, at least? There's got to be something you can use to figure it out. Do you have any idea how Libby's husband and daughter are feeling right now?"

"I—" Jordan began, but Sydney cut him off.

"I'll tell you. Mad. Sad. Horrified. Hopeless. Cheated out of all the years they thought they still had left with her. Robbed of the plans they'd made. Empty. Angry." Her voice had risen as she'd ticked off each sentiment, and her words were clipped and furious by the time she stopped. Her cheeks were flushed bright red, her jaw clenching and unclenching. She'd listed everything she herself was struggling with.

Savanna reached over and slid her hand into her sister's, covering it with her other one. "You're right."

Syd looked at her, and Savanna expected to see tears, but unlike her, Sydney didn't cry when she got angry. "I know I'm right!"

"He knows Anthony and Rachel are feeling all of that. And you know he's doing everything possible to find Libby's killer," Savanna said softly, her gaze moving from Sydney to the detective.

"I know." Sydney looked at Jordan. "I know you are. I'm sorry. This just isn't fair."

He nodded, his expression sympathetic, and rested his elbows on his desk. "It's not fair at all. We'll get to the bottom of this, Sydney. I promise you. I liked Libby too. She was a kind and caring woman. Her family needed her. Carson needed her."

The detective walked them out. He stopped them

before they parted.

"I do have a few leads I'm working on." He looked at Savanna. "You really don't have anything for me? No tiny detail you spotted Saturday morning that gives away our killer?"

"I seriously cannot read you sometimes," she said, shaking her head at him.

"I'm only half kidding." He unwrapped a red-and-white peppermint candy and popped it in his mouth. "Want one?"

She declined. "How long's it been since you quit smoking?"

"A long time. Too long," he said wryly. "But my wife's happy, and candy helps with the cravings. Anyway, let me know if anything strikes you. I mean it. You were instrumental in getting all the pieces to fall into place with Bellamy. You've got the eye."

Savanna beamed, feeling her heart swell. Last summer's race to find John Bellamy's killer had certainly challenged her attention to detail, from that discrepancy she'd spotted in his office to the crucial clue she'd uncovered with a friend's cell phone. She knew Jordan had indulged her input with some hesitation, but it was gratifying to know he took her clue-finding knack seriously. "Thank you. That means a lot coming from you, Detective."

He cleared his throat. "Talk soon." He turned and was gone inside the building.

Savanna smiled to herself. If she knew one thing for sure about the detective, he was perpetually uncomfortable with sentiment.

But Jordan's confidence in her only reinforced the idea that had started to take root outside the dance school. She squeezed Sydney's hand, which she still hadn't let go of. "We need to talk to Uncle Max tomorrow after school," she told her sister. "I have an idea."

Chapter Five

F ONZIE DIDN'T GREET SAVANNA WHEN she came in that evening. She went searching, having a hunch where she'd find him. Her dad had been at her house all afternoon, installing a set of French doors from the living room out onto the deck. He'd knocked out the small window and part of the wall to create room for the doors, after completing the vaulted ceiling project from unused dormer space, all based on plans Uncle Freddie had drawn up. It was as if Harlan and Uncle Freddie saw right into Savanna's head. They completely got her vision for the seventy-year-old home, and little by little, they were helping her make it a reality.

"Oh, wow! I love them—they look gorgeous," she said of the doors. Now when she sat on the couch at night, she'd have a full view of the dunes and the lake beyond.

"They're also the safest ones on the market. Let me show you how this works."

Savanna listened and nodded as her dad ran through all the security features: door sensors, shock sensors, glass break sensors, and even a special bar she could place over the inside handles to prevent a break-in.

"These doors are connected to the home security system I installed, just like your windows and the front and back doors. I'd recommend keeping the alarm active."

She looked up at her dad. She couldn't fault him for his concern, not after the handful of near misses she'd been involved in since coming home to Carson. She was always careful to make sure her sisters or Aidan knew where she was going, and last year, at Aidan's urging, she'd made sure to bring someone along when she'd been pursuing a hunch while trying to find the councilman's killer. But even so, she and Sydney both had landed in the hospital after the killer had targeted her. That incident alone was probably to blame for the new gray at her dad's temples.

"Don't look at me that way," he said, his voice stern. "Keep the alarm on."

"That means every single time I go through these doors to the deck, I'll have to type in the code?"

"You're right, that sounds so exhausting. Your poor fingers."

She laughed. "Okay, okay, I'll keep the alarm on. Unless, like, Aidan or Sydney or you and Mom are over and we're cooking out and all the bad guys who wanted to break in here agreed to delay their crime spree for another day."

He didn't even crack a smile. "Says the woman who was nearly killed by bad guys twice in less than two years."

Savanna bit her bottom lip, looking down at Fonzie. "I'll keep it on. And I'll use that special bar thingie. Promise." She hugged her dad. "Thank you. How do you feel about chicken parm sandwiches?" Her mother was probably not due home until Tuesday or Wednesday. She hated to think of her dad eating dinner alone, though he never seemed to mind.

"That sounds great—I'm starving. I'm in no rush."

At the round kitchen table, steaming, toasted chicken parmesan sub sandwiches on their plates, Savanna speared a forkful of salad and pointed the utensil toward the ceiling. "The skylight you put in makes this room so much brighter. And at night, I can see the stars. I love it."

"I'm enjoying the work. Now with the living room finished, we can get to the upstairs."

"I'm so happy here, Dad. It's perfect. Maybe I'll plan a dinner sometime next week so everyone can see what you've done. Don't worry about the upstairs. Your busy season's starting. We can wait until you have time."

"We'll see how it goes."

They ate together in silence for a bit. Savanna was perfectly comfortable sharing quiet space with her dad. When she was younger, calling to say hello every week from Chicago, she'd found it awkward and difficult to communicate when he'd answered the phone. Harlan said what he needed to say, but he didn't fill the pauses with small talk the way her mother did. Now that she was home again and older, she liked the quiet pauses between them.

Fonzie gave up waiting for scraps to fall and curled himself into a ball on Harlan's feet.

"He likes you," Savanna said.

"He just wants chicken."

She laughed. "Maybe. But he also likes you."

"I miss having a dog. It's been years. Your mother and I were throwing around the idea the other day."

"You were?" Savanna's voice rose excitedly. "What would you get? When? You know Sydney does grooming twice a month for that shelter in Lansing, right? Oh! Would you get a big guy this time? Or does Mom want another lap dog?"

Harlan laughed. "I don't know about any of that. I'm sure we'd adopt from the shelter if we did get a dog. But we're just talking."

"Okay, okay. I hope you do it! I know you love Pumpkin, but maybe he wants a dog friend."

"I'll keep you updated. Listen, I promised your mother I'd check with you about your birthday plans. We were thinking maybe we'd all go out for Sunday dinner. Giuseppe's or anywhere else you'd like."

"It's my turn to cook, though. I don't mind."

"She's not going to let you cook your own birthday dinner. Think about it and let us know. We could even move dinner to Saturday, if you'd like, since that's your birthday."

She shook her head. "No, Sunday's fine. It's tradition." Plus, Aidan had already asked her out for Saturday. At this time last year, they hadn't been steadily dating yet, what with Aidan's frequent trips back to New York for work, but somehow he'd remembered it was her birthday.

"All right." Harlan finished the last few bites of his sandwich, frowning.

"Is that okay? Did Mom want to move dinner?"

"Hmm? No. I was just thinking." He met her gaze. "About this Sunday. I don't know exactly how serious this thing is with Dr. Gallager, but you seem happy. Have you considered inviting him?" He put a hand up. "I know your mom and I joked about it last weekend, but maybe your birthday dinner would be a good time?"

She tilted her head, assessing her dad and feeling

her brow wrinkle. "Oh, wow."

He raised an eyebrow. "What?"

"You want to meet him. Like, officially."

"Meet him? I've known him longer than you have, Savanna."

"Not as the guy who's dating your daughter."

Harlan ran a hand through his hair and chuckled. "That's true. We'd like it if you invited him. It might help us work on thinking of him less as our doctor, and more as your, um…what did you all decide last Sunday? Boyfriend? Significant other? Special friend?"

"God, no!" She laughed. "Please never say 'special friend' again. Let's go with boyfriend. Are you going to do the whole third-degree dad inquisition on him?"

Harlan set his jaw and returned her gaze. He folded his arms across his chest, not gracing her impertinent question with a reply.

"Like you did with Rob?"

"A lot of good that did. I had him pegged from the moment I met him; you know that. He was a—"

Savanna reached over and put a hand on his arm. "I know. I didn't want to hear it. Don't worry. I've grown up since then." Rob Havemeyer had done her a favor by breaking off their engagement to travel the world and find himself. The experience had opened her eyes to the fact that she'd chosen a self-absorbed man-child to spend her life in Chicago with. Coming home to Carson had allowed her to get her bearings and start over. The relationship with Aidan still felt new in many ways, as they learned more about each other, but she'd known right away that he was nothing like her former fiancé.

"I'd never grill Dr. Gallager. I'm just putting it out there as an option. All right?"

"Yes." She nodded, having no clue whether she was ready to invite Aidan to Sunday dinner. "What about Sydney and Finn?"

"Oh. You think they're serious?"

"Well, I think she's more serious about him than I've seen her about anyone in a long time."

"Finn is just as welcome as Aidan, of course. That whole thing struck me as...temporary, I suppose? I thought he wasn't here to stay."

"I'm not sure. I think he isn't sure, either."

"I hope she doesn't get hurt," Harlan said. He stood and carried his plate to the sink. "Mind if I make a quick cup of coffee before I go?"

It was past ten when she waved goodbye to Harlan from her deck, the night warm for mid-May. She sat on her cushioned bench before going inside, closing her eyes and listening to the waves gently lap the shoreline. Her phone buzzed beside her with a video call.

"Hi there." She smiled at her phone screen.

Aidan's deep blue eyes crinkled back at her. He must be smiling, but at the moment all she could see was the upper half of his face and a vine-covered trellis behind him. He was on his back porch. "How are you? Hold on, let me—" The perspective shifted, and his head and shoulders came into view as he propped his phone up. He sat back.

"You're outside too? It's a beautiful night."

"I'd say your view is probably better than mine," he said. "I'll bet the water is still as glass right now."

"Almost. I can hear the waves, but it's very calm. My dad went fishing this morning; he's glad to have his boat in again. Have you ever taken Mollie out on the lake?"

"No. We've never been."

"What? How is that possible?"

"I don't know," Aidan said. "Constantly busy, I guess." He frowned and scrubbed a hand lightly over his five o'clock shadow, and Savanna swore she could smell his aftershave.

"Aidan. This is unacceptable. Let's go Wednesday. Just us, and then we can take Mollie another time."

He raised his eyebrows. "I'm not sure it's that easy. We'll need a boat, for one thing."

"That's not a problem. You do realize Carson has one of the largest marinas in the area, right? I know a guy."

He laughed. "You know a guy?"

"Gus at Sweetwater Boats. We can rent one. I'll call him in the morning. I don't want to take my dad's boat, not for your very first time on Lake Michigan." Her mind raced with plans. They could bring a cooler for dinner on the water. Should she take him south, toward Paradise Cove? Or north, toward Grand Pier? She'd have to wait and see how the wind was.

"Wait a second. Your guy, he's the captain? He'll drive the boat?" Something crossed his features, a fleeting look in his eyes Savanna hadn't seen before. Then it was gone. Was he nervous? About what?

"I'll drive the boat. Gus just runs the rental place." She paused. "My dad taught me, and I got certified when I lived in Chicago. We'll get a good-sized Catalina for a few hours, we'll wear life jackets, and the weather this week is supposed to be mild, no storms. It's perfectly safe, I promise."

He locked on her gaze through the screen. "You really want to do this?"

"If you do," Savanna said. She leaned toward the

phone. "We don't have to. I didn't mean to get carried away. Really, if there's some reason you'd rather not, we'll drop it." She was having such a hard time deciphering his expression. He seemed guarded suddenly, which hurt her to see; why would Aidan put his guard up around her?

"Let's do it. Call your guy. I'm game."

"Have you... Aidan, have you ever been out in a boat? Anywhere? Maybe it's a bad idea. Everyone is afraid of something. We could just shelve it for now." She reached out to touch the screen but didn't. She hated feeling so off-kilter with him, with miles between them.

He shook his head. "I trust you. I want to go. I'd love to see your captain skills firsthand. Wednesday?"

"Okay. If you're sure. Bring a jacket—it'll be chilly on the water."

The right side of his mouth went up in a half smile. "Yes, boss. I'll pick you up right after work."

She stifled a yawn. "Oops! Sorry."

"Go to bed. I'm glad I caught you in time to say goodnight." Now Aidan covered his own yawn with one hand, making Savanna laugh.

"I made you yawn. You'd better go to bed too. You have early rounds tomorrow, right?"

"I do. I'll see you soon."

She nodded. "Can't wait."

His screen shifted again as he picked up his phone. "I miss you. Sweet dreams, Savanna."

"'Night, Aidan."

The vague feeling of worry remained with her after they hung up. After locking up, brushing her teeth, and tucking Fonzie into his blanket by her feet, she dismissed it. She pulled her fluffy comforter up around her ears. Talking with Aidan before bed always promised good dreams.

Savanna paced outside the door to the teachers' lounge Tuesday morning. Not only had she forgotten to bring her own coffee this morning, but Jack was gone, at a librarian conference in Lansing today. The only chance of coffee between now and lunchtime was on the other side of that door.

Her 10:05 prep period seemed like the safest time to zip in, grab coffee, and zip out. Mornings before the first bell were always crowded in the teachers' lounge, and in another two hours, a good fifteen or so faculty would be in there eating lunch. She'd considered skipping her coffee altogether, but she knew that was a crazy idea. She took a deep breath and went in.

She was in luck! The large room was nearly empty. Only Rosa Taylor, one of the third grade teachers, sat at a table with a thick stack of cards and envelopes in front of her.

"Hi, Savanna. How are you?"

"Doing great, thanks! How about you?" She crossed to the coffeemaker on the counter against the far wall.

"Oh, shoot, I just took the last cup. I'm sorry. The new pot should be done in a few minutes."

"No worries. I'm glad you made more." She moved to Rosa's table. "What are you working on?"

"These? Wedding thank-you notes." She looked sheepish. "It's been months. I'm such a procrastinator. Trying to get a few done on breaks. George's aunt called the other day and yelled at him, thinking we'd skipped hers."

Rosa and George Taylor, Nick Jordan's partner, had gotten married before Christmas last winter. "That's ridiculous. People are busy! This looks like a big job."

"It is. I've still got another eighty or so to go, but George is helping. Oh! You were at Libby's Blooms the other day, right? George filled me in. Was it you who found her?"

Savanna sat down. What did Rosa mean, George had filled her in? Police officers and detectives couldn't share details of a case with anyone; at least, her extensive viewing knowledge from *Columbo* and her friendship with Detective Jordan had led her to believe that. Rosa seemed to have patchy information, so maybe her husband hadn't actually given her specifics. "My uncle found her. Did you know Libby?"

"She did our wedding flowers. She seemed like a nice lady, but I didn't really know her. I *was* at the bank a few weeks ago with her husband, though." Rosa lowered her voice and leaned toward Savanna. "I overheard the strangest thing. It popped into my head the moment I heard she'd been murdered."

Oh, jeez. Savanna had always been able to stay outside the gossip circle in this room, though it was impossible not to hear bits and pieces flying around. She shouldn't have come in here. Rosa looked at her expectantly, and Savanna played her role. "What happened?" She justified it to herself. Uncle Max was still a suspect. And Sydney had confided to her that she'd been having nightmares since Libby's death. Any information that led to the killer was good information to have, right?

Rosa rested her hands on the table near Savanna, keeping her voice at a whisper despite them being the only ones here. "Anthony Kent was freaking out. I was in line right behind him, so when he got called to the window, I couldn't help overhearing. The teller was trying to explain something about his investment account. He was arguing, saying she was giving him incorrect information—he kept saying the money was his whole retirement and their daughter's tuition. He was really upset. He insisted she re-enter his name and account number three different times, but I think she must've done it right all along, because he just got angrier and angrier."

Savanna's eyes were wide. "Oh my gosh." She tried to imagine Libby's husband angry and couldn't. She'd never seen him upset or ruffled. Granted, she'd never seen much of him at all, other than at Libby's when he'd come in to handle the flower shop's books. He was always pleasant.

Rosa looked up along with Savanna as a handful of teachers came through the door, chatting quietly. Tricia Williams, the teacher Savanna had hoped to dodge, wasn't among them, thank goodness. The teachers dispersed, two toward an empty table and the other three heading over to the coffee pot and reminding Savanna she still hadn't gotten her coffee.

She leaned forward, keeping her voice low too now. "What happened with Anthony?"

"They ended up calling him into the finance manager's office."

Pretty much everyone banked at the same place in Carson. Anthony must've been making quite a scene for the bank to pull him into the office.

"Mr. Fivell shut the door, and that was it. I wish I knew what the outcome was. If the bank messed up the

Kents' investment accounts, we should all be told. I'll take my business elsewhere."

"Good point. Well." Savanna sat back. "Maybe the bank made an error and they'll correct it."

"But what if they didn't? If Anthony and Libby lost their investments? George says domestic disputes turn ugly all the time. What if Anthony..." Rosa stared at Savanna with wide eyes, unwilling to say it. "You know."

It was a huge leap to murder from a possibly insignificant snippet of an interaction, obviously filtered through Rosa's imagination. "I don't know." Savanna shook her head. "I can't picture him doing anything crazy."

"Well. I told George about it. He's going to look into it." Rosa raised her eyebrows.

"I'm sure he and Detective Jordan will get to the bottom of it." Savanna stood. "I have to grab some coffee before it's gone. Good luck with those thank-you notes."

Savanna was on her way out with a delicious, steaming cup of French vanilla-flavored coffee when Missy Vonkowski, a fourth grade teacher, stopped her by the door.

"I wondered if you've heard any news yet?" Missy asked, keeping her voice low. About what happened at Libby's Blooms."

"I, uh...No. Nothing." Missy had barely said a word to her in nearly two years of teaching here. "Have you?"

The woman looked confused. "No, but you work there, don't you? My sister said you called and canceled her painting class until further notice."

"Jodie?" Savanna had been right to assume the Vonkowskis were related. She'd called each of her students yesterday to let them know the still life class was on hold for now.

"Right, yes," Missy said. "Jodie is thinking the shop might go under without Libby. I guess the husband has a black thumb—can't grow a thing, and that daughter's a whole other story. Anyway. My sister wondered what's going on and whether anyone is even taking care of the plants."

Put off by Missy's negative comments, Savanna took a swallow of her coffee. She hadn't been able to speak with Jodie yesterday—she'd had to leave a voicemail. "I'm not sure. I don't work there; Libby was just letting me host a class. I'd guess her family is probably working out what to do with the shop. I'm sure they're managing the plants."

"Right, right. I'll let my sister know you don't know anything."

Back in her classroom, Savanna spent the last few minutes of her prep hour sorting and unpacking everything she'd just heard. She sipped her coffee at her desk and stared straight ahead at the wall of her students' still life paintings. She really needed to talk to Uncle Max.

Chapter Six

TUESDAY AFTER SCHOOL, SAVANNA TURNED onto Wild Goose Lane from Sand Crane Way. Within walking distance of the Main Street shops, but set far enough apart to avoid tourist traffic, the luxurious townhome, Uncle Freddie had said, had called out to him when he and Max spent an afternoon driving by properties last summer. She wished Sydney was with her. Her sister had left her a message just before the end of the school day, saying the shop was busy and she couldn't make it. Savanna had called her back the moment her students had gone, but it had gone straight to voicemail. Something about the message seemed stilted, not like Sydney.

Savanna had worn her navy polka dot dress today with a cropped red cardigan and red ballet flats, and the full skirt swished around the backs of her knees as she climbed the steps to her uncles' front door. Their wide porch was a lush oasis of oversized hydrangea-filled planters, a bench swing hanging to one side of the front door, and inviting wicker furniture with plush floral cushions on the other. She rang the doorbell.

Once in the kitchen, Savanna sat at the island with Uncle Max and traced patterns in the granite countertop with a fingertip. Her uncles' adorable Welsh Corgi, Lady Bella, was curled up at Savanna's feet under the island. The space was open and elegant, comprised of varying grays with slate-blue accents, with rectangular clear-glass pendant lighting overhead. Max placed a tray with tea and lemon tarts between them, passing her a crystal sugar bowl with the tiniest spoon she'd ever seen.

"Is Uncle Freddie still at work?"

Max checked the time on the stove. "He's likely on his way home now. It's a bit of a drive, but he's like a child with a new toy with the Prius he bought. He hasn't complained at all about the commute. I think he enjoys being behind a steering wheel every day."

"I'm sure he does." Her uncles had lived in Chicago since Ellie was young. They'd primarily used public transportation and had gotten by with just an old Cadillac for occasional excursions until the move to Carson. "When is Ellie finished for the semester?"

"She's nearly done; exams start next week. She's coming home Friday so she can focus and get studying done this weekend. Freddie and I promised to leave her alone except for meals."

"I remember those days. She told me her roommates are a little wild; I'm sure she'll get caught up here. Do you think she'll make it for Sunday dinner?"

"Absolutely. She misses you—your sisters as well, but she's really missed you since you left Chicago. I think she's pleased to be close to your family again."

Savanna was a full thirteen years older than her cousin, but during the decade she'd spent in Chicago, they'd grown close. She'd regularly visited her uncles' penthouse apartment, and Ellie loved musicals as much as Savanna did. They'd probably seen over a dozen through the years, the last of which was *Hamilton* on its closing night in the city. "I can't wait to see her. It'll be so great to have her in Carson this summer."

"Now," he said, setting his teacup back in the saucer. "I have a feeling you're not here to talk about cars. What's on your mind, love?"

"Have you heard anything at all from Detective Jordan yet? Or from Anthony Kent?"

"No word from the good detective, but Libby's husband phoned yesterday. He plans to reopen as soon as he's given the green light, but he came right out and told me he's got no skills to speak of. So, I think it's up to me to keep it all alive and thriving."

Savanna raised her eyebrows. "He told you he expects that? That's a lot! Does he mean longer hours to cover the added responsibility? What about a raise?"

"Oh no, I couldn't go into all of that with him. He's just lost his wife."

"You're right, but you do need to clarify. Were you planning on making this a full-time job? Promise you'll talk to him, okay?"

"I promise. No worries."

"I know you walked into a terrible scene Saturday morning," Savanna said. She hated what she was about to ask, but it was important. "Would you mind giving me kind of a recap of what happened? A couple things aren't adding up for me."

"Really? I don't mind. Freddie was asking me about it last night. I slept better after we talked. I've not been sleeping well since it happened."

She squeezed his arm on the countertop. "I'm sorry. Sydney hasn't, either. She misses Libby."

He frowned. "Poor thing. I'm sure this is awful for her. All right, so your mother and I met at the diner for breakfast at seven that morning. I know it sounds like an ungodly hour for some, but I learned years ago that she and I are usually the first ones awake."

Savanna nodded. "Very true. She's never needed a lot of sleep."

"Opposite of her brother," Max said, grinning. "Your Uncle Freddie could sleep through a tornado; he's a bear if he doesn't get his full eight hours. But I'm getting off track, aren't I? Charlotte and I parted ways outside the diner, and I walked the block and a half to Libby's. She likes me to arrive at eight, to have things ready for customers by nine. I let myself in—"

"Wait, through the back or front door?"

"Back. Always."

"And it was locked?"

"Always. Even when Libby's arrived first. She's careful. She was." He paused, the corners of his mouth drawn down. "She was a sweetheart, and a smart business-woman. All right," he said, giving Savanna's hand a pat. "I'm fine. I knew Libby was there already because the lights were on and her sweater was on the coat rack. I called out for her, but not getting a reply, deduced she must be in the greenhouse. I walked through, turned on the office computer, put the drawer in the register. I went about my routine, providing care to the plants, and then headed up to the greenhouse."

"What time was that?"

"Close to eight-thirty, I know," he said, "because I passed the front window at Libby's and saw you and Skylar going into Fancy Tails with the pram. Your arms were full of coffees and treats. I've got to tell you, love, you've no idea how it warms my heart to see you three together. You young ladies have this way about you, thick as thieves, same as when you were girls. Never underestimate how fortunate you are." Uncle Max's gaze bored into hers, his eyes shining.

She took his hand in both of hers, her heart swelling in her chest. She loved him for noticing their close bond and mentioning it. "We don't, I promise."

"Good. So, I went through to the stairwell—"

"I'm so sorry," she interrupted again. "But you'd told Detective Jordan that door was locked too, right? You and Libby kept it locked on either side, even when she left her shop to go up to the greenhouse?"

He shook his head. "Oh yes, always. You know that stairway is used by several of us in the building—Miss Priscilla's, the yoga studio, anyone working at the flower shop, and the upstairs tenants too. She instructed me on my first day to keep our access door locked. It has a key deadbolt on both sides, so you can lock it after going through. Never know who might try to come into the flower shop that way, I suppose, though I know this is a safe little town."

"Okay, thank you for clarifying. So Libby must've come through the back entrance to the shop before you, locked that door after she entered, turned on the lights, and then used the access door to the building stairway, locking that after she went through, and went up to the greenhouse."

"You have it. Now, mind you, the door to the roof is always unlocked. I'm not sure why, but maybe it's a fire safety measure or the like. I used the access door to the stairs and went up to the roof and saw Libby before I even took two steps. I rushed over and tried to rouse her, but I think I already knew it was bad. There was so much blood. I called the emergency line, and they came straight away, but it was too late." He stopped abruptly and took a deep breath.

Savanna hadn't let go of his hand. "I don't know if you would've noticed, but did anything else that seemed...off? Out of place?"

He was quiet, thinking. "No. Nothing."

"Friday night, when I held my class, Libby was off working in the far corner of the greenhouse. You said something about a secret project, remember?"

"Oh, yes." He chuckled, relief crossing his features as they moved onto an easier topic. "Libby was cultivating an extinct flower."

Savanna's eyes widened. "What? How?"

"Now that is a good question. She never shared that with me. But she'd hoped to enter it into the upcoming Flower and Garden Show. It's called a Cry Violet. It's thought to have been completely extinct for the last fifty years or more."

"Wow! That's incredible."

"Does any of this help at all? Did something spark the need for the play by play?"

"There are just things nagging at me. Like, why would someone even want to hurt Libby? How did they get to her? It couldn't have been through the flower shop, since everything was all locked up when you arrived. And why did Libby's husband come in through the front door that morning? Why park out front, on Main Street? Unless he wanted everyone to see that he'd just gotten there?"

Uncle Max frowned. "I'm sure there's a good explanation."

Savanna sighed. "There are other things. The gossip is wild in the teachers' lounge. Det—" She cut herself off. She shouldn't reveal to her uncle that a police detective's wife had been speculating, possibly with tidbits of sensitive information. But maybe she should chat with Detective Jordan about that? She met Uncle Max's gaze and started over. "A teacher said she overheard Libby's husband at the bank, freaking out because there was some problem with his investment account. And then another teacher has a sister who's in my still life class, and it sounds like she's super curious about the flower shop and what's going to happen with the plants. Plus she sounded kind of mean about Rachel." She sat back, palms flat on the granite countertop. She hadn't realized she was keeping all those details filed away in her head until now, when she'd just spilled them all out in Max and Freddie's kitchen.

Uncle Max poured them each more tea. He lifted his small teacup to his lips and sipped. "Well. Rachel is a lovely girl. You could have a chat with her and see for yourself. So, there's that. I've no idea about the Kent's finances, so I can't help you there, I'm sorry. And who was this teacher who's interested in the fate of the shop?"

"Oh, no, it's a teacher's sister—Jodie Vonkowski. The teacher—Missy—said some unkind things about Anthony too. That whole conversation was weird."

"Jodie Vonkowski is the treasurer for Carson's Horticulture Society."

"What's that?"

"Apparently, it's a gardening club that's been around for years. Members use Libby's Blooms for seedlings and plant nutrients, mostly. Jodie told us the club likes the brand Libby carries better than the ones at Carson Greenery down Route 58—we're also local and more convenient."

"Fascinating," Savanna said, shaking her head. "I had no idea we have a garden club. And Jodie is—" She stopped and stared at Max.

He raised his eyebrows. "What is it?"

"Libby's secret flower. Was it taken? Stolen?"

"What? No, that's preposterous."

"You're sure?"

Uncle Max smoothed his silver-streaked dark hair and adjusted his tie. "No. I'm not sure," he mused. "Oh! But yes, the Cry Violet must be fine. Rachel knew her mother's intention to enter it into the Flower and Garden Show in Grand Rapids. I'm positive she's been caring for it these last few days. If it had gone missing, she'd have immediately raised an alarm with your detective. It must be fine."

Savanna bit her lip. "We need to make sure. I wish there was a way."

"I expect to hear about my own status very soon. Detective Jordan assured Freddie he'd verify my alibi today. I'd think, as long as I'm clear, I might be allowed in to check on the violet."

She nodded. "Yes, okay. And if not, I'll find Rachel and talk to her."

Uncle Freddie was getting out of his car as Savanna left Uncle Max. She met him halfway up the wide brick walkway and gave him a quick hug and kiss on the cheek. Lady Bella trotted in circles around Uncle Freddie's legs, excitedly huffing and whining, until he bent down and petted her.

"You're not staying for dinner?" He had a briefcase in one hand, his suit jacket slung over his shoulder. It was after six; he'd probably been in Lansing since eight o'clock this morning, and he looked invigorated rather than tired. "I just won the largest contract that office has seen this decade." He looked past her to a proud Uncle Max standing on the porch, and then returned his gaze to Savanna. "We're celebrating. Join us?"

"The champagne's chilled," Max said, smiling. "We always keep a bottle in the fridge. Just in case."

"I should go. I've got projects to grade and an early staff meeting in the morning. But that's amazing. Congratulations, Uncle Freddie!"

Her uncles stood on their porch, Max with his arm around Freddie's waist, the two of them already deep in conversation as she pulled out of the driveway. She honked briefly, and they both waved.

Savanna called Sydney on the way home.

Her sister answered in a breathless rush. "Hey Savvy, I can't talk, I'm sorry. can I call you later?"

"Sure, no problem. Are you— I just wanted to make sure you're all right. Doesn't sound like things have slowed down there."

"Not yet. I'm okay. I'm not, but y'know. I will be eventually."

Savanna frowned at the phone. The usual lilt in Sydney's voice was glaringly absent. "I could bring over brownie sundae stuff later," she offered. "We don't even have to watch *Columbo*. I'll let you pick."

Her sister sighed heavily into the phone. "No, not those."

"What?"

"Mrs. Sims, the basket to your right has the sale items," Sydney said, clearly not speaking to Savanna. "Not tonight."

"Um. Was that last part meant for me?" Savanna asked. "I can let you go, Syd."

"Yeah, sorry. I can't. I'm closing up in a minute. I just want to go home and crawl into bed. I'll see you tomorrow."

Savanna started to speak, but the line went dead. The silence that filled her car was thick with her own worry. Of the three of them, her younger sister was the open book. Her thoughts and feelings were always on display. She knew she'd caught Sydney in a rush at work, but she'd sounded terrible.

Savanna drove home on autopilot. She couldn't imagine what it must be like to lose a precious friend in such an awful way. The best way to help Sydney might be to untangle the truth about who killed Libby. She couldn't wait to hash things over tomorrow with her sisters and try to find a way to help with the investigation. She decided as she pulled into her driveway that she'd bring dinner over to Sydney's later. Her sister shouldn't be alone. She was not okay.

Sydney turned off her phone. She'd heard the concern in Savanna's voice, but she just couldn't deal with any of this right now. Her phone had kept dinging with unanswered text messages, and she'd known better than to take Savanna's call. There was no time. She rang up Mrs. Sims, putting on her best proprietor's smile, and glanced at the clock. She could lock up in ten minutes, but with Willow out sick, she was a long way from getting out of here. She hurried back to the grooming area and scooped the little Schnauzer mix up from his holding pen. She'd been almost finished with him when that irksome bell over her shop's front door had jingled for what had seemed like the hundredth time that day.

She tied one of her signature handmade bandanas around the sweet pup's neck and smoothed an errant bit of fur back into place on his newly trimmed scruff. "There. Very handsome, Fritz. I'm not locking you back up again—you can come out here with me." She set him back on the floor and headed out to the shop at the sound of the bell.

Fritz's owner had arrived with three more customers. Sydney gritted her teeth. Her mood had been foul since exactly 11:37 this morning, and it was just getting fouler. The back room looked like a tornado had struck, since she'd been running all day between grooming and selling and had done zero cleanup. And she'd never get to at this rate if people didn't stop showing up.

When the bell jingled once more as she was packaging bright yellow tennis ball cookies for one of her three patrons, her head snapped up. She'd tear that thing down with her bare hands before she let it ring one more time. "We're closed," she said, before looking over to find it was Finn. "Oh!"

His grin hit her right in the knees, making them feel like noodles for a second. "Hey there, Miss Fancy Tails. Business is booming, huh?"

"You could say that." She handed the dog cookie package to her customer, and the woman behind him stepped up the counter.

Finn went into the grooming area without another word, and she heard the vacuum kick on. God bless that man.

When she'd finally packaged the last treat and

cashed out the last customer, she followed the man to the door and turned the key in the lock, flipping the sign to *Closed*. She dragged a chair over from the waiting area, stood on it, and used a screwdriver to take the bell down. She thought she was home free until the last screw wouldn't come out. The thing had been hanging over her door since she'd opened the shop years ago; it was probably frozen in the threads. She wrestled with it, grunting and putting her weight into it. She caught movement from the corner of her eye and turned to find Finn leaning against her desk, watching her.

"What?" Sydney could feel the sweat at the back of her neck and knew she must look a sight after the day's trials.

Finn put his hands up, palms toward her. "Nothing at all. Need any help?"

"No! Yes," she amended. He started to come toward her, and she stopped him. "There's a hammer in the left middle drawer of my desk. Can you hand it to me?"

Finn did as she asked and stepped back.

She attacked the stubborn last screw with both the screwdriver and hammer, and the thin metal holding the bell in place abruptly snapped, releasing it and throwing her backward out of the chair.

Finn caught her unceremoniously around the waist, her legs flying.

Sydney burst out laughing. "Thank you. You have no idea the day I've had." She waited for him to let go of her, but he didn't.

"It must've been bad. You ignored all my texts." He fake-scowled at her. "I don't know if I'll ever get over it."

She kissed him and pushed gently against his chest, making him let go. They'd be here all night if she didn't get to work. She dropped the bell into the trash can next to her desk, feeling his gaze on her. "I hate that thing," she said simply.

He nodded. "I get it."

"Why are you here, though? Did I forget we had plans?"

"I picked up on your distress call," Finn said. One side of his mouth went up. "So I came."

Sydney knew he was kidding, but holy cats, his timing was perfect. It was probably just coincidence, his wanting to see her. Or the result of his string of unanswered messages. Either way, he was exactly what she needed. She moved back into his arms, hugging him and resting her head on his chest. She could afford the time it took for a hug. "Thank you, Finn." She was exhausted.

He kissed the top of her head. "What else needs to be done?"

She moved to the grooming area doorway and gasped. He'd not only vacuumed, he'd done everything. The holding pens were swept out; the scent of lemon disinfectant hung in the air. Her stainless steel table gleamed, and her grooming implements were all in the drying rack. She turned and stared at him.

"Because I've got pizza being delivered to your house in about..." He checked his watch. "Eleven minutes."

"I think you're my favorite person ever," Sydney said, smiling at him. Her dark mood was gray now instead of black, and getting better. She felt like she could finally exhale after a day of holding it all in.

Over veggie pizza in her living room, she told Finn what had happened. She hadn't woken up feeling like this. Granted, she'd been having bad dreams since Libby's death. She wasn't sleeping well, but she was handling it. Knowing Nick Jordan had some leads helped.

"I found a placemat from Jake's Shakes," she told Finn.

He gazed into her eyes, waiting for the rest, not asking any questions.

"I sat down for a minute to grab a granola bar before the noon appointment showed up. The placemat was folded in a little square behind the granola bar box in my desk. Libby and I had played hangman and tic-tac-toe on the back using crayons while we ate. It was from a few months ago. I remember folding the thing up and putting it in my purse, but I thought I'd lost it after that." She pulled the placemat from her back pocket and smoothed it out between them.

Finn took her hand and turned it palm up, covering it with his own. He leaned forward and scanned the doodles and notes scrawled with different crayon shades.

She got through the rest of the story without breaking down. "Libby wrote these five words to describe me, here. She had me do the same for her," Sydney pointed. Libby had written of Sydney:

Fun

Smart

Tough

Kind

Sassy

"She knew you well," Finn commented. "I know she was a good friend."

"I think our age difference gave us a stronger sense of how lucky we were to have become friends. Anyway, this right here is the date we picked for the next time we'd meet at Jake's—we tried to sit down over dinner and drinks every couple of months so we could brainstorm cross-promotion ideas for the shops." Sydney looked down at their linked hands.

"It was today." Finn's voice was quiet.

"Yeah."

"I'm so sorry." He brought her hand to his lips and kissed her palm.

"I'm just—" She hesitated.

He looked at her through black lashes, still holding her hand.

"How are Anthony and Rachel ever supposed to get over this? What if Rachel can't keep up with school after this? It meant everything to Libby that her daughter was going to be a nurse. And what if her flower shop has to close? And...what if she didn't even know how much I loved her?" Sydney sharply drew in her breath, her eyes burning. "What if she didn't? I canceled our morning tea the time before last," she confessed. "You know why? Because I wanted to sleep in. How selfish is that?" One tear overflowed and she frowned, swiping it away.

Finn pulled her into his arms. She curled herself into his embrace, tucking her face into the side of his neck, and squeezed her eyes shut tightly. Her chest was tight and her throat was full. She needed to cry. She knew she'd feel better if she could. But no more tears came.

She didn't know how long she sat that way, on Finn's lap and molded against him, his strong arms holding her.

His lips moved against her hair as he spoke. "Missing one morning with your friend to catch some sleep isn't selfish, it's human. And she knew you loved her,

Syd. Your heart is always on your sleeve." He gave the sleeve of her shirt a little tug. "Libby knew."

"I hope so," she said.

Savanna arrived ahead of schedule at Fancy Tails for lunch on Wednesday.

"I'll be right out! I'm just washing up." Sydney called from the grooming area in the back of the salon.

Savanna was relieved to hear Syd's voice sounding lighter than it had yesterday. She'd driven fettucine Alfredo over to her sister's house last night, but had turned around and gone home upon seeing Finn's car in the driveway. Whatever he'd done, it seemed to have helped. She eyed the deli sandwiches on the table and turned her chair so she had good view out the front window up and down the street. The vantage point from Fancy Tails offered visibility of pretty much all the storefronts on Main Street. She'd bet if she sat here long enough, she'd learn something new about every store owner and patron.

"Who are we spying on?" Sydney whispered by her ear, making her jump.

"For Pete's sake, don't creep up on people like that! I'm not spying, just looking."

The bell jingled as Skylar came through the door. "Shall I flip the sign?" When Sydney nodded, Skylar turned the sign with the drooling cartoon St. Bernard to the side that read: *Never trust a dog to watch your food! We don't! Closed for lunch.* "So," Skylar said, unwrapping her sandwich, "Nick has cleared Uncle Max."

"Finally!" Sydney exclaimed. "What took so long?"

"It was only a few days. He had to get a statement from the waitress at the diner who handled Mom and Uncle Max's breakfast order. I called to let Max and Freddie know."

"Well, I'm glad that's taken care of," Savanna said. "I know Max wasn't concerned, but Uncle Freddie was miffed."

"Have you heard if they've made any progress on his leads?" Sydney asked.

"Nick didn't say anything. But I've got to stop by and see him tomorrow. I can ask. I found something interesting that he needs to know." Skylar cocked one eyebrow at them and took a bite of her sandwich.

"Oh, you can't do that," Sydney said. "Drop the bait like that and then walk away. What did you find? Is it about Libby?"

She shrugged as she chewed.

Syd looked at Savanna. "I hate when she does that."

"She does it on purpose," Savanna said. "Come on, Skylar. There must be some detail you can share without breaking your lawyer-code thing."

Their older sister laughed. "My lawyer-code thing? You know I can't give you actual privileged information. But. I can tell you I'm the Kents' estate attorney. I represent both Libby and Anthony. And listen," she said, leaning in toward them with elbows on the table, eyes wide. "Nick is going to flip when I show him what I found."

Savanna tipped her head back, looking at the ceiling. "Ugh! Just tell us! Does it implicate Anthony?"

"The truth will come out eventually. But this might give the police a good lead. That's all I can say."

The three of them ate in silence for a few minutes.

Across the street, Kate exited her yoga studio and jogged across Main Street, going into the coffee shop down the block. Chef Joe Fratelli left the coffee shop and crossed at the light, heading back to his restaurant, Giuseppe's.

"You've got the best view in Carson," Savanna said. "What jacket did Chef Joe wear to work yesterday? Better yet, who is Mike at the real estate office secretly dating?"

"You're crazy. Like I have time to sit here and monitor everyone all day."

"What if Miss Priscilla is monitoring you?" Savanna pointed across the street. The dance school proprietor stood staring out the front window of one of the studios, hands on her hips, unmoving. Even from here, the woman looked lost in thought. She didn't appear to be monitoring anyone.

"Chef Joe wore his Detroit Tigers jacket yesterday," Sydney said, getting the attention of both her sisters. She laughed. "I wasn't peering out the window at him. He came in for dog treats."

"Skylar," Savanna said, "could I tag along when you see Nick tomorrow? There are some things I want to ask him about the case."

"I can't bring you with me, but I can't stop you running into me as I'm heading in to see him, right? What are you thinking?"

Savanna shared her thoughts on Anthony Kent, wondering aloud why he'd come in the front entrance the day Libby's body was found. She brought both her sisters up to date on the information provided through the teachers' lounge, and then filled them in about the extraordinary Cry Violet. "Now that Uncle Max is cleared, maybe he can get me up to the greenhouse so

I can check it out."

"It hadn't bloomed yet the last time I saw it. She was tending to it like it was her baby, but she was worried it might not flower. I hope it did before she died," Syd said softly.

"You saw it?" Savanna asked. "How did she even grow an extinct flower?"

Sydney shook her head. "No idea. I asked, but she went into something about germination and cleisto... clestog... some kind of science-y florist lingo and she lost me."

"She would've lost me there too," Skylar said, chuckling.

Savanna spoke. "There's one more thing. I realized something after talking with Uncle Max."

"What's that?" Skylar asked.

"Libby's killer didn't come in through the flower shop. They couldn't have."

"What? Why?" Sydney finished her sandwich in one large bite and uncapped her raspberry Mary Ann's soda.

"Because the shop was locked up tight. Uncle Max says all the doors were locked and Libby even turned the key in the deadbolt lock from outside the shop, in the building stairwell, when she went through to go up to the greenhouse. Only Libby, Uncle Max, and Anthony and Rachel Kent have keys to that access door."

"I'm sorry. I'm not following," Skylar said.

"If the killer came through the flower shop into the stairwell, he'd have had to lock the door behind him with a key. So, unless the killer was someone with the key, whoever killed Libby came from inside the building somehow," Savanna said.

"But it was so early," Sydney said. "The dance school,

Libby's, Kate's Yoga…none of those places were even open yet."

Savanna's gaze was on Libby's Blooms, in the middle between Kate's and Miss Priscilla's. "I wonder if Detective Jordan found any signs of a break-in. Did they check out the whole building, or just Libby's shop?"

"We can ask him tomorrow. Not sure he'll tell us, but it doesn't hurt to try," Skylar said.

"Good," Savanna said. "If they confirmed for sure there was no sign of someone breaking into the flower shop to get to Libby, they should've checked out the rest of the building."

As they watched, Mollie's tap instructor Marcus Valentine got out of the red convertible he'd just parallel parked in front of the dance studio. She expected him to go into Miss Priscilla's, but instead, he unlocked the plain door she'd noticed the other day and went in. Through the door's glass window, she watched him taking the stairs two at a time until he was out of sight.

Chapter Seven

"WHO WAS THAT?" SYD ASKED. "I've seen that car there before."

Savanna turned and looked at her sisters. "Marcus Valentine. Miss Priscilla's new tap instructor. But why would he go in that way? The dance school's open right now, isn't it?"

Now all three of them narrowed their eyes, looking across the street at the front door to Priscilla's Dance Academy.

"Maybe it isn't," Skylar said. "It's the middle of a weekday. Kids are in school."

Sydney tapped her phone screen. "It's closed right now," she confirmed.

"Maybe he's getting costumes or props or something from the storage space? Does that mean all of Miss Priscilla's instructors have a key to that door?" Savanna mused. "Or maybe he lives up there. Uncle Max said something about tenants living upstairs. I wonder how many there are? It's not a huge space." All she could think of was Marcus Valentine's shocking appearance Monday when he'd shown up for classes. "This might not have anything to do with Libby, but Marcus Valentine came to work on Monday with a pretty intense black eye."

"Oh my God." Sydney slapped the table. "Do you think it was him? What if Libby fought him off? Maybe she gave him the black eye. With him having that key, he easily could've gone right up those stairs and killed her. It explains why the flower shop was still locked up."

Savanna shook her head. She knew her sister needed someone to direct her anger toward, but... "That doesn't make sense. What would he have against Libby? And how would someone Libby's age and size be able to punch Valentine? He's, like, eight or ten inches taller than her."

"Maybe it wasn't a punch," Skylar said slowly. "If she was attacked, she'd have lashed out in any way possible. Elbows, feet, a ceramic pot—who knows?" "Was there a struggle? Did Nick mention anything like that?" Sydney asked.

"He hasn't mentioned much about anything," Savanna said. "You know how that goes. And I'm not trying to start rumors about Miss Priscilla's tap teacher. It's just weird timing. Maybe I'll ask him what happened to his eye when I take Mollie to dance tomorrow."

Skylar raised her eyebrows. "Really? All right, go for it. Just make sure you're in the lobby with people and not by yourself with him."

"Hey, Kate might know who lives in the building. Her yoga studio has been there forever. I can ask her," Sydney said.

"Oh, ask her!" Savanna sat forward in her chair and pushed Syd's cellphone on the table toward her.

Sydney placed the call and put her phone on speaker, but it went to voicemail. She left a message and then also sent a text for good measure.

Savanna tapped the screen on her own phone. "I can't find anything online about Marcus Valentine, other than what's on Miss Priscilla's website. What's the building address?" She squinted across the street, then returned her attention to her phone. "Well, that didn't work, either. It just says here the address houses apartments 201, 202, and 203. If Kate doesn't know who else rents there, I'll go ask Yvonne." Her friend Yvonne, a receptionist at the Carson Village Offices, was usually a wealth of information.

"Good idea," Skylar said. "Listen, I've got to get back, but you know we're doing your birthday scavenger hunt Saturday, right?"

"Oh! I sort of forgot. You don't mind doing it?" A stab of nostalgia hit Savanna. They'd started the tradition as teenagers, their mom helping create riddles the birthday girl would have to solve to determine the three or four destinations that were plotted out on their mini road-rally.

"Of course not. We've only missed a couple," Skylar said. "We've already got yours all planned out. You took care of the second stop?" she asked Sydney.

Their younger sister nodded. "All set."

Skylar stood. "We tried to make your clues harder this time. We went too easy on you last year!"

Savanna laughed. "Thanks a lot. You don't happen to know when we'll be back, do you?"

"I'm relieving Willow here at four, so not too late," Sydney said.

"Perfect." Savanna helped clear the table and stopped on her way out the door. She suddenly felt hopeful. They finally had a plan, some small ways to connect the dots and maybe contribute to the investigation. "Syd, are you okay? You seem better today."

Her sister nodded. "I'm all right. This is hard, that's all. Finn came by last night, and that helped a lot."

"Good. Hey, let me know what Kate says, will you?" Savanna asked. "If she doesn't know who lives in the building, I'll go talk to Yvonne."

Aidan was outside Sweetwater Boats chatting with the proprietor when Savanna arrived at the marina that afternoon. "I see you two have already met. How are you, Gus?" She leaned in and gave him a hug, and Augustus Connelly patted her on the shoulder.

Gus looked every bit of his seventy-five years, with permanently tanned and freckled skin and deep crow's feet around pale-blue eyes and sun-bleached eyebrows. He'd looked the same age since Savanna could remember, and she'd known him since she'd started coming to Carson Marina with her dad as a kid at least twenty years ago. "Can't complain," he said, his voice gravelly. "Your dad was out this morning. Caught a nice-sized silver he let me have. But you're not thinking fishing, right? You need a sailboat? Got one in mind?"

"How about a sloop? Maybe that twenty-six-foot Catalina, the red one?"

Gus dipped his chin once toward his chest, a quick nod. "Yep. She's prepped and ready. Had a feeling you'd pick her. Slip two twenty-three," he said, pointing.

"Oh, I'm so excited! I haven't been out since last summer—well, on Dad's boat, but there's just something about sailing," she said, grinning up at Aidan.

"You'll see."

"Um." Aidan took a few steps, following her toward the docks, but stopped, turning back toward Gus. "Mr. Connelly, what about life jackets? And shouldn't you, I don't know, help us back it out or something?" He cupped one large hand around the back of his neck, his bicep straining the short sleeve of his gray Henley.

"Nope. No worries, Dr. Gallager," the older man said. "Life vests are aboard, and this one knows her way around a rig." He spoke to Savanna, who'd just returned to Aidan's side and taken his hand. "The water's calm. Your sunset's at nine oh-four tonight. Take your time."

Savanna climbed aboard the small craft first, momentarily wrapping her fingers around the mainstay to steady herself. When she turned around, Aidan's expression conveyed volumes of concern, those twin lines between his eyebrows etched deeply; his stance was askew, as if he'd tried to reach to help her but then realized she was on the boat and fine. "Aidan." She made her voice soft, gentle. "What is it? Let's forget this—it's silly, anyway." She moved to climb back onto the dock, but he stopped her.

"No. I'm silly. That word is actually silly." He smiled sheepishly at her. "This is great. I want to go." He made no move to climb aboard. The sailboat, smaller than many in the surrounding slips, sat below the level of the dock, making the first step a big one.

A thought occurred to her. "One sec." She ducked down into the cabin briefly, reappearing with the two life jackets, and held one up to Aidan. "Put that on."

He raised one eyebrow at her. "I'm not worried about falling off the dock."

What *was* he worried about? Calm and collected

Aidan Gallager was certainly not himself, that was for sure. "All right." She dropped the vest and held out a hand to him. "Step onto the edge of the cockpit here, and use the shroud—that cable from the mast—to keep your balance."

Aidan took her hand and came aboard, his long legs making it look effortless. "No problem." He met her eyes, less than a foot from her in the small cockpit.

"Can we sit for a minute?" She didn't let go of his hand and sat facing him. "Aidan, if you feel unsure about going out, I promise it's okay. Some people just don't like boats."

"That's not it," he said, his voice low. "I'm fine. Really. Let's do this: tell me what to do. Doesn't every captain need a first mate? You're the boss of me for the next few hours."

"I am? That sounds nice."

"You are. I'll prove it. Give me a command." Aidan rested his elbows on his knees and leaned toward her, deep blue eyes gazing intensely into hers as he waited.

She swallowed. "Oh, the possibilities," she murmured, unable to avoid glancing at his inviting lips. She made the sensible choice. "Tell me what you're afraid of," she said quietly.

His eyes betrayed uncertainty. He took a breath, and she thought he was going to tell her, but then he looked down at their feet. When he met her stare again, that naked emotion—fear, sadness, something she couldn't place—was gone. "Give me a different command."

She sighed. She'd never seen him guarded like this. "Kiss me."

The corner of his mouth turned upward and he placed a hand on her jawline, fingertips in her hair. He leaned in and kissed her, sending a zing of electricity from her throat to her toes. The clean, slightly spicy scent of his aftershave, his warm hand on her skin and the other on her knee, gave Savanna the sense that all was well, even if she'd known that wasn't true minutes ago. She cupped her fingers around his forearm, and when he stopped and drew back, she frowned, searching his face.

Aidan kept his hand possessively on her knee through the denim. She'd worn jeans and her white Vans sneakers with a pink windbreaker. "Sailing's easy," he said.

Savanna laughed. "Are you ready? Or should we get out of here and go to Giuseppe's for dinner instead?"

"You kind of sold me on those sub sandwiches you brought," he deadpanned, clearly unwilling to talk about whatever was going on in his head.

She bit her lower lip. "Aidan. I seriously am happy doing anything, as long as we're together."

That elicited a full smile. "Let's go sailing." Aidan stood, donned his life jacket, and stepped out onto the deck, moving to the right around the cabin and steadying himself with the grabrail. He stopped at the bow, a hand on the mainstay, and looked back at her. "Are you ready? Should I untie her?"

She stared at him, starting to feel the way she did when she was furiously struggling to read Detective Jordan and couldn't. She shook her head. She'd wait until they were out on the lake and ask him again. "No," she called. "Hold on."

Once she'd stowed their things in the cabin, checked the lines, and flipped the switch to start the inboard motor, she gave him the go-ahead and watched as he tossed both ropes onto the dock, freeing the Catalina. He moved carefully from bow to stern, and then stayed in the cockpit with her while she steered them out onto Lake Michigan.

When they were far enough clear of the channel, she cut the engine, plunging them into a breezy silence. She glanced at Aidan. "When I raise the mainsail, it'll catch the bit of wind we've got, okay?"

"What can I do?"

"Honestly, nothing yet. Just stay put." Savanna moved along the length of the boom and tugged on the halyard to be sure it was loose, then pulled the mainsheet hand over hand until a good length of the rope was coiled up at her feet as the sail unfurled above them. She wrapped a length of rope around the winch and used the winch handle to bring the sail the rest of the way up, watching the telltales far overhead for wind direction. She trimmed the sail a little more and secured the mainsheet on the winch. They set out on a leisurely westward course, surrounded by blue water, no sounds but the water lapping the hull.

Savanna kept a hand on the tiller and breathed deeply, face turned into the wind. Every time she was on the water, she wondered why she didn't do it more often. She turned to find Aidan watching her.

"I have a million questions," he said. His expression was unreadable, but his tension was betrayed by the muscle in his jaw pulsing.

"I have some too. Ask me one. Or a million."

"Who taught you to sail? Did you ever have your own boat? Do you go out on the water often? And alone? Why did I never know this?" He took a breath. "And what is a silver, and why did your dad give it to

Gus?"

Savanna smiled. "A silver is a silver salmon. It's a good catch, better than a lake trout around here. Dad taught me to sail when I was thirteen, and I did have my own boat when I lived in Chicago," she said, enjoying Aidan's surprised expression.

"How cool. What happened to it?"

"I had to sell it when I moved back. My dad would've trailered it home to Michigan for me, but I didn't even know where I was going to live or if I'd find a job. It made more sense to get rid of it. I miss it."

"So, those couple of times last summer when you said you were going sailing, you literally meant you were going sailing. Here. Alone. In one of Gus's boats?" His voice went up at the end, his tone incredulous. "I just assumed you meant with your dad. But he doesn't sail now?"

"He sold his sailboat years ago and swapped it for a cabin cruiser. I think it fits his purposes better; he uses it to fish, and he and my mom even take it on trips together. When I say I'm going sailing, I usually mean here, either with one of Gus's boats, or sometimes my dad's friend takes us all out on his yacht—I'll have to show you when we get back to the marina. It's like something out of a movie. It's a fifty-five-foot X-Yacht, the biggest sailboat I've ever seen. He and my dad race in the regatta every fall."

Aidan was shaking his head, staring at her. "I'm sorry. I can't believe I've just discovered this hidden thing about you that I should've known."

"Aww, Aidan. Don't do that. You know a lot. You pay attention. I only went out last summer a handful of times, when you were working. And you assumed correctly that most of the time I was going with my dad, only on Sebastian's boat. I like to be safe, so I watch the weather—I've never been caught in a storm. And I don't go unless I can drag Sydney with me. Or maybe now you?"

He was silent. He didn't answer her, his gaze moving out onto the horizon, where the sun was dropping lower in the sky.

Savanna put the tiller lock on; she couldn't trust it for long, but she needed to not be tied to steering for a few moments. She touched his leg across from her, leaving her hand there until he looked at her. She was dying to ask him her question; she had only one. But she'd pressed him so hard earlier, and he still seemed closed off. Instead, she shifted to the bench next to him, hugging him and resting her head on his shoulder.

"I took Finn out on a sailboat the summer after I graduated high school." Aidan's deep voice was calm, quiet. "I worked at a yacht club in New Jersey, and I went through this phase... I guess we both went through a phase that lasted years after we lost our parents. I thought I knew what I was doing; I saw the sailors go out and come back all day every day, I knew all the terminology, and mainly I was just angry all the time. I was angry no one seemed to have the problems Finn and I had. We broke in after closing on a Sunday night. I stole a boat. We got all the way out onto the bay, but when I put the jib up—I know now I have no clue which sail to put up first—it caught the wind hard, the boat keeled, and the boom came across and knocked Finn into the water."

Savanna sat straight up and gasped. "Oh my God! And at night!"

"I got him. Obviously," he said, giving her a wry smile. "It took some maneuvering to get to him. Neither of us could swim, no life jackets...you can imagine. Finn almost died. It was a bad night."

She didn't know what to say. Why hadn't he ever told her?

"We've all got stuff," Aidan said. "Baggage. Right? My recklessness almost got him killed."

"But it didn't. And you were just a kid, one who'd been through too much already." Her heart ached for what he must be feeling.

"You sound like him. Listen, I need to put it to rest, I know that. I thought I'd moved past it until you brought up going out on the water."

"I wish you'd told me."

He shrugged. "Why? Look at this—" he made a sweeping motion over the vast blue lake. "I've lived here over ten years, and this is what I've been avoiding? It was a good idea, Savanna." Aidan pulled her into him, kissing her temple.

The sail above them rustled, going slack, and the boom slowly inched back toward the center of the boat.

He glanced up. "Anyway, Captain, I'm keeping you from your job. We're losing the wind. Would you do me a favor and put your life jacket on?"

She hugged him again, briefly this time, and put on her life vest before correcting their course.

They ate their submarine sandwiches on the sail back from Paradise Cove, where they'd watched the sun begin to set over the water. Aidan seemed fine after they'd talked, even when they'd unfurled the jib sail to pick up speed. They were still several minutes out from the marina, triggering that feeling—the mixture of sweetness and sadness Savanna always noticed toward the end of their time together. She knew it was ridiculous. They'd part ways, and then they'd usually talk again before she went to bed or the next morning. Even so, it was bittersweet.

"You're off the hook tomorrow," he said. "I'm leaving the clinic early to pick Mollie up from school to take her to dance. There are some forms I need to sign for the dress rehearsal and recital, and she wants me to see her tap number before they go on stage."

"You'll love it. I got a preview last week. Do you know much about the new tap teacher?"

He shook his head. "Just what I've heard in the lobby. He replaced Miss Cathy after Priscilla fired her. Mollie likes Mr. Marcus better, though she hasn't really said why."

"That, I can answer," Savanna said. "Mollie says he reminds her of her Uncle Finn."

Aidan chuckled. "Now it makes sense. No one's cooler than Uncle Finn in my daughter's eyes. Why do you ask?"

"I just wondered."

He scrutinized her. "Is this about Libby's murder?"

She looked up at the telltales on the sail, checking the direction of the ribbons to confirm they were still headed into the wind. He knew her too well.

"Because, if it's about Libby's murder," Aidan continued, "I'm sure Detective Jordan has that investigation handled."

She could feel him watching her and finally met his gaze. "I know he does. It's just, he only last night cleared Uncle Max, and Max and I were talking about the way he found Libby, and the fact that the flower shop was all locked up when he arrived that morning, which means the killer got up to Libby's rooftop greenhouse some other way, like possibly through one of the other businesses or the tenant access door."

"And you think Mr. Marcus could be the killer?"

"I didn't say that. Anyone in the building could be the killer. Even Sydney's friend Kate, by my logic." She hesitated, then pressed forward. "But we saw him go in through the tenant door today. When the dance school wasn't even open. So maybe he lives in the building. Aidan..." she leaned forward toward him. "He had a black eye on Monday. What if he was in a scuffle with Libby?"

"That's a big leap. How did he say he got the black eye? Did he even know Libby?"

"I don't know," she admitted. "I think I'm off base, anyway. The kids seem to love him. And you're right, he might not have known Libby. For all we know, she could've been killed by her own husband."

"Anthony?"

"You know him?"

"We're acquainted," Aidan affirmed, which Savanna had learned usually meant the person he was talking about was a patient. "Isn't that a cliché, though? The spouse as the likeliest murder suspect?"

"I guess so...but there's a reason it's a cliché, isn't there? I'm going to catch Skylar tomorrow and tag along as she's on her way in to see Detective Jordan. One of the teachers at school was at the bank a few weeks ago, and she says Anthony Kent was there yelling and making a scene. There was something wrong with his account. She said he was ranting that it was his entire savings and supposed to help toward his daughter's college tuition or something—he ended up being pulled into the office by Mr. Fivell. It is strange, the more I think about it. Anthony Kent is always calm, at least when I've seen him," Savanna said.

Aidan was frowning. "I think I already know the answer to this, but is it possible for you to sit this one out? Please?" His voice was thick with concern.

They were nearing the channel. Savanna dropped the jib, and Aidan helped retract the mainsail as she started the inboard motor. "I'm just thinking aloud," she said.

He nodded. "That's all? Because Libby's killer is still on the loose, and I still remember last year when trying to expose John's murderer almost got you killed."

She shifted her hand on the tiller and steered into the marina entrance, heading toward their slip. "I remember too, believe me. Nothing like that will happen again—don't worry."

After they'd secured the craft with the dock lines and said goodnight to Gus, Aidan stood with Savanna at her car. Theirs were the last two left in the parking lot, besides the Sweetwater Boats truck. The nearly dark sky still held remnants of oranges and pinks. Every so often, the distant light from Carson's lighthouse swept across them briefly and then left them in the gathering darkness.

She rested her fingertips lightly on the gray cotton of his shirt, between his chest and abdomen. He was close enough that she could see the few faint freckles across his cheeks and the way his black eyelashes curved out at the corners. Aidan's revelations tonight, the way he'd bared his vulnerabilities, made the constant magnetic draw she felt to him even stronger.

"Thank you for the sail," he said.

"Thank you for telling me about you and Finn. You can tell me anything, Aidan. You know that, right?"

"I do. Savanna, I don't want you to get mixed up in Libby's case."

"I'm not trying to," she said, hearing the evasive sound to her own words. "Nothing's going to happen. I'll stay out of it." She put her hands up in surrender. She'd try to stay out of it, after she had a chance to pass on what she'd seen and heard to Detective Jordan.

Aidan frowned at her. "You'll tell me if you decide to explore any of your suspicions further." It wasn't a question.

"I will." She meant it. She couldn't lie to him. Her breath caught in her throat as he pulled her to him and kissed her.

Chapter Eight

THURSDAY MORNING BEFORE SCHOOL, SAVANNA headed down Main Street from the coffee shop to Carson Village Police Station. Crossing the street, she noticed the yellow-and-black crime scene tape had yet to be removed from Libby's store. Miss Priscilla must be fuming by now. She perched on the low brick wall outside the village office complex and checked the time on her phone; Skylar was always on time, and it was still three minutes before eight.

Savanna looked up to find her younger sister crossing the street toward her. "Hey! How did you know I'd be here?"

Sydney pointed kitty-corner across Main Street. "I saw you walk past my window, and I remembered you were going to crash her meeting with Nick. I wanted to ask you something."

"Sure! What is it?"

"I know we sort of joked about it the other day, but should we invite the guys this Sunday? I'm sure Aidan would like to be there for your birthday dinner."

"Yes," Savanna said firmly. "I've been thinking about it too. Let's do it. It's time, right?"

Sydney pursed her lips. "Yes. I think it'll be good

they're both coming. Finn's next Med Flight assignment is in Colorado, but he'll be here for almost a whole
month until he goes. I hope he—" She cut herself off.
"Never mind. I just hope it goes well."

Savanna touched her sister's arm. "I'm sure it will!
Don't worry. Mom and Dad will be excited."

"I don't know how excited Finn will be. He's got this
thing about parents. He says they never like him."

Savanna frowned. "That's crazy. He's a good guy. And
really, I've seen how he looks at you. That's all they'll
need to see."

"Oh, there is no way. Nope," Skylar said, approaching from her law office next door. "It was already going
to be weird bringing one of you in there with me. This
is too much. Mine?" She took the black coffee from Savanna.

Savanna nodded. "Syd's not staying."

"Keep me updated." Sydney jogged back across the
street to Fancy Tails.

"She seems to be doing a little better," Skylar said of
Sydney when she'd gone.

Inside the police station, Savanna followed her sister past the desk sergeant down the hall to Nick Jordan's office. "Wait," she said, stopping her outside his
door. She dug a wet nap from Giuseppe's restaurant
out of her purse, tore it open, and carefully dabbed at
Skylar's lapel.

"What is it? I didn't even have breakfast yet—it
can't be food." Skylar looked down, trying to see.

"It might be Hannah's breakfast," Savanna said.
"There, all gone."

"Thank you." Her sister laughed. "You can dress me
up, but you can't take me anywhere."

Seated across the desk from the detective, as Skylar opened her briefcase and pulled out a manila file folder, Savanna suddenly felt much more intrusive than she'd thought she would. "Should I step out and let you go over your thing first?"

The detective shook his head. "I don't think that's necessary." Skylar handed the file to him, and he perused the documents inside. "Mm-hmm. All right, so there's a life insurance policy; not unusual."

Skylar waited, not answering.

"Well." He looked up at Skylar. "This is dated the end of April—not even three weeks ago."

"Yes. My office received the copies about a week before Libby died."

The suspense was killing Savanna. She scrutinized Skylar, her gaze then moving to Detective Jordan.

"He may regret the timing of this, even best-case scenario."

"Oh, no," Savanna said, unable to remain quiet. "Did Anthony, like, just take out life insurance on Libby? Right before this happened? That's crazy. Sorry." She put a hand up as they both frowned at her.

"I included the phone numbers and email addresses for his contact people there and at the bank, just in case you need them," Skylar said.

Detective Jordan closed the folder. "Thank you. I appreciate all of this."

"We appreciate you taking care of getting Max cleared," Savanna said. She was frustrated neither her sister or Jordan could tell her what was up, but she'd known that was how this would go. "Do you know yet when Libby's Blooms will reopen? Or even if it will reopen? I see Miss Priscilla hasn't torn your crime scene tape down yet."

Jordan lifted an eyebrow. "I'm a little surprised she hasn't gotten her husband to remove it. We'll be taking it down today. My evidence team is finished over there, and we had the cleaners handle the greenhouse yesterday. My partner already let Anthony Kent know he can reopen whenever he's ready."

Savanna shuddered. "Cleaners...that's something I've never thought about. Can I ask if there are any leads yet?"

"You can ask. But I can't tell you anything while we're still working the case."

"Okay. I wanted to talk to you about a few things I've noticed. It won't take long. First, did your team check out the whole building for break-ins? Or just Libby's shop?"

"We checked the building, since the stairwell to the greenhouse where Libby was found is a common access area."

"Oh, good! Was there any sign someone forced their way in somehow? Like, through the dance school or even the door for the tenants?"

"You know I can't release that information, Savanna."

"Right, okay. Sorry. Well, I'm sure you know the flower shop was locked up tight when Libby was in the greenhouse Saturday morning. Which must mean whoever killed her got to her some other way." She paused. His face gave nothing away. Had he already deduced that? Probably. "So, I know I don't know what exactly is in that file, but a teacher at work happened to be in line at the bank behind Anthony Kent a few weeks ago. She said he completely lost it—he was yelling at the teller because he thought they were giving him incorrect details on his finances. According to her, Anthony was upset and saying the account was for his retirement and his daughter's tuition."

"What was the outcome? Did the bank straighten it out?"

Savanna shook her head. "She didn't know. He went into Mr. Fivell's office, and that was it. But it's more than that. Did you notice he came in through the front entrance Saturday morning? He and Libby always parked out back, in the parking lot. Why would he park on Main Street and come in the front way, on that particular day?"

Jordan sat back in his chair, arms crossed over his chest. "Who knows? You don't know that Anthony never goes in the front. And as for the bank incident, they've screwed up my accounts before too."

"It'd be interesting to know whether the bank did make an error, or if he actually did lose his money. And honestly, with Anthony switching things up with where he parked the morning Libby was murdered, what better way for your officers to know he'd just arrived than for him to come in the front? What if he'd already been inside?"

"Savanna, I appreciate your concern. And you're great at noticing details. But none of this is helpful." He stood.

She and Skylar stood as well. She didn't want to argue, but she disagreed. "I understand. Those things just seemed odd, especially when you put them together. I'm acquainted with Anthony; he's always seemed calm to me. The scene Rosa described at the bank sounds—"

Detective Jordan interrupted her. "Hold on. Rosa, as

in Rosa Taylor?"

"Yes." Oh, boy. She didn't want to get Rosa or Detective Taylor in trouble. In spite of how she'd started the conversation, Rosa hadn't known any details. She'd just been speculating.

"Why was George Taylor's wife talking to you about the case?"

"She wasn't really," Savanna said. "I ran into her in the teachers' lounge and we chatted a little; most people know about my art class at Libby's. Rosa thought I might've been the one who found her. Then she told me about what she'd seen at the bank. I think it's natural in a small town. You know, to wonder about details. Another teacher that same day asked me whether anyone was taking care of Libby's plants. She thought I worked there because she knew her sister was in my art class in the greenhouse. People are just curious."

"Hmm." He held his office door open for them. "Why didn't the sister in your class just ask you who's handling the plants?"

"Oh. Because classes have been on hold. I haven't talked to her. But Jodie—the one in my still life class—probably knew about the special plant Libby was planning to submit to the Flower and Garden Show next week. I'm sure she was worried it might die while the shop was closed. I assumed that was why Mrs. Vonkowski stopped to ask about who was watering the plants."

Jordan stopped just outside his office, and Skylar and Savanna did the same. "Back up. This special plant—let me check something." He went back to his desk and pulled out a yellow legal pad, flipping through the pages before rejoining them. "That's the plant your uncle mentioned during his interview? Libby had come in early to tend to it, he said."

Savanna nodded. "Yes. Jodie is the Carson Horticulture Society treasurer. They used Libby's Blooms for all of their seedlings and supplies, so I'm sure she knew Libby was submitting something to the show."

The detective pressed his lips into a thin line. "All right. Thank you for that."

Savanna had meant to tell Jordan about Marcus Valentine's black eye and his building access. She started to speak, then thought better of it. It was going to come out sounding like a whole lot of nothing, just like her concerns about Anthony. She needed to find out first why the tap instructor had a key to the building—whether because he was a tenant or because he worked for Miss Priscilla.

"I think we're all set then?" Skylar asked Savanna.

"Yes, thank you for listening," she told the detective. "I've got to get to school."

The sisters parted ways at Skylar's law office. At the next building over, a police officer was removing the crime scene tape from Libby's storefront. Miss Priscilla and her husband stood outside in front of the dance school, watching him.

"What now?" Miss Priscilla called, the sharpness in her tone catching Savanna's attention and making her hesitate on her way across the street.

Startled, the officer looked over his shoulder at the Blakes. "What's that?"

"We've got a busy week coming up—lots of families in and out for recital prep. Is your investigation wrapped up? The shop's staying closed?" Dylan Blake asked.

The officer finished removing the last length, bundling it with the rest. "They've been cleared to reopen, but I have no idea what the owner's plan is."

Miss Priscilla spun and yanked the door to the dance school open, her husband behind her. She whipped her head back toward him and spoke vehemently. "I *told* you."

Dylan stopped in his tracks, giving her space before following her in. "It'll be fine, sweetheart." He nodded at the officer as he passed. "Listen, Pris, we're both hungry. Let's finish here and go grab breakfast." The door swung shut after him.

Savanna shook her head and resumed walking. Those two...she hoped they weren't as unhappy as they'd seemed to her the few times she'd been unfortunate enough to observe their interactions.

Why were they at the dance school so early on a weekday morning, anyway? She glanced back again and saw the answer right away. Both of the large front windows now bore bright, colorful banners bearing information about the upcoming dance recital. A whistling Dylan Blake came back through the door, carrying a ladder and the large vinyl banner that was strung over the door each year before the recital. Savanna smiled, picking up her pace in the last block to school. The whistling settled her worry about the Blakes. Miss Priscilla's husband was clearly not rattled; what looked like an argument to her was probably just stress over the upcoming recital in the face of a murder right next door.

She still wasn't sure what that little overheard exchange was about. Savanna couldn't see how whatever happened with Libby's would affect Miss Priscilla's. The dance school had thrived for two decades. It'd be fine.

Savanna forgot she wasn't taking Mollie to her Thursday dance classes until Aidan showed up in her classroom after the last bell. She was wiping the desks down and stacking chairs when he spoke from her doorway, making her jump.

"Ah, the less glamorous side of being a schoolteacher."

An embarrassing little yelp escaped her as she turned and saw him. "Ugh! Don't do that!" She went over to him, smiling, but stopped abruptly several feet from him.

"I thought I'd say hello. I told Mollie I'd pick her up today, but I think she forgot." He bent and caught Mollie as she threw herself at him in a wild hug.

The little girl giggled and squirmed out of his embrace, returning to her task at the whiteboard. "I have to do my job, Daddy." Her admonishment was stern and matched her expression. She used the dry eraser to continue clearing the marker on the surface.

"I'm so sorry. It's good you've put her to work," he told Savanna, winking.

"She begged," Savanna said quietly. "That's the only fun afterschool job in this room. She gets paid in stickers."

Aidan grinned. "Sounds fair. Can I help with anything?"

"I'm almost done, but thank you." Though they'd been steadily dating almost a year, she still had to work to quell the fluttery, excited sensation in her chest every time she was in his space. She'd almost run over and hugged him just like Mollie, before the thought of one of the teachers passing her door and catching them had popped into her head. It was exasperating some-times, having to think about who might spot them and fire up the rumor mill.

Aidan and Mollie walked out with her. Her car was in the teacher's lot, adjacent to the parent parking lot. The after-school pick-up circle in front of the school was slowing down, ten or twelve cars still in line and the crowd of kids thinning out. Tricia Williams wore the orange vest today, directing the sparse traffic. Of course, Savanna thought. Why not literally any other teacher? But since the encounter at the movie theater, Savanna had crossed paths with Tricia a couple of times in the hallways, and the woman had been noth-ing but pleasant.

Savanna looked up at Aidan. "I'll say goodbye now. My car's in the faculty lot. Have fun in class, Mollie. I can't wait to see your recital!"

Mollie beamed.

"I'll see you Saturday," Aidan said. "Let me know when you're home from your birthday treasure hunt, and I'll pick you up."

Tricia's back was still turned to them. Savanna knew she should get going, but she wasn't quite ready. "Where are we going? So I'll know what to wear."

"Can't tell you. But it doesn't matter what you wear." He leaned in toward her, lowering his voice. "You always look beautiful."

She met his gaze and forgot to breathe. Her cheeks burned. "Thank you."

"Bye, Ms. Shepherd!" Mollie took her dad's hand and waved as they crossed to the parking lot in Tricia Williams' direction.

Savanna forced the smile from her face, trying to look as if she hadn't just had a stomach full of butterflies stirred up by Dr. Gallager, and headed the opposite way to her car. Driving through town on the way home, she noticed the lights on at Libby's Blooms. The orange sign on the door was turned to Open. She had an idea.

She ran into Fancy Tails and bought a package of pupcakes from her sister. "I'm going to see if Uncle Max is over at Libby's. I'll be right back!"

She found him behind the cash register at the flower shop, which had no customers at the moment. The town probably hadn't realized yet they were open. Behind Max, she could see Anthony moving about in Libby's office. He'd wasted no time getting back to business. The scene in the bank and the oddity of him arriving Saturday morning at the front entrance notwithstanding, she couldn't imagine him as Libby's killer. She hoped he and his daughter could somehow got through the loss intact.

"Are you happy to be back?" she asked Uncle Max.

"I am," Max replied. "Four days off was plenty. Though it was nice getting to laze about with Lady Bella for a while."

"Aw, I doubt that. Speaking of Lady Bella, Sydney made these fresh today—her bacon pupcakes." She handed him the white box tied with string.

"You'll spoil her. She doesn't need more treats." He was smiling, and Savanna could tell she'd made him happy.

"Nonsense. She isn't spoiled. She's a sweet little dog, and she should have special treats as often as possible. Make sure you tell her they're from me."

"Thank you, love."

"Uncle Max." She dropped her voice to half volume, her gaze darting to Anthony Kent through the office door. "I have a favor to ask. Is it possible for you to show me Libby's project she was working on? The rare plant? I'm so curious."

He leaned toward her over the counter, lowering his voice conspiratorially. "I'd love to. I've been here since noon, I've taken care of all the plants, and there's nothing going on." He came around the counter, calling over his shoulder, "Anthony, my niece thinks she left her favorite paintbrush up on the roof. I'm taking her up. I'll be right back."

Savanna smiled and followed him through the stairwell access door and then up the two flights of stairs to the greenhouse. At the second-level landing, she lagged behind, stopping to peer through the window on the upper half of the door that led to the apartments and storage areas. Two hallways branched off on the other side of the door. One led around the corner, out of her line of sight, but down the other hallway were two apartment doors bearing brass numerical addresses.

Max was already halfway up the next flight of stairs to the roof and hadn't noticed she'd stopped. She reached out and grasped the doorknob, wishing and hoping for it to be unlocked—just as Uncle Max spoke and startled her. "The greenhouse is blooming beautifully. Rachel's done a great job managing the plants. Your easels got stacked and moved to the other end, likely during the investigation."

Savanna jerked her hand back and trotted up the steps. Max hadn't looked back; he'd been making conversation. She'd have to find some way to get a closer look at those apartments.

Max led her to the back corner of the greenhouse, where he unzipped a special mesh screenhouse Libby had erected around her project, then zipped them in once Savanna stepped inside the airy six-by-six-foot space. In the center, a majestic purple flowering plant sat on a pedestal.

"I give you the Cry Violet." Max made a flourish with his hands. "It really is quite remarkable. When Libby told me what she was up to, I did some research. All specimens of the Cry Violet have been extinct in the wild since 1930. There's some evidence that a few plants were cultivated by private owners, but those also went extinct around 1950. She was so excited to submit this to the Flower and Garden Show." His tone was reverent and serious. He shook his head. "I still can't believe she's gone."

"Wow." Savanna's eyes were wide. About five inches in height, it was a beautiful plant, the petals a warm violet hue, turning to a much darker, nearly indigo shade near the center. The leaves were thick and light green. "I've got to tell Sydney that it's flowering. She was hoping Libby was able to see it bloom before she died."

"Oh, yes," Max said. "It's been in full bloom for almost two weeks."

"It's so pretty. Mom lets the wild violets grow in her flower bed off the patio, but those are smaller. The purple isn't as vivid. How did the Cry Violet go extinct?"

Uncle Max nearly lit up. He loved talking plants. His hands clasped behind him, he rocked forward a bit toward the plant as he spoke. "Well, the species was native to France. The Cry Violet liked to grow along the Canal de Bourgogne and the south-facing sides of the limestone hills. She was actually named after the

French community of Cry. Apparently folks attempted to grow the violet in their gardens, on the brink
of her extinction around 1930, but even those efforts
failed. She's been officially extinct for seventy years."
He looked at Savanna, his eyebrows raised. Even with
all of his experience in the field, Uncle Max was clearly
enthralled with the story and Libby's project.

"So how..." She shook her head, watching him.

"How did she do it?"

"Yes! How on earth did Libby grow a plant that's
been extinct since 1950?"

He sighed. "We may never know. She never shared
her secret with me, and I don't get the feeling Rachel
knows, either."

"Holy wow," Savanna said.

"Holy wow, indeed. Rachel's going to bring the violet
to the show in Grand Rapids to honor Libby. She's a
good daughter."

"Definitely. I'm glad to see it's here and healthy. Detective Jordan may be checking in on the plant too,
based on a conversation we had this morning."

"He already has. He was here when we opened. Anthony brought him up here to see the plant, and he
seemed satisfied."

Jordan was nothing if not thorough. Savanna
wasn't sure what exactly she thought had happened
surrounding Libby's death and this plant and Jodie
Vonkowski in her still life class. But she was relieved to
know that Jodie's concern—expressed through Missy—
must simply be genuine horticultural interest.

Uncle Max let them both out of the enclosure. "I only
wish I knew how she did it," he lamented. "It's quite a
feat. A mystery that shall remain unsolved, I'm afraid."

"I appreciate you showing me."

"While I'm up here, I should prune those azaleas. Do you mind waiting for me?"

"Of course not." She followed him through a gorgeous array of flowering plants. An idea struck her. "Uncle Max."

"Yes, love?"

"My earring." She grabbed her earlobe before he could see her small gold earring, still safely in place. "I must've lost it on the stairway. Could I run and find it?"

"Yes, go on! Do you need another set of eyes?" He began taking off his gardening gloves.

"No," Savanna said quickly. She should've anticipated he'd do that. "I'll be right back, and I can help with the pruning if you give me some direction." She smiled at him. She so hated lying, especially to sweet Uncle Max. But it was for a good reason. He'd never be on board with what she hoped to accomplish in the next few minutes.

Chapter Nine

SAVANNA'S PULLED AT THE DOOR to the second-floor apartments, and her heart leaped when it swung easily open. She crept to the first apartment door, labeled with gold-tone numerals: 202. The door beyond it, 201, had an out-of-date Easter wreath with bunnies and ducklings below the apartment number. She turned a corner, finding another hallway. At the end of it, she found a steel door bearing the letters P.D.A.—Miss Priscilla's? It must be how the dance studio accessed their storage space.

She retreated back down the hall, passing apartments 201 and 202. She assumed the other hallway off the entry door led to storage areas and the third apartment. A bang came from somewhere below, and Savanna froze, instinctively backing up against the wall. Steps approached on the stairs outside the door she'd come through. What to do? A brief glance down that first hallway revealed only another closed door at the end; nowhere to hide.

A young woman appeared on the second-floor landing, and Savanna darted to the door, pushing it open as the girl pulled. "Oops! I'm so sorry," she exclaimed, stepping aside and letting her in. She looked to be around college age.

"That's okay," the young woman replied amicably. "Were you looking for me? Brianna," she offered, placing a hand on her chest. "Or maybe Marcus?"

"Um, yes! Actually. I was meeting him here. We're grabbing a bite. Maybe at the deli, but I don't know, maybe we'll get pizza instead. I'm not sure." *Oh jeez, Savanna, shut your mouth!* She stared wide-eyed at the woman, who must be Marcus Valentine's neighbor. Marcus really did live in the building. "I think I've got the time wrong, though. Maybe I'm early. He's not home." She was only making it worse. What if Marcus *was* home? And heard them in the hall talking? She backed up toward the still-open door.

The woman checked the phone in her hand. "It's four-thirty. Do you want to wait? His hours seem to be different every day, but I'm sure he'll be here."

"No, no, I'll come back. I'm way too early. Thank you, though!" The door was almost closed behind her when the young woman called to her.

"What's your name? I'll let him know you were here."

"Um." Savanna's mind raced. "Elizabeth. Thanks so much!" She nearly sprinted through the door and took two steps up toward the rooftop level before she realized the woman could see her and was probably wondering where the heck she was going. She spun and trotted slowly down the steps, heart pounding in her ears, halting on the step outside the access door to Libby's Blooms and leaning against the wall. Her middle name? Why on earth had she said *Elizabeth*? Now what? She glanced up the stairs, then slowly, stealthily went back up, ducking down under the door's window when she reached the second-floor landing so she remained hidden. She tried raising her head to peek, but changed her mind. If Marcus Valentine's neighbor was still in the hallway for some reason, she'd see her peeking, and how would Savanna even explain? She maintained her crouched-down posture, half squatting, half crawling, until she was four steps past the door. She let out a huge breath and hurried the rest of the way up and out into the greenhouse, breathing hard

Uncle Max gawked at her. He was a couple of feet away, gloves dangling from one hand. "Are you all right? You're pale as a sheet."

"Yes," she said, too brightly. "I'm great. Are you finished?"

He nodded slowly. "I see you found your earring."

"What? My—Oh!" She smacked a hand over her earlobe and the small gold earring there. "Right, yes." She swallowed hard, a pang of regret hitting her. She so hoped Uncle Max couldn't tell she was lying.

"I'm glad you found what you were looking for." He scrutinized her a moment longer, then pulled the door open. "Ready?"

That evening, Savanna sat outside on her deck and mentally sorted through the snippets of information she'd gained in the past few days. She was glad Uncle Max was now cleared in Libby's death, but she knew she could help Detective Jordan figure out who'd killed her. She had to, for Sydney. She'd seemed fine at lunch today, but that was because the three of them had been actively working on getting to the bottom of Libby's murder. The thought that perhaps Jordan wasn't looking at all the pieces in the case nagged at her. She'd have to let him know about Marcus living in the building, and the weirdly coincidental black eye he'd come to work with Monday after Libby had been killed. Her phone buzzed on the bench beside her. Sydney and Finn were walking on the beach and wanted to stop by.

Savanna added another small log to the fire in her fire pit and brought out two more glasses of lemonade. Fonzie came bounding up onto the deck from the dunes. Sydney and Finn were close behind. Sydney's long red hair was loose, the spiral curls on the ends damp like the hem of her skirt. Finn looked drier, though there were splash marks on his gray rock concert tee.

"You walked all the way from the park? And you went in? Isn't the lake still freezing?" Savanna asked.

"It's not too bad," her younger sister replied. "Almost warm enough to swim."

Finn laughed. "Speak for yourself. It'll have to be a lot warmer than that before I go in."

Sydney shrugged, she and Finn taking the adjacent bench. Fonzie curled up on Finn's feet. "So," Sydney said, "Finn's in for dinner on Sunday. Have you decided where we'll go? Did you ask Aidan yet?"

"I'm seriously fine keeping it at Mom and Dad's. I don't mind cooking."

"That's not happening. If you really want to skip the restaurant, I'll trade you weeks. Let me cook. I've got the perfect recipe."

Savanna gave in. "All right. That sounds good. I'm going to run it by Aidan tomorrow."

"It's your birthday dinner! I'm sure he'll come."

"He'd better," Finn said.

Sydney frowned at him. "Stop it. Don't be nervous.

You're going to love everyone, and they'll love you. And you don't want to miss what I'm making."

He put an arm behind her along the back rest and addressed Savanna. "I'm sure we'll have runs to Anderson Memorial tomorrow. Do you want me to find my brother and tell him?"

"I think I might try to meet up with him for coffee, but thank you." The three of them chatted a while longer as the sun dropped toward the horizon. Fonzie switched spots, sprawling out near the fire pit. The evening had gotten cool.

"This is my favorite spot in your house," Sydney said. "You've got the best view."

"I love it here. But I do miss being your roomie," Savanna said, smiling.

"That was the most fun," her sister agreed.

The teachers' lounge during Friday's lunch hour was packed. Carson's PTA was throwing their annual teacher appreciation luncheon. With only a month left of school until summer break, the remaining days were increasingly filled with events, assemblies, and field trips.

The spread was amazing. Savanna had to hand it to the parents. Three types of deli sandwiches, two choices of soup, several large, pretty bowls filled with fresh fruit, homemade potato salad, Michigan cherry salad, and a huge assortment of cookies and pies for dessert.

She wished she'd worn a more forgiving outfit today; the thin white belt on her blue linen dress was pinching her waist. She shared a table with Jack, Tricia Wil-

Tracy Gardner

liams, Rosa Taylor, and Jack's girlfriend Elaina Jenson, a third-grade teacher. Elaina and Jack had been dating for over a year, and they were adorable together. The two of them excused themselves a few minutes apart, leaving Savanna at the table with the teacher she was trying to avoid, and the teacher she was trying to avoid getting in trouble. She hoped Nick Jordan hadn't felt the need to say anything to his partner, George Taylor. The whole conversation she'd had the other day with Rosa had been pure speculation.

She picked at the cookies still on her dessert plate and asked Rosa if she'd been able to finish her wedding thank-you notes. That led to a discussion about newly married life, which led to kitchen appliances, brands, features, and finishes. Savanna jotted down notes as Rosa told her which model stainless steel side-by-side refrigerator was the best, making sure to ask more questions about the ice dispenser and the freezer space. She'd gotten a perfectly fine budget model last fall when she'd moved in, but she was determined to avoid meaningful conversation with both women until she could politely escape.

The parents began cleaning up, and Savanna was filled with relief as other teachers throughout the room began leaving. "Well, I'd better go. My afternoon classes are going wildflower hunting for a project, and I need to set up."

Tricia Williams put a well-manicured hand on Savanna's forearm. "No, I've been waiting to ask you about something." She shot a grouchy glance at Rosa, which surprised Savanna since she knew they were friends. It was her fault the table talk had been about appliances, not Rosa's.

"Sure, what's that?"

"You know Parker VanHelm?"

Savanna wondered where this was headed. Tricia had had her back turned the entire time Savanna and Aidan had been talking outside yesterday after school. She was sure of it. "Yes, he's a third grader, right?"

Tricia leaned closer, her elbows on the table. She glanced around briefly before speaking. "His mother stopped to talk to me in my pick-up line yesterday. After you and Dr. Gallager left."

"Dr. Gallager picked up his daughter after school. We happened to walk out together," Savanna clarified. Man, she wished she'd gotten out of here when Jack had.

"Parker's mom wanted to know if you two are dating."

"Based on what?" Savanna heard the defensive tone in her own voice but couldn't help it.

"She noticed the two of you together while waiting in the pick-up line. I don't know what she saw, but it was enough to make her ask. I told her I ran into you together at the movies Saturday night, so I knew you were friends." Tricia looked pleased with herself, as if she'd done Savanna a favor.

Savanna forced a smile. "Parker's such a sweet boy. I'm sure Mrs. VanHelm didn't mean to sound overly curious. I've really got to run." She stood.

"It's okay, I'll walk with you." Tricia turned to Rosa. "Don't forget we're going to yoga after school. I'll meet you out front."

Savanna thanked the parents for the delicious lunch on her way out. Tricia walked beside her to her classroom, Savanna gritting her teeth as the teacher continued to chat.

"Anyway, you should be careful. Not saying you are dating Dr. Gallager, but if you were, a lot of the parents would have a problem with that." Tricia's tone was sympathetic, but it was contradicted by the gleeful look in her eyes. "How do they know you won't give that parent's child preferential treatment? I'm not saying you would, of course. But you should be aware of what might happen if parents found out."

"If parents found out that a single elementary school teacher was dating a single parent." Savanna looked at Tricia.

"Yes. Not saying you are!" Tricia touched her arm again, making Savanna disproportionately angry.

"So, it's against the district rules?"

"Oh. Well, no, I don't think so. But I'm not sure—"

"And I'm sure there are mandates against any kind of inappropriate displays while at school," Savanna said. "If someone was dating a student's parent, they'd mainly need to make certain to keep the focus professional at school, and not show favoritism to the student."

"Yes, true—"

"Because if all boundaries were maintained, there'd be nothing for parents to be concerned about. Right?" Savanna stopped in her classroom doorway, one hand on the doorframe. Tricia Williams was not coming into her classroom.

"Yes," the teacher admitted, the wind completely taken out of her sails. She took a deep breath and sighed. "Okay then. I'll let you do your prep work, Ms. Shepherd."

"Sounds good." Savanna stayed in the doorway as

Tricia turned to go.

"Oh! I just remembered the other thing I wanted to ask you."

Savanna pressed her lips together, trying to arrange her expression into something more pleasant than what she felt. "Really? What's that?"

"With your uncle being accused in Libby's murder—"

"My uncle was never accused, Mrs. Williams." Savanna's eyes narrowed.

"Oh! Of course! I meant, you know, as the police are working through suspects. I'm not sure if your family is worried or not, but I thought you might like a bit of good news. I heard," Tricia said, coming back over to Savanna and speaking quietly, "Anthony Kent had just increased the life insurance coverage on Libby right before she died. Can you believe that? That's a pretty fishy coincidence."

Oh, boy. Well, the fact that Tricia had heard that was certainly significant. Savanna kept her expression neutral. "That's interesting."

"Interesting? I guess that's one word you could use. Why would he do that? It certainly makes him look bad."

"How do you know this?"

"Um. A friend told me. She's privy to some inside information now and then. Don't say I'm the one who told you!" Tricia's smug tone said otherwise. She'd probably have loved the whole school to know she had inside information.

"I won't."

"Your uncle won't have to worry. I'm sure now the police will be looking into Anthony as the murderer." The bell rang—*thank goodness*—and children began pouring into the hallway from the cafeteria down the hall. "Got to run!"

Literally saved by the bell, Savanna watched as Rosa exited the teachers' lounge and fell into step with Tricia. The friend with inside information was most definitely Rosa Taylor.

By the end of the day, Savanna was dying to talk to her sisters or Aidan or Detective Jordan—*someone*—about what Tricia had said. Not only had George Taylor's wife likely shared the news with Tricia about the life insurance policy, it seemed as if Rosa also knew who was being investigated as suspects. Why else would Tricia have even known about Max? Savanna would have to let Detective Jordan know about their conversation. Between Rosa and Tricia, important information that would tip off the murderer could be flying around town in no time.

Savanna was out of the school parking lot before most of the parents, and walking into Anderson Memorial a few minutes later. Carson's hospital was a small, one-hundred-thirty-bed, two-story-high full-service facility. Only fifteen years old, everything about it was state-of-the-art, and since Dr. Gallager had come to town a few years after it opened, Anderson Memorial had the highest ranked Cardiothoracic Surgery department in lower Michigan. While some complicated or severe medical cases were transferred to the larger Great Lakes Hospital farther north, Aidan's heart patients came from all over the state for his services.

Savanna ordered iced coffee at the kiosk in the lobby, a high, clean space full of natural light from the front wall of windows. She turned to see her boyfriend on his way down the open staircase, blue scrubs under his white lab coat. As he approached, she caught a glimpse of something small and pink pinned onto the scrubs under his lapel. Something new from Mollie, she guessed.

He met her halfway across the lobby, taking his fancied-up whipped cream and caramel-topped coffee from her and hugging her. She knew he typically took his coffee with plain cream and sugar, no frills, but she'd noticed last Saturday at dinner he'd asked for extra whipped topping on his pie. She was always learning something new about him. Including that today, in his scrubs and lab coat, he smelled different, antiseptic overlaying his usual spicy, masculine scent. Savanna reluctantly let go of him first and started to pull back; Tricia's words were still very loud in her head, despite the fact that she and Aidan were doing nothing wrong and she wasn't even at school anymore. But maybe he didn't want everyone at his hospital knowing about his personal life.

Aidan held on a beat longer, his lips near her ear through her hair. "You're gorgeous."

She laughed. "Maybe it's just the frou-frou coffee."

He held his up, checking it out. "Hmm. That's new, thank you. Or maybe it's because you dressed to match me today."

"I did?" Savanna glanced down. She was wearing almost the exact shade of blue as Aidan's scrubs. The white of her belt even matched his lab coat. "I did! That's so weird. Can I..." She peeked under the edge of his lab coat, curious about the bit of pink. "Oh! It's a little bunny!" She smiled up at him.

"Her newest find. Grandma Jean took her shopping Wednesday after the nature center. She got matching barrettes."

Savanna nodded. "I noticed them today! She's such a cutie."

"I've just finished rounds, and my charts will wait for me. Want to go for a walk? It looks so nice out."

"It's beautiful!" As they headed outside, she told him about her students' wildflower expedition. "I feel so lucky to have a job now where I can plan occasional nature hikes as part of my work day. In Chicago, I never had a clue what it was like outside most of the time."

"You were cut out to be a teacher. Did you ever imagine yourself as one?"

"A long time ago, when I was still in school. But I was so fascinated by the great artists and their techniques, and that led me to authentication, and I loved it. Well, most of it. I did love working with all of the beautiful pieces that passed through my hands." She bit her lower lip. "I always had this feeling, mostly in the mornings getting ready to leave for work. Like I was... I don't know. Living someone else's life? But now I feel like myself, in every part of my life. I'm not sure if that makes sense."

"It makes perfect sense to me." He took her hand as they walked.

She sipped her coffee. "So, I have an ulterior motive for coming here."

"No!" He tipped his head back and looked at the sky. "And I thought you just missed me."

"I did!" She laughed as she caught his expression, the slow smile that started with one side of his mouth and then took over his whole face, right up to the crinkles around his eyes. "Are you free Sunday evening? I wondered if you and Mollie would come to dinner at my parents' house."

"We'd love to."

"Awesome! Dinner's at six, but we all get there a little early. Sydney's taking my night to cook, since it's my birthday. Oh, and Finn's coming too."

Aidan's eyebrows went up. "Sydney got Finn to come?"

"She did. I think he'll be happy to hear you're on board now too."

His work phone buzzed in his pocket. He checked it and groaned. "I've got to go. Call me later? Look, speak of the devil." He nodded toward the ambulance bay they were approaching, where Finn was loading an empty gurney into the back of an ambulance.

Aidan left her with Finn, and she saw Aidan put his phone to his ear as he cut through the ER, breaking into a run at the end of the hallway. That couldn't be good.

"No coffee for me?" Finn made a sad face at her.

"I'd have gotten you one if I had known we'd see you." She stepped quickly to one side as his coworker carried a plastic bin past her and into the back of the ambulance.

"Ambu bags," Finn told the young man. "We're down to two."

"Already got 'em," the coworker said. He climbed into the back of the vehicle and began restocking the metal cabinets.

The double doors from the ER opened, and a group of scrub-clad hospital staff exited. It must be the end of a shift, Savanna thought.

"Savanna!" a familiar voice called out. She turned to find Libby's daughter Rachel waving. The young woman, wearing pink scrubs, came over to the ambulance bay. "I thought that was you. Hey, Finn."

"Hey, Rachel," Finn returned.

"How are you?" Savanna's voice softened with concern. It surprised her to see Rachel already back at work. She couldn't imagine how hard it must be.

Rachel sighed, shifting her backpack to her other shoulder. "I'm okay, I guess. It still doesn't seem real."

"It doesn't. I'm so sorry for your loss. Is there anything I can do, anything you or your dad need?" Tricia's words rang in her ears, but Savanna couldn't imagine Anthony Kent shooting his wife.

"No, thank you. We're okay. And so many people have brought food over, but neither of us feels like eating."

"I'm sure; I think that's normal. I'm sure they'd give you more time off here if you asked."

"Oh, they offered," Rachel said. "I won't need it. We aren't having a funeral. Dad wants a memorial service instead, so I'm planning that for next month. I'll get paid for bereavement days, but I'm just going to pocket the money and work through them. I was already short on my tuition money. I think nursing school might have to wait a while."

Ugh. Savanna's heart hurt for the poor young woman. "I'm so sorry." She impulsively reached out and hugged Rachel. "I know your mom was so proud you were going to be a nurse. Maybe you could try for student loans?"

"I already have as much as I can qualify for. My boyfriend thinks he might have a way to help me with the cost. I don't know." She took a deep breath, and Savanna watched her force her features into a sunnier expression. "It's all right. It'll all work out. I still have my dad, and Mom would love knowing her violet will still make it to the flower show next weekend. That would've made her happy."

"I saw it," Savanna said. "My uncle showed it to me. It's amazing she was able to somehow grow an extinct plant. I bet it'll win all kinds of awards."

"Mom thought it might too. Oh, shoot, that's my ride!" Rachel pointed to another scrub-clad woman who'd just pulled up in a car outside the ambulance bay. "Thank you, Savanna. You're a lot like your uncle. We just love him."

Savanna was quiet, watching Rachel leave.

"She's here all the time. At least it seems like it," Finn said. "Everyone has told her to take some time off. I mean, come on—her mom died."

"I know!" Savanna looked up at him. "It's awful she's so worried about money she can't take time to grieve."

All she could think about was that life insurance policy. Did Rosa and Tricia have bad information? Or maybe Anthony hadn't told Rachel yet about the money—if he'd even received it by now? She had no idea how that all worked.

Finn spoke, bringing up a good point. "Well, maybe she's handling it better staying distracted."

His words instantly reminded her that he knew what Rachel was going through. And he'd been even younger when he'd lost both his parents. "You're probably right. I'm sorry, you're working. I should go," Savanna said.

"We're just hanging out waiting for a run. You're good." No sooner had the words left his mouth than the emergency medical service radio crackled in the front of the vehicle. Finn's partner reached between the seats for it.

Finn pulled his sunglasses from the collar of his uniform shirt. His demeanor had subtly shifted with the call from dispatch; he was ready. Savanna could see how much he loved his career. It was nice having him here in Carson after his two-month-long absence. "Got something?" he asked his partner.

"Yep. Lake Haven Mall. Let's roll." The man closed the rear doors of the ambulance where Savanna was standing with Finn.

"I'm driving," Finn called over his shoulder. "Gotta run. Oh, and happy birthday, Savanna. You won't believe what my brother's got up his sleeve." He winked at her, donned his aviators, and grinned, and for a split second she saw exactly what Sydney must see. There was no one like Finn.

Chapter Ten

O N Saturday, Savanna woke on the morning of her thirty-second birthday before the sun was fully up. Pink light filtered into her room through her curtains, and she could hear the waves of Lake Michigan in the distance. She'd been sleeping with her window open since the snow had melted. Nothing lulled her to sleep at night like the shore.

She stared up at the ceiling, thinking of the exciting day ahead. Her mom and sisters would be here at ten to pick her up for her birthday scavenger hunt. She had no idea where they were headed. Then, later, Aidan would pick her up at five to take her out, but he wouldn't say where, either. Thirty-two must be the year for surprises.

Last year on this day, she'd awoken in the pink-and-yellow guest room at Sydney's house, wondering if she'd be living with her little sister forever. She hadn't known then whether the school was going to keep her on for next fall, with rumors of budget cuts. She and Aidan hadn't officially been a couple yet; he'd been running back and forth to New York, stretched far too thin with work, and they'd only gone on a few dates. So much could change in less than a year. Thirty-one had been the year of uncertainty. By that logic, thirty was definitely the year of change—a major move out of Chicago to her hometown, a broken engagement, and a career change. Things had gotten progressively better since coming home to Carson. She felt a tingle of anticipation at all the possibilities of the coming year.

Fonzie stirred at her feet, snoring softly, and tucked his nose under a fold in the bedding. He had the right idea. Savanna turned onto her side and snuggled down under the plush comforter, eyelids drifting closed. She'd sleep a few minutes longer.

When she opened her eyes again, sunlight streamed through every gap in her curtains. Fonzie was standing on the bed looking down at her and, seeing she was finally awake, he sprang across her and took off toward the stairway, ready to go outside. Savanna sped through her morning routine and was outside on her deck sipping a steaming cup of coffee when Skylar's car rolled into the driveway.

Sydney was in the front seat with Skylar, so Savanna got in the back with Charlotte. They were headed east, out of town, but that was all Savanna knew so far. She'd learned from last year to dress as nicely as possible without being formal, and to make sure to throw a pair of sneakers in her bag. Just in case the birthday scavenger hunt involved a two-mile hike, as it had for one of Sydney's birthdays.

Her mother reached into her purse and produced a bright blue envelope with a silver ribbon. "Here you go! You get two for the first destination."

Savanna didn't know who'd invented their birthday tradition, but she loved it. There was no winning or losing, other than the well-earned pride of solving the destination clues before arrival. She tore open the envelope, pulled out a long, narrow slip of paper, and read. "Clue number one: *A Sunday afternoon on the island of Water Lily Pond with the flower carrier leads us to a starry night.*" She frowned, her gaze going from Charlotte beside her to both her sisters up front. "What does that mean? *The Starry Night* is Van Gogh. A Sunday— oh! They're paintings."

All three women remained silent.

"A Sunday afternoon on the—that's Georges Seurat. *A Sunday Afternoon on the Island of La Grande Jatte* is the pointillist piece, the lovely scene in the park on the River Seine."

Charlotte nodded. "It's one of my favorite paintings. And?"

Savanna read the clue again. "*A Sunday afternoon on the island of Water Lily Pond—Water Lily Pond* is Claude Monet—*with the flower carrier leads us to a starry night.* All right, it ends with Van Gogh. This is my first clue? But we're coming back before nightfall today. Are we going to an island? No, we're heading east. A pond then? What's within an hour of Carson?" She drummed her fingertips on her purse in her lap, thinking.

Sydney spun around in her seat, pointing a finger at Savanna. "No phones! You know the rules."

"I know!" She raised her hands in the air, laughing. "Sunday afternoon on the island of Water Lily Pond with the flower carrier leads us... *The Flower Carrier* is Diego Rivera. So, you've got Rivera, Monet, Van Gogh, and Seurat. Maybe I should focus on the artists to solve the clue rather than the titles of the works. Or is it the era they're from?" Her family was no help.

"Would you like your second clue?"

"Yes, please."

Charlotte handed her a bright yellow envelope with another silver ribbon. Inside was a collage of four cut-outs, artistically placed side by side with decorative glitter swirls around them like a frame. The glitter had to be Sydney's work. Savanna held it up and smiled. "I love your arts and crafts."

"Thank you."

"Okay, pictures of three museums. The first is the Metropolitan Museum of Art in New York. Then my Kenilworth in Chicago, and this one is the Lansing Museum of Fine Art. And a white Panama hat on top of the Lansing Museum." She sucked in her breath, realizing what it meant. "Really? We're going now? And Britt knows? Oh, you guys!"

Skylar grinned at her in the rearview mirror. "We're having lunch with Britt at the museum."

Savanna let out a little squeal. She loved the museum, and Britt Nash, the art authenticator there, was a colleague and good friend. "I'm so excited! It's been too long since I've been, and since I've seen him! And oh my gosh, right now there's a whole Post-Impressionist exhibit going on at the museum. Did you—" she stopped herself. They were all smiling. "Of course you knew. I love you; you're all awesome. I've been dying to see it. Thank you."

"I told you the clues would be harder this time," Skylar said.

"They weren't too tough."

"Really?" Sydney glanced back at her. "You haven't even solved the whole thing yet."

"What? How? I figured it out."

"Not all of it."

Savanna looked down, studying the clues again. "Why did you include all three museums? Why not just Britt's?"

Her sisters in the front seat shrugged almost simultaneously. She looked at her mom beside her, but Charlotte's poker face was flawless.

"Ugh!" What on earth could it mean that all three museums were in the collage? The Met, the very first museum she'd ever visited, was where her love of fine art had blossomed into a career plan, nurtured, of course, by Caroline Carson. Kenilworth was obviously where she'd worked in that career. And the Lansing Museum was…what? It was where her colleague Britt worked. It was where she'd gone not long ago to use their lab in search of possible forgeries, just after she'd come home to Carson. What did the three have in common?

It turned out to be the only clue she couldn't solve. After they'd finished viewing the Post-Impressionist exhibit, Britt Nash joined them for lunch upstairs in the museum café, a lush, green oasis filled with live plants. Tall and slender, with white-blond hair and a tiny diamond earring in one earlobe, Britt hadn't changed a bit since she'd seen him last summer—or since he'd worked on contracts at Kenilworth with her years earlier, for that matter.

When they'd finished lunch and were sipping coffees, Britt turned to Savanna and solved the rest of the clue. "I have a proposal for you. Come and work with me."

Her eyes widened. "What do you mean? I can't leave my teaching job—I love it."

"Come and work with me this July," he clarified.

"We're getting an entire Marcellus DuBois collection in next month, and I'm going to need help with the provenances and authentication."

"Oh, wow! So, it'd be a temporary assignment?"

He nodded. "You're in commuting distance, unless you want to stay nearby, in which case the museum will put you up at a hotel. It'd just be a short-term summer job. With excellent pay and the added bonus of lunch with me every day."

Savanna got it. She turned in her chair and looked at the women at the table one by one. "A job! You already know about the job offer? That was the rest of the clue. You included all the museums where I've either worked or wished to work. Or something like that, right?"

"Exactly," Charlotte said.

"I still had Britt's number from the art festival last summer," Skylar said. "I called him to let him know we wanted to make the museum one of your birthday destinations, and he told us he'd been planning to call you about the authentication contract."

Charlotte stood, pushing her chair in. "Britt, I can't tell you how lovely it's been seeing you again. We're on a tight schedule, so we've got to run. But thank you so much for today."

There were hugs all around, and Britt pulled back from Savanna, smiling. "Is it a yes? I'll see you this summer? I can send you all the details before you decide, if you'd like."

"It's a definite yes. I'm so excited! And thank you for these." Savanna scooped up the bouquet of yellow roses Britt had given her. "We'll talk soon!"

On the drive back to Carson, Savanna was content,

caffeinated and basking in the glow of two more wonderful birthday destinations for which she'd fully solved the clues: a stop at a small shop she'd been wanting to check out, where her mom and sisters had her try on and choose an entire new outfit—their gift to her, followed by a favorite bakery in Lansing, where they enjoyed strong, sweet coffees in tiny cups and chocolate chip cannoli. Her thoughts drifted to this evening and the date with Aidan. The scant few minutes with him after work yesterday hadn't been nearly enough. She couldn't wait for tonight, and then dinner with him and her family tomorrow.

"Skylar." Now was as good a time as any to see if Tricia was right. "I heard yesterday at school that Anthony Kent increased Libby's life insurance policy right before she died."

Skylar looked at her sharply. "Who said that?"

"One of the teachers who has her nose in everyone's business. Tricia Williams."

"Her name doesn't sound familiar. Where would she have heard something like that?"

"I'd planned to mention this to Detective Jordan. I can't verify for sure where she got that information, but her best friend at school is Rosa Taylor."

"Rosa Taylor, as in Jordan's partner's wife? Rosa is the one who told you about Anthony Kent's tantrum at the bank, right?"

"Yes. Listen, I don't think she knows she's sharing information she shouldn't. I think George Taylor is telling her too much."

"The blame lies with her husband," Skylar agreed. "He knows better; he's a nice guy, but he's getting himself in trouble. I'll talk to Nick."

"That's a good idea. So the information passed to Tricia Williams is correct?"

Savanna could almost see the wheels turning in Skylar's head. Her sister was unfailingly close-mouthed about client information and always careful not to cross boundaries. "Okay. You know the Kents are my clients. Since you already have pieces of the truth, and Libby is gone, I'm comfortable telling you this, since it's her life insurance policy in question. Anthony Kent didn't just increase the policy on Libby; he doubled it. Two weeks before she died."

"Oh, my." Charlotte spoke from the back seat. "That sure doesn't look good."

"That was the information I gave to Nick the other day. He's looking into it, don't worry."

"Do you really think he could do that to Libby?" Sydney asked. "I mean, I don't know him very well, but he's had dinner with us on occasion. I can't really imagine him..." She shuddered, unable to finish the thought.

Savanna shook her head. "He's a quiet man. I can't imagine anyone killing Libby—that's the problem. But logistically, he could've done it. He has a set of keys; he could've locked the shop after going into the stairwell and up to the greenhouse early that morning. But the way she was killed—it was so up close and personal. You know..." she paused, thinking out loud. "Maybe we can ask Uncle Max. He sees Anthony almost every day."

"Tomorrow," Skylar said. "Let's ask him at dinner."

#

That night, Savanna stared at Aidan in the front seat of his SUV, positive he was kidding.

"I'm serious," he said. "I wouldn't make you if it wasn't necessary. But it'll only be for a few minutes."

She gave in. "Okay, fine. Go ahead." She turned away from him, faced the window, and closed her eyes as he gently tied a wide, silky length of material over her eyes and around her head. "Is that okay? Too tight?"

She touched the blindfold with her fingertips; it felt like a necktie. It smelled like him. She didn't mind so much. "Nope, it's good." She faced forward again, slivers of light sneaking in above and below the blue fabric. She turned toward him and lifted one side, narrowing her eyes and trying not to smile.

"You're so cute," he said, giving her that dimpled, crooked grin. *He* was cute. His gray linen dress shirt somehow made his eyes bluer, and his mildly unruly dark hair was neatly combed back tonight. Was it ridiculous that even after almost a year with him, and longer than that since they'd become friends, her heart still raced whenever he was close? If it was, she didn't care.

She leaned across the console, placed a hand on his cheek, and kissed him, a soft, brief encounter. His face was smooth, no trace of the usual five o'clock shadow that was standard by this time of night. She sat back and smoothed the blindfold down. "All right. I'm ready. You said it's a short drive, right?"

"I promise."

Less than ten minutes later, she felt the car come to a stop. She had no idea where they were; there'd been far too many turns and speed changes. Aidan came around and opened her car door, helping her out. She'd worn the outfit her mom and sisters had gotten her today at their second destination, a sleeveless aqua chiffon dress, and strappy gold sandals Sydney had chosen to go with it. She hoped she wasn't overdressed. "Can I take this off yet?" She heard seagulls, but that wasn't any kind of giveaway in a lakeside town.

"Almost. Come on, I'll help you." He slipped an arm around her waist, holding her loosely against his side, and she kept an arm locked through his bent elbow. He felt so much taller than her this way, even with her low heels on, as she carefully took his cues and walked alongside him. "Okay, now you can take it off. I don't need you falling into the water."

Savanna pulled the blindfold off, surprised to find they were at Carson Marina. He'd walked them past Sweetwater Boats to the third row of docks. At six-thirty, the sky had hints of pink, but the sun hadn't set. She supposed there was time for a quick sail. "Are we taking a boat out?"

"Not exactly." He took her hand and led her out onto the docks, past several boats and a few vacant slips, until they were almost at the end. He stopped at the second-to-last empty slip, where he'd tied the largest red ribbon and bow she'd ever seen on dock post 142.

She stared up at him, not understanding.

"Happy birthday! This is your future sailboat's slip. It's covered for the next two years, but we can renew after that unless you want to move to a different one. I wanted to get you the actual boat. I looked—a lot— since last Wednesday. Gus helped me, but there are way too many options and sizes and colors, and I decided you'd much rather choose her yourself, so I set up an account for you. You just have to decide what your dream sailboat is, and Gus will order her. But this way, you already have a place to—"

Savanna cut him off. She threw her arms around

him, half laughing, half crying, and kissed him, hard and firm and no holding back, as his arms tightened around her and her feet left the wooden dock. Her heart pounded so loudly in her ears she was sure he must hear it. When he set her down, her breathing was rapid and her cheeks were damp. She cradled his face in her hands, searching his eyes. One more small laugh escaped her lips, and she shook her head. "I can't believe you did this." She drew in a slow, shaky breath, trying to regain her composure.

"So." His deep, baritone voice was quiet. "You like it?"

She covered her mouth, feeling tears well up again. She fought them, looking up and blinking hard, and then met his gaze again. "You. Are. Crazy."

"About you."

She put a hand on his chest. She couldn't find the words. Any words. She bit her lip, taking deep breaths. She had to get control. Zen. Calm. *Om.* Something along those lines. "I love it," she finally said. "But I can't accept it. Any of it."

The look on his face made her instantly want to pull the words out of the air and take them back.

"I'm sorry!" She hugged him, resting her head against his chest. "I'm really sorry, but oh my God, this is way too much. It wouldn't be right; I can't let you do this." She pulled back and looked up at him, her eyebrows furrowed in worry.

"You're not *letting* me do anything. It's a birthday gift. If you don't want it, give it away to someone else." His voice was calm, but Savanna could hear the undercurrent of disappointment in his tone.

"Aidan, please. I don't want to ruin the evening. You're amazing. It's so wonderful you'd do this for me, but it's... I can't even imagine what all this cost. The slip alone is tons. And a boat? You can't do that."

He was quiet now, listening and watching her. A ship's horn sounded in the distance, and he glanced at his watch. "Oh, no. We've got to run. Right now—come with me!"

She took his offered hand and ran down the dock with him, past Sweetwater Boats, all the way to the public dock, where the marina's sunset cruise departed each evening during tourist season. They were the last ones to board the eighty-foot dinner yacht. Live music played from somewhere on the large cruiser. Aidan gave his name to the tuxedoed maître d', who escorted them to a window table on the upper deck.

When the man was gone, Aidan took Savanna's hand on the white-linen-covered table. "I'm sure you've been on this cruise dozens of times, but I thought it sounded nice. And different than dinner in a restaurant."

"I've never been on the *Moonstar*. Ever! I don't even know why. I've always wanted to."

His face lit up with a wide grin, easing her guilt a bit over declining his extravagant gift. "Really? Good."

They both avoided the elephant in the room throughout the four-course dinner. Savanna was loath to be the cause of that terribly dismayed look on Aidan's face again, and she suspected Aidan was remaining quiet and hoping she'd changed her mind.

When their table had been cleared, their waiter ceremoniously presented Savanna with an enormous hot fudge brownie sundae with lit sparklers jutting out the top. Four other waitstaff gathered around their little table, and Aidan joined them in singing "Happy Birthday" to her, making her cheeks burn furiously. She stared across the table at him, unable to stop smiling.

He brought up the elephant toward the end of the evening while they were dancing under the stars. The front man of the band on deck announced the cruise would soon be back in port, and they launched into Iz's version of "Somewhere Over the Rainbow." Aidan was a good dancer. His large, warm hand at the small of her back kept her close, her fingers rested on the back of his neck, and when he spoke, his lips moved against her hair. "I need you to keep the gift."

She closed her eyes. It was so hard to think logically like this. She stroked the edge of his silky hair against his neck, sliding her fingers across his skin.

"It would mean a lot to me," he said, his voice sending shivers down her spine. "I want you to have it. You deserve it. And I'd like you to teach me."

She looked up at him. "Teach you?"

He nodded. "I want to do it right. Sail. Learn how to control the boat."

"You can't control the boat. But you can guide it, and change your sails based on the wind."

He gazed into her eyes. "Will you teach me?"

This was as much about Aidan as it was about her, Savanna realized. Maybe he was trying to atone for the accident that had nearly killed Finn. He had nothing to atone for; he'd been a misguided, grieving kid. But she'd told him that already. "You really want to learn to sail?"

"I do."

"I could teach you on Gus's Catalina. That'd make the most sense."

He shook his head. "No. Savanna, I've seen you on the water. This makes the most sense. You need a sailboat, and I need to learn to sail. Look at it as a favor to me."

She tipped her head back, arching away from him for a second, and rolled her eyes. "A favor to you. I'm supposed to let you spend God knows how much on this crazy gift as a favor to you." It was the absolute craziest, sweetest, most personal gift anyone had ever given her.

"Forget about the money. It doesn't matter. Listen." He frowned at her, staring intently into her eyes. "Your reaction, the look on your face that instant out on the docks when you considered the possibility. That's what matters to me." He brushed a strand of hair back toward her temple. "Okay?"

How could she say no? "Thank you, Aidan. This is truly the best birthday I've ever had, and yours is the most perfect gift I've ever received. I'll think about it. Does that work for now?"

"It works," he said, smiling. He spun her, making her laugh, and then dipped her and kissed her.

Chapter Eleven

F INN GALLAGER STOOD ON THE porch outside Sydney's kitchen door Sunday morning. He raised
one hand in greeting as she gawked at him
through the window on the top half of the door. She'd
just woken up. He was over an hour early to pick her
up for breakfast at the diner.

She unlocked the door and ushered him inside,
running her fingers through her mussed bedhead and
shaking her hair out a little. Without makeup, Sydney
knew she looked much younger than her twenty-nine
years. Like, too much younger. She'd run to the coffee
shop early one day last week like this—but dressed—
and a woman she'd never seen before cautioned her to
hurry or she'd be late for school. Facing an unexpected
Finn now, with no makeup, wearing ruffled pink-and-
green summer pajamas with llamas all over them, she
was glad she'd already brushed her teeth. She put her
arms around his neck and kissed him; she didn't mind
at all that he was so early.

Finn wrapped both arms around Syd's frame, and
when the kiss ended, he pressed his face into her neck
and hair, simply holding her.

"Hey." She tapped him on the shoulder. "Finn. Is everything okay? You're super early."

He let go of her, nodding. "I'm all right."

"So…what's going on? Want some coffee?"

"God, yes." He followed her to the counter where she poured two cups.

"I'm guessing you just couldn't wait all the way until nine a.m. to see me? You didn't get enough of all this" —she made an exaggerated, sweeping motion over the llama PJs from her head to her toes— "last night at the arcade?" After Savanna's birthday scavenger hunt and then covering Kate's yoga classes, she and Finn had spent the evening at All Fun and Games, a huge go-kart and laser tag place they'd found in Grand Rapids.

Finn's slow, lazy grin deepened the shadows beneath his cheekbones. "There's no such thing as enough."

Oh snap, he was good. "That must mean you're not still mad I crushed you at Asteroids." She came around the counter and sat on a stool facing him. "What's up?"

"I got some news. I didn't want to tell you at the diner. I'm sorry it's so early."

She waited, now a little worried. He never sounded this serious.

"My H.R. guy called. With National Air Med Lifeteam. They need me to come now to Boulder. One of the medics just went on leave; his wife's baby came early."

She frowned. "But—you had another month here. There's more than only you, right? They can call someone else."

"It's the same assignment I'm already contracted for, just ahead of schedule. They'll bonus me for the short notice. It'd be crazy to turn it down."

"Okay…well, I'm sure the money's good, since they're asking you to drop everything and leave." She tried to hide her disappointment. She supposed if he went early, he'd be back in Carson sooner, giving them more of the summer together. "Would you still be here for our trip to Sleeping Bear this week?" It was one of Sydney's favorite places in Michigan. Finn had to see it. They'd planned to make it a day trip while Willow covered Fancy Tails.

He traced and retraced a small figure eight just above her knee. "Not exactly. They need me before Wednesday. But we'll go another time, I promise." He looked up at her, somber eyes green through dark lashes.

"You've already accepted." Sydney felt warmth creeping up into her neck and cheeks, irritation threatening to turn into something worse.

"Yes."

"But you'll be here for dinner tonight." She purposely made it a statement. He wouldn't flake on coming to dinner, on meeting her parents and uncles and basically her whole family. They were all expecting him to be there. He couldn't let her down like that.

He was quiet for a moment, gazing intently at her. "Syd."

She crossed her arms over her chest, moving on her stool so he wasn't touching her knee any longer. "You leave today? What, like, now? Does this at least stay a two-month assignment, or will you be gone an extra month now?"

"It'll make it three months."

She stood. He'd agreed to a whole extra month away from her, without any thought of how she'd feel. Her face burned, and she was sure her cheeks were flaming red. "You'd better go, then." She struggled to keep her voice level and pushed away the sudden urge to cry.

She would *not* cry in front of him.

"Syd." He reached out to her, and she stepped away. He stood but made no move toward her. "I didn't plan this. I'm sorry about the timing. I can't let my team down."

But he could let her down? She felt the first hot tear roll down her cheek and blinked hard, nodding. "Got it. We're just dating. You don't owe me anything." As she said what she assumed he wanted to hear, she realized the words were true. He'd made a decision about his job, that was all. But how could he think she wouldn't be upset?

"We'll reschedule dinner with your parents, I promise. Will you tell them I'm sorry to miss it?" The things he didn't say were even louder than his words. He didn't wrap his arms around her and tell her she was wrong, they weren't just dating. He didn't address what she'd said at all.

This was exactly what Aidan had warned her about last year. He'd said Finn could be unpredictable, never stayed anywhere long. Maybe she'd thought she was different—that he'd be different with her. How many other girlfriends had he put second to his job? She hated that she was now in that very un-special group.

Finn came over to her and pulled her into his arms, and she let him. "I'll fly back the first chance I get. I promise."

"You make a lot of promises," she said. She felt small.

"Hey now." He bent his head, hands on her upper arms, and waited until she looked up at him. "Syd, I love you. I'll be back as often as I can. It'll go fast."

She kissed him goodbye at the kitchen door and then wished she hadn't. Sad kisses were the worst. She watched him leave and wondered if she could talk herself out of loving him by the time he came back.

She shoved away the urge to go back to bed, and set out on a five-mile bike ride up Lakeview Drive that took her all the way north past Mitten Inn and back. She spent half the round trip crying out loud in earnest, not caring if anyone saw or heard her. The crying made her feel worse. She pulled into a scenic turnout and dropped her bike and sat in the cool grass, closing her eyes and struggling to use her calming yoga breathing techniques. She spent the ride back home summoning all the things that bugged her about Finn. His impulsive, unpredictable nature. His obsession with his career. His constant joking. His cocky attitude.

Sydney's mind supplied other Finn-traits against her will. His dedication to his niece Mollie. His instant willingness to help. His impulsivity—she couldn't even count all the times he'd come up with crazy, wonderful plans on the fly. His obsession with his career— how thoroughly he loved those risky, lifesaving runs. His joking nature—his ability to see things through a lighthearted lens. His cocky attitude—the confidence that had initially drawn her to him.

She was doomed. She didn't want to feel this way about someone who could just take off without warning, without even considering how it'd affect her. After a long shower and a stop at Happy Family Grocery, she headed to her parents' house to start dinner. She called Savanna on the way, hoping she might meet her there early to talk, but had to leave a voicemail for her. Her sisters could always help her find her footing, but she knew Skylar was with Travis and the kids at the zoo today. She needed Savanna.

The Shepherd family home was oddly silent as Sydney made enchiladas, Savanna's favorite dish, in honor of her birthday. She assembled them, put them in the oven, and set the timer. Then she wandered outside onto the patio outside her parents' kitchen. With time to kill before family arrived, Sydney curled up in the big canvas hammock with Pumpkin. She checked her phone, but Savanna hadn't returned her call yet. No word from Finn, either. The warm sun, the purring cat, and the slow swing of the hammock provided the soothing Syd needed. She'd just close her eyes for a minute.

Fonzie sprang to attention when Savanna turned into her parents' driveway. In the back seat, Mollie giggled as the little dog whined to be let out of the car. Aidan opened the door, and girl and dog came bounding out. Mollie took off across the lawn after him, her white-blond hair flying. Aidan laughed, glancing at Savanna.

"And you were worried she'd be shy," Savanna said. "Nolan should be here soon. He's a few years younger than Mollie, but I bet they'll have fun." Mollie had found the swing set. Harlan had updated the sisters' play area when Skylar had been expecting Nolan. He'd probably be thrilled to see another child enjoying it.

Savanna and Aidan came around the corner of the house to find Sydney just sitting up in the hammock, rubbing the sleep out of her eyes.

"Oh my God, what time is it?"

Aidan checked his watch. "About five-thirty."

Sydney looked relieved. "Okay, good."

Savanna followed her into the kitchen. "I listened to

your voicemail on the way over. I'm sorry I didn't hear it sooner. You sounded..." She frowned, assessing Sydney. Her normally vibrant, animated sister was quiet and subdued, something that had become too common since Libby's death. "Are you okay?"

Sydney had the oven door open and was removing the foil from the enchilada pans. She straightened up and looked at Savanna and Aidan behind her. "I don't know. Have you talked to Finn today?"

"Me?" Aidan asked. "No, why?"

"He's not coming." Sydney picked up the stack of square white plates from the counter and carried them to the long dining table.

Savanna's eyes widened as she met Aidan's confused gaze. He shrugged and shook his head. Savanna followed Syd with the cutlery and napkins. She set them out at each place setting, trailing Sydney around the table. "Hey. What happened?"

"Why do you even need to ask? You guys warned me about him. I should've listened."

"What did he do?" Aidan asked, his tone uncharacteristically clipped and angry.

Sydney stopped, plate in mid-air. "He's gone. Or if he's not, he will be any minute. He took a last-minute assignment. I guess I'm lucky he told me in person."

"Syd. What do you mean?" Savanna took the remaining plates from her sister's arms and set them on the table. "What assignment? When will he be back?"

Sydney dropped heavily into the nearest chair. "Three months. He was going to be around for a whole month until his Boulder contract. But they needed him now, so he went. He came over this morning to tell me."

"Oh." Savanna wrapped her arms around her sister.

"I'm sorry. It...I'm sure it was important?"

"He said one of the guys had to go on leave and they were short. We were supposed to go out to breakfast, but he came to the house and told me. He probably didn't want me to yell at him in the diner in front of everyone."

"Well, he wanted you to be able to yell at him, I guess," Savanna said. "Did you?"

Syd shook her head. "Not really. I'm just surprised he'd make a decision like that without any kind of discussion first. He's missing tonight, missing meeting Mom and Dad and Uncle Max and Freddie and Ellie, and plans we'd made for the next few weeks. Whatever. It doesn't matter."

"It matters," Aidan said. "I'm sorry."

"That's nice of you," she said. "You told me what to expect. I was hoping you were wrong."

Aidan looked crestfallen. "I was too," he said, his voice quiet. "Maybe I was; maybe they really did need him. He's been here in Carson longer than I've ever known him to stay in any one place. That's because of you, you know."

Savanna's gaze went from Aidan to her sister. He was such a good man. She loved seeing him try to make Syd feel better.

Sydney's stony expression softened. "That's good to know. I—" Her thought was interrupted by the rest of the family's arrival.

Skylar's family came through the kitchen door, No-lan followed by Travis carrying baby Hannah, Skylar, and Harlan and Charlotte behind them. Nolan did a lap around the kitchen island, snooping for any chance of a dessert preview, then ran back out into the yard where Mollie was playing. Charlotte set a large white bakery box tied with string on the countertop, its pink-and-black Main Street Sweets sticker the giveaway to something delicious inside.

Aidan said his hellos to her family. Why had she been nervous about inviting him? He already knew everyone. Harlan shook his hand, and she caught a snippet of their conversation—catamaran versus sloop, ketch versus yawl, tiller versus wheel. Oh, jeez. They'd plunged right into boat talk. Savanna hoped Aidan wasn't telling her father about the gift. She wasn't even sure what to do about that yet.

The oven timer rang, and Savanna grabbed Aidan's hand. "Sorry, Dad! We'll go round up the kids for dinner." She pulled Aidan with her outside, and began waving Mollie and Nolan in.

"I'm getting his input," Aidan said, reading her mind.

"Did you tell him you're buying me a boat?" She stared at him.

"Am I?"

"No. I don't know. Stop it," she said.

"I'm either buying one for you or for us. Let me know," he said, flashing a quick grin at her.

Uncle Max and Uncle Freddie arrived with Ellie. Uncle Max's arms were overflowing with a bright, cheerful sunflower bouquet, and Freddie carried a bottle of champagne. Ellie handed Savanna a gift-wrapped box and hugged her, wishing her happy birthday. Her cousin was effortlessly pretty, with stick-straight, long, dark hair with bangs that highlighted her large brown eyes.

"Thank you!" Savanna exclaimed. She made introductions between Aidan and her uncles and Ellie. "Ellie, this is Dr. Aidan Gallager. Aidan, my cousin Eloise May

Watson Quinn."

"Ellie," the girl said, as Aidan shook her hand.

"Ellie," he repeated. "What a great name, though. I've never known an Eloise."

"The only one I know of besides me is the one who lives at the Plaza Hotel," Ellie said.

"Those were Ellie's favorite books when she was little," Savanna said.

"My daughter loves them too," he said, as Mollie trotted over to them. "Mol, meet Eloise."

Mollie tilted her head, looking up at the girl. "You d-d-don't look like her."

Ellie smiled at Mollie. "I know! You look much more like Eloise than I do." Ellie tilted her head sideways and leaned a bit toward Mollie. "I did have a pet turtle though, when I was younger. I even named him Skipperdee, like in the books."

"You *did*?" Mollie re-emerged, dropping Aidan's hand and staring at Ellie, enthralled. "We just have Jersey and Cookie. Daddy says we have a dog and a guinea pig and we don't need a turtle."

"Life is so unfair sometimes," Aidan said, drawing down the corners of his mouth into a sad face for his daughter.

Sydney poked her head out of the kitchen. "Are you all joining us for Savanna's birthday dinner, or having your own little private party out there?"

There were twelve of them around the dining room table, counting Hannah in her high chair. Savanna had missed hearing Syd tell their parents why Finn hadn't joined them as planned, but she could tell her dad wasn't happy. He always doted on Sydney, but this evening even more so. For her own part, Sydney's mood seemed to improve a bit with her family gathered around her.

Savanna found an opportunity to broach the topic of Libby when most of the table was finishing their second serving of enchiladas. Uncle Freddie was grousing about the extra hours Max had to work lately.

"I don't mind," Max said. "Being surrounded by blooming flowers and plants is no hardship. I expect this is all temporary anyway, while Anthony sorts things out."

"Uncle Max," Savanna began. "Do you spend much time with Anthony Kent?"

"A fair amount now," he said. "He comes in much more often since Libby's passing. Rachel puts in hours as well. She's a sweet girl."

"How does he seem to you?"

"How do you mean, love?"

She knew it was too general a question. "I mean, I'm sure he's struggling. He and Libby were married a long time."

"Right, right. He's as you'd expect, I suppose. One day he's fine and the next day he snaps over every little thing, sometimes even at his daughter."

"What about when Libby was alive? Did you see them together often? Did they get along?"

Max's brow furrowed as he thought. "I can't say I had a sense of their personal relationship. Running a business is stressful. Most of their interactions involved things like finances, orders, inventory, parking."

Savanna latched on to the last point. "Why parking? They argued about having to use the lot behind the store?"

"Oh, no. They had an ongoing issue over designated

parking areas for each of the building's businesses. Libby's had the largest parking area—I assume because her shop was there first, wasn't it? The dance school and the yoga studio have much less. Priscilla Blake came over once to talk to Libby about using some of the lot during the lead-up to the recital, and Anthony wouldn't budge. I couldn't really tell whether Libby was on board with that or not."

"But that's crazy," Sydney spoke up. "How many customers can a flower shop have at once? A handful? Priscilla's is always packed. Why wouldn't the Kents have just given up some spots to Miss Priscilla?"

Uncle Max shook his head. "I don't know. I try to avoid eavesdropping when Anthony's in the office."

Charlotte spoke up. "I wonder if that's why Miss Priscilla won't use Libby's Blooms anymore for her recital flowers. Did you know that, Savanna?"

"No! They're right next door! Why? Just because of some dumb parking spots?"

Charlotte shrugged. "Libby's used to supply the flowers, but Priscilla switched to Carson Greenery way out on the highway during the second or third year you girls were in dance there. I always thought it was kind of a smack in the face."

"It is," Savanna agreed. "So, the bottom line is there was some animosity between Libby's and Priscilla's."

"But that doesn't mean anything," Skylar said, playing devil's advocate. "Animosity doesn't equal murder."

Chapter Twelve

O N MONDAY AFTERNOON, SAVANNA WAITED in the lobby of Priscilla's Dance Academy until Mollie went into her tap class. Mr. Marcus had already been in the classroom today when they'd arrived at the dance school, and his black eye was completely gone. Seeing Marcus Valentine interact with the kids the few minutes before class began, Savanna had to agree with Mollie's assessment of him; he was a fun teacher. With just over a week left until the recital, the energy in the studio was palpable, older kids rehearsing wherever they could find a few feet of floor space and younger ones trying to get headpieces and accessories fitted correctly. Today, Savanna had a plan to execute while Mollie was in class. She dropped her knitting into her oversized purse and went out the door to the parking lot.

A concrete walkway spanned the back of the building, with wooden benches and a few potted flowering plants. Savanna took a seat on the bench outside Priscilla's, opening a book on her lap but ignoring it. Now that Uncle Max had drawn her attention to it, she saw that the marked parking areas for each establishment—Priscilla's Dance Academy, Libby's Blooms, and

Kate's Yoga—weren't divided at all equally. In Priscilla's section, every single space was full, and two cars were illegally parked on the edge of the lawn. Libby's designated parking area had exactly three cars in it. All ten spaces in the area for Kate's yoga studio were full, which was odd, because the classes Savanna had attended there had been pretty small.

A minivan pulled into the lot and crawled up and down the rows on Priscilla's side, finally pulling into one of Libby's. A mom Savanna recognized from school unloaded two young kids, and the trio trudged toward her.

The woman narrowed her eyes at the back door to Libby's, and then spoke to Savanna on the bench. "I swear, if the Blakes don't do something about their stupid parking problem, we're not taking dance here next year."

"No!" The younger girl looked up at her mom.

The woman held the door to the lobby open for them. "I'm not kidding. I'd better not get another parking ticket. Ms. Shepherd, are you going to be out here for a little while? If you see anyone around my car, could you give me a holler?"

"Sure," Savanna agreed, her eyes wide. The Carson Village police department was really giving out tickets? How would they even know which cars were parked in the right spots and which weren't?

They couldn't possibly know. If Miss Priscilla's customers were parking in forbidden spaces and finding tickets on their cars as a result, it had to be due to someone from Libby's getting the Carson police to come over here and ticket them. The idea of it was ridiculous.

She checked the time on her phone. Mollie would

be out of tap in five minutes, and she'd be looking for Savanna. She stood to head back in just as two teenagers exited from Priscilla's lobby. Each girl had an armload of five or six costumes, and between them they lugged two duffel bags, two backpacks, two purses, and one black fedora. They were loaded up like pack mules. They made their way across the parking lot and the street beyond, then turned and headed down the side street another block to get to their car. It was painful to watch and obviously was due to the girls not wanting to park illegally in Libby's or Kate's spaces.

Although...Kate's spaces were full. Savanna nonchalantly wove her way up and down the two rows of parking spaces, trying not to look suspicious peeking into each vehicle she passed. At least half these cars had various dance accessories, tutus, or costume pieces in the back seats.

On a whim, she stepped into the yoga studio, encountering Kate herself folding clean white hand towels. The scent of lavender hung in the air, the establishment's atmosphere warm and welcoming with various peace-and-enlightenment-themed tapestries on the walls.

"Savanna! Hi! I'm so sorry, my next class isn't until six tonight."

Kate was Sydney's friend. With her perpetually sunny demeanor and constantly changing hairstyles, she'd always reminded Savanna of Phoebe from *Friends*. "That's okay! I have a weird question I'm hoping I can ask."

"I love weird. What have you got?"

"What's the deal with the parking in this building? Your spots are all full, but you're between classes right now." She tilted her head, making her tone higher-pitched as she feigned confusion. "Are people allowed to just park anywhere?"

"Oh, no. There's designated parking. I never need all the spots I have, so people at Miss Priscilla's know they can use mine. But not Libby's. Are you here bringing Dr. Gallager's daughter to dance? You didn't park at Libby's, did you?"

Savanna quickly shook her head. "I'm legal, don't worry. Do they actually enforce the designated parking areas?"

Kate sighed. "I've never understood why it's worth everyone getting so upset. It's just parking, for goodness' sake. But I was at Libby's once when Anthony called to make a complaint. An officer was already out there putting tickets on windshields by the time I walked back over here. That's when I told Miss Priscilla to put a note in her newsletter letting people know they can use my spaces, except for the handicapped ones."

"That's nice of you," Savanna said. "It is kind of crazy. The flower shop never has more than a few customers at a time. Can't the Blakes do something? Like, request a change through city council or something?"

Kate shrugged. "Dylan says they've tried that. It's… whatever. I don't mind sharing my spots. If my patrons come for a class and there's no parking, they just go a few blocks down and walk. Live and let live, right?"

"Absolutely. Oh shoot! I've got to run—I'm sorry."

Savanna sprinted back to the dance studio, coming into the lobby breathless. Mollie was sitting with her dance bag on the floor by the cubbies, pulling out her ballet shoes and repeatedly swiping at the hair hanging in her eyes.

"Hey," Savanna said, crouching down beside her. "Need any help?"

The girl donned her ballet shoes and forcefully flung her tap shoes into the bag. "Grandma cut my hair and now it won't stay in the bun," she said, frustration in her tone.

"That happens. Let me see." Savanna dug around in the zippered pocket of her purse, producing a few bobby pins. She quickly had the loose, shorter strands tucked neatly in place, and Mollie took off to Studio B, where Miss Priscilla was ushering children in with impatient swipes in the air. Priscilla Blake's stern, dissatisfied expression was etched permanently into her features.

With Mollie occupied in ballet, Savanna walked next door to Libby's Blooms. She really hoped Anthony was here today. If Uncle Max was working alone at the moment, she wouldn't be able to execute the second half of her plan, but it wouldn't be a loss. She always loved seeing her uncle.

Uncle Max greeted her from one of the displays, smiling widely. "Savanna! Come to talk to Anthony about your still life classes?"

She hadn't, but that was a great cover idea. She'd wanted to encounter Anthony Kent here and casually mention that she'd run into Rachel on Friday. If she could work her way around to the nursing school topic, she hoped to be able to gauge his reaction to Rachel fearing she wouldn't have enough tuition money to continue. If there truly was a life insurance payoff coming, neither Anthony nor Rachel should be stressed about money. But a murder investigation would definitely cause a delay in the process. "

Yes," she answered. "I was hoping to catch him."

"He's in the office," Max said. "I'll tell him you're here." He went behind the counter and through the door, and then opened it again and motioned Savanna over. "Go ahead in."

Anthony was at Libby's desk surrounded by papers and ledgers, an upside-down pencil in one hand poised over the desk calculator. Other than the desk, the office was neat and tidy—almost compulsively neat. The file cabinet drawers all bore labels, the large bulletin board on the wall listed promotions for the upcoming month, and the titles in the two tall, narrow bookcases were alphabetically arranged. Savanna's gaze drifted about the room, her art authenticator's brain telling her something, some minor detail, was out of place. But in her quick perusal she only saw order.

Anthony Kent set his pencil down and sat back, taking his glasses off to look at Savanna. "I'm due for a break. How are you?"

"Fine, thank you. How are you doing? I can't even imagine how hard this all must be." Her tone of concern was genuine. Libby's husband was older than Libby had been by a handful of years, but he looked much older than that today.

He nodded. "It's been difficult."

"I'm so sorry. How's your daughter holding up? The whole thing is so awful, for both of you."

"I lost my own mom in my twenties," he said. "You're never ready for that."

"I'm sure," Savanna said, then took her shot. "I ran into Rachel the other day as she was leaving work. She's such a sweet girl. She seemed quite stressed about nursing school..."

This was Anthony's opening. Anything he said would help her get a feel for what was going on—*yes, she's got tough classes? The tuition's expensive? It's a challenging profession?*

"I wouldn't know."

Savanna hadn't planned for that response.

His scowl drew deep creases between his eyebrows. "I never see her. Maybe if she took a break from all the time she spends with that hoodlum next door, she wouldn't be stressed about school."

Who? "Oh. Wow, I'm sorry." Savanna truly was. The man had a lot on his plate. Was there a tactful way to ask who the hoodlum was? Next door had to mean Miss Priscilla's. Could she be dating Marcus Valentine? All the other teachers were older women, and none of them seemed like a hoodlum to her. Neither did Mr. Marcus.

"Well, she's young," Savanna said. "I'm sure she'll figure things out. Have they been, uh, dating long?"

"Just since Dylan and Priscilla recruited him from God knows where to replace that teacher they fired. I hope you're right, Savanna. He's no good." Anthony cleared his throat. "Listen to me. None of this is what you stopped by for. Max says you wondered about starting your art classes back up?"

Savanna made it back to the dance studio with time to spare until Mollie's ballet class let out. Aidan had a new resident starting today and had offered to have his mother-in-law pick up Mollie from Miss Priscilla's, since he knew he'd run late, but Savanna had told him she'd drop Mollie off at her grandma's house after they grabbed a snack—the cheese stick and apple juice eaten on the way to dance were long gone. They zipped into Fancy Tails and picked up Fonzie, giving Mollie an opportunity to peek and giggle at the wildly fluffy Newfoundland pup on the grooming table in the back, and then got Grandma Jean's permission to stop at Lickety Split for ice cream.

Savanna got a hot fudge parfait and Mollie a strawberry sundae. Fonzie polished off his free Pup Sundae and then sat underneath the picnic table, catching bits of dripping ice cream from Mollie. While she chattered about the summer camp her dad had just signed her up for, Savanna's mind spun through all she'd learned in the last twenty-four hours.

Rachel was dating Marcus Valentine. Marcus hadn't shown up for work the Saturday Libby's body had been found, and he'd come to work the Monday after that with a black eye. Rachel might drop out of nursing school due to no funds for tuition. Anthony could be cashing in on Libby's large life insurance policy any day now, but it was likely on hold pending the completion of the murder investigation. If Anthony was found to be the killer, would the policy be completely voided, or would it go to Rachel? She'd have to pick Skylar's brain about how that worked. Did Rachel know about the policy increase?

She knew too much, and not nearly enough. On top of everything, as Savanna had been leaving Anthony's office after he'd agreed to let her resume her still life class, he'd cautioned her not to get too invested in holding the classes there.

"I'm no florist," Anthony had said. "This shop was always Libby's passion. It might be time to sell."

Chapter Thirteen

S AVANNA DIDN'T USUALLY WISH AWAY her time at Carson Elementary, but Tuesday seemed excessively long. She had plans to stop by and see her friend Yvonne after school, and then her still life class resumed at five today in Libby's greenhouse. She'd stowed her paint supplies for the class in her car so she wouldn't have to run home first.

Savanna and Yvonne had become close the year before, when Yvonne had ended up in the hospital after becoming an unwitting part of the mystery surrounding who killed a local councilman. It had been a very close call, but she'd recovered well. The visit Savanna planned for today wasn't entirely social, but she hadn't mentioned her ulterior motive to Yvonne yet. She hoped her friend wouldn't mind.

As soon as the last bell rang and she'd quickly cleaned up, she made a stop at Main Street Sweets before heading to the Carson Village Offices to meet Yvonne. After perusing the dizzying array of scrumptious desserts in the display case, she finally decided on a chocolate pecan brownie for Yvonne for now, and a package of raspberry kolacky cookies for her to take home, both her favorites. She couldn't leave without adding a dozen chocolate chip cookies for herself.

Just past Skylar's law office at the east end of Main Street, the two brown brick buildings that comprised Carson's government offices were connected by a curving sidewalk through a small courtyard between them. The rear building held Carson's public works and law enforcement departments. The smaller, more attractive building in front had gabled windows and an arched entryway and comprised Carson's Parks and Recreation department and the new mayor's office.

When Savanna pushed through the double glass doors, Yvonne hopped up from her desk outside Councilwoman Linda Rae's office and gave her a big hug. "How are you? How's your uncle doing? I heard he was the one who found Libby." Her large brown eyes were wide and full of concern.

"He's fine. He was a little shaken up. It's just so awful for her husband and daughter. How are you doing?"

With the large space empty besides the two of them, the mayor's assistant having already gone home for the day, Savanna sat across from Yvonne at her desk while they caught up. Yvonne brought two coffees over and a plate and plastic knife. She was thrilled at Savanna's chocolate pecan brownie gift and shared it, pushing the plate toward Savanna until she gave in and took her half.

"Oh my," Yvonne said after taking a bite of hers. She closed her eyes, shaking her head. "So good. Everything they make is amazing!"

"I know!"

"I do feel a little like I'm being buttered up." Yvonne narrowed her eyes at Savanna. "Not that I mind." She untied the string on the box of powdered sugar raspberry cookies, peeking in the box. "Oh! My favorites! So. Am I being plied with sweets for a reason?"

Savanna laughed. "You know me too well. But in my defense, I almost always bring food when I come see you at work."

"But usually it's sandwiches and pop," Yvonne reasoned.

"You got me." Savanna scooted her chair closer to the desk and leaned on her elbows, lowering her voice even though it was just them. "I have a small favor to ask."

"Anything."

"You've worked here a long time. I'm hoping you might know something about the bad feelings between Priscilla Blake and Libby Kent."

Yvonne gasped. "Do you think Miss Priscilla shot Libby?"

"I can't even imagine who could've done that to Libby. But between Sydney being good friends with Libby and then our Uncle Max having to be cleared as a suspect, we've started looking into who might've had motive and access. Syd and I are meeting with Detective Jordan tomorrow to let him know what we've learned," she said, deciding at that exact moment to do so. She'd been trying to avoid making things worse for her sister by involving her too much. Sydney had already been deeply affected by the loss of her friend, and now on top of it she was a mess because of Finn. But maybe getting more involved would make Sydney feel like she was doing something for Libby.

"Good," Yvonne said. "The detective should listen to you, especially after you cracked John's case last year. You know, I remember the Kents coming in here in person to file a complaint against the dance school a while back. Businesses and consumers can fill out the township's online complaint form for just about anything, so I wouldn't necessarily know if there were more. But Libby and Anthony came in. Let me check something." She frowned and turned to her computer screen, typing and clicking away.

After a minute, she sat back abruptly, her hands hovering over the keyboard and eyebrows raised in surprise. "Well." She pushed her chair back from her desk and looked at Savanna. "I'm supposed to pick up my prescription today. I'm worried I might not make it before they close."

Savanna checked the clock on the desk. "I think they close at six. You get off at five, right?"

"Yes, but I'm still worried," she said, and gave Savanna an exaggerated wink. "Would you mind just answering the phones for a few minutes? Here." She stood and motioned Savanna over. "Sit in my chair, and if the phone rings, say, 'Councilwoman Rae's office—how may I help you?'"

Savanna sat, looking up at Yvonne and then at the computer. The entire screen was populated with the online files the search had brought up: line after line after line, each one labeled either Libby's Blooms or Priscilla's Dance Academy.

Yvonne pushed the blue mouse over to Savanna, then grabbed her purse and marched across the lobby.

"Um, hey!" Savanna was half whispering now, grateful but a little nervous.

Her friend turned and looked at her, one hand on the door. "Thank you so much, Savanna. If a call goes into my voicemail, that's fine—don't worry about it. Linda Rae is gone for the day, anyway, though there are still a few staff in the back. Oh shoot, I didn't mean to leave my printer on," she said, pointing to it against the wall beyond her desk. "I'll only be a few minutes." She nearly sprinted through the door without looking back.

Savanna's gaze darted to the closed mayor's door, and then the door to the Parks and Recreation offices. *Sheesh!* What had she gotten herself into? She fervently hoped no one would come through either of those doors until Yvonne was back. Her friend had taken a huge risk. She'd better make good use of it.

She scrolled through, clicking each complaint one by one. They varied widely, but mud was slung from both sides. After she'd quickly read through the first several, she started printing. She needed something concrete to help fill in the gaps of what she'd heard, and also to give Detective Jordan. Once she'd sent everything she needed to the printer, she closed the window with the list of files. She'd just turned off the monitor for good measure and swiveled in the chair to face Yvonne's desk phone when the door behind her opened, making her jump. The printer was still making its whizz-clack sound as it worked through several pages.

She recognized the young man staring at her with a confused look on his face, a clipboard in hand. Jason Patterson had been helpful last year when Savanna had stopped by to talk to Yvonne and found her out sick. He'd told her Yvonne's no-call, no-show absence was completely out of character for her and he was worried, prompting Savanna to check on her.

"Jason! How are you?" she asked, her tone bright and cheerful. "I'm Savanna—we met last year."

"Oh, right! Savanna. Is Yvonne around somewhere?" He glanced around the large, empty lobby.

"She had to run and pick up a prescription. She asked if I could just sit here for a minute in case the phone rang. She ran across the street; I guess Bob called to remind her." Bob was the pharmacist over at Carson Apothecary, not exactly right across the street, and Savanna was a bad liar. She should stop talking before she made it obvious.

"Okay," Jason said, "no big deal. When she gets back, could you ask her to find me?"

"Absolutely."

He crossed to the offices beyond. Savanna held her breath, watching him through the window until he turned a corner, and then bolted out of the chair to grab her papers from the printer.

Yvonne came through the doors. "Are you good? Did I give you enough time?"

Savanna hugged her impulsively. "Thank you. Jason Patterson almost busted me. I think he believed my story. Oh, and he wants you to find him about something."

Yvonne laughed. "What story? That you were watching the phones for me?"

"Yes, sort of. I may have added something about Bob calling and bugging you to pick up your prescription. I talk too much when I'm nervous!"

"Don't worry about it. I hope it all helps. I don't care what kind of grudges the Kents and Blakes had going on—nothing was worth Libby's life."

"Exactly," Savanna agreed. "This might be a wild goose chase on my part. But they sure had a lot of issues with each other."

In her car, Savanna rifled through the stack of complaints, eleven in all. Both parties had reported the other at different times for lack of snow and ice clearing at the back entrances. The documents detailed griev-ances about an illegal sign, a noise disturbance, and a fire hazard complaint. There were others, but she was out of time; she'd have to go through these more closely tonight after her still life class.

She parked in one of the several empty spaces at Libby's Blooms and was on her way in when Libby's daughter pulled up outside the dance school. Savanna slowed her pace and raised a hand in greeting. Rachel waved back as Marcus Valentine came out of Miss Pris-cilla's and got in the passenger side of her car.

The young woman pulled up alongside Savanna on her way out of the parking lot. "Hi, Ms. Shepherd!"

"Hi, Rachel." She ducked down to peer into the car and say hello to the tap instructor as well.

Rachel looked uncomfortable. "I hate to ask you this, but could you please not mention seeing me to my dad?"

"Oh. Sure, no problem."

"Sorry. I know it's weird of me to ask. He's just…it's better for everyone if he doesn't know you saw us." She turned and glanced at Marcus beside her, whose ex-pression was stony and unreadable.

Savanna nodded. "That's fine; don't worry. None of my business," she said, feeling uncomfortable herself. Anthony certainly did dislike Marcus Valentine.

"Thank you, Ms. Shepherd."

She watched Rachel drive away. Ugh, she didn't envy either of them. Or Anthony. She'd only ever dated one guy her parents had truly disliked, but by then she'd been away at college in Chicago, which made it easier to avoid this type of problem. She still hadn't loved the feeling of knowing her parents were unhappy with her boyfriend. She couldn't blame Rachel for trying to be discreet.

The door to the florist office was closed; Anthony didn't even seem to be here today. Rachel had worried for nothing. Uncle Max stood behind the counter of the flower shop and for once, he didn't come around to greet her. He motioned her over, pointing down, and she leaned over the countertop to find Lady Bella looking up at her with her cute little Corgi grin.

"Puppy!" Savanna came around the side of the counter and kneeled, giving Lady Bella plenty of ear scratches and belly rubs. "How come you got to bring her to work?"

"She's not handling my longer hours well," Max said, making a sad face. "I got Anthony's permission to bring her with me some of the time, especially with Freddie's crazy schedule lately."

"Good. Poor baby." She kissed the top of the Corgi's head and stood, taking the large bouquet of tulips from her uncle. "These are gorgeous. The class will love painting them."

"You've a few students already up there, all thrilled your class is back in session." He walked with her through the shop to the stairway access door and unlocked it, opening it for her. "Don't lose any more earrings now."

She stared at him.

Uncle Max looked past her up the steps. "It's a smart idea, figuring who all has access to this stairwell. What isn't smart is getting mixed up in anything dangerous, love. Your Detective Jordan seems quite competent."

She should've known she couldn't outsmart him.

She kissed him on the cheek. "He is, and I'm fine. Don't worry, Uncle Max."

In the rooftop greenhouse, Jack Carson arrived just before Savanna started the class. Elaina Jenson was with him. "I convinced her to give it a try," Jack said, smiling at his girlfriend.

Savanna had worried people might not return to the rooftop greenhouse where Libby had died. It did give her the willies, standing a few yards away from where Max had discovered her friend's body. But her students all came, and class ended up being overfull when Sydney showed up.

"I told you I'd make it over here eventually," she said. "Willow's watching the shop and Fonzie. You can't make fun of whatever mess I make of this canvas, okay?"

Elaina spoke up. "Your sister promised she won't make fun of mine, either. I try, but even my third graders know how little artistic talent I have."

"Not true," Jack said. "I've seen the posters you make for your classroom. And Savanna's a good teacher. You might be surprised what you can do."

By the end of the class, all thirteen of Savanna's students had created the beginnings of lovely, colorful tulip bouquet renderings. The flowers would keep well enough in the refrigerator downstairs until Friday's class.

Savanna finally had a chance to talk with Sydney as everyone was cleaning up. She'd stopped by to check on her Monday evening and had found Sydney curled up on her couch under a blanket in her pajamas at eight p.m. Syd worked long hours and was entitled to have an early night, but Savanna had never seen her ready for bed so early. She hadn't been her usual bubbly, lighthearted self since Libby's death. Savanna had an idea of something that could help, if it panned out. She needed to hear from Kate next door before she said anything. But the fact that she'd come to class was encouraging.

"How are you doing?" Savanna asked, keeping her voice low.

Sydney shrugged. "Not great. I'm better when I'm busy. Sitting around feeling sorry for myself isn't going to bring Libby back or stop my boyfriend from running away from me."

"Syd, you know that isn't what he did. He—" She didn't have a good justification for Finn's adding a month on to his commitment and leaving abruptly. She recalled the look on his face, his whole attitude, in the ambulance bay. "He didn't do it right. He could've talked to you about it first. But he's kind of married to his job, you know? He really loves it."

"I know. I'm glad he loves it. That's the rational side of my brain talking. If I could get the rational side to communicate with the emotional side, all my sides would be perfect." She gave Savanna a wry smile.

"Has he been in touch since he left?"

"Every day, before and after work. And sometimes when he has a break. He says he couldn't let down his team. The guy he replaced has filled in for him before, and Finn felt obligated; that paramedic left the same day Finn flew out. His new baby was okay, but his wife had complications. I do get it now."

"That makes sense. These Gallager men and their sense of obligation." She couldn't help smiling. Finn's leaving town right away to help out a coworker reminded her of Aidan's abrupt departure last summer when he'd learned his former boss and mentor had had a heart attack and his wife would only let Aidan operate. Despite Aidan's reservations about his brother, Finn seemed to have the same commitment to doing what was right, even when it meant taking the harder path.

Sydney nodded. "I know."

Jodie Vonkowski approached them. "I'm sorry to interrupt."

"You aren't," Sydney said. "Thank you for the class, Savvy. Lunch at Fancy Tails tomorrow, right?"

"For sure. I'll text you later."

Jodie hung back while Sydney and the rest of the class filtered out. "I didn't want to bother you during class, but I wondered if I might be able to see Libby's Cry Violet. The Flower and Garden Show starts this Thursday. I'm so excited Libby's daughter is still submitting it. I just know it's going to wow the panel."

"Oh! Sure, it's in the back." Savanna headed toward the far corner of the greenhouse, Jodie following her. "It's such a pretty plant. I still think it's amazing she was able to grow it."

"Your uncle was probably close to Libby...did she ever let him in on her secret? I mean, I've been into gardening for years, I'm an active member of the Carson Horticulture Society, and I have no idea how she cultivated an extinct plant."

"He doesn't know, either. Libby never told him how she did it. And he doubted Rachel knew. It's a shame to think her secret is gone with her."

"It really is. I hope the violet gets the accolades it deserves. It's an incredible accomplishment."

They'd reached the Cry Violet's special mesh screenhouse. Savanna bent and unzipped it and held it open, letting Jodie enter. She heard the woman's gasp before she saw what had caused it: the pedestal in the center of the screenhouse was bare.

Chapter Fourteen

"**S**OMEONE STOLE IT!" JODIE EXCLAIMED, her eyes wide and her voice frantic.

"Wait," Savanna said. "We don't know that for certain." She pulled out her cell phone and called Max on speaker, downstairs in the flower shop.

He picked up on the first ring. "Hello there! Shall I come up and help carry things down?"

"No. Uncle Max, the Cry Violet. It's missing. It's just completely gone. Did you...maybe you brought it down there to keep a closer eye on it?" Savanna held her breath.

"No, I'm so sorry you've worried. Rachel picked up the violet this morning. She's taking it to Grand Rapids later this week for the Flower and Garden Show. She's so hoping the judging panel will be awestruck; I'm sure they will."

"Oh, good. Wonderful. Thank you, Uncle Max. We're on our way down."

"Whew," Jodie said. "I'm glad it's okay."

Savanna and Jodie parted outside in the parking lot, promising to update each other if either of them heard any news about the violet's standing in the show. Savanna was nearly home when she glanced over at

Fonzie hanging his head out the passenger side window and saw Mollie's stuffed bunny Mrs. Flopsy on the back seat. The little girl must've left it in her car before dance yesterday. *Ugh.* She'd probably been looking for it all over! The toy went everywhere with her and she slept with it every night.

Savanna turned the car around and a few minutes later, she was pulling into Aidan's driveway. The sound of piano music drifted through the air from the open front door when she got out of her car, bunny in hand. She'd never heard Aidan play the pretty Steinway piano that sat in his living room. On his porch, she was about to knock on the screened door but drew her hand back as the music stopped. Aidan's low voice and then Mollie saying something came through to her, followed by the tentative single notes that must be Mollie playing. Savanna recognized the strains of "Twinkle, Twinkle, Little Star." Abrupt silence, then voices again before Mollie resumed, continuing all the way through this time to the second verse.

How she'd love to watch the two of them, Aidan teaching his daughter to play piano. She reached out again to knock, but her hand froze before touching the door. Images flashed in her mind: she and her dad on his boat when she was a few years older than Mollie, him explaining to her how to read the sails to find the direction of the wind.

She quietly opened the screened door and set Mrs. Flopsy on the entryway table just inside. As she pulled out of the driveway, Fonzie barked once, likely putting in his two cents at not seeing his pal Jersey. "It's okay, buddy." Savanna patted his head. "Not this time."

She dreamed that night of the three of them—she

and Aidan and Mollie—out on the lake, wide white sails overhead against a pink sky.

Nick Jordan stared at Savanna Wednesday morning, incredulous, his eyes wider than she'd ever seen them. "And you didn't think this was important to mention to me, why?"

Sydney leaned toward him across the desk. "Nick." She spoke his name sharply, frowning at him. "You've literally told Savanna you wanted her input and then you pooh-pooh everything she tries to tell you. Even though it's very likely she's come across something you've missed. It's happened before."

Savanna turned a shocked stare on her little sister. Well, dang. Nobody spoke to Detective Jordan that way. Except apparently Sydney.

"What? You know I'm right." Sydney sat back in her chair and crossed her legs. She focused on Jordan. "And so do you. Go ahead, Savanna."

Oof. She'd sensed Sydney's sour mood when she'd stopped by Fancy Tails to grab her for the meeting she'd arranged. But she'd never seen her sister this abrupt with anyone before. One more thing to add to Savanna's *Reasons to Worry About Sydney* list. She and Skylar planned to sit down and talk with Sydney at lunch today.

Nick Jordan arranged his features into something closer to his usual poker face and folded his hands in front of him on his desk, eyes on Savanna.

"Detective," Savanna said, "when I mentioned Anthony Kent's tantrum at the bank, and how odd it was that he came in the front entrance the morning of Libby's murder, you brushed it all off as insignificant, and—"

He interrupted her. "Right. But a dance instructor coming in to work next door with a black eye two days after Libby was killed, after *missing* work the day she was killed, would fall into the significant category, especially if he's dating the daughter of the victim."

Savanna gritted her teeth, growing more irritated by the second. "I only just learned about Rachel dating him. And seriously, how am I supposed to know when I should tell you about things, when you act like it's all trivial? If I come talk to you, I obviously must think I have significant information."

The detective pressed his lips into a thin line. Savanna squelched her urge to apologize. She didn't mean to be disrespectful, but he was difficult to communicate with. He opened a drawer and set his yellow legal pad on the desk calendar. His expression softened. "You're right. Both of you. I'm sorry. The details you spot have always been helpful. You know I know that." He smiled, and it was the most forced, awkward thing she'd ever seen.

She laughed in spite of herself. "Okay. Yes, I do know that." Now she just wanted him to stop with the smile.

He narrowed his eyes at her. "Would you go through what you told me again?" He rested his penpoint on the paper in front of him.

"I was at the dance studio last Monday—a week ago—when he came in. He was running late for class."

"Marcus Valentine, the tap instructor at Priscilla's," he clarified.

"Yes, Marcus Valentine. He had sunglasses on, and

Miss Priscilla told him to take them off. When he did, and she saw his eye, she told him to put them back on."

"So he did, and did he say anything at all about it?"

She frowned, scouring her memory of that moment. "No. When he rushed into the studio, he said something to the kids about it being costume day, and then Miss Priscilla yelled at him—"

"Yelled?"

"No, sorry. She spoke to him, you know. Then he went in with the kids and shut the door, and that was it. He comes off as kind of jovial, charming. He wasn't ruffled by Miss Priscilla."

"Nobody there asked him how he got the black eye?"

"Well, no. The whole thing took, like, thirty seconds. I didn't see him after that. Oh—until the next day. No, wait, Wednesday. The three of us saw him from across the street. He pulled up in front of the building around lunchtime and went in through the tenants' door. So, when Libby's reopened, I was able to go up to the second floor and I found out Marcus Valentine lives in the building. He has an apartment over the dance school. He has access to that stairwell and the roof. And then I learned he and Libby's daughter are dating, and Anthony Kent is *not* happy about it." She stopped and took a breath.

Jordan was scrawling on his legal pad in cursive Savanna couldn't decipher. He caught up and looked at her. "You found out he lives there, and you learned about him dating Rachel and her father not liking it... how?"

"I can help with that, at least," Sydney spoke up, her tone calmer now. "I didn't know who Libby's daughter was dating, but I knew Libby wasn't happy with him."

"Oh, wow!" Savanna said. This was news to her. "What did she tell you?"

"She only said she didn't trust Rachel's new boyfriend. She never gave me details. I know it had hurt their relationship." She looked at Savanna. "I was thinking, it's probably why Libby made such a big deal over Rachel coming for dinner the night before she—before it happened. They'd been struggling."

"Oh." *Poor Libby. Poor Rachel, too.*

"Is that the same info you have, Savanna?" Jordan asked, his tone polite.

"There's a little more. I was visiting my uncle at the flower shop and I bumped into Marcus's neighbor from the apartment next to his." It was a mostly true summary, minus some snooping details. "She asked if I was looking for Marcus and said he wasn't home. And the lobby at the dance school is a rich source of, uh, information. It's common knowledge there that Rachel and Marcus are a couple." She finished with her encounter with Rachel at the hospital, Anthony's derogatory remark about his daughter's boyfriend, and Rachel's request that Savanna not tell her dad about seeing her with Marcus the other night.

"He actually called him a hoodlum?" Detective Jordan had the hint of a smirk. "It's hard to say if he's just an overprotective father or if he has a reason not to like Valentine. The black eye doesn't speak well for the guy."

"That was my thought too," she said, "though of course it could've been an accident. Like when you slipped in your shower last year and got that huge bruise on your forehead," she added to Sydney. "If you meet him, he's not really the way all this makes him sound."

"I'll meet him." The detective jotted something in the margin. "I don't see enough of a reason for him to want to kill his girlfriend's mom, though. Rachel running out of tuition money is weak, even if she or Valentine had knowledge about the life insurance policy."

Savanna nodded. The clock behind Jordan read eight thirty-five. School started soon, and Syd had to open the shop. "I do have a question for you, but we've got to get going."

"I'll walk with you. Shoot." He held his office door open for them, and they walked down the long hallway toward the exit.

"Do you know about any weird stuff going on between Priscilla's dance school and Libby's flower shop?"

"Weird how?"

"They've made complaints against each other for years about all kinds of stuff." She hoped the detective wouldn't ask how she knew what she knew. She couldn't betray Yvonne. "I wondered if you know about any of that? I mean, everyone knows Miss Priscilla can be a bit...terse. And the Kents have been sticklers about the parking situation over there." She glanced at Sydney, trying to be sensitive.

"We humor the Kents when they call about dance school patrons parking in the flower shop spots. My officers will go cruise through the parking lot, but once in a while they have to set an example and issue a citation. The Blakes hit back now and then with a call about lax snow removal outside Libby's, or delivery vans blocking their driveway." He sighed. "They've been this way ever since I've been with the sheriff's department. Maybe longer than that."

"I wonder if it's really about something else," Sydney

mused. "One of those situations where two parties are fighting, but it isn't really about whatever stupid issue they think they're fighting over. Like when your wife gets mad at you for throwing your socks on the floor."

He turned to her and grinned. Now that was a real Detective Nick Jordan smile. "I don't throw my socks on the floor."

"Right," Sydney said, and Savanna nodded along. "But it's not about the socks. Or the parking spots, or the snow. It's about a general lack of respect those actions communicate, right?"

He nodded slowly as they went outside into the morning sun. "Sure. So, the Kents and Blakes have a longstanding issue that stems from a basic feeling of disrespect. The petty complaints are symptoms of the real problem."

"Yes," Syd and Savanna both said at the same time.

Savanna laughed. "Jinx."

"I'm sure you're right," Jordan said. "But..."

"Yeah," Savanna said. "But none of that gives anyone motive to want to murder someone. Not the way Libby died. Right?"

"Right," he agreed. "I think Anthony Kent will run the flower shop and Priscilla and Dylan Blake will run the dance school until they're all well past retirement age, and they'll still be calling in complaints on each other."

"Maybe not, though," Savanna said. "Anthony said yesterday that he's thinking about selling."

"Really?"

"Really?" Sydney repeated. "Why? Libby loved that shop. How could he do that?"

Savanna bit her lip. She should've told Sydney first.

But it was just a possibility. "Honestly, I think he's in over his head. Libby was the florist, not him."

"Interesting," Jordan said. "That'd certainly make life easier for the Blakes. No more feud."

"You're thinking they did this to Libby to get rid of the shop?" Sydney's voice was incredulous.

He shook his head. "Not at all. I'm just listening. Considering all possibilities. No detail is completely insignificant." He cocked an eyebrow at Sydney, a smirk threatening around the corners of his mouth.

She sighed. "Okay. I'm sorry I yelled at you, Nick."

"Thank you. Not many folks would call me out like that."

Sydney twisted the end of her braid absently. "Yeah. It was out of line," she said, her tone saying she didn't care.

"It wasn't. You're fine." He looked at Savanna. "Thank you both. I appreciate your help. I'm looking forward to meeting Valentine."

Across the street, Savanna and Sydney stopped outside Fancy Tails. "Are we still having lunch today?" Savanna asked.

Her sister shrugged. "I don't care. Sure."

"Okay...well, Skylar or I will grab a pizza, I guess. If that sounds all right?"

"Whatever." Sydney scowled at something over Savanna's shoulder. She turned to find Miss Priscilla glaring at them through the dance school window.

"What the..." As they stared back at her, the woman whipped around and disappeared down the hallway toward the reception area. "What on earth was that about?"

Sydney frowned at Savanna. "She creeps me out.

Didn't you notice the dance school lights come on as we walked by on the way to the precinct this morning? Like, why? They don't open for hours. Every time I look over there, Miss Priscilla is peeking out her window at us."

"Wow." The woman had been staring at them the other day too, when they'd spotted Marcus getting out his car. "Though, that's not really peeking. She was standing there in full view glaring at us. What the heck?"

Sydney shook her head. "I don't know." She turned to go into Fancy Tails. "Gotta open the shop."

"Syd, could we sit down and really talk later? Maybe—"

Her sister cut her off. "I don't want to talk. I'm fine. See you at lunch." She yanked the door open and went inside.

Savanna's heart ached for Sydney. She and Skylar would make her listen at lunch today. Her sister had to let them help her.

Three hours later, Savanna crossed the street from a quick stop at Kate's Yoga and entered Fancy Tails. She was thrilled to find Skylar already here with Hannah. A Giuseppe's pizza box sat on the table. Savanna immediately stole the baby from her sister.

"You're getting so big! Aren't you? Look at this giant foot!" Savanna pretended to nibble her pink-socked foot. Hannah shrieked and giggled with her toothless smile and kicked her feet wildly. Her fuzzy socks matched her pink romper with a trio of satin ladybugs in purple hats on the front. She turned the baby to face outward against her chest, keeping her upright, as she loved laughing at Fonzie running around the shop. She bent toward Hannah's wispy blond hair and breathed in deeply. "Why do babies smell so good?"

Skylar laughed. "Sometimes they don't."

Savanna lifted the cover and peeked. "Ooh! I love their veggie pizza. How's Joe doing?"

Joe Fratelli, the owner and chef at the best Italian eatery in the county, was close to Harlan Shepherd's age and a good family friend. When he had been wrongly arrested for murder last summer, Savanna and her sisters had scrambled to prove he didn't do it. In typical fashion, Chef Joe harbored no grudges against Carson law enforcement for the gross error. He'd said he was just happy to be back in his kitchen at the restaurant. And ever since the sisters had helped clear his name, he wouldn't let them pay for pizza anymore.

"Joe's great," Skylar said. "He's happy. I have a feeling there might be a wedding in Carson sometime soon." She grinned at Savanna.

"Oh! That'd be wonderful. Good, I'm glad to hear everything's going well for them."

Skylar took a piece of pizza. "Do you mind keeping her for a minute so I can eat? She's so fussy when I put her in the carrier."

"Do I mind?" Savanna did slow turns with the baby in her arms, bouncing her and eliciting adorable baby gurgles every time they passed Fonzie, who was dancing at Savanna's feet. "Does it look like I mind, Hannah? Where is your other auntie, baby girl?" They were now on the grooming side of the shop and she peered into the back, past Syd's desk.

A very large, very furry Bouvier was on the grooming table, the short leash clipped to his collar. His dense, black, water-resistant coat was so long Savanna could hardly see his eyes, and his tail was wagging in wild arcs, flinging water everywhere. He was flanked by Sydney and Willow. Both women were drenched. Willow had one hand on the animal's back near his hindquarters and was scratching his ears with the other hand while she talked baby talk to the big dog. Sydney was combing out his undercoat, which looked to be a painstaking process.

Syd threw a look in Savanna's direction. "Save us a couple of pieces of pizza. This guy is new and nervous. Dad's friend Sebastian just adopted him. But Ringo's such a good boy, isn't he?" She patted him, reassuring the dog as she worked.

"Do you need help?" Savanna didn't know what on earth she could do to help, though.

"Nope, we've got it."

"Thank you, though!" Willow called.

Savanna rejoined Skylar, passing Hannah to her when she'd had a chance to eat. "There is no way I could do her job."

"Oh, tell me about it," Skylar said. "You should've seen the two of them getting that dog out of the bath. I think he's drier than they are. At least he seems like a sweet dog."

"Yes, he does." Savanna studied her older sister. "Spoken like someone who's growing to like dogs more all the time. Is Nolan still campaigning for one?" Savanna knew Travis was on board, but he wouldn't cross Skylar. They were always good at presenting a united front.

"Ugh. He wants a dog so badly, especially now with Uncle Max and Uncle Freddie here with Lady Bella. I just…"

Savanna frowned, waiting. Skylar sounded more

upset than the topic warranted. There was no deadline on whether or not to get a pet.

"I don't know if I can keep up this pace as it is. I can't add a dog to our lives when I'm already stretched so thin, some days I feel like I'm drowning." She met Savanna's gaze with eyes filled with tears.

Savanna was shocked. She leaned over and hugged her. "Sky, I'm sorry. What can I do?" Her sister never complained. Of the three of them, she was always the one who seemed to have it all together.

"No one tells you what it's like going from one kid to two," she said. "It's amazing. Truly, it's a miracle. The best thing Travis and I have ever done. Hannah and Nolan are more important to me than anything in the world. But I'm so exhausted. I've been ramping up to full-time at work the last few weeks, and I don't think I can do it."

"Then don't."

Skylar stared at Savanna as if she'd suddenly sprouted antlers. She shook her head. "That's not an option."

"Why not? Were you feeling okay when you worked three days a week? Part-time?"

"Better than this. I love my job. I can't quit—I don't *want* to quit."

"Well, of course not. We all know how much you love what you do. That's important. But why do you have to meet the status quo? What's compelling you to work forty or more hours a week with a new baby and a pre-schooler, if you don't have to financially?"

"We don't have to. We were all right with my part-time income and Travis' job. I don't know," Skylar said, her tone filled with angst. "I always imagined I'd be *that* attorney. Knocking out cases, never turning down work, making partner in record time."

"Is that still what you imagine?"

Skylar looked down at the baby in her arms. "Sometimes, yes. But sometimes, that stuff doesn't matter at all to me. Not right now. I mean, in a minute, they're going to be in school. Not everyone has the option to work less when they have a new baby. I'm fortunate I do."

Savanna nodded. "Yes, you are."

"I'll lose traction. My coworkers will pass me up by the time I'm back full-time."

"Yes, that's probably true."

Her older sister was quiet. The hum of the turbo grooming dryer in the back room was the only sound in the shop. After a long time, Skylar spoke. "I don't care about traction. I think I know what I have to do. Thank you for that."

When they'd finished their second slice of pizza, Savanna said what was on both their minds. "I don't know if we're going to get a chance to talk with her."

Skylar nodded. They'd exchanged a few messages this morning and were both on the same page. "She's the one who's always cautioning us about the dangers of stress." She'd lowered her voice to a whisper. "She's got to know she's off-kilter."

"I don't think she can see how much, though," Savanna said.

"Probably not. Should we push her to talk about it? Or give her space?"

"I'm too worried about her to give her much more space. I'm not sure how much of this is that dog back there and how much was planned by Syd to avoid us," Savanna whispered back.

Sydney made an appearance as Savanna and Skylar were cleaning up. "Hey," Syd called from the doorway behind her desk. "Sorry I missed it. Are you guys heading out?" Her pink Fancy Tails apron was soaking wet.

"Oh my gosh, you're drenched!" Savanna exclaimed. "We weren't leaving yet. I've still got time. We were waiting to talk to you."

"Um..." Sydney shot a look behind her, but Savanna spied Willow sweeping up. The Bouvier was finished. "Okay, let me scrounge up something dry to put on." She disappeared again.

Savanna exchanged looks with Skylar. Would she stall until they had to leave?

Sydney came out a few minutes later wearing one of their dad's construction company sweatshirts that came nearly to her knees. She hovered by the treat counter. "What's up?"

"Come sit down. Savanna has to leave soon."

Savanna pressed her lips together. Leave it to their older sister to cut through to the point. Sydney frowned but obediently joined them at the table.

"We're worried about you," Savanna began.

"You've just lost a good friend, and now with Finn leaving, we think this is kind of piling up on you," Skylar said.

"Sydney," Savanna said, waiting until her sister met her gaze. "Aidan says this is grief. He says the stages of grief don't always happen in order. Sometimes they get all tangled up, and it can take time and help to find your way through."

"Why would you talk to him about this?" Sydney wailed, startling them both.

Savanna sat back. "He asked about you. He was concerned."

"Because his flaky brother did what he's best at, and now, thanks to you, Finn will hear all about how terribly I'm handling it." Red color crept up Sydney's neck toward her cheeks.

"Aidan's not going to tell Finn anything. He's not thrilled with him, either."

Skylar spoke. "Syd, just let us help. Please. I'm sure there are grief support groups around here. We could go with you."

Sydney laughed, and it was a scary, mirthless sound. "I don't need a support group. I need to know who killed my friend. You know what I keep thinking about? All those early mornings we had tea on her roof. She'd call me or I'd message her, just spur of the moment. So why not that Saturday? Why? What if I'd reached out to her and asked if she wanted a quick cup of tea with me? Would she still be here? We'd have been together and I bet the coward who snuck up that stairwell and shot her point blank wouldn't have had the nerve. That's all it would've taken! A cup of tea! Me stepping out of my own little world and asking her to have tea with me!"

Savanna jumped up and pulled Sydney into her arms. She could feel her slight body shaking. Skylar put an arm around Sydney, baby Hannah babbling and plucking at Syd's damp red braid. Savanna met Skylar's gaze over her head, both their expressions reflecting their sister's torment.

"It's not your fault," Skylar said. "There was no way for you to know what would happen that morning, Syd."

Savanna expected to feel sobs from Sydney, she was so distraught, but there were no tears. She and Skylar relaxed their grip. Sydney's cheeks were beet red, and there were faint gray circles under her eyes.

"She was much better at setting up our morning dates than I was. She was a much better friend than I was," Sydney said quietly. "All I had to do was reach out. That's it."

"You did. I know you did. And Libby knew how much you cared about her. I think you know that," Savanna said.

Willow startled them from the doorway. "I don't mean to eavesdrop. But we only have two appointments left today. Why don't you give yourself the afternoon off, boss? It's what you'd tell me. You need it."

The three of them looked at Willow, Sydney's twenty-year-old assistant, whose brightly colored nails and multiple earrings matched her perpetually sunny demeanor.

"That's a great idea." Skylar buckled Hannah into her stroller. "All I'm doing today is working on motions. I can do that later tonight. What do you say, Syd? Let's get some sun and go for a walk."

The words brought Fonzie to life in an instant. He leaped up from under the table and sprinted toward his leash hanging by the door. Sydney laughed, and it was music to Savanna's ears, so much better than how she'd sounded minutes ago. "Can we take your dog with us?"

Savanna clipped his leash on. "I think you have to." She looked over her shoulder at Willow. "Thank you. You're sure you're okay on your own here?"

The young woman nodded. Sydney's lack of protest told them how right Willow was—Sydney needed to relax.

Outside on the sidewalk, Savanna stopped her sisters before they headed in the opposite direction. "Wait. This is for you." She handed Sydney a Kate's Yoga flyer, the lotus flower logo at the top. Kate had pulled this together in less than two days when Savanna had told her she was worried about Sydney.

"I already got this month's newsletter," Sydney said.

"It's an update." Savanna pointed at today's date in the corner. "Did you know Kate has a class called Stress Less Yoga?"

Sydney stared at her. "You don't even believe in yoga."

"What? I do! I'm just bad at it," Savanna said. "But I believe it's good for our minds and bodies. I've learned that from you." She flipped to the back page of the pamphlet, turning it back toward her sister. "It ends with twenty minutes of Savasana yoga."

Skylar peered over their shoulders. "I want to go. What's Savasana yoga? Never mind, I don't care. I want to go."

"Savasana is a way to reach deep relaxation, the space between sleeping and wakefulness," Savanna said. "Don't look so surprised," she chided Sydney. "I've done my research. Kate says these yoga sessions are meant to help the mind reach a state of peacefulness."

Skylar took the pamphlet, turning it over and reading the sticker with class times. "We're going. Tomorrow at four p.m., Syd. Me and you."

Chapter Fifteen

S AVANNA WAS ON HER DECK Wednesday evening, ready for Aidan to pick her up, when her phone buzzed with a video call from him. His handsome, scruffy face filled her screen. His lab coat collar and the V-neck of his blue scrubs told her why he was calling before he did.

She smiled involuntarily; it happened whenever she saw him. "Still at work?"

"I am. I've been trying to leave since four, but my post-op Triple A—sorry, aortic aneurysm—won't stabilize." He wore an aqua surgical cap that made his eyes look even bluer, and the phone jostled as he took off his lab coat. The screen lost him for a second and when he reappeared, he was sliding his arms into a surgical gown as someone else held the phone for him. "I'm so sorry, Savanna. I'm going to be here a while."

"Don't worry about it. Go save your patient."

He nodded once. "I'll call you later. Sorry." He held her gaze a moment longer, then looked beyond the phone and said, "All right, let's go." The screen went black.

Savanna sighed. They hadn't had anything big planned, just a picnic on the beach—the first of the season, as it was finally warm enough. Fonzie hopped up on the bench beside her and bumped her arm with his nose. She rested a hand on his back. "It's okay. This is dating a surgeon. I get it," she murmured. Aidan's job wasn't simply important, it was life or death. She hoped his patient would pull through. It was a little crazy that he'd called her as he was going to scrub in. Other guys might've not even bothered, or maybe sent a quick text. Aidan was certainly not like other guys.

Savanna had an idea. She placed a quick call to Caroline Carson, packed the picnic dinner she'd prepared for herself and Aidan into a backpack, and headed down along the shoreline with Fonzie. The dog scampered ahead, pouncing on the tide. Twenty minutes later, they made their way through the sand dunes into Caroline Carson's orchard. She hadn't come through this way since she was a teenager. She guessed it was about a mile's walk from her house, and the weather this evening was perfect for it. The town matriarch was standing at the railing of her large, wraparound porch waiting for them.

Savanna walked into Caroline's open-armed hug, awed as always by the ninety-one-year-old woman's verve and vigor. She let go, noting the cane in Caroline's hand. The yellow scarf at her neck perfectly complemented the yellow-and-lavender linen pantsuit she wore today; her lipstick was perfectly applied and her white hair beautifully coiffed. "You look fabulous, as always," Savanna told her. "I'm glad you were free!"

"I was about to fix myself some soup for dinner when you called. How are you? How are your parents?" Caroline went through the wide doors into the parlor, chatting as she walked. Her two little fluffy white poodles had found Fonzie and were already in the yard playing.

"We're all doing well." Savanna unshouldered her backpack. "I hope you like what I brought. We've got cold fried chicken from Happy Family, homemade potato salad, coleslaw, honeydew melon, and chocolate chip cookies from Main Street Sweets for dessert."

"Oh, lovely! Much more palatable than my soup." Caroline stopped in front of the floor-to-ceiling mural Savanna had painted for her when she'd first come home to Carson. Situated in Caroline's parlor in plenty of natural light from the many windows, it was a depiction of Lake Michigan with the dunes and the wide, beautiful sky; Caroline's late husband's yacht sailed over the blue waves, among others. "What a wonderful gift you've given me. When I'm relaxing in my chair here every evening, your artwork provides me such a sense of tranquility and joy."

"That's the perfect compliment." Savanna smiled warmly at her.

Caroline resumed walking. "Let's eat in the shade outside the kitchen."

Savanna served them each a plate and fetched two glasses of lemonade from the kitchen. Caroline had been like a grandmother to Savanna and her sisters ever since they were little. Long summer days spent on this very porch and races through the orchard to the dunes and the lake beyond had been staples of Savanna's childhood. She'd seen her first real-life Claude Monet painting in this house, as Caroline's late husband Everett had been an avid collector. When Savanna had discovered shortly after moving home from Chicago that someone was trying to kill the town matriarch, she, her sisters, and Aidan had become embroiled in the race to save the woman's life.

"Tell me. To what do I owe this fun surprise?" Caroline asked.

"I've missed you! I've been meaning to come by. Plus," Savanna added, wanting to be completely honest, "my plans tonight with Dr. Gallager fell through, and this seemed like a good backup plan. He had to go into an emergency surgery."

"Life with a surgeon," Caroline said. "I recall what that's like. Have I told you my father was a surgeon? And my brother and his daughter—my niece. Runs in the family."

"I remember." Savanna had missed Caroline, and she was glad she'd gotten to see her tonight.

"My mother would get so aggravated with my dad. He missed a lot. That's the truth."

Savanna nodded. "I'm sure. How did you feel about that?"

"It's funny. I think kids take their cues from their parents. When I was small, I remember being constantly disappointed at missed school plays, birthdays, piano recitals, that sort of thing. But something shifted when I was eleven or twelve. I'll never know what caused it, but my mother began planning around the likelihood he'd be called away. She'd have us perform our scene in the play in the living room for him when he'd trudge in the door late at night after an emergency surgery. She'd sit and eat a few bites with us when he missed dinner, and then take her dinner with him later on. She began explaining to us what a surgeon does, how they have a hand in saving lives. Maybe it simply took time for her to adjust. But I don't recall ever feeling upset with him after that. He was always there when he could be.

And when he was, he was one hundred percent there, invested, ours. It was enough."

Savanna sat still, processing her words. She might as well be describing Aidan. When he was present, he was the most amazing, attentive man she'd ever met. It was hard to imagine being angry or irritated with him when he was only doing his job.

"My brother's a retired neurosurgeon. His story is different. He didn't marry until he was nearly fifty. His wife is an accomplished cellist with the Detroit Symphony Orchestra, and plenty busy herself. They only have the one daughter. Their relationship seems to work well." She stopped, taking a drink of her lemonade, her gaze searching Savanna's expression before she went on. "My niece has had a different path than both her father and grandfather. Her first marriage ended in divorce. She'd tell you herself it was because her husband was so unhappy with her unpredictable schedule. Her second husband became a stay-at-home father to their three children. They've always seemed happy to me."

Savanna spoke. "Very interesting, all three relationships. It sounds like there's not necessarily one right way to handle being with someone who isn't always in control of their own time."

"Exactly. I believe it works when both parties are willing to make it work. When it's a burden, or the benefits aren't worth the sacrifices, it doesn't work."

"That makes sense. For any relationship. You're all kinds of wise, Caroline."

The other woman shook her head, making a dismissive sound. "Not really. I only know what I know. I know *you*. You've got a lot on your mind."

"Oh," Savanna said. The woman was amazing. Perceptive, sharp, and concerned...no wonder she and her sisters always felt at home here. "I suppose I do. As I said, very wise of you."

"Well, we're skirting around the real issue, aren't we? Have you put serious thought into how you feel about our Dr. Gallager, my dear?"

The question caught Savanna completely by surprise. They'd been speaking purely in generalities. She began to answer, and then stopped. She couldn't. She knew, without question. She couldn't tell Caroline Carson how she felt before she spoke the truth where it belonged. She was in love with Aidan Gallager.

On Thursday morning, Savanna was in the middle of demonstrating to her third graders how to piece together their felt cut-outs, pieces of fabric, and other items to create a friendly monster, Carson Elementary's receptionist appeared at her door with an enormous bouquet of flowers in a glass vase. She only knew it was Karen because she recognized the receptionist's trademark leopard print loafers at the end of a pair of legs coming out of the biggest collection of pink-and-red double peonies she'd ever seen.

Her students reacted before Savanna could—the classroom was filled with *"Oooohs"* and giggles rippling throughout the kids. She met Karen and took the bouquet, her eyes wide. "What in the world?"

"Aren't they gorgeous? Smell them!"

Savanna did, closing her eyes and inhaling. "Oh, wow." She opened the tiny envelope—which was already open—and read the card, what there was of it to read:

Sorry about last night. Raincheck Saturday?

Love, Aidan

"Are these from Dr. Gallager? What did he *do*? If it was me, I'd forgive him in a heartbeat," Karen said in low tones, lifting her eyebrows. "Get it? A heartbeat."

A nervous laugh escaped Savanna. "Ah, right, because he's a heart surgeon—clever. Thanks for bringing these down, Karen." She carried them to her desk; they were surprisingly heavy. She fussed with the arrangement, straightening a few stems in hopes the receptionist would take her cue and go, and she did. The bouquet was so beautiful. She only wished he'd sent it to her house. Jack's words rang in her ears, advising her to fly under the radar. She couldn't help wondering how many other staff had seen the woman carrying this bouquet fit for a queen down the main hallway.

Within seconds of her dismissing her class after the last bell, Jack poked his head around the corner into her classroom. His library was kitty-corner across the hall from her, where he taught computer classes. "Savanna and Aidan, sitting in a tree, k-i-s-s-i-n—"

She aggressively shushed him and pulled him by the elbow into the room, shutting the door behind him. "Have you ever even seen such a gorgeous bouquet? I've never gotten flowers before at work. It's so nice," she said, hands clasped together in front of her. "But…"

"But?" Jack leaned forward and smelled the flowers. "Mmm."

"Well, I hope no one but Karen saw them come down the hall. Karen and you," she corrected.

Jack's expression was skeptical. "You do understand, if Karen knows, everyone knows, right?"

"Oy. I was worried about that."

Jack leaned on her desk and crossed his khaki-clad legs at the ankles, laughing. "I'm a little surprised that he didn't just send them to your house. I'd pegged him for the demonstrative but discreet type. But honestly, who cares? Half the teachers here probably wish their partners were as awesome as yours."

"He remembered how much I love peonies," Savanna said. "I just hope no one makes an issue of it."

"Try not to worry. What are they for, anyway? I thought your birthday was last weekend."

"It was. These are because Aidan had to cancel our date last night. He had an emergency surgery. They're so unnecessary."

"But very sweet," Jack added.

"Yes, they are. You're right, I should be happy he sent me flowers and quit stressing about breaking a rule we don't even know for sure is real."

The bouquet was seat-belted into the back seat beside Mollie on the way to dance Thursday after school. Savanna snapped off one pretty rose-pink bloom and stuck it into Mollie's bun before they headed into Miss Priscilla's. This would be the last time this year Savanna would be bringing the child to dance, since the dress rehearsal and recital would take place next week. She pulled out her knitting and worked on Hannah's baby blanket while she waited, paying careful attention to the discussion topics in Priscilla's lobby. She picked up no good gossip at all. All the parents were focused on the recital, what color tights they still had to buy, who'd correctly assembled which headpieces for various classes, and which classes their children were planning to take next fall. That long list of complaints between the Kents and the Blakes was still fresh in Savanna's mind; they were all mean-spirited and petty. There was even one made by Libby and Anthony when the dance studio had erected an expensive new custom-made sign on their storefront. The Kents had dug up an odd, decades-old statute prohibiting the use of any type of sign with lighted red lettering, and the city council had forced Miss Priscilla to remove it. And yet they were surprised the dance school refused to use their florist services? Savanna didn't like seeing this new side of her late friend.

Mollie's grandma picked her up at the end of her ballet class, and Savanna walked next door to see if Uncle Max was ready to leave yet. She was having everyone over for dinner tonight to see the finished result of her, Harlan's, and Uncle Freddie's hard work on her house. She'd made a lasagna last night after walking home from Caroline's, and she just had to put it in the oven for an hour when she got home. Aidan had already told her not to expect him, as Thursdays were his late days at the clinic. She'd called him on her lunch break and thanked him for the lovely flowers, taking Jack's advice to try to stop worrying.

Uncle Max looked especially dapper today in a brown checkered linen suit and burgundy bow tie. "I'm just finishing up. You're sure you don't mind if Lady Bella comes along?"

"You know you don't even need to ask," she said.

"I wondered what you..." Max's voice trailed off as he went into the office behind the counter.

"I'm sorry, what?"

"Oh, my fault, love." He leaned out of the office so she could hear him. "Come back here while I add today's orders to the inventory log."

Savanna felt strange going behind the flower shop's counter without Anthony here, but she did. She stood just inside the door to the office. "You were saying?"

"Yes! What did you think of your flowers?"

"They're so beautiful! Did you help him pick out what to send?"

"He didn't need my help. He knew exactly what he wanted. He said evening delivery, but he apologized for putting in his order on short notice this morning, so I figured I'd get them out to you the moment I'd finished the arrangement."

Now it all made sense. Savanna didn't have the heart to tell her uncle he might have created a problem for her at work. She hoped she was wrong; she supposed she wouldn't know for sure until tomorrow. "Thank you. I was so surprised." She crouched down to pet Lady Bella, tipping her head sideways to read the titles on the bookshelf. That jarring sensation needled her again, same as the last time she'd been in here. The space was so meticulously neat, except...

She raised her gaze to the top of the bookshelf, which had not a book out of place. On top was a lone, old hardcover lying on its side, rather than filed alphabetically like the others. She stood and squinted at the title: *The Common Sense Book of Baby and Child Care* by Benjamin Spock.

"Uncle Max," she called over her shoulder, frowning at the book. The black and green of the spine was faded and quite weathered.

"Yes?" He closed the laptop on Anthony's desk and came over to her, following her gaze up to the book.

She stood on tiptoe and stretched out her fingers, reaching for it. She was a few inches shy. "What is that doing here? Isn't it kind of strange? Do you think it's Libby and Anthony's, from when Rachel was a baby?"

Max plucked the book from the top of the bookcase. He handled it gingerly, turning it over in his hands, and then passing it to her. "It's certainly old. I can't imagine why they'd have a childcare book in the office."

Savanna carefully opened the cover and read the title page. "1946. But it hasn't been here long. It isn't dusty." She thumbed through the pages, catching a lovely whiff of dated paper and ink—her favorite thing about old books. She gasped. "What was that?"

Max peered over her shoulder.

She slowly paged backward from the direction she'd been flipping through and stopped when she found the thing that had caused that split-second flash of color and startled her. "Oh, my." Her words came out as a whisper. "Is this what I think it is?"

Uncle Max turned and grabbed a ream of white tissue paper, spreading it out on the table near the door. "Go ahead, turn the book sideways. Let's take a closer look."

She did as she was told, and a pale, dried flower slid out of the book onto the tissue paper. As Max bent to examine it, Savanna held the book over the paper and thumbed through one more time, but nothing else fell out.

Uncle Max donned one of his white cotton gardening gloves and moved the flower slightly to one side. "Look at this. You've discovered how it was that Libby

215

was able to grow an extinct Cry Violet. There are still four seeds left. I wonder how many tries it took before she got one to grow. Goodness gracious, I wonder how she came by this book."

"You think the flower has been in this book since the 1940s or '50s?"

"It only makes sense."

Savanna brushed her fingertips over the page the violet had been closed against all these years. She felt slight depressions and ridges. "You're right. You can tell where it's been pressed into the paper."

Max followed suit, nodding. "Those small areas must be where the pistol and stamens were lying on the page. Probably for decades." He looked stunned. "The sheer complexity of this, getting the seed to germinate... I'm impressed."

"She was committed. It's a shame she won't see her plant win this weekend."

Uncle Max smiled. "I hope it wins all the awards. It certainly deserves it. Let's put this right back the way Libby had it. Anthony and Rachel will be excited to learn about it." He carefully set the flower back in its depression. As he closed it, he and Savanna jumped at the sound of the stairwell door slamming.

Anthony stormed into the office, oblivious to the discovery they'd just made. Mumbling under his breath, he snatched his keys from the desk and hurried toward the door. "Sheriff's got my daughter in for questioning. I've got to go. Max." He stopped in his tracks and turned toward her uncle. "The sprayers are still on upstairs; I forgot them. I know you have plans, but could you take care of those? Then you can lock up early and leave. I don't care." He was gone.

Savanna stared after him. "What—"

"They brought Rachel in? How strange." Max patted his pocket, double-checking for his keys. "Let me run up to the roof. Then we can go. My goodness."

Savanna stayed where she was in the office, unsure what to do. Sometimes she didn't understand Nick Jordan at all. She bit her lip, staring straight ahead at nothing while she tried to imagine why he'd brought Rachel in. The label on a file cabinet drawer came into focus, and she frowned, moving closer. Each drawer of the tall metal cabinet was marked with the contents inside:

Mortgage & Finance

Employees & Contractors

Insurance—Health, Dental, Life

Legal

She knew what Sydney had said in Detective Jordan's office about the nitpicky behavior between Libby's and Miss Priscilla's: it hadn't been about parking or lighted signs. So what was it about? An old grudge? Money? Some perceived slight?

Savanna pulled open the drawer labeled *Insurance*. Quickly scanning the hanging file folders inside, she ignored the multiple files listing health insurance providers and dental plans. She sucked in her breath as she thumbed quickly toward the back and spotted a folder titled *Policy update 2020*. She plucked it out, closed the drawer, and opened the next one, suppressing her urge to peruse it right this second. In the drawer marked *Legal*, she grabbed one that caught her eye—a formal-looking notice on Carson's law firm's letterhead. She closed that drawer and repeated the process twice more, doing her best to grab anything that might be significant. She scanned whatever she could pertaining to complaints, insurance changes, property value changes, even one labeled *Tuition*.

She shot a furtive glance over her shoulder. When Max came back into the shop from upstairs, she'd probably hear the bang of the door from the stairwell. She slid all the documents into one slim stack and shoved them into the top feeder on the copy machine next to the file cabinet, hitting the green start button. The large machine kicked on with an extraordinary amount of noise; she'd never hear Max now.

Savanna couldn't recall ever being this nervous. She darted over to the door, peering out into the shop, and then zipped back to the copier when it quieted, grabbed the originals, haphazardly stuffed them back into folders, knowing they were out of order, yanked the file cabinet drawers open, and put them each back.

She froze with her copies in hand at the sound of the stairwell access door closing, and then the jingle of Uncle Max's keys as he locked the deadbolt. *Oh, snap!* She shook open one of the brown Libby's Blooms bags from under a shelving unit and threw the papers in, adding a handful of baby's breath branches on top as he came through the office door.

"I need a few of these for a project at school. Could I pay for them?" She sucked in air, struggling not to appear out of breath.

"Those aren't fresh. No worries, you may take as many as you need." He was preoccupied with the closing routine.

Savanna's conscience was jabbing her in the ribs. *Ugh.* "Uncle Max."

He stopped and looked over at her. "Yes, love?"

"I'm sorry." She dumped the paper bag upside down on the counter. "I'm so sorry. I can't lie to you. But I'm so close to figuring out who killed Libby. I think a few of these records could help Detective Jordan solve the case."

Max moved to her side and perused the papers. "I see." He glanced at her. "You're quick."

Savanna hugged him. "I'm sorry, Uncle Max. I promise next time I'll just ask you if I need something."

He returned her hug. "My dear, I appreciate your honesty. I'd have been none the wiser this time—you didn't have to confess. But I'm glad you did. I only have one question."

"Anything."

"Do you really believe the clue to who killed our Libby is in here?"

She nodded vigorously. "I really do."

"All right. Then we've got to get them to the detective." He scooped the papers up and deposited them in the bag, handing it to her.

"Thank you. Can I help with anything?"

"I believe we're all set," he said, waiting as she stepped out of the office and locking it behind her. She followed him through the darkened shop into the parking lot, Lady Bella on their heels. "Lucky for us, Anthony doesn't mind closing up early now and then. This is the second time in a week."

Chapter Sixteen

S AVANNA OPENED THE DOOR TO welcome Uncle Freddie and her parents, who were all arriving at the same time. The aroma of lasagna and garlic bread filled the house. Sydney and Uncle Max stood at the kitchen sink, rinsing vegetables and assembling the salad. Skylar had unfortunately called to say Travis and Nolan were both fighting a bad cold; their family was staying in for the evening.

"Oh my gosh," Charlotte exclaimed. "Look what you've done." She clasped her hands at her chest and stood taking in the grouping of framed pictures Savanna had hung on the stairway landing wall facing the foyer.

She'd gone through old photos in her parents' basement and had had a few blown up. She'd painted the naked wood frames herself and had artfully arranged them over a four-foot-high hand-painted mural of a cherry blossom tree just like the one in the backyard of her childhood. The photos above the pale pink flowers on the tree were a mixed collection of Savanna and her sisters as kids and now: Skylar and Travis in a seaside cabana on their honeymoon; Nolan on the couch looking lovingly down at baby Hannah in his little arms;

Sydney cutting the wide red ribbon at Fancy Tails & Treats' grand opening; Charlotte and Harlan on their anniversary cruise in Alaska; Freddie, Max, and Ellie on move-in day at her campus; and Savanna with Caroline at her ninetieth birthday party, on her porch under the tiny globe lights.

Her mother slid an arm around her waist and smiled, her eyes shiny. "I'm so proud of you. Show me what else you've done."

Savanna couldn't help falling in love with her modest little home all over again as she conducted a tour through each room, pointing out the renovations. Freddie's architectural expertise had proved invaluable when it came to changing the floor plan and figuring out structural issues. Harlan made sure to show Charlotte the security system he'd installed at each point of entry, stressing that their daughter had promised to be consistent in using the safeguards.

They were in the family room at the back of the house when the doorbell rang, triggering Savanna's organic alarm system. Fonzie sprinted to the front door, followed by Lady Bella, both barking all the way. Aidan stood on the front porch, holding a bottle of wine with a silver bow on it.

"Hi!" Savanna ushered him in. "What are you doing here? Your clinic doesn't close for another hour!"

"Sanjay offered to cover for me. I didn't want to miss this too. I'm s—"

She cut him off. "No. Don't do that. No more flowers and multiple apologies when you're just doing what you committed to. I understand."

He shook his head. "I appreciate that, but this type of thing can become a problem. I don't want you to doubt your importance to me."

She frowned up at him. Clearly, the flowers, the apologies, his current worried expression were about much more than last night. Had this been a sore point with his late wife? The conversation with Caroline floated through her thoughts. Aidan had obligations to meet. But when he was with her, he was present, invested, all in. It was enough. "Aidan. You've never given me any reason to doubt you. We are okay—we're good. I know who you are." *I love who you are. I love you.* The words were on the tip of her tongue, true, vital. But conversation from her family drifted to them from the other room.

Aidan cradled her jaw, his fingertips at the back of her neck, and kissed her too briefly. He drew back. His lips parted; he was about to speak.

"Let me ask Savanna—the corkscrew has to be somewhere." Uncle Freddie came through from the kitchen just then, halting when he saw them. "Oh. Sorry, we were trying to get into the wine."

Aidan held up the bottle he'd brought. "Start with this. Good to see you, Freddie."

Savanna followed the two men into the kitchen; they immediately launched into conversation about an office plaza in New York that Aidan had learned Freddie was responsible for designing.

Savanna had noticed right away that Sydney's edges were a little less sharp tonight. "How are you feeling?" she asked. They were setting the table. "How did Stress Less Yoga go?"

Sydney handed her the last two plates. "It was amazing. Skylar got as much out of it as I did. I signed up for the next few sessions." She narrowed her eyes.

"That wasn't coincidence. Did you ask Kate to add that specific class just for me?"

Savanna shook her head. "I just asked if there were any types of yoga that could help with extreme stress or loss. She took it from there. She's been concerned about you too, Syd."

Sydney gave her a quick hug. "Thank you for looking out for me. I feel a little more like myself. I can't really fix any of the stuff that's happened."

"No," Savanna agreed. "I'm glad it helped." She wasn't saying a single word to her sister about Libby's daughter being brought in for questioning. No need to undo all the benefits of her yoga session.

The evening passed much too quickly. Savanna said goodbye to Charlotte and Harlan on the deck, while Sydney toasted marshmallows over the firepit. Uncles Freddie and Max eventually stood to take their leave.

Aidan shook Max's hand. "Thanks again for your help this morning with the bouquet. And for your advice on my hostas. I was starting to think I'd have to dig them all up and start over."

"Anytime. And if you really want to share a cutting of your clematis vine, I'd love it. It sounds like yours has really taken off."

"I'll give it to Freddie," Aidan said, shaking Savanna's other uncle's hand now. "I'll see you for our tee time Saturday morning."

"Eight sharp," Freddie agreed.

When Savanna hugged Uncle Max goodbye, he made her promise to let him know if she heard anything about why Jordan had brought Rachel in.

Savanna thought of the copied documents still in the trunk of her car. She'd be up late tonight; she couldn't wait to go through them. "I'm hoping to see the detective tomorrow. I'll find out. Thank Anthony from me for letting you close early, if you think of it."

He nodded. "I will. I'm really not sure Anthony will keep the shop. He's more irritable every day he's there. And then who knows what it might become if he sells? I'll be out of work."

"I doubt you'd be out of work very long."

"I'm not worried," Uncle Max said.

"That's got to be a heartbreaking decision for Anthony Kent," Savanna mused. "Keep the flower shop his wife loved, or let it go and move on." In the back of Savanna's mind was the nagging question of whether Anthony was waiting for something. For his life insurance payout? For someone to be arrested for his wife's murder? For the assurance that it wouldn't be him?

Friday morning, Savanna delivered homemade chicken noodle soup and a new Star Wars Lego set to Skylar's front porch. She'd been saving the Legos for Nolan's birthday, but she felt bad that the poor little guy was sick. She set the package on Skylar's porch bench outside the front door and then texted before pulling out of the driveway; she didn't want to take a chance on waking anyone. Then she headed to Sydney's salon with the rest of the unfinished pie from last night. She had so many goodies in her house it wasn't even funny; they needed to be dispersed.

Sydney handed her a cup of coffee. She flipped on the switches in the grooming area, opening the shop for the day. "I had such a good time last night. I love having our uncles here in Carson. And your house doesn't even look like the same place you bought last year. Except for the deck—still my favorite spot."

"Thank you. I really love it; it feels like mine." Savanna hung the oversized purse she'd brought today on the wall hook. It was full of documents she intended to hand over to Detective Jordan later today. "Do you need me to sweep or anything?"

"Nope, did that last night. You could restock the treat case if you want."

A flash of movement caught Savanna's eye, and she looked up from the yellow tennis ball dog cookies she was organizing in time to see Dylan Blake strolling by the wide front window with two coffees. "Like clockwork," she murmured. School started in a half hour, which always seemed to be the time of morning Dylan made his coffee run. She bent to resume her task behind the display counter but halted, tennis ball cookie in midair. Something was very wrong across the street at Libby's Blooms. "Syd!"

"Hold on," her sister called from the grooming area.

Savanna went to the front window to get a better look. "Sydney! Get out here!"

"Hold your horses, woman," Sydney said, carrying a large box and slowly moving toward the treat side of the salon with it. "No, that's all right, don't bother to help. I love carrying boxes full of heavy leashes and collars,"

Savanna rushed over and took one side, helping her sister get it to the pet accessory wall. Once they'd set it down, she dragged Sydney to the window by her sleeve and pointed. "Look."

"Oh my gosh! The whole front window's shattered!"

Savanna and Sydney went outside in front of Fancy

Tails and gawked at the flower shop.

"Has no one even noticed this yet?" Sydney asked.

"Did it just happen?" Savanna answered her question with a question.

"Uncle Max isn't there, is he?"

"No. Look, it's dark inside. He says Anthony has him start later than Libby used to. I don't think anyone's there. But—Miss Priscilla's husband just walked by. Didn't he notice it?" Savanna pulled out her phone to call the police.

"Well, you'd think he should have!" Syd exclaimed.

Across the street, Dylan Blake came through the front door of the dance studio and called over to them, waving his cell phone. "I'm on it, ladies. I just spoke to the police."

"Come with me," Savanna said to Sydney, and crossed the street to where Dylan stood outside the door to the dance studio. "Good. We were just about to. Are they sending someone?"

He nodded. "I don't know who I talked to, but she said an officer would be right over. None of us has an alarm system, apparently. Maybe it's time I thought of getting one."

Savanna got closer to Libby's Blooms, looking out for glass. Most of it had fallen inside the shop. The enormous picture window was basically gone, large pieces hanging in shards from the edges. A hole at least six or eight feet in diameter went through into the store. Several floral and plant displays in the front window had been knocked over. Dirt and pottery and displaced greenery lay all over the tile floor.

"I wonder if it was a break-in or vandalism. We're lucky they didn't get us too." Dylan looked at the front of the dance studio. The lights inside were on, and as they talked, Miss Priscilla appeared, pulling a rolling cart full of trophies behind her. She left it and came outside.

She nodded at Savanna and Sydney. "Girls."

"Hi, Miss Priscilla," they said together, then looked at each other, embarrassed.

She stood near her husband and frowned at the destruction. "Huh. Well, that's a mess. I thought you were exaggerating," she said to Dylan. "What happened?" She turned her intense stare on the Shepherd sisters.

If Savanna didn't know better, she'd swear she was ten and in trouble for talking in ballet class. She gazed wide-eyed at the older woman. "We don't know."

A black-and-white police cruiser pulled up at the curb, hitting the siren once, and the man Savanna remembered was Officer Whitney got out. He walked from one side of the shattered storefront to the other, assessing the situation. "No one's hurt? Can someone tell me what happened?" He pulled a small notepad and pen from his shirt pocket.

"I was walking back from getting coffee," Dylan said, pointing down the street toward the coffee shop, "and found it like this."

"Did you see anyone? On foot or in a car?"

"No. And I'm sure it wasn't like this when I left. I'd have noticed. It must've just happened."

"Mrs. Blake, you were here working in the dance school when it happened? Did you hear anything?"

Priscilla Blake shook her head. "I didn't. Though I am a little hard of hearing." Other shop owners were emerging from doorways up and down Main Street, peering toward the officer and the small group in front of Libby's.

"We didn't hear or see anything, either," Sydney offered. "Which is strange, since we have a clear view over here from my window. I see pretty much everything if I happen to be looking. We somehow missed what happened, but my sister spotted the broken window."

"Officer," Savanna said, "can you tell by looking what happened? It looks like something got thrown through the window, right?"

Whitney nodded. "That's what I'd say. But I'll need to get inside and check it out." He put his notepad away and pulled his radio from his shoulder and spoke into it, calling an evidence tech to the scene. "Mr. and Mrs. Blake, Ms. Shepherd—both of you," he said, addressing the group around him on the sidewalk. "Can you think of anyone who'd do this? It seems pretty antagonistic, right after the florist was killed."

Detective Jordan came around the corner on foot from the police station and joined the group. No one had an answer to Whitney's question. Jordan addressed the sisters. "Kent and your uncle aren't at work already, right? Any damage to your place?" he asked the Blakes, who shook their heads.

Officer Whitney cleared his throat. "I, uh, I haven't cleared the flower shop yet. I was about to."

"Wait for Evidence. Callie's working today," Jordan said.

At that moment, the lights all came on inside the shop. Seconds later, Anthony Kent stood looking through his broken window at the gathering group on the sidewalk. Kate had come out now, as well as the tenant Savanna had run into on the second floor, and the deli owner across Main Street. A quick glance to her left told Savanna that Marcus Valentine was at home. His red convertible was parked at the curb. Had he not heard the commotion? Or maybe he had, and was staying out of the way?

Jordan motioned to Anthony. "Mr. Kent, I need you to come out here. Now."

Anthony looked shocked when he came through the front door. "Who did this? Why would someone throw a rock through my window?"

"You found a rock? Just now?" Sydney asked. "That's what happened?"

Detective Jordan looked at her sharply, then back at Libby's husband. "Where? Show me."

"What? Oh no, no." Anthony shook his head, running a hand through his thinning hair. "I just meant that's what it looks like. Right? I didn't see any rock. I don't know what could've happened." He narrowed his eyes as he looked past Sydney to the mess of glass.

Sydney slipped her hand through Savanna's arm, leaning close to whisper into her ear. "That was weird. Why would he assume that?"

"We're pretty sure no one had shown up yet to open the shop," Savanna told the detective. "Max says his starting time is later now since Libby's gone."

"We may have questions once we go through the debris," Jordan said, looking from the Blakes to Kent to Savanna and Sydney. "If any of you remember anything, let me know."

Dylan and Priscilla Blake headed back inside the dance studio.

"The seeds," Savanna said, looking at Detective Jordan.

"What seeds?" Anthony Kent asked, looking confused.

"Uncle Max and I found the seeds to Libby's extinct plant—the Cry Violet. Maybe this is crazy, but I wonder if someone was trying to steal them. I'd think there'd be some money in growing extinct plants."

"Really?" Jordan looked at her, his tone intrigued. "You found seeds? So there are more left? This may not be a straight vandalism job. Whitney, come with me." He put a hand on the door and looked back at Savanna. "Where were the seeds?"

"The office. In the big book on top of the bookshelf." To Anthony, she said, "We found them by accident. Max placed them back exactly where we'd found them. We thought you and Rachel would want them."

"Go back to your shop," Jordan told Sydney and Savanna, his voice stern. "Mr. Kent, Kate, people. Please move away. We don't even know yet that the perpetrator is gone and not inside." He and Whitney went into the flower shop, each with a hand on his holstered gun.

Savanna and her sister retreated back across the street but stayed outside, watching. "What do you think happened?" Sydney asked.

"I don't know. My first thought was the seeds, but that seems unlikely. Maybe someone just targeted the shop because no one was there yet? Is there money in there?"

Sydney frowned, thinking. "There's a safe, yes. Libby deposited the earnings in the bank twice a week, so in between, there's always money in the safe."

"But why would someone break in in broad daylight?" Maybe Savanna was off base. "What if it was a warning or something? To convince Anthony Kent to sell?"

"I don't know," Sydney said. "Uncle Max seems pretty sure Anthony's already planning to sell. The vandalism isn't really necessary."

"Right." Savanna peered through the grooming salon window at the wall clock. "Oh my gosh, I have to run! First bell rings in three minutes!" She darted inside and grabbed her purse.

"I'll text you if anything happens," Sydney called, as Savanna pulled away from the curb.

Savanna's relaxing, productive morning of soup and Lego and pie delivery had turned into a mad rush into Carson Elementary. She ran from the faculty lot into the building, abruptly slowing to a fast walk once inside. Her first class began at nine, and it was 9:02. She arrived breathless and frazzled.

Tricia Williams sat at Savanna's desk at the head of her classroom, arms crossed, the children all unusually quiet. "There she is!" Tricia held an arm out to Savanna. "We were just wondering if you'd be here today, Ms. Shepherd."

"Of course," Savanna said. "Thank you so much for waiting, Mrs. Williams." She flashed the fakest smile in the history of fake smiles at the teacher and addressed her class. "Who's ready to finish their monster today?"

Tricia left, and the students visibly relaxed. *For Pete's sake.* Tricia Williams must've stressed them all out, sitting here telling them Ms. Shepherd was playing hooky from work or something equally wild. Everyone ran a minute or two late once in a while.

Savanna questioned her own logic an hour later when she was summoned to Mr. Clay's office. Karen had hand-delivered the little pink note at the beginning of her prep hour. "He says now would be fine, unless

Monday is better for you," the receptionist told her, and turned to go.

"Karen! Wait. Is this because I was late? I've never been late before. It was my first time in two years."

The woman gave her a sympathetic shrug. "I don't know."

The hallway to the office seemed extra-long as Savanna headed down to talk to her principal. She tried to prepare a defense in her head, but it was impossible. She was either being called to the principal's office because she'd been two minutes late, or because Karen or one of the teachers had told Mr. Clay she'd gotten a huge bouquet yesterday from a parent. Could she simply say the bouquet was a nice gesture of friendship? Or possibly a thank you for being a great teacher? Probably not. Aidan's card had been incriminating, and someone had opened the envelope and read it.

Mr. Clay waved her in. She'd liked him since the first time they'd met, right here. She'd been back in her hometown less than a week, hadn't considered the possibility of teaching since sophomore year of college, and had been so nervous she'd felt nauseated. That feeling came back to her instantly now; her stomach was doing backflips.

Now, just as he had two years ago, Mr. Clay tried to put her at ease. "Savanna, thank you for coming to see me. I've got to say, it's hard to believe you're only in your second year of teaching. The students and parents are very happy with you and your class."

"Thank you. That's so nice to hear."

"I do have a small concern, however." Mr. Clay folded his hands in front of him on the sturdy old wooden desk. "This is a little awkward."

"It's all right, Mr. Clay. I think I know." He was so nice. She couldn't help trying to make his job a little easier. "I promise I won't let anything like that happen again. It was completely unprofessional."

He frowned. "I'm... Well, I appreciate that, but it isn't something you can control. I've addressed it with the other party on my end."

Savanna sat up straighter and sucked in her breath. Her eyes were huge. "You—you have? Already?"

"Oh, yes. This isn't the place for that kind of thing. I know no harm was meant, but I think there's a much clearer understanding now of the boundaries."

"Yes," she said, her voice sounding small to her own ears. "I'm so sorry."

"No need to be. I don't expect it'll happen again."

"No, absolutely not," Savanna said. "I'm curious, since I tried so hard to be discreet and get the bouquet out to my car without anyone seeing it. Was it Karen who mentioned it to you? Or possibly Tricia Williams?"

Mr. Clay sat back in his chair, looking confused. "I'm not sure we're discussing the same thing."

"Um..."

"I'm talking about our friend Rosa Taylor and her mishandling information she was given in private. She has a good understanding now of police business and detective work and inappropriate sharing of information. She'd passed on some minor details of Libby Kent's murder investigation to a good handful of the staff here, including you, as I understand it, and that caused some issues for her husband, George. I believe he's in his third year as Nick Jordan's partner. The whole ordeal was probably a good wake-up call for both of them."

"Oh." *Wow.* She hadn't seen that coming. At least she

didn't need to feel guilty for getting Rosa or George in trouble. It sounded as if they both were much too lax with confidentiality. Savanna must not have been the only one to notice.

"I wanted to talk to you to make sure you know not to share anything you may have heard, through Rosa or someone she spoke to."

She quickly shook her head. "Of course—please don't worry. I'm glad it sounds like it's all taken care of. So," she said, starting to stand. "All set then?"

"Almost," Mr. Clay said. She stayed seated. "I believe you were referring to your flower delivery from Dr. Gallager yesterday, yes?"

Oh, snap. She'd given herself away. "Yes." Well, she'd already said her apologies when they'd been miscommunicating; she hoped Mr. Clay would take that into consideration.

"Receiving flowers from a significant other here at school isn't a problem, Savanna. I saw your bouquet. It was beautiful."

She could actually breathe again. "Yes, it was, thank you. Mr. Clay, since we're talking, can I ask, am I breaking any district rules? Am I allowed to date the single parent of a student?"

"In general, yes. It's only a problem if staff or parents begin to feel the child of that parent is receiving special treatment."

"I'd never do that. We've been dating almost a year, and I don't think most folks here even noticed. I think our approach was working fine until yesterday, and that was a big mix-up at the florist. I swear nothing like that will happen again."

"I'm not worried," he said.

Savanna felt as if a heavy weight had been lifted from her shoulders. She hadn't even realized she'd been harboring anxiety over whether her relationship with Aidan would cause problems at school. Tricia had planted those seeds at the movie theater two weeks ago, and they'd been growing ever since. She'd wasted too much negative energy over nothing.

Before her prep hour ended, she texted Detective Jordan. She hated to bother him with everything he was probably dealing with this morning, but she needed to show him what she'd found. She asked him if she could stop by after school today and show him something. He replied seconds later.

Can't, sorry. I'm in court after 2:00.

Okay, she texted back. *It's important. Should I leave it with George?*

No. I'll come to you. What time's your lunch break?

12:30.

See you then.

Chapter Seventeen

SAVANNA MET NICK JORDAN OUTSIDE on her lunch break, on one of the picnic tables along the school's walking path. The tables were only ever used for field day and occasional outdoor activities.

She took the stack of copies from her purse and set them in front of Jordan, keeping one hand on them. "I have to tell you what I found out about Libby's. But I have a couple of questions first. Is everything all right with Rachel? Can you tell me why she was brought in for questioning yesterday? Is she a suspect?"

The detective fished around in his pockets, first the ones on the sides and then the inside breast pockets. He produced a handful of Jolly Ranchers and set them on the table between them, unwrapping one. "I got sick of the mints. Rachel is fine. She was in and out in an hour. We told her to go ahead to that flower thing in Grand Rapids. I get that it was important to her mother."

"But then why did you bring her in?"

"I wanted insight into Marcus Valentine. We're ruling Rachel out as a suspect. Her alibi is iffy, but I don't feel she had access to the type of weapon used. She wasn't very forthcoming about Valentine, unfortunately."

"So, he is a suspect then? Are you going to bring him in for questioning too?"

"No. We're not bringing him in until we've got enough to hold him. That's in the works now."

That sounded serious. "You think Marcus Valentine might've done it? For what, the money Rachel will be getting? Have you talked to him yet? Do you know if he has an alibi or motive?" Savanna rested her forearms on the picnic table, leaning a little closer as they talked, even though there wasn't a soul around.

Jordan gave her his best poker face, quiet for a moment. "I met him. I found a reason to catch him on his way into the building, and we talked for a few minutes."

"Really?" She raised her eyebrows. "What did you think? I'm right, right? He's kind of charming."

"I don't know about all that. Rachel is his alibi, which is problematic. The odd thing was, when I mentioned Anthony and his relationship with Rachel, he made it sound like everything was peachy. Like they're all on great terms. But Rachel admitted her dad isn't crazy about her boyfriend. I had Taylor do some digging, and we found out why a prestigious dance school alum would want to move to Small Town, U.S.A. for what's likely a modest income and a tiny studio apartment."

Savanna was afraid to say a word. She usually had to work to pull information from Detective Jordan. The fact that he was sharing must mean he'd settled on the dance instructor as his primary suspect. She waited for him to fill in the blanks—why had Valentine settled in Carson?

"Anyway." He opened another candy and eyed her

Wonder Woman lunchbox. "Shouldn't you eat your lunch?"

"Oh!" She'd forgotten about it. She unpacked it, opening a Tupperware container with carrots and ranch dip and another with grapes, and then picked up her turkey sandwich. "Thanks. You were saying? About why he came here?"

"It's just background information. Might speak to motive. But you said you had something for me?" He put a hand on the stack of papers she'd set on the table.

Shoot. It'd been too much to hope he'd reveal Marcus Valentine's secret past to her. So frustrating! She knew when not to push. "So, remember my uncle works at Libby's and sometimes handles stuff like inventory, ordering, getting contractors for repairs, paying the lease. A lot of different aspects of the business." She'd rehearsed her wording; she had to make it sound as if she'd been given access to the information, and not that she'd snuck around the office and discovered it. Her conscience had been immediately lighter after confessing to Max, but she didn't want to get him in trouble with Anthony Kent. She continued. "We were in the office last night, and I made some copies from the flower shop records and found a few really strange things."

Detective Jordan took the first stapled-together packet of documents she passed him.

Savanna jumped in. "This is a purchase agreement. Mike at Carson Community Homes put it together"— she pointed to the signatures at the bottom—"two years ago. It's signed by Dylan Blake and Anthony Kent, here. This is for the purchase of Libby's Blooms."

He raised his gaze and stared at her.

"But. This is where Libby's signature belongs." She

pointed to the blank line underneath Anthony's signature.

"I'll be darned." Detective Jordan scrubbed a hand over his chin, frowning at the paper in his hand. "And we don't know what happened? I don't recall Libby's ever being for sale."

"It wasn't. Look." She passed him another set of pages on Carson Community Homes letterhead. "Six years ago. Same thing. But this one doesn't have Libby's or Anthony's signatures."

"Can I keep these?" Jordan's usual intensely serious demeanor was dialed up even higher. "What else do you have?"

"A couple other things. But first, I called Mike last night when I found these. He was my real estate agent. He remembers drafting the newest purchase agreement. The other one was under an agent who's since quit. Mike says Dylan Blake and Anthony Kent seemed civil the one time he sat down with both of them; he says Anthony scheduled a follow-up meeting to go over the purchase with Libby there, but it never happened. He didn't know anything beyond that."

"Thank you for checking with him. This is significant. It gives both Dylan Blake and Anthony Kent a motive."

She nodded. "I kind of thought so. The next thing I found is weird." She passed it across the table to Detective Jordan. "I think it's a complaint made to the IRS. The Kents' statement is here." Savanna pointed at the section of the form that allowed for narrative. "They're alleging that the dance school was committing tax fraud. This is the confirmation letter Libby and Anthony received back, stating that the IRS takes incidences of tax fraud seriously and all reports will be investigated; it appears to be a form letter."

He scanned the pages while she talked, and she went on. "The next one is from Dylan Blake to Anthony and Libby." She handed him a copy of a short legal warning on letterhead from Black, Jones, and Sydowski. She let him read before continuing. She couldn't help viewing the Kents and the Blakes in a different light after all she'd learned last night. Most of what had snowballed into truly mean, vindictive measures had started with petty disagreements. What might've happened if they'd just found a way to work things out early on?

"This is basically a cease and desist," he said, glancing up from the document. "Saying the Blakes are going to sue the Kents for defamation—libel and slander against the dance school—unless they drop their tax fraud claim against them. All of this is from January this year."

She nodded. "I sent Skylar a picture of that; it was drafted by Jillian Black. Skylar didn't know about Priscilla and Dylan threatening to sue the Kents, but she said she could have Jillian call you and fill you in on her meeting with the Blakes in January."

Nick Jordan placed the cease-and-desist letter on the thin stack of papers in front of him. "You have one more?"

"I'm not so sure this last one is even important. I think you've already got the information from Skylar about the life insurance policy. This is a letter from Anthony Kent to his financial advisor—listed right there—and it pretty much details what he was so upset about at the bank that day. According to this, he's angry about some bad investments that depleted his account. He used what was left of it toward the cost of doubling his life insurance."

Jordan took the paper. "I knew some of this, as far as the finance part, but not why. He's telling his advisor why he needs to liquidate his account and close it. Daughter's tuition, interest increase on the mortgage payments for the flower shop, commercial tax rate went up…that kind of thing. He's concerned if something happened to himself or Libby, Rachel would be crushed by debt. It does explain his thought process with the life insurance policy increase, though his timing is wildly suspicious."

"Detective," Savanna said. "Can you tell me—that policy, is it only the spouse who benefits? Is Anthony set to receive the entire amount, or does it get divided between him and Rachel?"

"That all depends on how the policy is written and who the beneficiaries are. Rachel is a co-beneficiary on the policy, getting an equal share along with the surviving parent. That's how Anthony set it up when he doubled the policy."

She shook her head. "Rachel doesn't know there's any money coming."

Jordan raised his brows. "What makes you say that?"

"Well, the day I ran into her at the hospital. She just seemed so stressed about money for school. She said that's why she hadn't taken any bereavement days off."

He frowned. "Hmm."

Savanna knew there was more to his noncommittal response than it appeared. He'd head back to his office and dig into all this. "Do you think she was bluffing? Could she be involved somehow?"

"Not sure." He stood. "You've outdone yourself here. I assume Anthony Kent isn't aware you and your uncle looked through his files?"

"No, he isn't aware."

"Good to know."

She packed up her wrappers and empty containers into her lunch box and walked with Jordan on the winding path around the school to the parking lot. "Detective, what about the gun? The ballistics report must be in by now. Is there a way to tell if the killer used a registered gun?"

"The report is in and our investigation is ongoing," he said.

"What about the casing markings?"

He frowned at her. "We're working through a short list of registered firearms in the county that match the casing markings. But I'd be surprised if someone used a weapon registered in their own name to commit a murder."

"Ah." Savanna sighed. "So I guess unless you find the weapon at an actual suspect's residence or the killer uses it again and is caught with it, the gun's a dead end?"

"Cripes, Savanna. Maybe you should've gone into law enforcement instead of art."

She chuckled. "That's sweet of you." She had a feeling he hadn't said it to be sweet. She was irritating him now, she could tell. Well, she was almost done. "One last question, if you don't mind."

"Shoot."

"What do you think happened at Libby's this morning? Nobody seems to have seen or heard anything at all. It doesn't seem random. Was it a robbery? Because if someone wanted money, they'd be smarter to break into Lakeview Fine Jewelry down the street instead. Plus, it's farther away from you—from the police station."

"It wasn't a robbery. We're still looking into it."

That was about as specific as she was going to get from him.

He stopped before getting into his car. "I've always said you've got a good eye for detail. I appreciate all the work that went into this, Savanna. Thank you. I'll keep you in the loop on where it leads us."

She walked back into the school, still puzzling through everything she'd learned between last night and today. The shattered flower shop window was throwing her off. Was it possible it wasn't connected to Libby's death? However unlikely, that would help explain a lot. Anthony Kent wouldn't destroy his own window, would he? That'd just cost him money, or at least a renter's insurance claim. It didn't make sense to think Dylan Blake had done it, either. He was the one who'd discovered it and called the police. Plus, she'd seen him on his coffee run—how would he have had time to do it? Marcus Valentine and Rachel Kent popped into Savanna's head. She still wasn't certain if Rachel could have had anything to do with Libby's death, or if it might've been Marcus acting alone. Rachel should be in Grand Rapids at the flower show today, so she couldn't have done it. What about Valentine? Living in the building, it'd be quick and easy for him to throw something through the window and run back upstairs. But for what purpose?

Savanna dove into the projects her afternoon classes were working on, happy to think about nothing else but the large, colorful versions of friendly monsters her students were finishing up.

Handling the pick-up line after the last bell Friday afternoon seemed to take forever. As soon as she was done, she dropped the compulsory yellow-and-orange vest on her desk and headed for Fancy Tails. She showered Fonzie with pats and scratches and praise when she arrived and poked her head into the grooming area. Sydney had their uncles' Lady Bella on the grooming table. The Corgi spotted Savanna and attempted to leap off the platform, her stout, furry body wagging along with her tail.

Sydney laughed. "Now you have to come back here and calm her down."

Savanna went through the half door and stood petting the sweet dog's head while Sydney continued trimming her. "Has there been any action across the street since I left this morning?"

"I know it looks like I just play with dogs all day," Syd joked, "but I almost never get time to go stare out the window and spy on everyone."

"Hey, don't judge me. I have my reasons for spying." Savanna smiled back at the smiling Corgi. "You're so cute!"

"She's seriously the cutest," Sydney agreed. "Don't tell Fonzie. And to answer your question, I do know there's been a whole lot of action across the street since this morning. Willow was grooming today until she left, so I was at the treat counter."

Savanna chuckled, parroting Sydney from a minute ago. "'I never have time to look out the window!'"

"So, you don't want an update then?"

"Come on, tell me what you saw!"

"Well, I had the first grooming appointment, so I'm not sure what happened right after we left. But Willow got here an hour later, and Jordan and his partner were inside the flower shop, along with Callie from their evidence team—she's got the biggest, goofiest Great Dane mix," Sydney interrupted herself with dog facts.

Savanna was used to it. She nodded as her younger sister continued.

"Anthony Kent showed up in the middle of them, checking everything over. There was a lot of arm-waving and pointing and shouting. It was kind of like a silent movie on this side," Sydney noted.

"Who was doing the yelling? Pointing where?"

"Anthony Kent appeared to be yelling at Jordan and Taylor. He kept pointing toward Miss Priscilla's. I'm sure he probably thinks they did it. The detectives left, but Callie stayed to finish up; she was snapping photos and measuring things with that red string you see on crime shows. Then Uncle Max came in, even though we texted him about what had happened. It's probably good he did. It was a plant massacre over there." She stopped, looking slightly nauseated. "So uncalled for. Uncle Max tried to scoop up and save as many as possible. Anthony just stood there watching and getting in Callie's way. Trade ends with me—I have to do her ears."

It took Savanna a second to separate the silent movie narrative from Sydney's grooming command. She swapped places with Sydney for the dog's back end, which wasn't as much fun as seeing her smiling face.

"Okay, and then after Callie left, a utility truck pulled up and started working on the glass. The cleanup took a really long time. Once they got it all, those guys took their own measurements, left, and came back with the plywood you can now see covering almost the whole entire store front where the glass is missing. I'm guessing they have to special order the replacement window. That's all I know. You're gorgeous, Lady Bella!" She unclipped the short leash and hugged the dog, lifting her and setting her down on the tiled floor, where Fonzie instantly began prancing in circles around her.

"You know everything," Savanna said. "Thanks for the rundown. Can she come play, or do you have to put her in a pen?"

"She knows the owner, so she's allowed to come out and play," Sydney said, opening the half door and following Savanna and the Corgi through.

Sydney crossed through the wide daisy archway to the treat side of the salon, grabbed two waters from the mini fridge, and flounced into the chair by the window. Savanna sat at the table. Across the street, Anthony had flipped the *CLOSED* sign on the flower shop door. She'd already called her students and canceled tonight's still life class. She was starting to wonder if she should cancel for good. But the people in her class seemed to really enjoy it.

They gazed out the window for a while in silence.

"Have you heard from Finn? How's Boulder?" Savanna asked.

"He says it's beautiful. He can see the Rocky Mountains from his sublease—the company puts him up in temporary housing, and it sounds like they try to find good places. He went rock climbing last night," she said. "I've always wanted to try that outside a gym."

"Y'know, do you think you'd ever want to take, like, a long weekend and go meet him on one of his assignments? It could be a lot of fun. I'd help Willow with the shop."

Sydney nodded. "I've thought about it. He wanted me to come to Phoenix. Thank you for the offer, but the shop isn't stopping me. Willow would be fine; I could schedule light for a day or two. Kate would help out too."

"Why don't you?"

Sydney pulled her legs up and sat with them criss-crossed in the comfy chair, elbows propped on the arm-rests. "I don't know. I know I'm super late to the party realizing this, but I think the reality of his job is hitting me. Hard. I can feel myself pulling back." She met Savanna's gaze, her forehead crinkled with worry.

"Oh, Syd. Don't do that."

"I don't want to!" Anguish filled her tone. "I'm trying not to. You and Skylar were right when you had your mini-intervention last year and made me see I have a habit of bailing before things get too serious. I do that. I know that now. But you know what? You were also right when you said this thing with me and Finn wouldn't end well. It can't. He's never in one place long enough, and I'm the definition of staying in one place." She spread her arms out, encompassing the salon. "I love it here. If I didn't, I wouldn't have opened a dog salon."

"I know," Savanna said. Her poor sister. Savanna had wished for Sydney to truly connect with someone someday, but she sure didn't envy her this dilemma. The issues with Finn were tough.

"Part of me is head over heels in love with him, and part of me wants him to stay in Boulder for good and never come back. Because I can't think straight when he's around, and I hate this feeling" —she clutched her stomach, grasping the cotton of her shirt—"when he's gone."

Savanna's eyes abruptly welled up. She covered her mouth with one hand, but it couldn't conceal her smile.

"What? What is wrong with you?"

She took her hand away and swallowed hard. She'd never seen Sydney like this. "Do you hear yourself?" Her voice was soft. She had no solutions, no words to help her figure out what to do. It was an odd feeling, her heart simultaneously swelling and breaking for her sister.

Sydney held Savanna's gaze. Her expression shifted with tangled emotions as she realized what she'd said. Sydney put her head in her hands. "Oh my God. What did I get myself into?"

———————————————

Sydney was in love with Finn. No wonder she hadn't recognized it—she'd never before felt this horrible and wonderful at once. All she knew was that she constantly wanted to be near him when he was here, and she had this crushing, hollowed-out feeling when he was gone.

After Savanna left, Uncle Freddie came to pick up Lady Bella and accidentally threw salt in her Finn-related wounds by innocently asking when the family would get to meet her boyfriend. He didn't mean to upset her, but it highlighted the problem. *When, indeed?* How had she fallen so hard and fast for someone she'd been warned about? Aidan had cautioned her, and so had Savanna: Finn was impulsive, unpredictable, never stayed anywhere long. Her boyfriend had come with a huge warning label, and she'd totally ignored it.

That night when she crawled under her fluffy comforter, she checked her phone one last time before she went to sleep. No call or text from Finn. He'd been calling every day after work, but tonight there'd been nothing.

Sydney believed in energy. She didn't believe in magic, exactly, but she strongly believed in energy and connections and signs. Maybe, hundreds of miles away in Boulder, Colorado, Finn was picking up on whatever energy she was emitting into the universe, and on some level he sensed her confusion and was allowing her space to process. She knew this was the kind of thing Skylar would probably laugh at, and Savanna might be curious about at first but would ultimately decide was just Sydney doing her woo-woo thing.

She set her phone on her bedside table, switched off her lamp, and tucked her arm back under the bedding. She was just floating off to sleep when her phone buzzed. She fumbled with it and saw it was a video call from the man in question. She should decline it and go to sleep. Her head would be clearer tomorrow morning. But she answered it, staying where she was under the blankets. "Hi."

"Hi, baby. I'm sorry I woke you up." His eyes were extra green in the dark of her bedroom.

"You didn't. How are you?"

He frowned, his face moving closer to the screen. "Are you sick?"

She laughed. Nice. "No. I was almost asleep. Do I look sick?"

"You look beautiful. I miss you."

"I wish you were here."

"Oh. Hey now. I will be tomorrow."

"What? Shut. Up." She sat up in bed. "Why?"

"Are you free around five?"

"Sure!" She was awake now. She opened her mouth to ask how long he'd be in town and then decided against it. She didn't want to know. Any answer he gave wouldn't be good enough.

His wide grin filled her screen. "Perfect."

Chapter Eighteen

S AVANNA SET OUT FOR A walk on the beach Saturday morning, Fonzie racing ahead of her as usual. After a while, they took the footpath from the dunes through the trees, emerging on the far end of lush, green Carson Park. Savanna and Fonzie headed across to where the gazebo and the proud, twelve-foot-tall statue of Jessamina Carson stood. Beyond the park was the beginning or end of Main Street, depending on your perspective. Around this time last year, Savanna had discovered Jessamina beheaded, with a spray-painted threat across the pedestal just before Carson's hard-won Art in the Park festival had kicked off. The beloved town landmark was now intact, thanks to the restoration team.

They were passing the playground area when Fonzie found Nolan playing on the jungle gym. Her nephew looked summery in his orange-and-white striped polo shirt and shorts, making Savanna yearn for her first summer in her house. She'd been making lists of flowers she wanted to plant in garden boxes on her deck, but she needed Uncle Max's advice before she got started with the project.

Savanna spotted Skylar a few yards away on a park

bench and joined her. "Nolan looks like he's feeling better."

"He and Travis are both doing a lot better. Your soup and Lego set helped perk Nolan up yesterday. No fever since Thursday night, so I thought some sun would be good for him."

Savanna had been thinking about Aidan's gift to her all week. She had a possible compromise...maybe Skylar would lend her objective opinion. "I think I know what I'm going to do about the boat slip."

"Really?"

"What if I told Aidan I accept the gift, but just that part of it?"

"What do you mean?" Skylar asked.

"Well, he bought the dock assignment for two years, and opened an account with Gus for whatever type of sailboat I want. Which sounds even crazier when I say it out loud," Savanna said, shaking her head and smiling.

"It's quite a gift," her sister agreed.

"What if I keep the slip but tell him he cannot buy me a boat? I mean, that's way too extravagant. You know the slip alone is an over-the-top birthday gift. And it gives me an excuse to start saving to get another sailboat like the one I gave up in Chicago."

Skylar nodded slowly. "I like that. I think he'll be okay with your solution. I miss Dad's sailboat—could you hurry and save so you can take me out on yours?"

Savanna laughed. "Sure, no problem." Her phone jingled beside her. She grabbed her hoodie off the park bench and pulled it from the pocket. "Hi, Uncle Max! How are you?"

Skylar watched her and listened, waiting, until she

hung up.

"He's coming over here—he's at Fancy Tails right now. He says he's got news. I wonder what's going on?" That reminded her. "Hey. I've been meaning to pick your brain about something."

"Sure, what is it?"

"Okay, just hypothetically, if the beneficiary of a life insurance policy is found guilty of murdering the insured person, what happens to the payout? Would the policy be voided? The killer couldn't get the payout, I assume?"

"Hypothetically, if the primary beneficiary is convicted of any involvement in the insured party's death, that only voids their right to receive the payout. But if there is a secondary or what's sometimes called a contingent beneficiary, that person would then receive the payout as long as they weren't also implicated in the insured party's death."

So Savanna had been right in her assumption. Though it still didn't clear anything up in terms of Anthony's or Rachel's or even Marcus's possible involvement in Libby's death. "Thank you."

They spotted Uncle Max walking past Jessamina toward them. Savanna waved and Fonzie ran over to him, prompting Nolan to follow suit.

Max caught Nolan and scooped him up. He carried him the rest of the way. "Well, hello, young sir! I see we're completely recovered and full of beans this morning."

Nolan pushed off Uncle Max's chest. "I only eat beans when Mama makes me."

Max chuckled and set him down, and the boy darted off toward the slide, blond hair flying and Fonzie at his heels.

Savanna scooted over for her uncle. "Sit. Tell us your news!"

"Libby won!"

"Oh, wow!"

"The Cry Violet took first place overall. Anthony got word from Rachel this morning. The judges were a little befuddled when Rachel couldn't explain how Libby had cultivated an extinct plant, but it didn't stop them from awarding it the placement it deserves. Rachel said they were captivated with the entry, and the Cry Violet will be on the cover of *Plant Life* next month."

"I'm so thrilled." Savanna hugged Max around the shoulders. "I suppose Libby's secret stays with us."

"Well," Uncle Max said, "not entirely. I showed Anthony the book you found. I offered to help him or Rachel try and raise another plant from the remaining seeds, but they're giving them to me. I'm so excited, love. I've already sent a message to an old colleague in London, and we're going to collaborate on how best to get them all to germinate. It might even be something one of the botany journals would be interested in."

"Nice!" Savanna smiled at him. "I think Libby would be happy knowing her work had an impact."

She stopped at Halle's Berries before heading home. The fresh farm stand was a staple of Carson's downtown and even busier on weekends than during the week. Savanna came away with homemade strawberry rhubarb jam, bright red radishes, and blackberries to pack for the picnic she and Aidan had planned this afternoon, and fresh asparagus and zucchini for Sunday dinner tomorrow. It was her turn to cook, and she was still working through her menu.

In her sunny kitchen, Savanna packed the picnic

basket she'd borrowed from Aidan. She'd told him it was her turn to plan their evening. She was taking him back to the secluded spot he'd found for a picnic date they'd had last year. That was the night she'd first felt that whatever was between them was solid, somehow intentional and magical at the same time. It was a strange combination of contentment and excitement, the same way she felt every time Aidan was close.

When her phone rang an hour before he was due to pick her up, an unwelcome sense of déjà vu accosted her. She answered his video call from her bedroom. She'd pinned her wavy auburn hair back on one side, and was in the middle of figuring out what to wear. She might go with what she had on: a wispy pink skirt that just brushed her knees and a black fitted top. "Hi, Aidan," she said, sitting in the window seat Harlan had built for her. She made her voice cheerful and pushed away the sudden worry that he was canceling.

Aidan's smile was only at half wattage, and he looked fatigued. Once again, he was in blue scrubs and surgical cap. "Hi there. I'm so sorry... I'm going to be late."

That wasn't so bad. "Okay, no big deal. I understand."

"I'm just out of an emergency surgery, but I need to hang out for a bit to make sure there are no issues. I should be there by seven, all right?"

"Sounds good. Really," she stressed. "If it's later than that, I'll know why. Don't worry."

He didn't react, and she thought their connection had frozen or dropped. Then she saw the subtle shift as his expression changed, his brow relaxed. "Thank you, Savanna. I'll see you soon."

The time flashed on her screen when they hung

up: five p.m. Sydney popped into her head. She'd probably just arrived at the small Lake Haven airport Finn had told her he was flying into. He'd shocked Savanna last night when he'd called her. Aidan had given him her number. He had an out-of-the-box idea for his date with Sydney, and wanted a restaurant recommendation in the area he was thinking of. Savanna had been happy to help. She was excited for her sister. She was sure she'd be thrilled with where Finn was taking her.

Aidan made it to her a little sooner than he'd planned. After she put the picnic basket in the back seat and sat in the front, she had him turn left at the end of her street onto the main road. She hadn't told him where they were going, and planned to navigate while he drove.

He turned south—the wrong direction. "We have a quick stop to make first." He glanced at her. "It won't take long."

"Okay." The only thing inside Carson limits to the south was the marina. "Aidan, I've been thinking a lot about your birthday gift to me. It's so unique and thoughtful…but much, much too generous. Seriously."

The muscle in his jaw pulsed. He kept his eyes on the road. "Don't refuse it, Savanna. I thought you'd love it."

She turned in her seat so she was facing him. "It was an amazing idea, and I do love it. I can keep part of it. I'd like to keep the slip for my future boat, okay? It's such an incredible gift, and it motivates me to get a boat again soon. I can still teach you to sail using the ones at Sweetwater. You just cannot buy me a sailboat."

He sighed. "I had a feeling you were going to say that."

"I'm sorry. I love the gift." She put a hand on his forearm, tanned from his early morning golf session with Uncle Freddie.

"Okay." He met her gaze briefly as he made the right turn into Carson Marina.

While they were here, they could reserve the little Catalina again for a sail later next week. She'd done the math, and if she set aside a portion of her paycheck every two weeks, she'd be able to get a small pre-owned sailboat within a year. Most of the inventory at Sweetwater Boats was used; it wouldn't be hard to find a nice one.

Aidan held out a hand to her, and they crossed the parking lot and headed toward the docks.

"Are we checking on the slip?" she asked.

He nodded. "I had Gus's guy install the dock ladder. I just want to take a quick look."

"I think they're still open," Savanna said, craning to see the front of Gus's shop as they approached. "You could stop and have him close that account while we're here."

"Yeah, I could do that," he said. His tone sounded strained. He must be upset, even though she'd tried to turn down the boat portion of his gift as compassionately as possible. He raised a hand in greeting as they walked by Sweetwater Boats.

Gus leaned in the doorway, leathery arms crossed on his chest. He nodded back and met Savanna's gaze.

"Hey, Gus, how are you?" she asked.

"Hey there, Miss Savanna. Dr. Gallager." His gravelly voice was low and quiet. An uncharacteristic grin broke his weather-worn features. "You two have a nice evening." He turned and went inside his shop.

"That was weird."

"Was it?"

Now she wondered whether possibly Aidan's emergency patient earlier today hadn't done well. But she hated to ask and completely ruin his mood. They turned down the row of docks that led to hers. When they got close enough, she saw why he was preoccupied. In slip 142 floated a gorgeous blue and white Catalina 355, a thirty-five-foot cruising yacht. She felt her jaw literally drop. She turned in what felt like slow motion and looked up at Aidan.

His gaze was on her. He'd been watching her reaction. That smile, the one that always got her straight in the heart, began at one corner of his mouth, hesitant. He raised his eyebrows when she still hadn't spoken. "Mad?"

She started to speak but nothing came out. She had no words. She shook her head once, briskly, to clear it. And looked again at the boat. And then again back at him. Everything about him was overwhelming. She finally found her voice. "Aidan. You can't keep doing this."

"Hold on," he said, squeezing her hand and then letting go. He pulled a white envelope from his back pocket and handed it to her. "I didn't buy you a boat. It's not just yours. I bought it for us."

"What? What is this?" *Holy wow.* What went on his head? Who just upped and bought a sailboat on a whim? When they couldn't even sail? She opened the envelope and silently scanned the official-looking document.

"Title of ownership. I didn't buy you a boat," he repeated. "This belongs to both of us." He pointed to where both their names were typed in the owner box on the form.

Savanna stared again at the beautiful Catalina.

"You bought a yacht. I mean, do you even... I can't believe you did this."

"All right. Let's go take a look." He stepped down onto the decking.

She took off her inappropriate-for-boating wedges off and followed him, barefooted. He stepped onto the boat, more easily this time than he had when they'd gone out on Gus's small Catalina sloop, and then steadied her as she climbed aboard.

The cockpit and deck gleamed. This was a much larger boat than she was used to sailing. Tipping her head up, she took in the mast and jib sheet, and noted there was even rigging for a spinnaker, the large, colorful sail that could be unfurled at the bow.

"I know it's big. But we really need this size for the lake; it's safer. We'll stick to days when the water's like glass, to start with, while you teach me." He motioned to her. "Check this out."

She went down the five steps after him into the cabin. Warm, highly polished mahogany and plenty of recessed lighting made the large space look clean and inviting. There was a complete kitchenette, a table with bench seating, two sleeping quarters—the works.

"And—come on!" He disappeared through the far set of doors, and she heard a clang. Following him, she saw he'd opened the hatch and was hoisting himself up through it, something she hadn't seen anyone do except for herself and her sisters on Harlan's boat when they were little.

She giggled, peering up at him through the open hatch that led out to the bow. "Oh my God, Aidan, you're ridiculous."

He leaned over and stuck a hand through, waiting.

She grabbed it, pushing off the hardwood as he helped her climb through.

She closed the hatch and straightened up. "I don't know what to say."

Aidan was already moving along the side decking. He hopped back down into the cockpit.

Two slips over, an older couple was cleaning up and tucking their boat in for the night. The woman waved to Savanna and Aidan. "Hi, neighbors!"

As naturally as if he'd been a sailor his whole life, Aidan waved back and called out, "Hi there! That's a great Pearson you've got. I've always admired that model."

"We love her," the man replied. "Yours must be new. Haven't noticed it here before."

Aidan nodded. "Secondhand new. But she's in good shape." He propped a hand on the large steering wheel at the stern. As *if!* As if he'd even know how to handle the wheel out on the water. He was crazy.

"Nice," the man said. "Heading out for a night sail?"

"Thinking about it! Looks like you just came in. How's the wind?"

Savanna was frozen near the starboard halyard, halfway between the bow and cockpit, staring bug-eyed at Aidan. If she didn't know better, she'd swear she'd never seen this man before.

"It's a little choppy—and will probably pick up even more. Watch yourselves out there," the woman answered.

"Will do," Aidan said.

The couple climbed onto their dock and headed toward the parking lot, carrying their things.

Savanna unfroze herself and joined Aidan in the

cockpit. "Who *are* you?" She grabbed a handful of his maritime-blue dress shirt with the shirt sleeves rolled up, the tiny white polka dots of the fabric lending him a nautical air. Here on his Catalina yacht. Wearing— she glanced down, realizing she hadn't even noticed them until now—brand-new Sperry boat shoes. Chatting with their new boating neighbors. "What in the world are you thinking?" She searched his face and couldn't help smiling. He looked like a kid, his expression was so joyful, and there was something else there. A hint of worry?

"So...you're not mad?"

She shook her head. "How could I be mad? You're so excited." She glanced over her shoulder, taking in the entirety of the surprise boat before turning back to him. "Look at this beauty."

His focus remained only on her. He held her gaze and slid an arm around her, the warmth of his hand on her back radiating through the thin silk and chiffon of her skirt. "Savanna. I'm so in love with you."

Her breath caught in her throat, and her neck and cheeks flushed hot. She reached up and wrapped her arms around him and kissed him, standing on tiptoe, her fingertips in his hair. When he loosened his hold on her, she kept one hand on each side of his neck near his jawline. "I love you too. Sometimes I think I conjured you from wishes and daydreams."

He smiled. "I'm glad you did."

***

Sydney arrived at Lake Haven Airfield a few minutes early and drove around the small complex until she found the parking area Finn had directed her to. Rather than wait in the car for him, as she had no idea whether his plane had landed yet or not, she got out and headed toward the triple-warehouse-sized blue hangar. She was almost to the hangar entrance when she spotted him coming around the corner of the building in his navy-blue Air Med Lifeteam jacket and aviators. They met in the middle. Sydney went to hug him, and he scooped her up, her feet leaving the ground as he kissed her.

He put her down, shades still on, and scrubbed a hand across his thick black hair. "Hot dang, Syd. I've missed you."

She reached up and took his sunglasses off. "Better. It seems like you've been gone a month."

"I know."

She peered past him and then over at the airport hangar. "Did you just get in? Should we go?"

He nodded. "We're leaving from here. Go grab your purse if you want it."

She frowned at him. "What do you mean? It's in my car—"

"We're not taking your car." He raised an eyebrow at her. "We've got other plans."

Sydney stared at him, startled. "Um. All right, be right back." She retrieved her purse and jacket and walked with Finn around toward the opposite side of the blue hangar, where a helicopter sat on the tarmac.

He kept walking, and when she didn't follow, he came back over to her, taking her hand. "Let's go."

"You're kidding, right?"

He shook his head. "Nope."

"Finn. I've never been in one of these. I've only ever

been on a plane once in my life. I know you do this all the time but…could we just drive?"

He grinned. "It'd take too long. I promise you'll be safe." He stood facing her, not letting go of her hand. "Trust me?"

She narrowed her eyes at him. "That's not fair. You know I do."

"Okay. How about this? It's up to you. We can take the Ultralight." He turned and made a sweeping gesture toward the helicopter. "Or we can drive to someplace closer. I really don't care. I'm just glad to be home with you for a minute."

Sydney hugged him impulsively. He'd said "glad to be *home*." She took a deep breath, staring past him at the chopper. "Let's do it. I might scream a little," she warned him. She wasn't afraid of heights, but sheesh, she was betting riding in one of these things would feel like being on a roller coaster.

Finn harnessed her into the passenger seat and had climbed in behind the controls before it hit her that *he* was the pilot.

She looked at him and tried to turn her body toward him in her seat, but her harness didn't allow it. "Wait! You're driving? Flying? I thought you said someone else flies you guys? When you're on the medevac flights?"

He nodded. "Right. But you know I have my pilot's license. I got it with my FP-C. I do fly some of the Air Med flights, depending on who's with us."

"Oh."

"Syd. I promise you're safe. Trust me."

"I do. Okay. I'm ready." She gripped the edges of her seat. It got loud, even through the headset Finn had placed over her ears. She felt the helicopter lift off the ground, and as they rose, her stomach did that weight-less swooping thing that happened when she went on the swings with Nolan. "Where are we going?" she shouted.

Finn's voice came through her headset at a normal level, and he squeezed her knee, making her look at him as he spoke. "Push this button to talk." He pointed on his own headset. He adjusted the small microphone in front of hers. "Go ahead and try it."

She pushed the button. "Where—oh, cool—where are we going?"

"We have a stop before dinner, but the restaurant is called Northpointe."

"Oh! That's the place out on the pier up near Sleeping…" Sydney smiled widely at him. "It's near Sleeping Bear Dunes. That's why we needed the helicopter?"

"It's about a forty-five-minute trip by air."

"Unbelievable," she murmured, without hitting the talk button. When Finn had called her last night to say he was flying in, she'd thought they'd have a rushed few hours at Giuseppe's and then the beach, or something similar. She hadn't imagined he'd make good on his promise to reschedule their trip. Finn might be un-predictable, but he was never unreliable.

After a good while running up the dunes and racing back down, taking in the elevated view of the lake, and then shaking the sand out of their clothes and hair, Finn secured them an Uber to Northpointe on the pier ten minutes farther north. Sydney ordered the wall-eye, and Finn got the New York strip steak. They were fortunate to be seated along the railing, facing west across Lake Michigan, far enough away from the live band to enjoy it but still easily talk.

After their table was cleared, Finn moved over next to her, resting an arm along the back of her chair. A light breeze lifted and dropped tendrils of Sydney's hair, and she brushed a piece off her face. The sun was on its slow descent into the lake on the horizon.

"I took a different job," Finn said. "Training."

She turned to look at him. "What does that mean?"

"It means I'll be working mainly for Anderson Memorial, and I'll be gone six days a month to train new flight paramedics for Air Med."

Sydney's eyes widened. "Really? You'll be here then, most of the time?"

He kissed her temple. "I'll be here."

"Oh!" She wrapped her fingers around his forearm, smiling at him.

Finn pushed his chair back and dropped to his knee in one smooth motion, pulling a small black box from his pocket.

Sydney gasped, one hand resting flat on the skin near her throat. She'd stopped breathing. She could hear her own heartbeat in her ears.

Finn gazed up at her. "I love you, Syd. I've never met anyone like you. And you see me in a way no one else does. If you'll let me, I—" He broke off at her reaction. He cupped a hand around the outside of her thigh, a calming gesture.

Her eyes burned with tears at his words. She fought against them spilling over and ducked her head down for a second, swallowing hard. When she met his gaze again, he continued, now smiling too.

"If you let me, I'll spend every single day trying to make you look this happy."

She couldn't speak. He was completely amazing.

He moved a little closer to her, his voice quieter. "You are happy, right? The tears shouldn't throw me?"

She laughed, tipping her head toward the sky and then focusing on him again and nodding.

"Will you marry me, Sydney?" He opened the box, revealing the most unique engagement ring she'd ever seen. A large, sparkling round diamond set in white gold was flanked by two small yellow-gold daisies.

She put a hand on his cheek, and he kissed her palm. Her voice came out in a whisper. "Yes."

Chapter Nineteen

S YDNEY SAID GOODBYE TO FINN early Sunday morning. They'd gotten back to the airport late, and pulled up to her house after midnight. Now, at barely seven a.m., she stood on her porch and leaned into him one last time, hardly able to believe last night was real. It'd be a month until she saw him again. It was still dark as he climbed into his cab. The car rolled down the street and her gaze caught the beautiful ring on her left hand. She went back inside and locked the door and crawled back under her plush comforter, pulling it over her head. She closed her eyes and ran her fingertip over the unique daisy engagement ring. The fact that Finn had found one with her favorite flowers didn't even surprise her. At this point, nothing about him would.

Sunday dinner tonight was going to be interesting.

She woke again with a start and sat straight up in bed. She'd heard a crash. Hadn't she? Sydney waited, but heard nothing else. Maybe she'd dreamed the noise.

She swung her feet out of bed and padded barefoot to the kitchen, looking around, but there was nothing amiss. She felt as if she'd slept hard for another couple of hours after Finn had left, but it had only been an hour. The sky was that pre-dawn shade of pink. She pulled a robe and slippers on, made a cup of coffee, and moved through her house, finding no sign of any disturbance. The crash she'd heard was still vivid in her head, but it must've been in her dream. Unless...

Sydney unlocked the connecting door to Fancy Tails and tentatively peered into the large grooming area that spanned the back of the salon. She flipped on the lights. All seemed fine. She moved through to the front of the shop and halted in her tracks by her desk. The scene Friday morning at Libby's was mirrored in her once-pretty customer waiting area. On the floor was a large red brick surrounded by a mass of shattered glass. The huge front window now had a gaping hole in the center. The brick had come through with such force it'd knocked over one of her red-and-chrome chairs.

Sydney flew to the front door and darted outside to the sidewalk, looking up and down Main Street. But she'd spent too long ambling through her house before checking the shop. Whoever had done this was long gone. Carson's Main Street was deserted at this hour on a Sunday. Across the street, the front of Libby's bore a wide piece of plywood where the window should be. Now Fancy Tails would have one too. She shuddered. This was no coincidence. She darted back into the shop, locked the door, turned out the lights, and locked the salon door behind her when she made it back to her own house.

In the time it took for her to throw clothes on and call Nick Jordan, her dad, Savanna, and Skylar, in that order, Sydney had time to come up with who could have done this. Her mind kept returning to two things.

Crabby old Miss Priscilla constantly glaring across the street at her, from the day they'd seen Marcus park his car at the curb to just the other day, when she and Savanna had gone to the police station to talk with Jordan. And Anthony Kent Friday morning. It was so odd the way he'd blurted, *Who threw a rock through my window?* And then when Jordan had seized on that and demanded he show him where he'd seen the rock, Libby's husband had backtracked.

What if this was a warning?

At Charlotte and Harlan's house, Savanna nearly wore a path back and forth between the kitchen island and the front window, waiting for Syd. She and Skylar had seen Sydney briefly this morning, in the chaos of Detectives Jordan and Taylor taking down what she'd heard and discovered while their evidence tech looked for any trace of the culprit, and Sydney asked questions about filing a claim under her lease to get the replacement window covered. Harlan had gotten there before the glass truck did and had already begun boarding up the window once Jordan had said he could. Sydney had remained cool and collected, hands in her pockets, nodding and answering everyone's questions calmly. Savanna had thought that either the yoga really was helping, or Sydney was in shock.

Aidan had answered that question. He'd surprised them by showing up even though Savanna hadn't called him. Finn had sent him. Aidan had checked Sydney's blood pressure and pulse and made her sit down with a glass of water. It wasn't quite good enough for

Harlan, who got Detective Jordan to promise to keep a patrol car assigned to her until they had answers.

Savanna tried to focus on the meal she was making for her family—sundried tomato wraps with turkey and avocado, cucumber slices, and her homemade dressing. A platter of fried zucchini and a vegetable medley salad was already on the table. She'd made a completely vegetarian wrap for Sydney, and her signature baked macaroni and cheese waited in the oven for Nolan and Mollie. Two weeks in a row of having Aidan and his daughter included for family dinner was becoming a nice habit.

Sydney poked her head into the kitchen from the patio. "Psssst! Savanna!" Her voice was a hissed whisper.

Savanna looked up. "Syd! Get in here, you weirdo."

"Are Mom and Dad around?"

"Not yet. What's wrong with you? Are you okay?" Savanna dropped the sandwich she was working on and crossed to the kitchen door. Jeez, her sister had her in a constant state of worry lately! She'd seemed so disproportionately fine this morning in the middle of her vandalized salon. Now she was trying to be sneaky about something?

Sydney came inside carrying a chubby, fuzzy yellow puppy in her arms.

Savanna squealed. "Oh, my goodness, what a baby! Whose is he? Are you grooming him?"

Sydney shook her head. "She's a girl. I don't know what to do with her. You know the Wilsons, right? They've been bringing their dogs to me since I opened. They're moving overseas and Daffodil just had puppies three months ago, and they've all been adopted except this one."

"Why?" Savanna put her face into the ultra-soft puppy fur around the sweet little dog's neck, and the dog paddled her floppy front paws on her arm. "Nobody wanted you?" Her gaze rose to Sydney's. "Oh, no. What did you do? Syd. What did you do? Didn't you say you don't have time for your own dog with the shop? Are you okay? For real, after this morning? Maybe you shouldn't make any snap decisions for a while."

Sydney tipped her head back and laughed. "Dude, I'm totally okay. Really. I'm great, I promise. I'm not worried about the window. Well, I mean, I'm worried, but now I've got a cop following me until you and Nick get a handle on this. I'm sure it's the same person who killed Libby. I'm betting on Miss Priscilla." They'd both agreed this morning that the dance instructor's behavior had gone from her usual rudeness to an uncomfortable level of animosity.

"I wish I knew. I'm not so sure. You didn't see the look Anthony shot at you when you jumped on him saying someone had thrown a rock through the glass. It's all connected somehow."

Sydney nodded. "That's what Nick says too."

"So...this little pup? Maybe now's not the best time for major changes?"

"I can't give her back."

"You can't? Why not?"

"I can't. I kind of told the Wilsons last week that I'd work on finding a home for her. I didn't mean I'd take her! They're moving literally tomorrow. Look at this face! How could I say no? I'm her only option."

Savanna scratched the puppy around her ears. "So you got a dog," she said. Fonzie was trying to climb up their legs to see what the fuss was about. Savanna reached down and gave him lots of pats too.

"I did not get a dog. I can't keep her. She's a golden retriever mixed with something else, and obviously super sweet. I thought maybe Skylar would take her? Nolan and Trav—"

Savanna's expression stopped Sydney's thought mid-sentence. "No."

"Why not? They've been trying to convince her for so long."

"She can't. This would put her over the edge. She's so overwhelmed right now with the new baby and everything else. She just cut back on her work hours and *oh my God, Sydney, what is this?*" She'd suddenly spotted the sparkling diamond on her sister's left hand, partially covered by the puppy in her arms. "Give me the dog." She took the puppy, cradling her, and made Sydney hold out her hand. "Is this what it looks like?"

Sydney met Savanna's gaze. "Yes," she said softly. "I think so, yes. Maybe."

"Oh, wow. 'Yes, maybe?' What does that mean?"

"Are we talking about Finn?"

Charlotte spoke from the doorway beyond the dining room, startling them. She must've come in the front door.

The both spun around, facing her. "Mom."

"Girls," Charlotte said, her focus now on the puppy who'd just come around the kitchen island behind Fonzie. "Did you adopt a puppy?"

"Oh! Shoot," Sydney said. "I'm sorry. This is, um. She's..." Syd looked helplessly at Savanna.

Savanna scooped up the animal and carried her to Charlotte. "She's a gift from Sydney to you and Dad. We know you've been thinking about getting a dog. Isn't she adorable?"

Charlotte petted her. "Oh, my. I don't know. We hadn't decided anything. She is sweet." She frowned at the dog. "Did you show your father yet? I'm leaving it up to him, and I don't think he's ready. Where did she come from?"

"I wanted to surprise you guys," Sydney said. "The Wilsons' dog Daffodil had puppies."

Charlotte moved to the refrigerator and took out a pitcher of iced tea. Her beige wrap dress and the tortoiseshell clip holding up her hair were accented with small gold hoop earrings and the necklace Harlan had gotten her for Christmas. "I thought they were moving, weren't they?"

"They're moving tomorrow. They couldn't find a home for their last puppy—the rest have been adopted. This little girl can't go with them."

"Ah. And if your dad says no?"

Sydney glanced at Savanna. "Then maybe Fonzie needs a sister?"

Savanna laughed. "Oh, no. I don't think so, sweet as she is." She bit her lip, eyes on Syd. She could hardly wait for her sister to share her big news.

Sydney took a deep breath. "Mom?"

Charlotte looked up from pouring three iced teas. "Hmm?"

Sydney sat on one of the stools at the island and pushed out the one next to her. "Come sit down."

Charlotte did, her expression concerned now.

Sydney opened her left hand, palm down, on the countertop between them, watching Charlotte's face.

Charlotte took in the ring, and then raised her eyes to Sydney. She slid her hand under Sydney's, folding her fingers around her daughter's, and looked again at the beautiful diamond-and-daisy ring. "My goodness. Finn certainly knows you. You said yes?"

Sydney pursed her lips, her brow furrowed. "Sort of."

Charlotte pulled her into a hug, and then let go and cupped Sydney's cheek in one hand. She shook her head. "I can't believe you're old enough for this. You were just a little girl not that long ago."

"Mom, I'm twenty-nine. I think I'm old enough," Sydney said, smiling.

"What does 'sort of' mean, honey?"

"I said yes. He took me on this whole whirlwind helicopter adventure last night and the way he proposed... the things he said to me... I said yes and I meant it. But he's making plans to live in Carson full-time and work through the hospital EMS. He'd only fly out a few days each month to train new flight paramedics. I don't know what to do. If I marry him, will he regret giving up working all over the country for me? Will he resent me?" Sydney stopped and took a breath. She looked at Savanna and then back at her mom. "Do you know how scary that possibility is? Maybe I shouldn't have said yes."

Charlotte was quiet, thinking. "I wish I'd had the benefit of meeting him by now."

"I know." Sydney hesitated. "Last Sunday couldn't be helped. And you and Dad not meeting him before that is completely on me. I could've set something up a long time ago."

"I don't recall you ever dating anyone for as long as you've been with Finn," Charlotte mused.

"He's not like anyone I've ever dated. He's different."

"You're different with him," Savanna finally spoke.

"You've had strong feelings for him since the beginning."

Charlotte raised her eyebrows at that. She turned on her stool and faced Sydney. "Let me ask you something. Imagine you tell Finn you've made a mistake, and you can't marry him. He flies out, and maybe you cross paths occasionally when he comes to Carson to visit his brother. Maybe you even remain friends somehow. How does that make you feel?"

Sydney had begun shaking her head halfway through Charlotte's hypothetical situation. Her hand was on her middle. "How do I feel imagining that? I feel sick. Everything you just said sounds like a nightmare." Sydney's mouth was drawn down in a grimace at the idea.

Charlotte nodded. "All right. Well, I know how he feels about you. He's willing to give up part of what makes him love his career because he wants a life here with you. You said he'd stay with that company for a few training assignments? I'd think that might help him adjust to being in one place, wouldn't it?"

Sydney nodded. "Probably."

"And now we know exactly how you feel about him. So, I don't see how you can say no. It doesn't sound like that'd be fair to either of you."

"Mom's right. Your first answer was the right one."

Sydney smiled at them. "You're both right. Okay."

Savanna let out a little scream. She grabbed her little sister by the shoulders. "You're getting married!"

"I'm getting married!" Sydney laughed. "Thank you. I'm so relieved—thank you for talking that through with me." She kissed her mom on the cheek.

Charlotte stood and hugged her. "You have two surprises now for your father."

"Oh, boy," Savanna said. The dogs were circling her legs in the excitement. She bent to hold Fonzie back "Fonzie, give the baby a break! They're playing so rough."

"Take them out in the yard," Charlotte said. "It's been a long time since we had a puppy, but I do remember how often they need to go out. Sydney, I don't want to put a damper on your day, but I hope you have a backup plan for that dog if your dad says no."

"Of course." She carried the puppy through the door to the patio, Savanna and Fonzie following.

"*Of course*," Savanna mimicked quietly. "Mom's being hardnosed, but you know she'll come around once Dad agrees."

"He's easy. I can convince him," Syd bragged.

"You have about a minute to figure out what you're going to say." Harlan turned into the driveway on his motorcycle and parked just past the police cruiser that had accompanied Sydney today. He stopped to talk with the officer sitting behind the wheel and then headed toward them.

He was accosted by the small yellow fluffball halfway across the grass. He bent to pet the puppy, and she flipped over, baring her belly, her whole body wiggling. Savanna and Sydney giggled, watching. Harlan straightened up and came toward them, laughing as the little dog chased at his heels, barking her cute, high-pitched puppy bark. "Sydney, that officer will be swapped out with an Officer Whitney for the night shift later. Just so you know. And I picked up the alarm system I mentioned for your house and shop. I'll install it tomorrow. Now, which one of you got a dog?"

"You did!" Sydney grabbed the pup mid-bark and

held her up against her chest, facing Harlan.

"Funny. No. I think we took that off the table for now."

Syd moved closer to her dad and held the puppy out to him. "I'm serious, though, if you could just think about it? Please? She's the last puppy from the Wilsons' dog, and they're moving. She doesn't really have any options." The puppy squirmed in Sydney's grasp, whining.

Harlan unwillingly took the little dog rather than leave her suspended in the air between them. She wormed her way up toward his neck and licked his chin. He frowned.

"You and Mom have been talking about getting another dog," Sydney said. "She's half Golden Retriever, and they think her dad was some kind of Lab. So she's a water dog. She'd love your boat," Syd said, trying her hardest to sell him on the idea.

"She sure loves you," Savanna said. "She didn't act that way with us."

The puppy had her nose tucked into Harlan's neck, her body stretched out along his chest, floppy feet dangling beyond his hand. She'd become instantly calmer when he'd taken her. He looked over his daughters' heads to the kitchen door, where Charlotte stood.

"I told them I didn't think so. It's your call," his wife said.

"Ah, make me the bad guy. Puppies are a lot of work. And we'd have to make sure we have the time to invest." He looked down at the puppy, not an easy feat with how closely she was snuggled into him. "She's sweet."

Charlotte came over to him and ran a hand over the dog's fur. "She's very sweet." She looked up at her husband. "What do you think?"

"We did talk about getting a dog who would go on the boat with us. We'll have to get the dog bed and crate down from the attic. And she'll need a name." Harlan exchanged looks with Charlotte. His eyes were bright. "Well. I guess it's about time."

Sydney forcefully hugged her dad. "Thank you. You won't regret it. I think she's going to be a good dog." Harlan hugged her back, and then began to move toward the house. She stopped him with a hand on his arm. "Dad. I need to tell you something, before everyone gets here. I'll tell them all, but I need you to know first."

"Sounds serious." He glanced at Charlotte, who slipped her arm through his.

"It is." Charlotte nodded at Sydney.

"Dad, Finn asked me to marry him, and I said yes." She paused, and then barreled forward. "He's changing his life for me. He'll be staying in Carson, working for Anderson Memorial, and he'll go train flight paramedics a few days a month for a big pay bump. And I'm sorry I haven't made an effort to bring him around, but I promise you'll like him when you meet him."

Savanna realized they were all hanging on Harlan's reaction; when he passed the puppy to Charlotte and grabbed Sydney in a bear hug, she finally took a breath. Harlan released his daughter and kept his big hands on her upper arms. "I want to meet him soon. This week. He makes you happy? He's a good man?" He looked over at Savanna for the last query.

Savanna nodded vehemently. "Yes, he is. He's a lot like Aidan, Dad. Syd and I figured that out recently." Finn and Aidan were both similar to Harlan in many ways, too. "You'll like him."

He nodded. "I'd better." He kissed the top of Sydney's

head. "Honey."

She looked up at her father.

"You're sure? Finn's the guy for you?"

Sydney nodded. "He is the guy. I'm sure. I—Daddy, I've never felt this way about anyone before. I promise you'll understand when you meet him."

Savanna followed her family into the house and saw her dad swipe at one eye with his thumb, clearing his throat.

Savanna set an enormous platter of halved wraps in the center of the dining room table next to the steaming baked mac and cheese casserole dish. Everyone was here except Ellie, who was, unfortunately, consumed with her exams. Uncle Max and Uncle Freddie were bringing her home later in the week for the dance recital.

Sydney stood and made her happy announcement to the family around the table, plus Aidan and Mollie. As she circulated to show off her beautiful, unique engagement ring, Aidan stood.

"Best news ever," he said. He hugged her, and she hugged him back, smiling. "My brother called me this morning before flying out. Sydney, I want you to know, I've never seen Finn the way he is now. I know I'm hard on him. But this past year, he's proven me wrong on multiple counts, and I'm glad. I told him the same. He's a very lucky guy, and I know he'll make a good husband to you."

Sydney's eyes filled with tears. "Thank you, Aidan. You have no idea how much that means to me."

When the sandwiches were gone, Savanna replaced the empty platter with the chocolate cake she'd spent the better part of the afternoon making. She set a fresh pot of coffee and vanilla ice cream out, for those so inclined.

Uncle Max spoke first, fork in mid-air. "Savanna. Oh, my. This is absolutely scrumptious."

"I agree. We'd have moved here years ago if we knew about your Sunday dinners," Uncle Freddie added.

Near the sink, Harlan stood up from playing with Fonzie and the new puppy. "These two need some room to run—I'm taking them outside. The pup needs a name, Syd."

"She's your dog; you'll have to come up with one," she said, smiling.

"I'm thinking Daisy," he said, winking at his youngest daughter. "Come on!" He held the kitchen door open, and the dogs sprinted out.

When Mollie and Nolan made motions to follow, Aidan stood, excusing himself. "I'll go help Harlan keep an eye on them." He looked down at Savanna, a hand on her shoulder. "All right?"

She squeezed his hand. "Thanks." She loved that he was going to hang out with her dad.

At the far end of the table, Uncle Freddie, Uncle Max, and Travis were engrossed in conversation about Freddie's Detroit project last year for the Modern Art Museum renovation. Uncle Max was detailing the botanical gardens he'd devised for the building's two courtyards, which led seamlessly into Travis asking if Max had any time to consult on a lakefront hotel his civil engineering firm was working on.

Savanna joined her mom and sisters at the opposite end of the table.

"I was sure I'd just dreamed the crash," Sydney said. "I wish I'd gotten out front fast enough to see who did it."

"Nick is sure this is all the same person," Savanna said. "Whoever killed Libby is not happy with us poking around. I can't help thinking it was a warning to you. Or us."

Skylar nodded. "I don't like how close to home this has gotten. What's next? Your house?" she asked Savanna. "Mine? The Blakes and Anthony and Rachel Kent and even that tap instructor Marcus can see when we're getting together and exactly how often we go talk to Nick at the precinct. We're making the killer nervous."

"Which is a terrible thing to do!" Charlotte said, looking at each of them in turn. "Please, can't you three step back and let the detective wrap this up?"

"We mostly are now," Savanna said in their defense. "But there are things he wouldn't have been able to learn without our help. All three of us."

Charlotte sighed. "I'd feel better if each of you had a police officer with you until this is over. I might call him and tell him that myself."

"Mom," Skylar said. "Let me do that. It's a good idea if we're really thinking Sydney's window is a warning. I'll call him tonight. We've got to stay safe—I've got kids in the house and Savanna's house is so secluded. We're all easy targets."

Charlotte squeezed Skylar's hand. "Thank you. If he won't do it, let us know. Your dad will talk to him."

That elicited chuckles from the sisters. "Don't sic Dad on him," Savanna said. "He doesn't deserve it. Listen, I dug up some things in public records through my friend Yvonne." Her mind raced; was it plausible the information she'd taken from Libby's file cabinet could also be a matter of public record? She hoped she wouldn't be getting Yvonne in trouble.

"What kind of details? What did you two find?" Sydney asked.

Skylar chimed in. "Did Nick say whether he ever talked to Fivell at the bank?"

"I'm not sure," Savanna said. "But I found the complaint of tax fraud filed against the dance school by Libby and Anthony Kent. That was what I called you about, Skylar, to ask about the lawsuit the Blakes were threatening against the Kents. It would've been for defamation of character or something like that, I think. I passed that all on to Nick. He was going to talk to Jillian Black at your firm about it."

"Wait a minute." Charlotte spoke. "What are you saying? The Blakes were going to sue the Kents? Why did the Kents accuse Priscilla and Dylan of tax fraud?" She shook her head. "I know things had been ugly between the two businesses for years, but not at that level. I'd thought it was all petty complaints over signs and things like that."

"That's what I thought too," Savanna said.

"About Libby's window, and now Sydney's," their mother continued. "Has Detective Jordan entertained the idea that Anthony did it himself?"

"Why would he do that to his own window?"

"To deflect guilt? If he thought Detective Jordan was leaning toward him as the killer, his own shop window being smashed in certainly takes the focus off him," Charlotte said.

"And if Anthony did kill Libby for the life insurance money, he'd be scrambling to lead the police to arrest someone who isn't him," Skylar added. "He can't collect on the policy until he's completely cleared as a suspect."

She stood with Hannah and began pacing; the baby was fussy and rubbing her eyes.

Savanna spoke. "We know Anthony was stressed about money. I'd heard through the grapevine that his meltdown in the bank that day was because his investment account was nearly gone. He was worried about the flower shop's mortgage payments and Rachel's tuition," she said, summing up the letter to his financial advisor.

"It's a good theory," Sydney agreed. "But Savvy, did you tell Nick about Marcus living in the building and his black eye right after Libby's body was found?"

She nodded. "I did. He had access, living there, and if Rachel told him about the policy, he'd know that if he could somehow frame her father for murder, the money would all go to her—to the two of them, he was probably thinking. It's pretty apparent the Kents did *not* like Marcus Valentine. My guess is the feeling was mutual."

"Is that why Rachel got called in for questioning?" Uncle Max asked, moving over to Skylar and joining the conversation. He held his arms out for the baby. "Give her to me."

She handed a cranky, sleepy Hannah to him. He cradled her, lightly patting her back, and made a slight side-to-side swaying motion. The baby instantly quieted, her eyelids drooping.

"Like magic," Skylar marveled.

"Yes," Savanna said, answering Max's question. "Nick talked to Rachel because he's looking closely at Valentine. Rachel is Valentine's alibi, which Nick considered iffy. But Rachel truly didn't seem to know about the life insurance policy."

Charlotte stood and began clearing dishes, carrying

them to the sink. Harlan got up and helped.

"There's one more thing," Savanna said. "If we're thinking the murderer smashed the window for the same reason they killed Libby, then maybe the Blakes make the most sense. Revenge over the tax fraud claim, or more likely, because they'd tried to buy the flower shop twice in the last six years, and Libby was the reason the sale didn't go through."

Chapter Twenty

EVERYONE IN THE ROOM WAS now tuned in to Savanna, including Uncle Freddie and Travis, who'd only been half listening before.

Savanna continued. "I talked to my real estate agent at Carson Community Homes. Mike was the one who wrote the purchase agreement. Libby's Blooms was never on the market, but that didn't stop Dylan and Priscilla from making an offer on it. The latest instance was two years ago. Mike said he sat down with Dylan Blake and Anthony Kent to go over paperwork. It's only missing Libby's signature. With all the bad blood between them, I didn't quite believe Anthony would've signed, but the Blakes' offer was way over market value. Mike said it was ridiculously generous. A follow-up meeting was set to include Libby, but it never happened. He never learned why, just that the Kents weren't selling."

"Would the Blakes kill Libby to get the shop?" Sydney asked the room.

"And the parking?" Savanna added.

Sydney looked at Charlotte. "Mom? You've known all of them longer than all of us."

Charlotte frowned, considering, a plate in each hand. "I'm sorry. I can't get this to make sense, the idea that Priscilla getting more parking space for her dance school was worth Libby's life. I honestly cannot imagine Anthony as a murderer, or Rachel. I don't know this Marcus Valentine, but he sounds young and in love with Rachel. Killing his girlfriend's mother for money, even if it was for the two of them, is extreme."

Savanna sighed and nodded. "I know."

"I know that isn't helpful. I'm sorry," Charlotte repeated. She set the plates down and moved closer to the group at the table. "Honestly, I don't like any of you being involved in this. I'm also not thrilled about my brother-in-law risking his life working in this environment—I can't imagine you're comfortable with this, either?" She appealed to Freddie, who was already nodding.

"Max," Freddie said, moving to stand beside him and resting a hand on his shoulder, "you'd told me about the window, but it seems like there's a dangerous undercurrent of continued risk. I'd feel better if you'd take some time off. Just until this all gets settled."

Max looked up at his husband. "I'll think about it. I don't mean to worry you. But that would leave the shop with no one, and it'd be quite unfair to Anthony and Rachel. Not to mention the plants. That shop was Libby's life." He took Freddie's hand and held it between his. "I haven't felt unsafe for a moment, I promise you."

Savanna couldn't help feeling responsible for at least some of the worry in the room. "Listen, I'm pretty sure this will all be wrapped up in a couple of days. I have a plan I'm going to talk to Nick about tomorrow. I think it'll help flush out the guilty party. And all it involves is having a cup of coffee. Detective Jordan will be right there with me. You can't get safer than that. *And,*" she added, "I'll go into the precinct through the rear entrance tomorrow to present my plan. I never have to hit Main Street. No one will know I'm going to talk to him."

Seeing her mother wasn't satisfied, Savanna spelled out her idea. She was a little relieved Aidan was outside with her dad. Charlotte wasn't exactly on board, but it couldn't be helped. Savanna had a feeling Uncle Max's promise to "think about" taking time off was also simply an empty appeasement.

The family was treated to a preview of Mollie's and Nolan's recital numbers on the patio before they separated for the evening. Mollie performed a tapless tap dance while Aidan played the music through an app on his phone, and then Nolan recited his lines—the ones he remembered—from the drama skit he'd been rehearsing. Their enthusiasm for the upcoming show was infectious.

***

Savanna mentally ran through her role one last time Tuesday morning. She was nestled in the big aqua chair in front of the window at Fancy Tails a few minutes before eight a.m., when she was set to meet Detective Jordan.

Sydney spoke from the gourmet treat counter where she was restocking pupcakes. "Okay, so you and Nick are going to grab a table at the coffee shop—"

"Near the register. We need to be close enough to where they take the orders."

"Right," Syd said. "You'll be at a table near checkout, having coffee, when Dylan Blake makes his eight fifteen morning coffee run. Which I still find a little creepy that you've kept track of, just so you know. I mean, we were all kind of kidding last week about watching everyone from my window."

"I wasn't kidding," Savanna said.

"Again. Creepy. So you and Nick will be talking about the case? About Libby or the broken window or something like that?"

"Yes, but more importantly, I'm going to have these folders here," Savanna said, tapping the set of dummy file folders she'd created, "on our table." She'd made sure to use large, dark block lettering on the front of each to write a word or two summarizing each folder's "contents."

Sydney came over to the nook by the window, reading them aloud. "Lawsuit, Purchase Offer, Financials, Life Insurance."

"Nice! What's in them?" Sydney flipped open the *PURCHASE OFFER* folder. "Oh! How did you get these?"

Savanna grinned. "They're fake! But you looked right at them and thought they were real. I typed a made-up address and printed them from a real estate website. I even thought about trying to whip out my mirrored compact at some point, to keep an eye on him at the counter, but that might be too obvious."

Sydney laughed. "Nice! Like you're a spy on a covert mission."

"Well, I kind of am, right?"

"Do you have a backup plan in case Miss Priscilla doesn't send her husband for coffee this morning? Skylar said dress rehearsals start this afternoon. What if their schedule's different today?"

"Don't jinx me!"

Sydney looked over her shoulder at the wall clock.

"Eight o'clock. Don't you have to go?"

Savanna stood and gathered her things from the table. "Wish me luck!" She walked the half block to the coffeehouse and was pleased to find Detective Jordan already seated near the register. She took the chair opposite him and fanned out the folders on the small table. Then, scrutinizing them, she messed them up a little, moving them around. Then changed her mind and stacked them neatly. They had to look authentic. Maybe messy was better? Was this too obvious a set-up? Savanna's mouth was suddenly too dry.

"Savanna," Jordan said. He put a hand on the folders. "Sit back, take a breath. Here's your coffee." He pushed a cup over to her.

"Sorry." She took a sip and grimaced. It might as well be black. He'd added the tiniest amount of cream and no sugar.

"I've no idea how you take your coffee. Apparently not like that," he said, smiling.

"It's fine, thank you. What time is it?"

"We've still got about ten minutes." He jerked his head in the direction of the cream-and-sugar station at the end of the counter. "Go fix your coffee. Don't rush. We're fine."

Jordan's calm did nothing to settle Savanna's nerves. She went quickly to the counter and added three sugars, her hands trembling enough to scatter sugar granules all over the granite. She didn't trust herself to pour the cream. She was back in her chair in a flash. She leaned across the table, keeping her voice low. "Have you thought about what we should talk about while he's in here? We can't rely only on him looking at the folders."

The detective sat back in his chair and crossed his legs. "Listen, this was a great idea. Really. But you have got to relax. If you telegraph the body language of someone who's being sneaky or furtive, with nervous movements and speech, this won't work. It'll have been a waste of time, and worse, we'll have trashed our one shot at using what we know to learn more. This negates any chance of me using the same type of information to interrogate him in a conventional setting."

Oh, for the love of Pete! Savanna swallowed hard and bugged her eyes out at him. She began to speak and then stopped, mirroring his actions. She sat back in her chair and picked up her coffee. She narrowed her eyes at Nick Jordan and spoke severely. "Everything you've just told me makes me a thousand times more nervous. So thanks for that."

Jordan raised his eyebrows in surprise, saying nothing.

Oof. She'd have to apologize for her tone later; she never spoke to anyone that way. "I'll be fine. It's fine. I want this to go well, the same as you," she said, mindful of her voice.

"I'm going to ask you some questions. All you need to do is answer them. That's it. Okay?"

"That'll work? But he'll be unable to hear us at least part of the time he's in here." She hoped the detective knew what he was doing. She'd imagined they'd talk about complaints being filed, lawsuits, life insurance—subjects with key words Dylan Blake would hear.

"It'll work." He moved the folders about on the tabletop, making it appear as if they'd been going through them. He pulled the edge of a page out the bottom of one and turned another to face himself instead of Savanna.

She reached to nudge some pages from another one, and he put a hand out, palm down in the air over their table. "All good." He pulled a pen and small notebook from inside his jacket and flipped the notebook open to a page that already had something written on it.

She focused on the chalkboard on the wall behind Jordan, reading the price list for the specialty drinks.

Jordan cleared his throat. "Showtime." He sat forward, elbows on the table, and Savanna did the same. He waited, timing his first question. As Dylan Blake crossed her peripheral vision, approaching the register, Jordan asked, "Can you prove what you're telling me?"

She frowned at first, and then understood what he was doing. "Yes, I can. Let me show you." She opened the first file folder and turned it around to face Detective Jordan, pointing at the middle of the first piece of paper. "This part goes over the property details for Libby's Blooms."

"I see," Jordan said. He clicked his pen and jotted something illegible down in his notepad. "What about this?" He pulled a page from behind the first one.

Now Blake was directly behind Jordan and in Savanna's line of sight, a few feet from their table.

With the ambient noise in the coffee shop, Savanna could only hear words and snippets of conversation from those around her, even from the two women at the next table over. Jordan must be figuring an occasional meaningful word or phrase would float to Blake's ears.

Savanna spoke up. "That's the purchase agreement Mike told me about."

"Interesting." He flipped the folder closed and reached for another one. "And these are the files on the Kents' finances?"

"That's right. I know they used a financial advisor to invest their money."

Jordan flipped through the papers in the open folder, stopping to write down a few things. "Now as far as the investment losses, do you have something that covers that?"

"Yes," she said, pointing at nothing on the lines of text in front of him. "There's some information right here. And you know about the complaint they filed, right?"

"What complaint do you mean? There have been dozens through the years."

Blake paid using a card, and should've stepped to the end of the counter to wait for his order, but instead he only moved a few feet down. He stooped and looked into the biscotti-and-scone case. His normally handsome profile was skewed by the grimace on his lips, his jaw set forward. Blake's brow was furrowed, and his body appeared rigid as he stood quite still. He had to be listening.

"The one to the IRS—there's paperwork in here going over the details." Savanna passed the detective another folder.

He made a good show of perusing the dummy documents in the folder. "Do you know if there was any legal action taken?"

"There was, actually. It's toward the back," she said, reaching across and pointing. "It's on letterhead from Black, Jones, and Sydowski, the law firm down the street."

"And all of this happened in the last several months, you said?" Jordan pulled a page from the back of the folder and set it down, picking up his pen again and jotting several lines of scrawled cursive in his note-book. "Good, very good," he said as he wrote.

Now the next customer had paid, and Dylan Blake was forced to move to the end of the counter, where Savanna couldn't see him well without making it obvious.

Jordan sorted the folders into a neat stack on the table between them. "This was very helpful. And I can keep these? Your information should lead us in the right direction. I appreciate you coming to me."

A splash of yellow and blue registered in Savanna's peripheral vision as Dylan Blake's name was called for his coffee, and he took it and left.

"He's gone," Jordan confirmed. "I hope he caught enough of that. You did great!"

She finally relaxed; she'd been sitting with all her muscles tensed and not even realizing it. "Really? Thank you. I couldn't see him most of the time. How did he look when he left?"

"Hard to say. But if he's got anything to hide, I'm sure we'll know."

She nodded. "Good. All right, I've got to get to school before I'm late."

Jordan checked his watch. "It's eight twenty-two."

"What? Oh, wow. That was stressful. Seven minutes from when he arrived? It felt like an hour," she said, laughing at herself.

She and Jordan walked together as far as Savanna's car, parked in front of Fancy Tails. As she watched the detective cross the street and head toward the precinct, she had a stroke of genius. Or at least a decent idea; she wouldn't know until she tried it. She knocked on Fancy Tails until her sister let her in. The salon was still closed.

"Did it go okay?"

"It went great. Give me your glasses."

"What? Why?"

"I'll bring them back. You don't need them right now, anyway—you aren't driving anywhere."

Syd moved to her purse and handed her glasses over. Savanna piled her hair into a messy topknot and grabbed the rust-colored chiffon scarf off her sister's desk, tying it around her hair like a headband. "How do I look?"

"Um. Like Savanna in a scarf and glasses."

She groaned. "I'm working on an idea and I only have a few minutes before I have to run to school. I need something...do you have any obnoxious lipstick in your purse? Or eyeliner, maybe?"

Syd darted to her desk and turned her purse upside down. "Yes! Ooh, this color looks awful on me. You can keep it. Here."

Savanna used the dark magenta lipstick and then stood in front of Sydney while she drew dark brown eyeliner in wide rims around her eyes.

Syd stepped back, appraising her. "Not bad. Not so much Savanna anymore."

"I'm hoping Marcus Valentine doesn't pay much attention to the parents in the lobby. I don't think he'll have a clue who I am."

"Okay, I have no idea what you're up to, but none of this works if he watches you walk back across the street afterward and get into your car that you park in front of my shop almost every single day. Give me your keys, and I'll put it out back."

Breathless now, Savanna stood in front of the *Owners / Occupants Only* door between Libby's Blooms and

Priscilla's Dance Academy. The stairway through the window was empty. Before she could lose her nerve, she pushed the buzzer for apartment 202. She waited. A minute. Two whole minutes. She pushed it again. This was Marcus Valentine's apartment, she was positive. When she'd run into his neighbor Brianna that day up on the second floor, she'd been in the hallway with apartments 201 and 202, and 201 had a cute bunny and duckling Easter wreath on the door. She didn't know Marcus Valentine at all, but she was betting her entire plan that he was in 202.

The speaker on the intercom crackled with a man's voice. "Hello?"

Savanna tried her hardest to sound like she was breaking up, leaving gaps between a few words. "I— dropping—there?" It had happened all the time in her Chicago apartment; the intercom had constantly been in need of repair. She stared at the speaker expectantly.

"I can't hear you. Who is this?"

"Sorry—documents—promised—morning." She clutched the folders in one hand and rocked back on her heels, looking up and down Main Street. It was still pretty quiet this early in the morning. She wasn't at-tracting any unwanted attention.

"Hold on, I'm coming down." He sounded irritated.

She'd woken him up. Marcus descended the stairs in bare feet and pajama pants, pulling a T-shirt over his head on the way down, and pushed the door open. "Hi. The intercom must be broken." He tapped it.

"I'm so sorry. Now I'm not sure I have the right ad-dress? Is this not 3705?" She took two steps backward to look up at the building and purposely stumbled, opening her fingers and letting the folders fly out of her hand.

She and Valentine watched the papers drift to the sidewalk. He bent to help Savanna gather them up as she did her best to flip the folders face up with the block lettering visible. "I can't believe I did that," she said.

"This building is 3695," he said. "You probably want the law office next door." He stood up and pointed east.

"Yes! That's exactly what I was trying to find. And I've mixed up all the Kents' important files now," she said, smacking her own forehead. She stacked the file folders in the crook of her arm and looked at the young man. She so wished Nick Jordan had told her what he'd found out about him, why he was living in Carson. She'd hoped to push him, if he was responsible for Libby's death. Maybe he'd see her files and start worrying he'd been found out. What safer place to prod a potential killer than in public in broad daylight?

But Valentine didn't appear bothered. "Good luck." He went back inside and upstairs. The only drawback to both of her plans this morning was the lack of instant gratification. It wouldn't be apparent until sometime later today or maybe tomorrow whether she'd struck a sensitive nerve with a murderer. Now they'd have to wait and watch.

Savanna hurried around the block to the back of Fancy Tails, where Sydney had left her keys on the front seat of her car. She took the glasses and scarf off and headed to school with a few minutes to spare. She'd completely forgotten about her dramatic new eyeliner look until Elaina Jenson gave her the strangest stare when she delivered her students to Savanna.

Savanna sat beside Aidan in the darkened auditorium of Carson High School, waiting for Mollie's ballet number. There were still several ahead of her, and then her tap dance was nine songs after that, plenty of time to change costumes. Dress rehearsal ran for two days, with a one-day break before the recital this Friday. When Aidan had asked if she had any interest in coming with him tonight, she'd immediately said yes. She fondly remembered her dancing days, and all the magical excitement surrounding rehearsal and the spring recital. Plus she needed an excuse to keep an eye on the Blakes and Marcus Valentine.

In the large holding area backstage, she'd carefully styled Mollie's fine blond hair into a bun, using dabs of hair gel when the silky strands wouldn't stop slipping through her fingertips. She'd finally gotten it perfectly centered, with most of the fly-aways tucked into bobby pins, then told Mollie to hold her breath while she'd spritzed it with hairspray before sending her over to her group—a dozen or so children around her age, wearing sparkly, poufy pink ballet costumes with springy tutus.

Aidan had arrived before her and snagged them seats dead center in front of the stage, in the sixth row, which, he told Savanna, was the perfect distance from the stage for pictures and video—far enough away to be able to see the full dance, including the feet, but close enough to see detail. In full dad-mode tonight, his camcorder was on a tripod in front of him and his camera was ready for still shots. Photos and video weren't allowed in the auditorium during the recital, only in rehearsal. She could see he'd done this before.

She hadn't shared with him her ulterior motive for wanting to come to dress rehearsal tonight, but she needed to know if her and Jordan's ploy this morning had had any effect at all. Now, as the jazz instructor helped her students find their marks onstage, Miss Priscilla was visible in the wings at stage left, talking with her husband. With the dim lighting, it was impossible to get a feel for their interaction.

Five or six songs later, Mollie's group came onstage. Aidan went to work filming and snapping photos, while Savanna had the pleasure of sitting back and enjoying the dance. Miss Priscilla returned to the stage to give them notes, reminding them the most important thing to do was to smile. Savanna leaned over and offered again to operate the camcorder or camera, but Aidan declined. He turned to her. "Look how great she did on just the first run-through!"

She nodded. "She's very focused, you can tell. And she had the biggest smile up there."

While they waited for Mollie to come back to them in the auditorium after the ballet dance was over, Savanna scanned the instructors in the front row for Marcus Valentine. Maybe he was running late? According to the program, Mollie's tap rehearsal was another six songs—or about a half hour—from now.

When Miss Priscilla took center stage a few numbers later to announce that Mr. Marcus had had an emergency come up and all remaining tap numbers would be postponed to Wednesday instead of today, Savanna was only mildly surprised. The parents in the row ahead of her put their heads together and consulted the program with the light from their phones.

Savanna leaned forward. "Excuse me. What happened to Mr. Marcus, do you know?"

The woman who always sat across from Savanna in the lobby during tap classes turned to reply. Her little boy, Andy or Alex or something like that, was in Mollie's class. "No," the woman said. "He was here earlier, but he left a few numbers ago."

Outside the high school in the cool evening air, Savanna congratulated Mollie on a beautiful job well done. She parted ways with Aidan and his daughter, with the plan to meet them here tomorrow to watch Mollie's tap number.

It was dark by the time Savanna pulled into her driveway. Coming through her front door, she found it was unlocked. She must've forgotten to lock it. Her dad would be so upset with her if he knew.

She whistled for Fonzie. Then she hung her sweater and car keys on their hooks, dropped the tote of projects she had to grade, and sank into her plush couch by the front window. She hadn't realized how tired she was until just now. When she called Fonzie's name again, she heard yelping and scratching coming from the bathroom.

Had she accidentally closed him in there after work today, when she'd been rushing to get to the auditorium? Poor dog! "Fonzie, I'm so sorry, buddy," she called. She hurried down the hallway and flung the bathroom door open. The little dog catapulted out onto the hardwood, his feet skittering and clacking as he barked and whined at her, pawing at her legs. Savanna bent and scooped him up, hugging him. "It's okay! I can't believe I locked you in there!" He leaped out of her arms and raced toward the kitchen. *Sheesh.* He must need to go out.

She moved down the hallway and halted abruptly in the doorway to her kitchen. Every cabinet and drawer stood open.

A quick glance over at the dining room confirmed someone had been—or was still—in her house.

Chapter Twenty-One

P ANICKED AND WIDE-EYED, SAVANNA GRABBED
the closest thing to her—a metal soup ladle.
Fonzie was barking at the back door off the
kitchen. Savanna darted to the knife block by the
sink and swapped her soup ladle for a butcher's knife,
though she didn't know what she thought she'd do
with it if it came to that. She was terrified.

She stood for a second in the double doorway between her kitchen and dining room, her heart pounding, and looked around, taking in as much of her small
house as possible from that vantage point. The stairs
to the bedrooms, the hallway where she'd just been, the
door to the basement. What if the person—or persons—
were still in here?

Fonzie slid into her legs. He'd run over to her, barking, and now scurried back through the kitchen to the
back door, where he dug at the tile, whining. Sucking
in air, her heart racing, Savanna followed him. She was
accosted by a strong scent right by the back door and
shook her head, bringing the back of her hand with the
knife in it up to her nose.

When she opened the door, the little Boston Terrier
took off across the yard, barking. Savanna chased him

in the dark, around the corner of her house, and spotted a figure running toward a truck she hadn't noticed parked down the street from her driveway.

"Fonzie!" Her frantic scream to get her dog out of the way of the truck hurt her own ears. The dog reversed and came back, and Savanna sprinted back inside through the open back door, snatched her keys from the hook, and went out the front. Fonzie was on the passenger seat the moment she yanked her car door open. She threw the car in reverse and hit Detective Jordan's name on her phone as she pulled out of her driveway. She could barely glimpse one dim red taillight way down the road. He picked up on the second ring.

"Someone was in my house!"

The detective's voice came through her Bluetooth. "Right now? Stay on with me." She heard him talking to someone else but couldn't hear what he was saying.

"No! Someone was in my house and they ran out and they're speeding down my street and I'm behind them but I can't see the plate yet and it looks like they've got a burned-out taillight—"

"Savanna, no!" His typically calm tone was gone. "Pull over. I don't want you involved in a chase. Cars are on the way to you right now. So am I."

Then it hit her. The smell, it was still in her nostrils; that stinging, overly strong evergreen-and-musk combination. "It was Dylan Blake. Just him, or maybe both of them, I don't know. They broke into my house and went through my things. I can still see the truck—it's turning onto the highway now."

"Which direction?" His police radio crackled in the background.

"South."

"All right, pull over. Now." He issued the order again. "How do you know it was the Blakes?"

"Dylan Blake was in the house. His cologne. I've noticed it before in the dance school. Maybe you have too—Oh!" Fonzie tumbled onto the passenger side floor as she took the same turn the truck just had. "Come on, boy, I'm sorry!" Once he'd climbed back up, she fumbled around one-handed and attached his safety harness on the front seat. She was relieved she could still see the single taillight far ahead of her on the two-lane highway.

"Why does it still sound like you're moving?" Jordan's voice came through the speaker.

"I can't stop now. Your guys will never find him! What happens if you don't catch him fleeing from my house? He can just deny he was there!"

"That's not necessarily true. I'm a mile from your street, and the patrol cars I sent are a little ahead of me. You'll see us in a minute."

The truck disappeared from sight. "No! What—" Savanna squinted into the darkness and flipped on her high beams. It had to have turned. She slowed, head whipping to the right as she passed Sandpiper Avenue, Warbler Way, Lighthouse Lane...a single taillight was visible in the distance on Lighthouse Lane. Savanna pulled onto the shoulder and reversed all the way back to the street, gravel kicking up as she took that turn.

"Lighthouse Lane. They turned again." She heard sirens in the distance. Lighthouse Lane was the long, winding dirt road that ran right along the water, curving around areas of century-old trees and through hilly ups and downs. The sirens quieted the farther she followed the truck, and then the red taillight in front of her blinked out. "I lost it again! What the heck?" She kept going, squinting into the dark.

In her rearview mirror, she saw the truck pull out from a stand of trees and take off the way she'd just come, tires squealing.

"They're coming back toward the highway!" She took the scenic pullout on her right and turned around, getting back on the road.

"Savanna, stop pursuing now!" Nick Jordan barked. She heard the crackle of his police radio and then him citing some numbers.

She couldn't see the taillight anymore from the curving portion of road she was on. She wasn't purposely disobeying Jordan. She wasn't exactly pursuing, was she? She had no way of pulling anyone over, and in her little car, it was no wonder she kept almost losing the truck.

She came around the next bend in the road and stomped on her brakes, wrestling with the steering wheel to keep control on the dirt road. The truck was blocking the road a hundred yards ahead. She heard the gunshot at the same time she registered the dark figure in the driver's seat sticking his arm out his window and aiming at her. Dirt and rocks just outside her door exploded in a cloud around her, and she screamed and threw her car in reverse, slamming her foot down on the gas pedal.

"Savanna! Are you okay? What was that?" More police radio crackling just behind Jordan's questions to her.

The back end of her car fishtailed, and she worked to stay on the road. Driving backward was awful! Why did it always look so easy in the movies? Another gun-shot sounded, and then a deafening metal clang as the speed limit sign she'd just passed went down, and she shrieked again, picking up speed and trying to avoid skidding toward the ravine. There was a side street fast approaching; she could attempt to turn around to get away from him, but it'd slow her down. Through her windshield, the Blakes' truck barreled toward her.

Red and blue lights were right behind it, sirens wailing. Savanna made the snap decision to keep go-ing backward rather than chance turning around. The truck would catch her if she tried. More gunshots broke the siren-filled air. Savanna ducked down as much as possible and saw the truck go into a wild spin, three of its four tires shredded, and two police cruisers plus Jordan's sedan surrounding it as it rocked over on one side and then finally slid to a stop.

Savanna hit her brakes, breathing hard, her pulse pounding in her throat and her hands suddenly damp and clammy on the wheel. She sat, unmoving, as five officers converged on the truck and pulled the figure out of the driver's side. Shouts joined the sirens, and then Dylan Blake, hands cuffed behind his back, was escorted into the back of a police cruiser.

Savanna became aware of Fonzie's cold nose on her arm, nudging her and whining. She started to turn to-ward him, and the car lurched backward, still in re-verse. She slammed it into park, then unwrapped her fingers from the death grip she'd had on the steering wheel and tried to take slow, deep breaths. She rolled her window down for Nick Jordan.

He bent and peered in at her. "You're not hit?"

She shook her head, but then looked down, patting

herself, making sure she was fine. She ran her hands over Fonzie's wiggling frame too just to make sure. "No, I'm all right. Oh my God." She burst into tears. Her effort at calm and slow, steady deep breaths was futile. Adrenaline still coursed through her; it had to be why she was still so shaky and breathless and now sobbing after the fact. Embarrassed in front of the detective, she swiped at her eyes with a trembling hand. "Sheesh. I'm fine. For real. I'm fine," she said, the last time to herself. She really was, despite all that had just happened.

Jordan opened her car door as an ambulance pulled onto the scene. The vehicle stopped near the cluster of police cruisers and Blake's truck, and paramedics walked over to her car. Detective Jordan waited with her. She looked up at him.

"I'm really okay. You didn't need to call them."

"They were already on the way—standard procedure with shots fired. Let 'em check you out. Then I'll drive you home in your car." He frowned at her, his jaw set, almost like a challenge.

She didn't argue. "Thank you."

Miraculously, Savanna's car was unharmed, and Savanna checked out well too. Her blood pressure was close enough to normal that the two medics were comfortable letting her leave, rather than advising a trip to Anderson Memorial. Fonzie had settled down by the time she and Jordan rolled past Dylan Blake in the back of one of the police cruisers. His head was bent down but he glanced up, glaring at her in the brief moment they made eye contact. Her stomach lurched and she bent forward, squeezing her eyes shut. He'd nearly killed her.

The detective put a hand on her shoulder, not

speaking. She waited until the sudden wave of nausea had passed and sat back in her seat, trying again at deep breaths.

"Okay, Savanna?" he asked quietly.

She nodded.

He handed his car keys through Savanna's window to an officer, who would take his car to Savanna's home for him. They were back on the highway before he spoke again. "Do you see now why I told you to stop pursuing?"

"Yes."

"But you didn't. Do you know how close you came to being shot tonight? What if you had been? Or if your dog had been?"

As much as she couldn't wrap her head around the fact that she could've been shot, the thought of Fonzie being struck with a bullet got through to her. Blake's bullets had hit the dirt right outside her window, and then the sign only seconds after she'd passed it. She could've easily been shot.

"You could've been killed." He scowled at her. "Do you get that, Savanna?"

"Yes," she said, tears threatening again. She swallowed hard and clenched her teeth. "Yes. I get it now. I'm really sorry." Her voice broke. She turned away, staring out the window. She hadn't been thinking. The whole time she'd been behind the truck, she'd only been focused on keeping it in her sights until Jordan and his team got there. But it'd never even crossed her mind he could have a gun, could try to kill her. "It was reckless and stupid and incredibly irresponsible," she said, mad at herself now.

"Yes, it was." He softened. "I appreciate everything

you've done, Savanna. Your idea for our act at the coffee shop this morning flushed Blake out. I'm sure he thought he was about to be arrested for Libby's murder when he took the risk of going to your house. I'd thought we made it obvious that I was keeping the files, but I guess he didn't hear that part. I never would've gone along with it if I thought you'd be in danger."

"I know that. Don't worry."

"I also heard through the grapevine about the odd visit Marcus Valentine received this morning." He glanced sideways at her. "You didn't mention your plan had a phase two."

"Oh. How did you hear?"

"I brought him in for questioning this afternoon. He did explain his incriminating black eye and why he missed dance class the Saturday Libby was killed."

"Ooh. You're really going to tell me what the missing pieces are this time?"

"It was relevant to the case before, so I couldn't. Now we know he didn't do it, so it doesn't matter. He came clean today with me and Taylor. When Priscilla Blake accepted his overqualified application to be the new tap instructor, Valentine probably dodged a much worse fate than a simple black eye. He'd run up some significant gambling debt in New York. Cards. He says he got in over his head and the only way out was to get as far away as possible. He'd met with one of the people he owes money to the night before Libby was killed— he says he made a partial payment on his debt, but I guess it wasn't enough. Rachel lied for him. He didn't get back into Carson until Sunday."

"Why would Rachel lie for him? Oh. I think I know. She lied because if you found out about the kind of people he dealt with, it'd just make him look more guilty? She must've been positive he didn't kill her mom."

"Well, yeah. I mean, when Rachel talked about getting her mom's plant to that show, it seemed highly unlikely that she was involved in the murder. And more unlikely that her boyfriend would go behind her back and kill her mom, even for all that money."

"So, Anthony will get his life insurance payout. Anthony and Rachel both will. Right? She can finish school, and he can keep the shop going. That's got to be a relief for them."

Jordan nodded. "I'm sure it is. Anthony Kent's timing with the life insurance policy change was pure coincidence." They rode in silence the rest of the way until he turned onto her street. "Listen, just so we're clear," he said. "I do appreciate you leading us to Blake. But I swear to God, if you ever willfully disregard what I'm telling you when you know it's about keeping you safe, I'm never speaking to you again."

A little laugh escaped her, and she pressed her lips together. They pulled into her driveway.

"I'm serious." He put the car in park and turned to look at her.

"I know you are. I'm sorry. It just sounded funny. I know it's not," she added.

"I'm glad you're all right. You're going to let someone know what happened? Maybe you shouldn't be alone tonight."

She nodded. "Good point."

Detective Jordan walked her in so he could check doors and windows for signs of the breach. When he discovered Savanna's alarm pad at both doors had darkened screens, and the deck and porch lights wouldn't come on, they checked the circuit breaker box in the utility room. One had been switched off. Savanna threw the breaker, getting full power back. Jordan found Dylan Blake's point of entry at the kitchen window over the sink, where the screen had been cut to allow the window to be unlatched and raised. Going through the high-tech alarm system keypad in her foyer, Jordan showed Savanna how he'd done it.

"Your system allows sixty seconds to turn off the alarm after a window or door is opened when it's set. You did set the alarm when you left today. This memory function shows that. It also shows the kitchen window was accessed tonight at eight fifty-two p.m., and then there's a power outage. Blake must've disconnected the battery first, and then cut the power. Your circuit breaker panel looks brand new; I'm assuming your dad installed that for you?"

She nodded. "Yes, he had to bring the electric and plumbing up to code. I labeled the circuit breakers in case the power goes out," she said, pointing to the panel.

"With everything so neatly labeled, it was probably easy to only kill the power to the alarm, so he'd still be able to rifle through your house looking for those files. Might be a good idea to have your dad rewire it so it has an independent circuit or another backup. And then don't label the circuit that has the alarm."

"We'll do that tomorrow." She was thinking. "You said eight fifty-two? He was at dress rehearsal tonight. I saw him talking to Miss Priscilla...but that would've been earlier. Because I think he was still in my house when I got home." She was running the evening backward in her head, to when she'd arrived at the high school auditorium and what time Mollie had gone on stage. "I saw him an hour before he was here. What about Miss Priscilla? Do you think she was part of this?"

"I'm not sure. We won't know until later tonight when we question both of them. Taylor was on his way to pick her up when we left the scene. I'll keep you updated."

Aidan arrived as Detective Jordan was leaving. Savanna had texted him as soon as they'd pulled in the driveway.

In her comfy family room, Savanna was cozied up under her favorite throw between Fonzie and her boyfriend. She'd put *I Love Lucy* reruns on TV, the volume low; after the excitement of tonight, it was just too soon to jump back into her *Columbo* marathon. Dr. Gallager had insisted on re-checking her blood pressure, and it was perfect.

He gave his own version of the same speech Nick Jordan had given her, regarding putting herself in the middle of an armed car chase. "You're sure you're okay?" He pulled her closer and she leaned into him.

"My own personal doctor made a house call for me. I'm a thousand percent better than okay." She smiled up at him.

Chapter Twenty-Two

T RUE TO HIS WORD, NICK Jordan stopped by Savanna's house Friday after work with news. She let him in, motioning for him to follow her; she was in the middle of slicing strawberries for her get-together tonight. She handed him a glass of lemonade.

"We've fixed the screen," she said, pointing at the kitchen window. "And my dad rewired the circuit for the alarm. I know which one it's on, but I rewrote the labels and left it off—I should've been smarter about that. Perils of being a first-time homeowner, I guess."

"I'm glad you took care of it so fast. I wanted to let you know, we have an airtight case against Dylan Blake, and we know now that he acted alone. The bullet casings from the unregistered gun he shot at you with matched the one that killed Libby."

"Oh, wow! How do you know Miss Priscilla wasn't involved? What did she say?"

"It was more how she reacted. We got a warrant to search their house and business, and we found items in Dylan Blake's home office that were enlightening. Not only did he have professionally done plans for his expansion of the dance studio into the flower shop space, but we found a new purchase agreement already drawn up by a real estate agency in Grand Rapids. He also had a detailed spreadsheet with the revenue increase he expected once the dance school had double the space. With the extra classes and competition division teams he'd planned to add, he was anticipating more than a hundred percent increase in profits. Blake was likely just waiting for Anthony to either be sole owner of the flower shop he didn't want, or better yet, be arrested for Libby's murder. He'd also kept all of his bank deposit slips for an account under his name alone."

Savanna narrowed her eyes. "How did that help you?"

"He'd been funneling money from the dance school, putting a portion of customer payments into his personal account. He had enough for a big down payment on the flower shop. It's also a good way to hide small business income, for tax purposes—if he hadn't been found out. The Kents' fraud claim against the Blakes was spot on. Anyway, we brought Priscilla in for questioning. We had no evidence to tie it to her, and when we began laying all this out for her, her reaction was extreme. She didn't have a clue what her husband was doing."

"Good. That actually makes me feel better," Savanna said. "I know she's not a warm and fuzzy person, but I've known her since I was a kid. I'm glad to know she wasn't involved in Libby's death. How did Anthony and Rachel take the news? Uncle Max says he's hardly seen either of them since last week."

"I believe Anthony Kent is dealing with some guilt despite being cleared of murder. With all of this out in the open, Rachel knows now that her father tried to sell her mother's shop. He didn't entertain the Blakes' first offer years ago, but I suppose everyone has a price."

Savanna sighed. "It sounded to me like he was stressed about money. Maybe he thought he could convince his wife to sell for the big money Blake offered the second time. The shop was Libby's passion, not his. But he didn't kill her."

Mollie and Nolan's recital that evening went off perfectly, despite a conspicuously absent Miss Priscilla. Marcus Valentine stepped in and handled emcee duties; he thanked the audience for coming and shared that Miss Priscilla had been devastated upon learning what her husband had done. She hadn't been up to being part of the event, but she and an overwhelming majority of the dance parents had felt the show must go on out of respect for the students' months of hard work. Mollie executed her ballet and tap dances beautifully, just as she'd done in dress rehearsal. Nolan thoroughly enjoyed his theater skit onstage among his classmates, despite the full thirty seconds he forgot a line. He'd stood staring into the bright lights, even though most of the audience could see the theater teacher in the wings whispering it loudly to him. At bows after the finale, Nolan ran over to Mollie, took her hand, and marched the two of them to the edge of the stage for their bow, gaining extra applause.

Both families got a sweet surprise on the way out of the crowded auditorium. Finn Gallager was waiting just outside the exit, wearing a suit and tie and holding two beautiful bouquets of roses in his arms. Sydney spotted him first, but Mollie was right behind her.

"Uncle Finn! You came!" The little girl sprinted over and launched herself at him.

He laughed and caught her, shifting the flowers. "Of course I came!"

"But did you see me?" She pushed off his chest with both hands, scrutinizing him.

"I saw you in both numbers." He set her down. "I even saw when you did that extra spin at the end of the tap dance. You were a-ma-zing." He drew the word out and Mollie beamed up at him. Finn placed the pink roses in her arms. "These are for you, Mols." He straightened up and met Sydney's gaze.

Sydney had hung back near Savanna, letting Mollie bask in the attention from her uncle.

He murmured greetings to Aidan and his in-laws as he moved through the little gathering, but his focus was on Sydney. He handed her the bouquet of red roses. "And these are yours. Hey there, Syd."

She'd seen him less than a week ago, and they'd talked every night. But now, Sydney felt like she would burst with happiness over him standing here in front of her. She was acutely aware of being in the middle of both their families. Despite the conversation and laughter, she swore she could feel her parents watching them. "I don't understand," Sydney said, keeping her voice low. "What are you doing here? You'd said your next trip home wouldn't be until the end of June."

"I wanted to meet your mom and dad. I want to meet your family. And I didn't want to let Mollie down." He grinned. "There was just way too much at stake."

Sydney curled her fingers around the lapel of his suitcoat. She stood on tiptoe and planted a kiss on his cheek. "Thank you. Do you have to go right back?"

"I've got until Sunday."

"Oh, good! Sounds like forever."

Finn leaned down and put his lips near her ear, sending a shiver through her. "I like the way that sounds." He looked over toward Harlan and Charlotte on the opposite side of the gathering, and then back at Sydney. "Ready?"

She took his hand and smiled. "Come on. They can't wait to meet you."

***

The Shepherd and Gallager families gathered at Savanna's house for post-show ice cream sundaes. She'd set up an assembly line across her kitchen counter with three kinds of ice cream, hot fudge, strawberries, flavored syrup, and a wide array of other toppings. She opened the French doors onto her deck, and the group drifted in and out, talking and enjoying dessert. It was a beautiful night, just warm enough, with a light breeze that brought the welcome lake air into the house.

Savanna joined Aidan on her deck, where he was talking with Harlan and her uncles.

"It's definitely worth considering," Uncle Freddie said to Max.

"What are we considering?" Savanna asked, late to the conversation.

Uncle Max's eyes were bright with excitement. "Did you happen to see the 'For Sale' sign in Libby's window today?"

"What? No, I didn't! Anthony's moving on, then. I guess that shouldn't be a surprise."

"And," Uncle Freddie said, "we thought, what a perfect opportunity for a seasoned botanist to take over running the flower shop."

"Oh!" Savanna exclaimed. "Oh, my goodness. Uncle Max, would you really do it? It'd be wonderful if Carson could still have its lovely Libby's Blooms. You'd be a natural fit."

Uncle Freddie put an arm around his husband. "I think it's a great idea. I can see it now—two members of our family with successful shops across the street from each other."

Max smiled. "I might be ready for a new adventure."

"You and Sydney could run cross promotions!" Savanna exclaimed. "It'll be fun! I'll get in touch with my real estate agent first thing in the morning and ask him to call you."

"Speaking of tomorrow morning..." Freddie said, looking at Aidan. "Are we still on for golf?"

The other man nodded. "Maybe we can convince the rest of you to join us?"

"Nope. I have the pleasure of babysitting my niece and nephew," Savanna said. "Skylar and Travis have a breakfast date." She was so happy Skylar was giving up a little control and letting her sisters help out.

Uncle Max shook his head too. "I wouldn't subject you to my golf swing," he told Aidan. "My brother-in-law here knows—he'll tell you. It's not pretty."

Harlan shrugged. "It's not all that bad. It's about on par with mine." He winked at Savanna.

"Ha ha," she said, giving him a half smile. "Nice dad joke."

"I aim to please. Besides, I'm taking my boat out fishing tomorrow morning. No time for golf."

There was her opening. Savanna slipped an arm

through Aidan's. "Dad," she began, "remember when you were teaching me to sail and I said that someday, I wanted a sailboat just like yours?"

"Sure I do."

"Well, I now own half a sailboat. A beautiful thirty-five-foot Catalina. She's amazing. Would you want to check her out tomorrow and leave yours in the slip?"

"I can't tomorrow," he said. "Darn it. If you'd just caught me a little earlier. Since I'll be done fishing early enough, Dr. Gallager here actually just invited me out on *his* Catalina thirty-five-footer tomorrow afternoon." He smirked at her.

She turned and stared at Aidan. "You could've stopped me anytime. You already told him?"

"I didn't! I wouldn't do that—you wanted to tell him. I'd planned for us to tell him on our boat tomorrow."

"You can't even sail!"

"No, but both of you can." He grinned at her.

"The Catalina is Aidan's very generous birthday gift to me," Savanna said. "Well, my half of it anyway, along with the slip." She leaned a head on his shoulder, smiling. "I tried to turn it down, but he wouldn't let me."

Harlan laughed. "Good man. You two are going to love it. One of the best decisions you'll ever make."

On Sunday morning, Savanna glanced at Mollie in the back seat of Aidan's SUV. She raised one eyebrow at her and tilted her head to the side. "So let me get this straight. You know where we're going, and your dad knows where we're going, but neither of you can let me in on the secret?"

Aidan had asked if they could pick up Savanna for a Sunday drive, and of course she'd said yes. But Mollie's whole cat-who-ate-the-canary demeanor was a giveaway that she and her dad were planning something. She giggled and put her fingertips to her lips and turned them as if turning a key in a lock. She held the invisible key out in front of Savanna, then tossed it out the window and crossed her arms over her chest.

Savanna laughed. "All right, I can see I won't get anywhere with you."

"Don't even start on me," Aidan warned her. "I'm forbidden to tell you anything."

They were heading south. She had a feeling they might be taking Mollie for a sail on the new boat. "Did Finn leave today?"

"I think he had an early flight," Aidan said, nodding. In another mile or so, he made a right into the marina, confirming Savanna's suspicions. It was perfect sailing weather. She was so excited for Mollie to test out this fun new experience.

They greeted Gus as they passed Sweetwater Boats, Mollie's small hand in Savanna's larger one. Savanna spotted the dozens of balloons tied to the Catalina from two docks away.

"What is that?" She looked from Mollie to Aidan. "What did you two do?"

Mollie pulled on her hand, moving faster. "Come and see!"

The three of them climbed into the cockpit, and Savanna tipped her head way back, looking up at the balloons tied to the boom and side stays. "Wow! They're so pretty." The pastel-colored balloons against the blue sky were moving gently in the breeze.

"Mollie said there had to be balloons," Aidan said. His voice was strained, different. She met his gaze, and then looked at Mollie, sitting on the bench opposite them.

The little girl held out a small white gift box wrapped with a big purple bow. "Ms. Shepherd, I made this for you."

Savanna took it, puzzled. "Mollie, you're so sweet! You made a gift for me?"

Mollie took a deep breath in, puffing her chest out. She looked at her dad.

"Go ahead, Mollie. You've got this," he assured her. Savanna slid her gaze in his direction. "She's been planning this for a while. We both have, but we had to get our ducks in a row. Right?" he asked his daughter.

She giggled. "I w-want to ask you something," she told Savanna. "I want you to—" Mollie paused and frowned. She took the box back from Savanna's open palm and untied the ribbon. "Here."

Savanna slowly removed the lid to reveal a bit of tissue paper covering up something pink. "Should I look?" she asked Mollie.

The girl nodded, then took the tissue paper away herself. "See?"

Savanna gasped. Her eyes instantly filled with tears. She reached in and pulled out a braided pink-and-purple bracelet with a small pink bunny charm woven into the strands. "Oh, Mollie." Her voice came out thick and quiet.

"This is Mrs. Fluffypants," the girl said, excitement in her tone. "She's just like mine and Daddy's, see?" Mollie displayed the one like it on her own wrist and then leaned across Savanna and pushed up her dad's sleeve, revealing a matching pink-and-purple bracelet. She took the bracelet from Savanna and painstakingly tied it around her wrist.

While she did, Savanna finally looked at Aidan sitting silently beside her. Her tears overflowed, and she didn't even care. She had no words. He kissed her temple, and she closed her eyes, swallowing hard.

"So now you have the same one as us," Mollie said. Savanna smiled at her and nodded, struggling to find her voice. Mollie patted her arm. "Could you please be part of our family now?"

Savanna nodded vigorously, smiling and unable to stop crying. "Yes, Mollie. Yes, I'd love to be part of your wonderful family. Thank you." She folded Mollie into her arms and hugged her. Holy ever-loving cats. This little girl had just claimed her heart in the time it took to tie a bracelet to her wrist.

When Mollie let go, Savanna took a deep breath and turned, smiling, to Aidan.

"My turn," he said, a small black box in the palm of his hand. "We wanted to do this a while ago, but it took some time to get this from storage in New York."

Savanna forgot to breathe, watching him. She was completely overwhelmed. Her heart thumped at the base of her throat. She hadn't expected this—any of this.

Aidan opened the box and took her hand. The ring was stunning, a large round transitional cut diamond in a vintage gold setting. "Savanna, that day on Caroline Carson's front porch, when you tangled the poodles around my legs, was the luckiest day of my life."

She laughed.

"I love you. I'm completely in love with you. So is my

daughter. We need you in our life, now and always. Will you marry me?"

Savanna looked up at the balloons, blinking rapidly. Goodness, she wasn't prepared for any of this. He constantly surprised her.

Aidan leaned toward her, worry furrowing his brow. "It was my grandmother's ring," he said. "But we can choose a new one if you'd like. And maybe this seems fast. I don't know, maybe it is. But I know how I feel about you, Savanna. We can take any amount of time you want; I'm not going anywhere. Just please, say yes."

Savanna cupped his face in her hands and kissed him. She had to before her heart raced right out of her chest. "Yes."

The End

Acknowledgements

Writing the third book in the Shepherd sisters series was an experience I'll never forget. Two weeks before learning that Hallmark wanted to continue the series with *Still Life and Death*, I was laid off from my home health RN position in the midst of the developing pandemic. I was grateful to be put on leave by my physician, who made the decision with my best interests in mind after I'd had a life-threatening lung issue a year earlier. This leave from my job marked the first time since I was fifteen—thirty-five years ago—that I've been unemployed.

But of course I wasn't really unemployed. I was lucky to be able to immerse myself in the Shepherd sisters' world for the third time in two years, and I don't think I'm overstating it when I say they saved me. Savanna and her sisters and beau and the little town of Carson provided me with a sense of peace and calm during a time of uncertainty, fear, and upheaval. I think this story is infused with a little of the grace I felt while writing it—thankful to be healthy and surrounded by my family and knowing how truly fortunate that made me. The nurse portion of me firmly, painfully grasps this history-making, horrific time, while the writer portion is grateful beyond words to be here, drawing breath and sharing my stories.

I'm also thankful to have the most amazing advocate in my corner, Fran Black with Literary Counsel. Thank you, Fran, for all the everything all the time.

Your dedication is something to aspire to. Thank you to Hallmark Publishing's Stacey Donovan, who took a chance on a debut author and allowed me to bring the Shepherd sisters and their world to life. You gave me my shot. Huge thanks to super patient and kind editor Rhonda Merwarth, whose keen eye and skilled work in three books' worth of edits have given me valuable tools I'll carry forward. Thank you to Eunice Shin and the Hallmark Publishing team for all you do.

So much love and gratitude to my sweet, supportive, jokester husband Joe, our kids Katy, Joey, and Halle, and my always-first reader and beloved concert wife, Ann Sullivan. Many thanks to WHMI's Jon King for always generously including this local author in book events and opportunities to be interviewed. Thank you to Angela Hart, wonderful booktuber and author supporter. Thank you to Kalie Holford, the talented artist who creates most of my gorgeous marketing graphics. As always, thanks a million to those who believe in me and lift me up on my publishing journey: Julie, Mom, Rocsana, Jimmy, the Hallmark author group, and an even wider group of family and friends.

Much love and gratitude to you, wonderful reader. I hope you find something of yourself in the sisters and their world. Enjoy!

About The Author

Tracy Gardner is a metro Detroit native who writes mystery and romance novels. A daughter of two teachers, she has been writing since she could hold a pen. Tracy grew up on Nancy Drew mysteries and rock and roll. Her drive to understand the deeper meaning of things serves her well as an author of compelling, relatable characters and stories.

Tracy splits her time between being a nurse, a writer, and a baker, because brownies are an important staple in her home, which she shares with her husband, two fun-loving teens, and a menagerie of spoiled rescue dogs and cats.

Chocolate Pecan Brownies

In *Still Life and Death,* when Savanna Shepherd needs information about people on her personal list of murder suspects, she knows who to turn to: Yvonne, her friend who works in the city council office and has access to important files. To persuade Yvonne to help, Savanna brings her treats from the local bakery, including a chocolate pecan brownie that's to die for. File this scrumptious recipe away for any time you need to talk someone into something. Hey, it worked for Savanna!

- **Prep Time:** 15 minutes

- **Cook Time:** 25 minutes
- **Serves:** 16

Ingredients

- 1/2 cup unsalted butter
- 5 (1 ounce) squares unsweetened baking chocolate
- As needed no-stick cooking spray
- As needed flour
- 4 medium eggs
- 2 cups granulated sugar
- 1 teaspoon vanilla
- 1/2 teaspoon Kosher salt
- 1 cup flour
- 1/2 cup pecan pieces
- 1 handful good-quality dark chocolate chips

Preparation

1. Preheat oven to 350°F.
2. Combine butter and chocolate squares in a small skillet or heavy saucepan and heat over low heat until melted. Set aside to cool.
3. Spray a 9-inch x 12-inch baking pan with no-stick cooking spray and dust lightly with flour.
4. Combine eggs, sugar, vanilla, and salt in mixing bowl; beat on high speed for 3 minutes.
5. Add cooled chocolate mixture to mixing bowl; whisk by-hand until blended.
6. Add flour to mixing bowl; whisk by-hand until blended.

7. Add nuts and "secret ingredient" to mixing bowl; whisk by-hand until blended.

8. Using a rubber spatula, pour batter into baking pan; spread evenly and bake uncovered for 25 minutes. Cool.

9. Cut into 16 rectangle-shaped pieces and serve.

Thank you for reading *Still Life and Death*! If you enjoyed the book, please support the author by leaving an online review.

You might also enjoy these books from Hallmark Publishing:

Out of the Picture: A Shepherd Sisters Mystery
Behind the Frame: A Shepherd Sisters Mystery
Murder By Page One: A Peach Coast Library Mystery
Dead-End Detective: A Piper and Porter Mystery

For information about our new releases and exclusive offers, sign up for our free newsletter at hallmarkchannel.com/hallmark-publishing-newsletter

You can also connect with us here:

Facebook.com/HallmarkPublishing

Twitter.com/HallmarkPublish

Turn the page for a bonus excerpt from

MURDER BY PAGE ONE

A PEACH COAST LIBRARY MYSTERY

OLIVIA MATTHEWS

CHAPTER 1

"**I** WAS PROMISED CHOCOLATE."

I directed the reminder toward my new best friend, Jolene Gomez, after entering the bookstore. I threw my gaze into every visible nook and cranny of To Be Read in search of chocolate-covered pecan clusters.

Jo owned To Be Read, an independent bookstore on the southeast side of Peach Coast, Georgia. It wasn't that I needed the food bribe to come to her bookstore— or any bookstore—especially when a bunch of authors were signing their books. It was just that, well...promises had been made.

"Marvey." The tattooed businesswoman's tan features warmed with a welcoming smile. Her coffee-colored eyes shifted to my right. "Spence. I'm glad you both made it."

Jo seemed relieved, as though she'd worried we wouldn't come. Why would she have thought that? I kept my promises, especially those made to another book fanatic. Jo and I had bonded over our love of books, our newcomer status—she was from Florida and

I was from New York—and chocolates, which reminded me today's stash was still conspicuously absent.

"Of course we came. We're readers. On top of that, we're here supporting our friend." I nudged Jo's shoulder with my own.

"The others are on their way," Spence said, referring to the members of the Peach Coast Library Book Club.

Spence and I had walked over from the library after our Saturday afternoon meeting. It was about a fifteen-minute walk, and the weather on this May Day had been comfortably warm. As geographically challenged as I was, I'd been glad to have Spence with me. On my own, I probably would've still been circling the library's parking lot.

Spencer Holt was a local celebrity, although he'd deny it. The Holts were the richest family in Peach Coast and one of the wealthiest in Camden County. They owned a bed and breakfast, a hotel, a local bank, and the town's daily newspaper, *The Peach Coast Crier*. It was considered required reading among the residents, and Spence was the publisher and editor-in-chief.

The family was also philanthropic: Peach Coast's answer to Gotham City's Wayne Foundation. Spence's mother, for example, served on the board of directors for the Peach Coast Library—which technically made her my boss.

For all his money, prestige, power, and good looks—think Bruce Wayne with a slow Southern drawl—Spence was very humble. He was more interested in listening than talking about himself, and he seemed to prefer comfort over fashion. I once again noted his brown loafers, faded blue jeans, and the ruby-red polo shirt that showed off his biceps and complimented his warm sienna skin.

Spence shifted his midnight gaze to mine. "If you want pecan clusters, we can get some at the coffee shop after the signing."

After the signing? "It wouldn't be the same." Translation: that would be too late. Far too late. I continued scanning the store, my mind rejecting the truth my eyes had confirmed.

"I haven't put the chocolates out yet, but I'll get you some in a minute." Jo waved a hand as though the treats weren't important. The right sleeve of her citrus-orange knit sweater, which she'd coupled with leaf-green jeans, slipped to reveal the University of Florida Gators logo inked onto the inside of her small wrist. Jo was a proud alumna. "First, let me introduce you to Zelda Taylor. She's the president of Coastal Fiction Writers. The authors who're signing today are members of her group. Zelda, you know Spence."

"Ms. Zelda, it's nice to see you again." Spence's greeting rumbled in his Barry White voice.

"Mr. Spence, it's always such a pleasure," the redhead gushed. Her porcelain cheeks glowed pink. "How is your mama?"

"She's very well, ma'am. I'll tell her you asked after her." Spence's smile went up a watt. The poor woman seemed dazed.

I tossed Spence a laughing look. "Is there anyone in this town you don't know?"

Spence's smooth forehead creased as he pretended to consider my question. "Well, nearly one thousand people reside in Peach Coast. I'm sure I've yet to meet one or two of them."

Jo gestured toward me. "Zelda, this is Marvella Harris. She moved here from New York—the city—four months ago. She's the library's new director of community engagement."

Zelda tugged her attention from Spence. Her appearance was flawless: well-manicured nails, perfect makeup, and salon-styled hair. She was camera-ready for a photo spread in a Southern homes magazine.

"Oh, yes. I read the article about you in the *Crier* a couple of months back." Her voice was now imposing, as though she were reading a town proclamation. "Welcome to Camden County. What brings you all this way, Ms. Marvella?"

Referring to the county of residence instead of the town was taking some getting used to. I supposed it was like New Yorkers saying we were from Brooklyn, The Bronx, Queens, or Staten Island. Only people from Manhattan said they were from "the city."

"Just Marvey, please." The Southern custom of adding a title to a person's name was charming, but it was a lot to say before getting to the point. "I want to help the library increase its outreach and services. Do you have a library card?"

Zelda's eyes widened. "Why, yes." Her commanding tone had faded. "Yes, I do."

Although suspicious of her response, I gave her the benefit of the doubt. "Excellent. I look forward to seeing you at the library. You should join our book club. We meet the first Saturday of each month."

"Oh. That sounds nice." Zelda smoothed her silver cotton dress in a nervous gesture. I sensed her casting about for a believable excuse to get out of the meetings.

Spence offered an incentive. "Marvey serves Georgia

Bourbon Pecan Pie and sweet tea after every meeting—but you have to stay till the end of the meeting for the refreshments."

Panic receded from Zelda's eyes to be replaced by interest. "Oh, well, now. That would be nice indeed."

I turned my attention from Zelda to survey To Be Read. I loved the store. It was like a giant welcoming foyer, flooded with natural light. Closing my eyes briefly, I drew in the scent of crisp new paper from thousands of books and magazines. Fluffy furnishings in pale earth tones popped up at the end of aisles and in quiet nooks. A multitude of blond wood bookcases stuffed with stories offered the promise of adventures and the thrill of knowledge.

A couple of Jo's employees were setting up for the book signing. They'd already arranged the wooden chairs and matching tables. The twenty-somethings transferred books from wheeled metal carts to each author's assigned table. Jo's third employee processed purchases at a checkout counter while engaging each customer in conversation as though they were lifelong friends. Every now and then, a burst of warm laughter rolled across the store.

But there still wasn't a single chocolate-covered pecan cluster in sight.

"I'm sorry I missed the meeting." Jo's gaze swung between Spence and me, twinkling with curiosity. "How was it?"

"It was great," Spence said. Slipping his hands into the front pockets of his jeans, he turned to me. "I'm impressed you were able to get the club up and running so quickly, within a month of your arrival."

"We librarians are known for our efficiency." It was a struggle to keep the smugness from my tone.

Spence's compliment filled me with a massive sense of achievement—and relief. Even though it was only our third meeting, I'd known the book club would be a success. We'd already attracted twenty-five book lovers, all from diverse backgrounds and each strengthening our argument for a bigger budget. *That* continued to be my motivation.

Leaving my parents and older brother in Brooklyn to relocate to Peach Coast with my cat had been hard. My roots were in Brooklyn. I'd lived my entire twenty-eight years in the New York borough, but I'd grown increasingly frustrated by my lack of opportunities to shine in my public library system. There, I was just one of many small fishes in a very big pond. I couldn't generate any waves. Not even a ripple. But I'd been confident that, if given a chance, my ideas for growing the community's interest in and support of the library could make a big splash. Here, in this small town, I'd finally be able to try. The library's success would make at least some of my homesickness worth it.

Jo grinned. "So who came in costume, and what did they wear?"

Spence ran a hand over his close-cropped hair. His voice was devoid of inflection. "Mortimer painted himself blue and called himself Aquarius."

This month's member-selected read was the latest paranormal fiction release by Bernadine Cecile. I loved paranormal stories. This one featured a world in which meta-humans used the power of their zodiac signs to defeat villains—hence Mortimer's costume. He wasn't the only one who'd gotten carried away. Most of the members hadn't wanted to read *Born Sign*, but the first rule of book club was to keep an open mind. To my relief, the novel had been a hit.

Zelda spoke over Jo's laughter. "Marvey, if you don't mind my saying, that's a lovely pendant." Her gaze had dropped to my sapphire cotton T-shirt, which I wore with cream khakis and matching canvas shoes.

"Thank you." I touched the glass pendant. I'd suspended it from a long antique silver chain. It held a silver-and-black illustration of the cover of Lorraine Hansberry's *A Raisin in the Sun*, the version depicting the Younger family's dream home.

Jo inclined her head toward me. Her long raven ponytail bounced behind her narrow shoulders. "Marvey makes those herself. And the matching hair barrette. She draws the pictures and puts them in the pendants and barrettes."

Zelda glanced at my shoulder-length, dark brown hair, but she couldn't have seen my barrette, which gathered my hair behind my head.

"You're very talented." Her eyes glinted with admiration—and longing. "Do you sell them?"

This question came up a lot. Each time, I stood firm. "No, it's just a hobby. I'd like to keep it that way."

I'd been making those pendants and barrettes since high school. The craft fed my love of art and jewelry making, and allowed me to pay homage to great works of literature. It was the kind of activity I could do while listening to an audiobook. Although I often gifted sets to family and friends for birthdays and holidays, the hobby was something I did for enjoyment, not for money. If I mass-produced them, it wouldn't be fun anymore.

Jo's dark eyes twinkled with mischief. "With all the

interest people have shown in your pendants, you may have to break that rule."

Spence flashed his silver-screen smile. His perfect white teeth were a dentist's dream. "Maybe you should give a class. That way, you can teach people how to make their own pendants."

"That's a great idea. The course could be a fundraiser for the library." New books. Updated software. Additional periodical subscriptions. Every little bit would help. I shelved the idea to consider in depth later.

"Ready for another great idea?" Spence's lips twitched with humor. "Run the Cobbler Crawl with me."

The man was relentless. I responded to his winning smile with a chiding look. "For the fourth time, no, I will not."

The Peach Coast Cobbler Crawl was an annual three-and-a-half-mile race to raise money for the local hospital. Each two-member team had to stop and eat a large, heaping spoonful of peach cobbler at the one-, two-, and three-mile points. The first team to cross the finish line together won.

"I can't enter the Cobbler Crawl without a running partner." Spence had been trying to convince me to form a team with him almost since the day we'd met.

I was running out of ways to say no. "Why don't we both just give a donation and watch the event from the sidelines?"

Jo laughed. "You should do it, Marvey. You run six miles every day. Three and a half miles will feel like nothing."

Now they were ganging up on me. "If we only had to run, I wouldn't hesitate. But I don't think I can run *and* keep down the cobbler." I shuddered to think of the consequences.

Zelda came out of her spell, dragging her attention from my pendant. "I'm the exact opposite. I could eat the cobbler, no problem. But I couldn't run a mile in a month of Sundays."

Determined to change the subject, I turned to Zelda. "How many members of the Coastal Fiction Writers are published?"

"We're a small group, but we're growing. At the moment, there are twelve of us. Four of our members are published."

"Five." Jo lifted the requisite number of fingers. "I ordered books for five members. I think you're missing Fiona." She addressed Spence and me. "Fiona Lyle-Hayes just released her first book, *In Death Do We Part*. It's a mystery, and it's gotten great advance reviews."

Spence sent me a look before switching his attention to our companions. I could tell he wasn't giving up on the Cobbler Crawl. "We ran a piece about her book in the *Crier*."

"Oh, yes. How could I have forgotten Fiona?" Zelda clutched her pearl necklace. Her smile seemed fake. That was curious.

"Fiona helped coordinate the signing." Jo glanced at her employees who were setting out the books before returning her attention to Spence and me. "She's also the writing group's treasurer."

"Yes, Fiona manages our money. She's good at that." Zelda flashed another tight smile, then looked away. Tension was rolling off her in waves. I really hoped it didn't bubble over and ruin Jo's event.

I glanced toward the entrance again to see more of

our book club members arriving, as well as quite a few strangers—each one a potential new library cardholder. Four of the newcomers made a beeline for Jo, who identified them as the local authors who were signing today. I concentrated on the introductions, but keeping names and connections straight strained my brain. Of course, Spence knew all of them. I resolved to stick to him like gum on his shoe.

The authors dressed up their displays with promotional postcards and trinkets. Jo's employees put the finishing touches on the arrangements, which included the bowls of the long-promised-but-seemingly-forgotten chocolate-covered pecan clusters. Jo and I had only been friends for four months, but I'd known she wouldn't let me down. I began drifting toward the signing area—and the chocolates—when Jo's voice stopped me.

"I wonder what's taking Fiona so long?" Jo checked her silver-and-orange wristwatch. A frown cast a shadow over her round face. "The signing starts in ten minutes. I thought she'd have her books out long before now."

Zelda scanned the store. "Fiona left our writers' meeting early, saying she needed to get ready. Where is she?"

Jo jerked her head toward the back of the store, sending her ponytail swinging. "She's been in the storage room. She wanted to examine her books and bring them out herself."

Weird. "Why?"

Jo shrugged nonchalantly, but I saw the aggravation in her eyes. "She didn't say, but I suspect it's because she thought my staff and I would damage her books."

Zelda's smile didn't reach her eyes. "Fiona can be a pain in the tush. Bless her heart."

Bless her heart. That was a Southern phrase I'd heard before. It didn't mean anything good.

CHAPTER 2

WHILE I HUNG OUT WITH Spence and Zelda, Jo checked on the authors who'd taken their seats on time.

Spence's voice drew my attention from the bowls of chocolate. "Nolan, I'd wondered if you'd make it to Fiona's first signing."

Nolan was a few inches shorter than Spence—perhaps an even six feet—and fit. Despite his graying close-cropped brown hair and tired brown eyes, he seemed youthful. It could've been the casual clothes he wore: powder green jersey, dark blue jeans, and blue sneakers. That's right, sneakers.

Southerners—and admittedly, much of the rest of the country—referred to "sneakers" as "tennis shoes," but that felt wrong to me. Not all sneakers were tennis shoes. Some were running shoes or cross trainers. To me, it was like referring to all carbonated soft drinks as "Coke." Yes, Georgia was home to The Coca-Cola Company, but New Yorkers called it "soda." You could take the woman out of Brooklyn, but you couldn't take Brooklyn out of the woman.

Spence made the introductions. "Nolan Duggan, I'd like for you to meet Marvella Harris. Nolan's the co-owner of Lyle and Duggan CPA, along with Fiona. Marvey is the director of community engagement with the Peach Coast Library."

Nolan regarded me with an odd combination of welcome and wariness. "I read the interview with you in the *Crier*. You're from New York." I swear it seemed like he'd said, "You're an alien."

"It's nice to meet you, Nolan." I tilted my head and gave him my best nonthreatening smile. "Do you have a library card?"

Nolan gave me a blank stare. "I've never needed one. I'm at the bookstore all the time." His gaze drifted to Jo and lingered before returning to me.

"Everyone needs a library card, Nolan." I increased the wattage of my smile. "Why don't you stop by the library Monday? I'll help you with the application."

"All right." Nolan dragged out the two-syllable consent as though hesitant to make the commitment.

"Great!" Another customer. Another step toward a bigger budget.

An older woman and two younger men entered To Be Read. The woman marched with purpose, leading her contingent toward the signing area. If this had been New York, I would've suspected the trio was out to start something.

The woman's face flushed as she brought her posse to a stop in front of Jo. "Where's Fiona?"

I didn't like her tone. Not one bit. All of my protective instincts toward my friend went on high alert. I glanced at Spence. "Who is she?"

Spence lowered his voice. "That's Betty Rodgers-

Hayes and her son, Bobby Hayes. Bobby is Fiona's step-son. I don't know who the other man is. I don't think he's a local."

Nolan solved the mystery. "That's Willy Pelt, Fiona's friend from Beaufort, South Carolina. I met him when he was introducing himself to Ms. Betty and Bobby out in the parking lot."

Now I was even more confused. "It's nice of them to attend her event, but why are they so angry?"

Concern for Jo made me want to get a closer look at the wannabe mob. And I couldn't deny myself the clusters any longer. I wandered over to stand behind Jo and reached for one of the individually wrapped candies.

"Wow!" Jo's shout distracted me from my goal. She'd gestured toward Bobby's right arm. Her voice was reverent. "Who did your ink?"

My attention shifted from the candy dish to the bold rendering of a large, well-fed, and vicious-looking snake drawn onto Bobby's tanned arm. The orange, black, and brown serpentine illustration extended from his thick wrist, past his elbow to disappear beneath the sleeve of his faded red T-shirt. I suppressed a shudder. Snakes. I disliked them. A lot.

Bobby smiled shyly. As he turned his arm, I noticed several scratches on the back of his hand. "I got it done at a place out in Vegas."

But...a snake? I had to ask. "Why did you choose a snake?"

He shrugged. "I like 'em."

Why? But I let it go.

Betty's sniff was unfiltered maternal censure. "Well, I'm sure I don't know what got into his head to do such a crazy thing. It makes him look like a ruffian! And a *snake*? It's evil."

"Snakes aren't any more evil than humans, Mama." Bobby's voice was quiet and respectful.

But Betty was on a roll. She continued as though her son hadn't spoken. "Of course, he works in a hard-ware and repair shop full of ruffians. Well, I told him it's a good thing he does. Otherwise he wouldn't have any kind of job with filth like that covering his body."

Bobby gave a long-suffering sigh. "They're good guys, Mama."

"Your body is a *temple*, Bobby. *A temple*." Betty was breathless. Her brown hair fluttered above her sturdy shoulders with indignation. "Well, he can't ever get a de-cent job working in a decent place, now can he, looking like *that*?"

Bobby shook his head, never once raising his voice. "Just let it alone, Mama."

Jo pushed up the left sleeve of her sweater to reveal the silver, black, and gold sketch of a decorative cross inked onto her forearm from wrist to elbow. "If he ever wanted to try a new career, I'd hire him here at the bookstore."

Betty's brown eyes stretched wide. "Well, yes..." As Betty appeared to struggle to contain her true reaction, her son studied Jo's cross with avarice.

If the older woman had asked me first, I would've warned her that Jo was the absolute wrong person to turn to for a sympathetic ear on the topic of tattoos. But she hadn't asked me. And for the record, yes, I was amused by Betty's predicament.

Personally, I wouldn't get a tattoo. I couldn't fathom withstanding that much pain. But if I were to—and the odds were slim to none—it would be an image of Batgirl. I'd always admired the superhero. And—bonus!—Batgirl's alter ego, Barbara Gordon, was a librarian.

"It's nice that you've all come to support Fiona." I turned to Fiona's friend. "Especially you, Mr. Pelt, coming from South Carolina."

Willy glanced up from his wristwatch. He seemed surprised that I knew his name, then he noticed Nolan. Willy inclined his head in a silent greeting to Fiona's business partner, the expression on his pale, square face pleasant but vague. He drove his fingers through his shock of thick auburn hair. "I've known Fiona's family for years."

"I wonder what Fiona will do now?" Nolan's attention bounced from Jo to the rest of the group. "Will she give up her share of the business to write full-time?"

It was a good question, although I knew most authors continued to work full-time. Popular media's depiction of fiction writing as a lucrative career was greatly exaggerated.

Betty snorted. "Well, she doesn't *need* a job, now does she? Not like the rest of us. When Buddy died, he left *her* well provided for. The rest of us have to *work* for a living."

The bitterness in her voice seemed to come from far more than envy of another person's good fortune—literally and figuratively. Then I made the connection: Fiona Lyle-*Hayes*. Betty Rodgers-*Hayes*. There was a story there, one that could explain Betty's hostile disposition.